LOG OF Cape Otway LIGHTHOUSE STA[TION]

.13470.

Day and Date.	Hour.	Wind. Direction.	Wind. Force.	Weather.	Bar	Ther.	
Sunday 6"	6 a.m.	NW	4	cm	29.66	60	Employed at Lighthouse
	Noon	NE	2	Bcm	29.79	62	& Shipping duties changing
	6 p.m.	ENE	3	cm	29.69	61	Burners & Vapourizers from 6-10pm
	Mdgt.	NW	2	Bcm	29.70	59	till 6.30pm
							Ths Lowry
Monday 7"	6 a.m.	North	2	Bcm	29.30	59	Employed testing Vapourizers
	Noon	NE	2	Bcm	29.39	67	& Burners Mr Telford
	6 p.m.	NW	3	cqm	29.52	59	arrived 4.20pm with load
	Mdgt.	WNW	3	cm	29.44	58	of Kerosene completing
							cartage of Stores
							Ths Lowry
Tuesday 8"	6 a.m.	West	5	cqmp	29.26	57	Keeper & Assist. Johansen
	Noon	NW	4	sqmp	29.25	57	to Glenaire for meat —
	6 p.m.	West	5	cqmp	29.25	56	Left Station 9.30am
	Mdgt.	West	5	cqm	29.26	53	returned 2.30pm
							Ths Lowry
Wednesday 9"	6 a.m.	West	5	oqmp	29.15	53	Employed in Bedroom
	Noon	WNW	5	cmqr	29.99	59	& Stairs
	6 p.m.	West	5	cqmp	29.19	53	
	Mdgt.	West	5	cqmp	29.20	52	Ths Lowry
Thursday 10"	6 a.m.	West	6	cqmp	29.22	54	Assist. Meyers & Assist.
	Noon	West	5	cmp	29.28	56	Warcham employed in
	6 p.m.	West	5	oqm	29.39	56	the Tower Mr Beauvais
	Mdgt.	West	6	oqm	29.29	56	& Mr McHarg linemen
							arrived 4.20pm
							Ths L[owry]

The LIGHT BETWEEN OCEANS

A Novel

M. L. STEDMAN

Scribner
New York London Toronto Sydney New Delhi

Scribner
A Division of Simon & Schuster, Inc.
1230 Avenue of the Americas
New York, NY 10020

Map by Neil Gower

First Scribner hardcover edition August 2012

Designed by Carla Jayne Jones

Manufactured in the United States of America

1 3 5 7 9 10 8 6 4 2

Library of Congress Control Number: 2011050244

ISBN 978-1-4516-8173-4
ISBN 978-1-4516-8176-5 (ebook)

Detail from lighthouse logbook courtesy of the Australian National Archives.

In memory of my parents.

AUSTRALIA
INDIAN OCEAN
PACIFIC OCEAN
GREAT SOUTHERN OCEAN
Tropic of Capricorn
NORTHERN TERRITORY
QUEENSLAND
WESTERN AUSTRALIA
SOUTH AUSTRALIA
NEW SOUTH WALES
VICTORIA
TASMANIA
Great Sandy Desert
Great Victoria Desert
Brisbane
Byron Bay
Sydney
Melbourne
Hobart
Maatsuyker Island
Adelaide
Kalgoorlie
Point Moore
Geraldton
Perth
Hopetoun
Janus Rock
Albany
Point Partageuse
500
Miles

PART ONE

27TH APRIL 1926

On the day of the miracle, Isabel was kneeling at the cliff's edge, tending the small, newly made driftwood cross. A single fat cloud snailed across the late-April sky, which stretched above the island in a mirror of the ocean below. Isabel sprinkled more water and patted down the soil around the rosemary bush she had just planted.

". . . and lead us not into temptation, but deliver us from evil," she whispered.

For just a moment, her mind tricked her into hearing an infant's cry. She dismissed the illusion, her eye drawn instead by a pod of whales weaving their way up the coast to calve in the warmer waters, emerging now and again with a fluke of their tails like needles through tapestry. She heard the cry again, louder this time on the early-morning breeze. Impossible.

From this side of the island, there was only vastness, all the way to Africa. Here, the Indian Ocean washed into the Great Southern Ocean and together they stretched like an edgeless carpet below the cliffs. On days like this it seemed so solid she had the impression she could walk to Madagascar in a journey of blue upon blue. The other side of the island looked back, fretful, toward the Australian mainland nearly a hundred miles away, not quite belonging to the land, yet not quite free of it, the highest of a string of under-sea mountains that rose from the ocean floor like teeth along a jagged jaw bone, waiting to devour any innocent ships in their final dash for harbor.

As if to make amends, the island—Janus Rock—offered a lighthouse, its beam providing a mantle of safety for thirty miles. Each night the air sang with the steady hum of the lantern as it turned, turned, turned; even-handed, not blaming the rocks, not fearing the waves: there for salvation if wanted.

The crying persisted. The door of the lighthouse clanged in the distance, and Tom's tall frame appeared on the gallery as he scanned the island with binoculars. "Izzy," he yelled, "a boat!" and pointed to the cove. "On the beach—a boat!"

He vanished, and re-emerged a moment later at ground level. "Looks like there's someone in it," he shouted. Isabel hurried as best she could to meet him, and he held her arm as they navigated the steep, well-worn path to the little beach.

"It's a boat all right," Tom declared. "And—oh cripes! There's a bloke, but—"

The figure was motionless, flopped over the seat, yet the cries still rang out. Tom rushed to the dinghy, and tried to rouse the man before searching the space in the bow from where the sound came. He hoisted out a woolen bundle: a woman's soft lavender cardigan wrapped around a tiny, screaming infant.

"Bloody hell!" he exclaimed. "Bloody hell, Izzy. It's—"

"A baby! Oh my Lord above! Oh Tom! Tom! Here—give it to me!"

He handed her the bundle, and tried again to revive the stranger: no pulse. He turned to Isabel, who was examining the diminutive creature. "He's gone, Izz. The baby?"

"It's all right, by the looks. No cuts or bruises. It's so tiny!" she said, then, turning to the child as she cuddled it, "There, there. You're safe now, little one. You're safe, you beautiful thing."

Tom stood still, considering the man's body, clenching his eyes tight shut and opening them again to check he wasn't dreaming. The baby had stopped crying and was taking gulps of breath in Isabel's arms.

"Can't see any marks on the fellow, and he doesn't look diseased. He can't have been adrift long . . . You wouldn't credit it." He paused. "You take the baby up to the house, Izz, and I'll get something to cover the body."

"But, Tom—"

"It'll be a hell of a job to get him up the path. Better leave him here until help comes. Don't want the birds or the flies getting at him though—there's some canvas up in the shed should do." He spoke calmly enough, but his hands and face felt cold, as old shadows blotted out the bright autumn sunshine.

Janus Rock was a square mile of green, with enough grass to feed the few sheep and goats and the handful of chickens, and enough topsoil to sustain the rudimentary vegetable patch. The only trees were two towering Norfolk pines planted by the crews from Point Partageuse who had built the light station over thirty years before, in 1889. A cluster of old graves remembered a shipwreck long before that, when the *Pride of Birmingham* foundered on the greedy rocks in daylight. In such a ship the light itself had later been brought from England, proudly bearing the name Chance Brothers, a guarantee of the most advanced technology of its day—capable of assembly anywhere, no matter how inhospitable or hard to reach.

The currents hauled in all manner of things: flotsam and jetsam swirled as if between twin propellers; bits of wreckage, tea chests, whalebones. Things turned up in their own time, in their own way. The light station sat solidly in the middle of the island, the keeper's cottage and outbuildings hunkered down beside the lighthouse, cowed from decades of lashing winds.

In the kitchen, Isabel sat at the old table, the baby in her arms wrapped in a downy yellow blanket. Tom scraped his boots slowly on the mat as he entered, and rested a callused hand on her shoulder. "I've covered the poor soul. How's the little one?"

"It's a girl," said Isabel with a smile. "I gave her a bath. She seems healthy enough."

The baby turned to him with wide eyes, drinking in his glance. "What on earth must she make of it all?" he wondered aloud.

"Given her some milk too, haven't I, sweet thing?" Isabel cooed, turning it into a question for the baby. "Oh, she's so, so perfect, Tom," she said, and kissed the child. "Lord knows what she's been through."

Tom took a bottle of brandy from the pine cupboard and poured himself a small measure, downing it in one. He sat beside his wife, watching the light play on her face as she contemplated the treasure in her arms. The baby followed every movement of her eyes, as though Isabel might escape if she did not hold her with her gaze.

"Oh, little one," Isabel crooned, "poor, poor little one," as the baby nuzzled her face in toward her breast. Tom could hear tears in her voice, and the memory of an invisible presence hung in the air between them.

"She likes you," he said. Then, almost to himself, "Makes me think of how things might have been." He added quickly, "I mean . . . I didn't mean . . . You look like you were born to it, that's all." He stroked her cheek.

Isabel glanced up at him. "I know, love. I know what you mean. I feel the same."

He put his arms around his wife and the child. Isabel could smell the brandy on his breath. She murmured, "Oh Tom, thank God we found her in time."

Tom kissed her, then put his lips to the baby's forehead. The three of them stayed like that for a long moment, until the child began to wriggle, thrusting a fist out from under the blanket.

"Well"—Tom gave a stretch as he stood up—"I'll go and send a signal, report the dinghy; get them to send a boat for the body. And for Miss Muffet here."

"Not yet!" Isabel said as she touched the baby's fingers. "I mean, there's no rush to do it right this minute. The poor man's not going to get any worse now. And this little chicken's had quite enough of boats for the moment, I'd say. Leave it a while. Give her a chance to catch her breath."

"It'll take hours for them to get here. She'll be all right. You've already quietened her down, little thing."

"Let's just wait. After all, it can't make much difference."

"It's all got to go in the log, pet. You know I've got to report everything straightaway," Tom said, for his duties included noting every significant event at or near the light station, from passing ships and weather, to problems with the apparatus.

"Do it in the morning, eh?"

"But what if the boat's from a ship?"

"It's a dinghy, not a lifeboat," she said.

"Then the baby's probably got a mother waiting for it somewhere onshore, tearing her hair out. How would you feel if it was yours?"

"You saw the cardigan. The mother must have fallen out of the boat and drowned."

"Sweetheart, we don't have any idea about the mother. Or about who the man was."

"It's the most likely explanation, isn't it? Infants don't just wander off from their parents."

"Izzy, anything's possible. We just don't know."

"When did you ever hear of a tiny baby setting off in a boat without its mother?" She held the child a fraction closer.

"This is serious. The man's dead, Izz."

"And the baby's alive. Have a heart, Tom."

Something in her tone struck him, and instead of simply contradicting her, he paused and considered her plea. Perhaps she needed a bit of time with a baby. Perhaps he owed her that. There was a silence, and Isabel turned to him in wordless appeal. "I suppose, at a pinch . . ." he conceded, the words coming with great difficulty, "I could—leave the signal until the morning. First thing, though. As soon as the light's out."

Isabel kissed him, and squeezed his arm.

"Better get back to the lantern room. I was in the middle of replacing the vapor tube," he said.

As he walked down the path, he heard the sweet notes of Isabel's voice as she sang, "Blow the wind southerly, southerly, southerly, blow the wind south o'er the bonnie blue sea." Though the music was tuneful, it failed to comfort him as he climbed the stairs of the light, fending off a strange uneasiness at the concession he had made.

CHAPTER 1

16th December 1918

"Yes, I realize that," Tom Sherbourne said. He was sitting in a spartan room, barely cooler than the sultry day outside. The Sydney summer rain pelted the window, and sent the people on the pavement scurrying for shelter.

"I mean *very* tough." The man across the desk leaned forward for emphasis. "It's no picnic. Not that Byron Bay's the worst posting on the Lights, but I want to make sure you know what you're in for." He tamped down the tobacco with his thumb and lit his pipe. Tom's letter of application had told the same story as many a fellow's around that time: born 28 September 1893; war spent in the Army; experience with the International Code and Morse; physically fit and well; honorable discharge. The rules stipulated that preference should be given to ex-servicemen.

"It can't—" Tom stopped, and began again. "All due respect, Mr. Coughlan, it's not likely to be tougher than the Western Front."

The man looked again at the details on the discharge papers, then at Tom, searching for something in his eyes, in his face. "No, son. You're probably right on that score." He rattled off some rules: "You pay your own passage to every posting. You're relief, so you don't get holidays.

Permanent staff get a month's leave at the end of each three-year contract." He took up his fat pen and signed the form in front of him. As he rolled the stamp back and forth across the inkpad he said, "Welcome"—he thumped it down in three places on the paper—"to the Commonwealth Lighthouse Service." On the form, "16th December 1918" glistened in wet ink.

The six months' relief posting at Byron Bay, up on the New South Wales coast, with two other keepers and their families, taught Tom the basics of life on the Lights. He followed that with a stint down on Maatsuyker, the wild island south of Tasmania where it rained most days of the year and the chickens blew into the sea during storms.

On the Lights, Tom Sherbourne has plenty of time to think about the war. About the faces, the voices of the blokes who had stood beside him, who saved his life one way or another; the ones whose dying words he heard, and those whose muttered jumbles he couldn't make out, but who he nodded to anyway.

Tom isn't one of the men whose legs trailed by a hank of sinews, or whose guts cascaded from their casing like slithering eels. Nor were his lungs turned to glue or his brains to stodge by the gas. But he's scarred all the same, having to live in the same skin as the man who did the things that needed to be done back then. He carries that other shadow, which is cast inward.

He tries not to dwell on it: he's seen plenty of men turned worse than useless that way. So he gets on with life around the edges of this thing he's got no name for. When he dreams about those years, the Tom who is experiencing them, the Tom who is there with blood on his hands, is a boy of eight or so. It's this small boy who's up against blokes with guns and bayonets, and he's worried because his school socks have slipped down and he can't hitch them up because he'll have to drop his gun to do it, and he's barely big enough even to hold that. And he can't find his mother anywhere.

Then he wakes and he's in a place where there's just wind and waves and light, and the intricate machinery that keeps the flame burning and the lantern turning. Always turning, always looking over its shoulder.

If he can only get far enough away—from people, from memory—time will do its job.

Thousands of miles away on the west coast, Janus Rock was the furthest place on the continent from Tom's childhood home in Sydney. But Janus Light was the last sign of Australia he had seen as his troopship steamed for Egypt in 1915. The smell of the eucalypts had wafted for miles offshore from Albany, and when the scent faded away he was suddenly sick at the loss of something he didn't know he could miss. Then, hours later, true and steady, the light, with its five-second flash, came into view—his homeland's furthest reach—and its memory stayed with him through the years of hell that followed, like a farewell kiss. When, in June 1920, he got news of an urgent vacancy going on Janus, it was as though the light there were calling to him.

Teetering on the edge of the continental shelf, Janus was not a popular posting. Though its Grade One hardship rating meant a slightly higher salary, the old hands said it wasn't worth the money, which was meager all the same. The keeper Tom replaced on Janus was Trimble Docherty, who had caused a stir by reporting that his wife was signaling to passing ships by stringing up messages in the colored flags of the International Code. This was unsatisfactory to the authorities for two reasons: first, because the Deputy Director of Lighthouses had some years previously forbidden signaling by flags on Janus, as vessels put themselves at risk by sailing close enough to decipher them; and secondly, because the wife in question was recently deceased.

Considerable correspondence on the subject was generated in triplicate between Fremantle and Melbourne, with the Deputy Director in Fremantle putting the case for Docherty and his years of excellent service, to a Head Office concerned strictly with efficiency and cost and obeying the rules. A compromise was reached by which a temporary keeper would be engaged while Docherty was given six months' medical leave.

"We wouldn't normally send a single man to Janus—it's pretty remote and a wife and family can be a great practical help, not just a comfort," the District Officer had said to Tom. "But seeing it's only temporary . . . You'll leave for Partageuse in two days," he said, and signed him up for six months.

There wasn't much to organize. No one to farewell. Two days later, Tom walked up the gangplank of the boat, armed with a kit bag and not much else. The SS *Prometheus* worked its way along the southern shores of Australia, stopping at various ports on its run between Sydney and Perth. The few cabins reserved for first-class passengers were on the upper deck, toward the bow. In third class, Tom shared a cabin with an elderly sailor. "Been making this trip for fifty years—they wouldn't have the cheek to ask me to pay. Bad luck, you know," the man had said cheerfully, then returned his attention to the large bottle of over-proof rum that kept him occupied. To escape the alcohol fumes, Tom took to walking the deck during the day. Of an evening there'd usually be a card game belowdecks.

You could still tell at a glance who'd been over there and who'd sat the war out at home. You could smell it on a man. Each tended to keep to his own kind. Being in the bowels of the vessel brought back memories of the troopships that took them first to the Middle East, and later to France. Within moments of arriving on board, they'd deduced, almost by an animal sense, who was an officer, who was lower ranks; where they'd been.

Just like on the troopships, the focus was on finding a bit of sport to liven up the journey. The game settled on was familiar enough: first one to score a souvenir off a first-class passenger was the winner. Not just any souvenir, though. The designated article was a pair of ladies' drawers. "Prize money's doubled if she's wearing them at the time."

The ringleader, a man by the name of McGowan, with a mustache, and fingers yellowed from his Woodbines, said he'd been chatting to one of the stewards about the passenger list: the choice was limited. There were ten cabins in all. A lawyer and his wife—best give them a wide berth; some elderly couples, a pair of old spinsters (promising), but best of all, some toff's daughter traveling on her own.

"I reckon we can climb up the side and in through her window," he announced. "Who's with me?"

The danger of the enterprise didn't surprise Tom. He'd heard dozens of such tales since he got back. Men who'd taken to risking their lives on a whim—treating the boom gates at level crossings as a gallop jump; swimming into rips to see if they could get out. So many men who had dodged death over there now seemed addicted to its lure. Still, this lot were free agents now. Probably just full of talk.

The following night, when the nightmares were worse than usual, Tom decided to escape them by walking the decks. It was two a.m. He was free to wander wherever he wanted at that hour, so he paced methodically, watching the moonlight leave its wake on the water. He climbed to the upper deck, gripping the stair rail to counter the gentle rolling, and stood a moment at the top, taking in the freshness of the breeze and the steadiness of the stars that showered the night.

Out of the corner of his eye, he saw a glimmer come on in one of the cabins. Even first-class passengers had trouble sleeping sometimes, he mused. Then, some sixth sense awoke in him—that familiar, indefinable instinct for trouble. He moved silently toward the cabin, and looked in through the window.

In the dim light, he saw a woman flat against the wall, pinned there even though the man before her wasn't touching her. He was an inch away from her face, with a leer Tom had seen too often. He recognized the man from belowdecks, and remembered the prize. Bloody idiots. He tried the door, and it opened.

"Leave her alone," he said as he stepped into the cabin. He spoke calmly, but left no room for debate.

The man spun around to see who it was, and grinned when he recognized Tom. "Christ! Thought you were a steward! You can give me a hand, I was just—"

"I said leave her alone! Clear out. Now."

"But I haven't finished. I was just going to make her day." He reeked of drink and stale tobacco.

Tom put a hand on his shoulder, with a grip so hard that the man cried out. He was a good six inches shorter than Tom, but tried to take a swing at him all the same. Tom seized his wrist and twisted it. "Name and rank!"

"McKenzie. Private. 3277." The unrequested serial number followed like a reflex.

"Private, you'll apologize to this young lady and you'll get back to your bunk and you won't show your face on deck until we berth, you understand me?"

"Yes, sir!" He turned to the woman. "Beg your pardon, Miss. Didn't mean any harm."

Still terrified, the woman gave the slightest nod.

"Now, out!" Tom said, and the man, deflated by sudden sobriety, shuffled from the cabin.

"You all right?" Tom asked the woman.

"I—I think so."

"Did he hurt you?"

"He didn't . . ."—she was saying it to herself as much as to him—"he didn't actually touch me."

He took in the woman's face—her gray eyes seemed calmer now. Her dark hair was loose, in waves down to her arms, and her fists still gathered her nightgown to her neck. Tom reached for her dressing gown from a hook on the wall and draped it over her shoulders.

"Thank you," she said.

"Must have got an awful fright. I'm afraid some of us aren't used to civilized company these days."

She didn't speak.

"You won't get any more trouble from him." He righted a chair that had been overturned in the encounter. "Up to you whether you report him, Miss. I'd say he's not the full quid now."

Her eyes asked a question.

"Being over there changes a man. Right and wrong don't look so different any more to some." He turned to go, but put his head back through the doorway. "You've got every right to have him up on charges if you want. But I reckon he's probably got enough troubles. Like I said—up to you," and he disappeared through the door.

CHAPTER 2

Point Partageuse got its name from French explorers who mapped the cape that jutted from the south-western corner of the Australian continent well before the British dash to colonize the west began in 1826. Since then, settlers had trickled north from Albany and south from the Swan River Colony, laying claim to the virgin forests in the hundreds of miles between. Cathedral-high trees were felled with handsaws to create grazing pasture; scrawny roads were hewn inch by stubborn inch by pale-skinned fellows with teams of shire horses, as this land, which had never before been scarred by man, was excoriated and burned, mapped and measured and meted out to those willing to try their luck in a hemisphere which might bring them desperation, death, or fortune beyond their dreams.

The community of Partageuse had drifted together like so much dust in a breeze, settling in this spot where two oceans met, because there was fresh water and a natural harbor and good soil. Its port was no rival to Albany, but convenient for locals shipping timber or sandalwood or beef. Little businesses had sprung up and clung on like lichen on a rock face, and the town had accumulated a school, a variety of churches with different hymns and architectures, a good few brick and stone houses and a lot more built of weatherboard and tin. It gradually produced various shops, a town hall, even a Dalgety's stock and station agency. And pubs. Many pubs.

Throughout its infancy, the unspoken belief in Partageuse was that real things happened elsewhere. News of the outside world trickled in like rain dripped off the trees, a snippet here, a rumor there. The telegraph had speeded things up a bit when the line arrived in 1890, and since then a few folks had got telephones. The town had even sent troops off to the Transvaal in 1899 and lost a handful, but by and large, life in Partageuse was more of a sideshow, in which nothing too evil or too wonderful could ever happen.

Other towns in the West had known things different, of course: Kalgoorlie, for example, hundreds of miles inland, had underground rivers of gold crusted by desert. There, men wandered in with a wheelbarrow and a gold-pan and drove out in a motorcar paid for by a nugget as big as a cat, in a town that only half ironically had streets with names like Croesus. The world wanted what Kalgoorlie had. The offerings of Partageuse, its timber and sandalwood, were small beer: it wasn't flashy boom-time like Kal.

Then in 1914 things changed. Partageuse found that it too had something the world wanted. Men. Young men. Fit men. Men who had spent their lives swinging an ax or holding a plow and living it hard. Men who were the prime cut to be sacrificed on tactical altars a hemisphere away.

Nineteen fourteen was just flags and new-smelling leather on uniforms. It wasn't until a year later that life started to feel different—started to feel as if maybe this wasn't a sideshow after all—when, instead of getting back their precious, strapping husbands and sons, the women began to get telegrams. These bits of paper which could fall from stunned hands and blow about in the knife-sharp wind, which told you that the boy you'd suckled, bathed, scolded and cried over, was—well—*wasn't*. Partageuse joined the world late and in a painful labor.

Of course, the losing of children had always been a thing that had to be gone through. There had never been guarantee that conception would lead to a live birth, or that birth would lead to a life of any great length. Nature allowed only the fit and the lucky to share this paradise-in-the-making. Look inside the cover of any family Bible and you'd see the facts. The graveyards, too, told the story of the babies whose voices, because of a snakebite or a fever or a fall from a wagon, had finally succumbed to their mothers' beseeching to "hush, hush, little one." The surviving children got used to the new way of setting the table with one place fewer, just as they grew accustomed to squishing along the bench when another sibling arrived. Like the wheat fields where more grain is sown than can ripen, God seemed to sprinkle extra children about, and harvest them according to some indecipherable, divine calendar.

The town cemetery had always recorded this truthfully, and its headstones, some lolling like loose, grimy teeth, told frankly the stories of lives taken early by influenza and drownings, by timber whims and even lightning strikes. But in 1915, it began to lie. Boys and men from across the district were dying by the score, yet the graveyards said nothing.

The truth was that the younger bodies lay in mud far away. The authorities did what they could: where conditions and combat permitted, graves were dug; when it was possible to put together a set of limbs and identify them as a single soldier, every effort was made to do so, and to bury him with a funeral rite of sorts. Records were kept. Later, photographs were taken of the graves, and, for the sum of £2 1s 6d, a family could buy an official commemorative plaque. Later still, the war memorials would sprout from the earth, dwelling not on the loss, but on what the loss had won, and what a fine thing it was to be victorious. "Victorious and dead," some muttered, "is a poor sort of victory."

As full of holes as a Swiss cheese the place was, without the men. Not that there had been conscription. No one had forced them to go and fight.

The cruelest joke was on the fellows everyone called "lucky" because they got to come back at all: back to the kids spruced up for the welcome home, to the dog with a ribbon tied to his collar so he could join in the fun. The dog was usually the first to spot that something was up. Not just that the bloke was missing an eye or a leg; more that he was missing generally—still missing in action, though his body had never been lost sight of. Billy Wishart from Sadler's Mill, for example—three little ones and a wife as good as a man has a right to hope for, gassed and can't hold a spoon any more without it sputtering like a chaff-cutter and spraying his soup all over the table. Can't manage his buttons because of the shakes. When he's alone at night with his wife he won't get out of his clothes, and just hugs himself into a ball on the bed and cries. Or young Sam Dowsett, who survived the first Gallipoli landing only to lose both arms and half his face at Bullecourt. His widowed mother sits up at night worrying who'll take care of her little boy once she's gone. There's not a girl in the district'd be silly enough to take him on now. Holes in Swiss cheese. Something missing.

For a long time, people wore the bewildered expression of players in a game where the rules had suddenly been changed. They tried hard to take comfort from the fact that the boys hadn't died in vain: they had been part of a magnificent struggle for right. And there were moments where they could believe that and swallow down the angry, desperate screech that wanted to scrape its way out of their gullets like out of a mother bird.

After the war, people tried to make allowances for the men who'd come back a bit too fond of a drink or a stoush, or the ones who couldn't hold down a job for more than a few days. Business in the town settled down after a fashion. Kelly still had the grocer's. The butcher was still old Len Bradshaw, though young Len was itching to take over: you could tell by the way he took up just a bit too much of his dad's space at the counter when he leaned past him to pick up a chop or a pig's cheek. Mrs. Inkpen (who never seemed to have a Christian name, though her sister called her Popsy in private) took over the farrier's when her husband, Mack, didn't make it back from Gallipoli. She had a face as hard as the iron the lads used to nail onto the horses' hooves, and a heart to match. Great hulks of men she had working for her, and it was all "Yes, Mrs. Inkpen. No, Mrs. Inkpen. Three bags full, Mrs. Inkpen," even though any of them could have picked her up with barely more than a finger.

People knew who to give credit to, and who to ask for money up front; who to believe when they brought goods back and asked for a refund. Mouchemore's draper's and haberdasher's did best around Christmas and Easter, though the run-up to winter brought them a swift trade in knitting wool. Did a profitable line in ladies' unmentionables, too. Larry Mouchemore used to pat his pointed mustache as he corrected mispronunciations of his name ("It's like 'move,' not like 'mouse,'"), and watched with fear and bile as Mrs. Thurkle got it into her head to open a furrier's next door. A fur shop? In Point Partageuse? If you please! He smiled benignly when it closed within six months, buying up the remaining stock "as an act of neighborly charity" and selling it at a tidy profit to the captain of a steamer bound for Canada, who said they were mad for that sort of thing there.

So by 1920, Partageuse had that mixture of tentative pride and hard-bitten experience that marked any West Australian town. In the middle of the handkerchief of grass near the main street stood the fresh granite obelisk listing the men and boys, some scarcely sixteen, who would not be coming back to plow the fields or fell the trees, would not be finishing their lessons, though many in the town held their breath, waiting for them anyway. Gradually, lives wove together once again into a practical sort of fabric in which every thread crossed and recrossed the others through school and work and marriage, embroidering connections invisible to those not from the town.

And Janus Rock, linked only by the store boat four times a year, dangled off the edge of the cloth like a loose button that might easily plummet to Antarctica.

The long, thin jetty at Point Partageuse was made from the same jarrah that rattled along it in rail carriages to be hauled onto ships. The wide bay above which the town had grown up was clear turquoise, and on the day Tom's boat docked it gleamed like polished glass.

Men beetled away, loading and unloading, heaving and wrestling cargo with the occasional shout or whistle. Onshore, the bustle continued, as people went about with a purposeful air, on foot or by horse and buggy.

The exception to this display of efficiency was a young woman feeding bread to a flock of seagulls. She was laughing as she threw each crust in a different direction and watched the birds squabble and screech, eager for a prize. A gull in full flight caught a morsel in one gulp and still dived for the next one, sending the girl into new peals of laughter.

It seemed years since Tom had heard a laugh that wasn't tinged with a roughness, a bitterness. It was a sunny winter's afternoon, and there was nowhere he had to go right that minute; nothing he had to do. He would be shipped out to Janus in a couple of days, once he had met the people he needed to meet and signed the forms he needed to sign. But for now, there were no logbooks to write up, no prisms to buff, no tanks to refuel. And here was someone just having a bit of fun. It suddenly felt like solid proof that the war was really over. He sat on a bench near the jetty, letting the sun caress his face, watching the girl lark about, the curls of her dark hair swirling like a net cast on the wind. He followed her delicate fingers as they made silhouettes against the blue. Only gradually did he notice she was pretty. And more gradually still that she was probably beautiful.

"What are you smiling at?" the girl called, catching Tom off guard.

"Sorry." He felt his face redden.

"Never be sorry for smiling!" she exclaimed in a voice that somehow had a sad edge. Then her expression brightened. "You're not from Partageuse."

"Nope."

"I am. Lived here all my life. Want some bread?"

"Thanks, but I'm not hungry."

"Not for you, silly! To feed the seagulls."

She offered him a crust in her outstretched hand. A year before, perhaps even a day before, Tom would have declined and walked away. But suddenly, the warmth and the freedom and the smile, and something he couldn't quite name, made him accept the offering.

"Bet I can get more to come to me than you can," she said.

"Righto, you're on!" said Tom.

"Go!" she declared, and the two of them began, throwing the pieces high in the air or at crafty angles, ducking as the gulls squawked and dive-bombed and flapped their wings at one another furiously.

Finally, when all the bread was gone, Tom asked, laughing, "Who won?"

"Oh! I forgot to judge." The girl shrugged. "Let's call it a draw."

"Fair enough," he said, putting his hat back on and picking up his duffel bag. "Better be on my way. Thanks. I enjoyed that."

She smiled. "It was just a silly game."

"Well," he said, "thanks for reminding me that silly games are fun." He slung the bag over his broad shoulder, and turned toward town. "You have a good afternoon now, Miss," he added.

Tom rang the bell at the boardinghouse on the main street. It was the domain of Mrs. Mewett, a woman of sixty-odd, as stout as a pepper pot, who set upon him. "Your letter said you're a bachelor, and you're Eastern States, so I'll thank you for remembering you're in Partageuse now. This is a Christian establishment, and there's to be no taking of alcohol or tobacco on the premises."

Tom was about to thank her for the key in her hand, but she clutched it fiercely as she continued, "None of your foreign habits here: I know what's what. I change the sheets when you leave and I don't expect to have to scrub them, if you know what I mean. The doors are locked at ten, breakfast is served at six a.m., and if you're not there you go hungry. Tea's at five thirty, and likewise applies. Lunch you can find somewhere else."

"Much obliged, Mrs. Mewett," said Tom, deciding against a smile in case it broke some other rule.

"Hot water's an extra shilling a week. Up to you whether you want it. In my book, cold water never did a man your age any harm." She thrust the room key at him. As she limped off down the passageway, Tom wondered whether there was a Mr. Mewett who had so endeared men to her.

In his small room at the back of the house, he unpacked his duffel bag, setting his soap and shaving things neatly on the one shelf provided. He folded his long johns and socks into the drawer, and hung his three shirts and two pairs of trousers, together with his good suit and tie, in the narrow wardrobe. He slipped a book into his pocket and set out to explore the town.

Tom Sherbourne's final duty in Partageuse was dinner with the Harbormaster and his wife. Captain Percy Hasluck was in charge of all the comings and goings at the port, and it was usual for any new Janus lightkeeper to be invited to dine with him before setting off for the island.

Tom washed and shaved again in the afternoon, put Brilliantine in his hair, buttoned on a collar and hauled on his suit. The sunshine of the previous days had been replaced by clouds and a vicious wind that blew straight from Antarctica, so he pulled on his greatcoat for good measure.

Still working on Sydney scales, he had left plenty of time to walk the unfamiliar route, and arrived at the house rather early. His host welcomed him with a broad smile, and when Tom apologized for his premature arrival, "Mrs. Captain Hasluck," as her husband referred to her, clapped her hands and said, "Gracious me, Mr. Sherbourne! You hardly need to apologize for gracing us with your presence promptly, especially when you've brought such lovely flowers." She inhaled the scent of the late roses Tom had negotiated to pick, for a fee, from Mrs. Mewett's garden. She peered up at him from her considerably lower vantage point. "Goodness! You're nearly as tall as the lighthouse yourself!" she said, and chuckled at her own wit.

The captain took Tom's hat and coat and said, "Come into the parlor," after which his wife immediately chimed, "Said the spider to the fly!"

"Ah, she's a card, that one!" exclaimed the Captain. Tom feared it could be a long evening.

"Now, some sherry? Or there's port?" offered the woman.

"Show some mercy and bring the poor devil a beer, Mrs. Captain," her husband said with a laugh. He slapped Tom on the back. "You have a seat and tell me all about yourself, young man."

Tom was rescued by the doorbell. "Excuse me," said Captain Hasluck. Down the hall Tom heard, "Cyril. Bertha. Glad you could come. Let me take your hats."

As Mrs. Captain returned to the parlor with a bottle of beer and glasses on a silver tray, she said, "We thought we'd invite a few people, just to introduce you to some locals. It's a very friendly place, Partageuse."

The Captain ushered in the new guests, a dour couple comprising the plump Chairman of the Local Roads Board—Cyril Chipper and his wife, Bertha, who was thin as a yard of pump water.

"Well, what do you make of the roads here?" launched Cyril as soon as they had been introduced. "No politeness, mind. Compared with over East, how would you rate them?"

"Oh, leave the poor man alone, Cyril," said the wife. Tom was grateful not only for that intervention but also for the doorbell, which rang again.

"Bill. Violet. Grand to see you," said the Captain as he opened the front door. "Ah, and *you* get lovelier by the day, young lady."

He showed into the parlor a solid man with gray whiskers, and his wife, sturdy and flushed. "This is Bill Graysmark, his wife, Violet, and their daughter . . ." He turned around. "Where's she got to? Anyway, there's a daughter here somewhere, she'll be through soon, I expect. Bill's the headmaster here in Partageuse."

"Pleased to meet you," said Tom, shaking the man by the hand and nodding politely to the woman.

"So," said Bill Graysmark, "you think you're up to Janus, then?"

"I'll soon find out," Tom said.

"Bleak out there, you know."

"So I hear."

"No roads on Janus, of course," threw in Cyril Chipper.

"Er, well, no," Tom said.

"Not sure I think much of a place with no roads at *all,*" Chipper pursued, in a tone that implied there were moral implications.

"No roads is the least of your problems, son," rejoined Graysmark.

"Dad, lay off, will you?" The missing daughter now entered as Tom had his back to the door. "The last thing the poor man needs is your tales of doom and gloom."

"Ah! Told you she'd turn up," said Captain Hasluck. "This is Isabel Graysmark. Isabel—meet Mr. Sherbourne."

Tom stood to greet her and their eyes met in recognition. He was about to make a reference to seagulls, but she silenced him with, "Pleased to meet you, Mr. Sherbourne."

"Tom, please," he said, speculating that perhaps she wasn't supposed to spend afternoons throwing bread to birds, after all. And he wondered what other secrets lay behind her playful smile.

The evening proceeded well enough, with the Haslucks telling Tom about the history of the district and the building of the lighthouse, back in the time of the Captain's father. "Very important for trade," the Harbormaster assured him. "The Southern Ocean is treacherous enough on the surface, let alone having that under-sea ridge. Safe transport is the key to business, everyone knows that."

"Of course, the real basis of safe transport is good roads," Chipper began again, about to launch into another variation on his only topic of conversation. Tom tried to look attentive, but was distracted out of the corner of his eye by Isabel. Unseen by the others, thanks to the angle of her chair, she had begun to make mock-serious expressions at Cyril Chipper's comments, keeping up a little pantomime that accompanied each remark.

The performance went on, with Tom struggling to keep a straight face, until finally a full laugh escaped, which he quickly converted into a coughing fit.

"Are you all right, Tom?" asked the Captain's wife. "I'll fetch you some water."

Tom couldn't look up, and, still coughing, said, "Thank you. I'll come with you. Don't know what set me off."

As Tom stood up, Isabel kept a perfectly straight face and said, "Now, when he comes back, you'll have to tell Tom all about how you make the roads out of jarrah, Mr. Chipper." Turning to Tom, she said, "Don't be long. Mr. Chipper's full of interesting stories," and she smiled innocently, her lips giving just a momentary tremble as Tom caught her eye.

When the gathering drew to a close, the guests wished Tom well for his stay on Janus. "You look like you're made of the right stuff," said Hasluck, and Bill Graysmark nodded in agreement.

"Thank you. It's been a pleasure to meet you all," said Tom, shaking hands with the gentlemen, and nodding to the ladies. "And thank you for making sure I got such a thorough introduction to Western Australian road construction," he said quietly to Isabel. "Pity I won't have a chance to repay you." And the little party dispersed into the wintry night.

CHAPTER 3

The *Windward Spirit,* the store boat for all the light stations along that part of the coast, was an old tub, but trusty as a cattle dog, Ralph Addicott said. Old Ralph had skippered the vessel for donkey's years, and always boasted he had the best job in the world.

"Ah, you'll be Tom Sherbourne. Welcome to my pleasure launch!" he said, gesturing to the bare wooden decks and salt-blistered paint as Tom came aboard before dawn for his first journey out to Janus Rock.

"Pleased to meet you," said Tom as he shook his hand. The engine was idling and the diesel fumes filled his lungs. It wasn't much warmer in the cabin than in the biting air outside, but at least it blunted the snarl of the wind.

A mess of red corkscrew curls emerged through the hatch at the back of the cabin. "Reckon we're ready, Ralph. She's all fixed now," said the young man they belonged to.

"Bluey, this is Tom Sherbourne," said Ralph.

"Gedday," replied Bluey, hauling himself through the hatch.

"Morning."

"Talk about brass-monkey weather! Hope you've packed your woolen underduds. If it's like this here, it'll be a bloody sight worse on Janus," said Bluey, breathing on his hands.

While Bluey showed Tom over the boat, the skipper ran through his final checks. He gave the brine-smeared glass in front of him a wipe with a scrap of old flag, then called, "Ropes at the ready now, lad. Prepare to cast off." He opened the throttle. "Come on, old girl, off we go," he muttered, to coax the boat out of its berth.

Tom studied the map on the chart table. Even magnified on this scale, Janus was barely a dot in the shoals far off the coast. He fixed his eyes on the expanse of sea ahead and breathed in the thick salt air, not looking back at the shore in case it made him change his mind.

As the hours passed, the water deepened below them, its color taking on the quality of a solid. From time to time Ralph would point out something of interest—a sea eagle, or a school of dolphins playing at the bow of the boat. Once, they saw the funnel of a steamer, just skirting the horizon. Periodically, Bluey emerged from the galley to hand out tea in chipped enamel mugs. Ralph told Tom stories of evil storms and great dramas of the Lights on that part of the coast. Tom talked a little of life at Byron Bay and on Maatsuyker Island, thousands of miles to the east.

"Well, if you've lived through Maatsuyker, there's a chance you'll survive Janus. Probably," Ralph said. He looked at his watch. "Why not grab forty winks while you can? We've got a way to go yet, boy."

When Tom re-emerged from the bunk below, Bluey was speaking in a low voice to Ralph, who was shaking his head.

"I just want to know if it's true. No harm in asking him, is there?" Bluey was saying.

"Asking me what?" said Tom.

"If . . ." Bluey looked at Ralph. Torn between his own eagerness and Ralph's bulldog scowl, he blushed and fell silent.

"Fair enough. None of my business," said Tom, and looked out at the water, which had now turned seal-gray, as the swell rose around them.

"I was too young. Ma wouldn't let me bump up me age to join up. And it's just that I heard . . ."

Tom looked at him, eyebrows raised in question.

"Well they reckon you got the Military Cross and that," Bluey blurted. "Told me it said on your discharge papers—for the Janus posting."

Tom kept his eyes on the water. Bluey looked crestfallen, then embarrassed. "I mean, I'm real proud to be able to say I've shaken the hand of a hero."

"A bit of brass doesn't make anyone a hero," Tom said. "Most of the blokes who really deserve the medals aren't around any more. Wouldn't get too worked up about it if I were you, mate," he said, and turned to pore over the chart.

"There she is!" exclaimed Bluey, and handed the binoculars to Tom.

"Home, sweet home, for the next six months." Ralph chuckled.

Tom looked through the lenses at the landmass which seemed to be emerging from the water like a sea monster. The cliff on one side marked the highest point, from which the island sloped down gently until it reached the opposite shore.

"Old Neville'll be glad to see us," Ralph said. "He didn't take kindly to being dragged out of retirement for Trimble's emergency, I can tell you. Still. Once a keeper . . . There's not a man in the service'd leave a light go unattended, however much he carried on about it. I warn you, though, he's not the happiest corpse in the morgue. Not much of a talker, Neville Whittnish."

The jetty stretched a good hundred feet out from the shoreline, where it had been built up tall, to withstand the highest of tides and fiercest of storms. The block and tackle was rigged, ready to hoist the supplies up the steep ascent to the outbuildings. A dour, craggy man of sixty-odd was waiting for them as they docked.

"Ralph. Bluey," he said with a perfunctory nod. "You're the replacement," was his greeting to Tom.

"Tom Sherbourne. Pleased to meet you," Tom replied, putting out his hand.

The older man looked at it absently for a moment before remembering what the gesture meant, and gave it a peremptory tug, as if testing whether the arm might come off. "This way," he said, and without waiting for Tom to gather his things, started the trudge up to the light station. It was early afternoon, and after so many hours on the swell, it took Tom a moment to get the feel of land again as he grabbed his kit bag and staggered after the keeper, while Ralph and Bluey prepared to unload the supplies.

"Keeper's cottage," said Whittnish as they approached a low building with a corrugated-iron roof. A trio of large rainwater tanks ranged behind it, beside a string of outbuildings housing stores for the cottage and the light. "You can leave your kit bag in the hallway," he said, as he opened the front door. "Got a lot to get through." He turned on his heel and headed straight to the tower. He might be long in the tooth, but he could move like a whippet.

Later, when the old man spoke about the light, his voice changed, as though he were talking about a faithful dog or a favorite rose. "She's a beauty, still, after all these years," he said. The white stone light tower rested against the slate sky like a stick of chalk. It stood a hundred and thirty feet high, near the cliff at the island's apex, and Tom was struck not only by how much taller it was than the lights he had worked on, but also by its slender elegance.

Walking through its green door, it was more or less what he expected. The space could be crossed in a couple of strides, and the sound of their footsteps ricocheted like stray bullets off the green-gloss-painted floors and curved, whitewashed walls. The few pieces of furniture—two store cupboards, a small table—were curved at the back to fit the roundness of the structure, so that they huddled against the walls like hunchbacks. In the very center stood the thick iron cylinder which ran all the way up to the lantern room, and housed the weights for the clockwork which had originally rotated the light.

A set of stairs no more than two feet wide began a spiral across one side of the wall and disappeared into the solid metal of the landing above. Tom followed the old man up to the next, narrower level, where the helix continued from the opposite wall up to the next floor, and on again until they arrived at the fifth one, just below the lantern room—the administrative heart of the lighthouse. Here in the watch room was the desk with the logbooks, the Morse equipment, the binoculars. Of course, it was forbidden to have a bed or any furniture in the light tower on which one could recline, but there was at least a straight-backed wooden chair, its arms worn smooth by generations of craggy palms.

The barometer could do with a polish, Tom noted, before his eye was caught by something sitting beside the marine charts. It was a ball of wool with knitting needles stuck through it, and what looked like the beginnings of a scarf.

"Old Docherty's," said Whittnish with a nod.

Tom knew the variety of activities the keepers used to while away any quiet moments on duty: carving scrimshaw or shells; making chess pieces. Knitting was common enough.

Whittnish ran through the logbook and the weather observations, then led Tom to the light itself, on the next level up. The glazing of the light room was interrupted only by the crisscrossing of astragals that kept the panes in place. Outside, the metal gallery circled the tower, and a perilous ladder arched against the dome, up to the thin catwalk just below the weather vane that swung in the wind.

"She's a beauty all right," said Tom, taking in the giant lens, far taller than himself, atop the rotating pedestal: a palace of prisms like a beehive made from glass. It was the very heart of Janus, all light and clarity and silence.

A barely perceptible smile passed over the old keeper's lips as he said, "I've known her since I was barely a boy. Ah yes, a beauty."

The following morning, Ralph stood on the jetty. "Nearly ready for the off, then. Want us to bring out all the newspapers you've missed next trip?"

"It's hardly news if it's months old. I'd rather save my money and buy a good book," replied Tom.

Ralph looked about him, checking everything was in order. "Well, that's that then. No changing your mind now, son."

Tom gave a rueful laugh. "Reckon you're right on that score, Ralph."

"We'll be back before you know it. Three months is nothing as long as you're not trying to hold your breath!"

"You treat the light right and she won't give you any trouble," said Whittnish. "All you need is patience and a bit of nous."

"I'll see what I can do," said Tom. Then he turned to Bluey, who was getting ready to cast off. "See you in three months then, Blue?"

"You bet."

The boat pulled away, churning the water behind it and battling the wind with a smoky roar. The distance pressed it further and further into the gray horizon like a thumb pushing it into putty, until it was subsumed completely.

Then, a moment's stillness. Not silence: the waves still shattered on the rocks, the wind screeched around his ears, and a loose door on one of the storage sheds banged a disgruntled drumbeat. But something inside Tom was still for the first time in years.

He walked up to the cliff top and stood. A goat's bell clanged; two chickens squabbled. Suddenly these pinpricks of sound took on a new importance: sounds from living things. Tom climbed the 184 stairs to the lantern room and opened the door to the gallery. The wind pounced on him like a predator, slamming him back into the doorway until he gathered the strength to launch himself outward and grip the iron handrail.

For the first time he took in the scale of the view. Hundreds of feet above sea level, he was mesmerized by the drop to the ocean crashing against the cliffs directly below. The water sloshed like white paint, milky-thick, the foam occasionally scraped off long enough to reveal a deep blue undercoat. At the other end of the island, a row of immense boulders created a break against the surf and left the water inside it as calm as a bath. He had the impression he was hanging from the sky, not rising from the earth. Very slowly, he turned a full circle, taking in the nothingness of it all. It seemed his lungs could never be large enough to breathe in this much air, his eyes could never see this much space, nor could he hear the full extent of the rolling, roaring ocean. For the briefest moment, he had no edges.

He blinked, and shook his head quickly. He was nearing a vortex, and to pull himself back he paid attention to his heartbeat, felt his feet on the ground and his heels in his boots. He drew himself up to his full height. He picked a point on the door of the light tower—a hinge that had worked itself loose—and resolved to start with that. Something solid. He must turn to something solid, because if he didn't, who knew where his mind or his soul could blow away to, like a balloon without ballast. That was the only thing that had got him through four years of blood and madness: know exactly where your gun is when you doze for ten minutes in your dugout; always check your gas mask; see that your men have understood their orders to the letter. You don't think ahead in years or months: you think about this hour, and maybe the next. Anything else is speculation.

He raised the binoculars and scoured the island for more signs of life: he needed to *see* the goats, the sheep; to count them. Stick to the solid. To the brass fittings which had to be polished, the glass which had to be cleaned—first the outer glass of the lantern, then the prisms themselves. Getting the oil in, keeping the cogs moving smoothly, topping up the mercury to let the light glide. He gripped each thought like the rung of a ladder by which to haul himself back to the knowable; back to this life.

That night, as he lit the lamp, he moved as slowly and carefully as one of the priests might have done thousands of years earlier in the first lighthouse at Pharos. He climbed the tiny metal stairs that led to the inner deck around the light itself, ducked through the opening and into the apparatus of the light. He primed the oil by lighting a flame under its dish so that it vaporized and reached the mantle as a gas. He then set a match to the mantle, which transformed the vapor into a white brilliance. He went down to the next level and started the motor. The light began to turn with the exact, even rhythm of the five-second flash. He picked up the pen, and wrote in the wide, leather-bound log: *"Lit up at 5:09 p.m. Wind N/NE 15 knots. Overcast, squally. Sea 6."* Then, he added his initials—*T.S.* His handwriting took over the telling of the story where Whittnish had left off only hours before, and Docherty before that—he was part of the unbroken chain of keepers bearing witness to the light.

Once he was satisfied everything was in order, he went back to the cottage. His body craved sleep, but he knew too well that if you don't eat you can't work. In the larder off the kitchen, tins of bully beef and peas and pears sat on shelves beside sardines and sugar and a big jar of humbugs, of which the late Mrs. Docherty had been legendarily fond. For his first night's supper he cut a hunk of the damper Whittnish had left behind, a piece of cheddar and a wrinkled apple.

At the kitchen table, the flame of the oil lamp wavered occasionally. The wind continued its ancient vendetta against the windows, accompanied by the liquid thunder of waves. Tom tingled at the knowledge that he was the only one to hear any of it: the only living man for the better part of a hundred miles in any direction. He thought of the gulls nestled into their wiry homes on the cliffs, the fish hovering stilly in the safety of the reefs, protected by the icy water. Every creature needed its place of refuge.

Tom carried the lamp into the bedroom. His shadow pressed itself against the wall, a flat giant, as he pulled off his boots and stripped down to his long johns. His hair was thick with salt and his skin raw from the wind. He pulled back the sheets and climbed in, falling into dreams as his body kept up the sway of the waves and the wind. All night, far above him the light stood guard, slicing the darkness like a sword.

CHAPTER 4

Once he has extinguished the light at sunrise each morning, Tom sets off to explore another part of his new territory before getting on with the day's work. The northern side of the island is a sheer granite cliff which sets its jaw stiffly against the ocean below. The land slopes down toward the south and slides gently under the water of the shallow lagoon. Beside its little beach is the water wheel, which carries fresh water from the spring up to the cottage: from the mainland, all the way out along the ocean floor to the island and beyond, there are fissures from which fresh water springs mysteriously. When the French described the phenomenon in the eighteenth century, it was dismissed as a myth. But sure enough, fresh water was to be found even in various parts of the ocean, like a magic trick played by nature.

He begins to shape his routine. Regulations require that each Sunday he hoist the ensign and he does, first thing. He raises it too when any "man o' war," as the rules put it, passes the island. He knows keepers who swear under their breath at the obligation, but Tom takes comfort from the orderliness of it. It is a luxury to do something that serves no practical purpose: the luxury of civilization.

He sets about fixing things that have fallen into disrepair since the decline of Trimble Docherty. Most important is the lighthouse itself, which needs putty in the astragals of the lantern glazing. Next he gets rottenstone and sands the wood on the desk drawer where it has swollen with the weather, and goes over it with the wolf's-head brush. He patches the green paint on the landings where it is scuffed or worn away: it will be a long while before a crew comes to paint the whole station.

The apparatus responds to his attention: the glass gleams, the brass shines, and the light rotates on its bath of mercury as smoothly as a skua gliding on currents of air. Now and again he manages to get down to the rocks to fish, or to walk along the sandy beach of the lagoon. He makes friends with the pair of black skinks which reside in the woodshed, and occasionally gives them some of the chooks' food. He's sparing with his rations: he won't see the store boat for months.

It's a hard job, and a busy one. The lightkeepers have no union—not like the men on the store boats—no one strikes for better pay or conditions. The days can leave him exhausted or sore, worried by the look of a storm front coming in at a gallop, or frustrated by the way hailstones crush the vegetable patch. But if he doesn't think about it too hard, he knows who he is and what he's for. He just has to keep the light burning. Nothing more.

The Father Christmas face, all red cheeks and whiskers, gave a big grin. "Well, Tom Sherbourne, how are you surviving?" Ralph didn't wait for a reply before throwing him the fat, wet rope to wind around the bollard. Tom looked as fit and well after three months as any keeper the skipper had seen.

Tom had been waiting for supplies for the light, and had given less thought to the fresh food which would be delivered. He had also forgotten that the boat would bring post, and was surprised when, toward the end of the day, Ralph handed him some envelopes. "Almost forgot," he said. There was a letter from the District Officer of the Lighthouse Service, retrospectively confirming his appointment and conditions. A letter from the Department of Repatriation set out certain benefits recently allowed to returned servicemen, including incapacity pension or a business loan. Neither applied to him, so he opened the next, a Commonwealth Bank statement confirming that he had earned four per cent interest on the five hundred pounds in his account. He left until last the envelope addressed by hand. He could not think of anyone who might write, and feared it might be some do-gooder sending him news of his brother or his father.

He opened it. *"Dear Tom, I just thought I'd write and check that you hadn't been blown away or swept out to sea or anything. And that the lack of roads isn't causing you too many problems . . ."* He skipped ahead to see the signature: *"Yours truly, Isabel Graysmark."* The gist of the middle was that she hoped he wasn't too lonely out there, and that he should be sure to stop by and say hello before he went off to wherever he was going after his Janus posting. She had decorated the letter with a little sketch of a keeper leaning against his light tower, whistling a tune, while behind him a giant whale emerged from the water, its jaws wide open. She had added for good measure: *"Be sure not to get eaten by a whale before then."*

It made Tom smile. The absurdity of the picture. More than that, the innocence of it. Somehow his body felt lighter just to hold the letter in his hand.

"Can you hang on a tick?" he asked Ralph, who was gathering his things for the journey back.

Tom dashed to his desk for paper and pen. He sat down to write, before realizing he had no idea what to say. He didn't want to *say* anything: just send her a smile.

Dear Isabel,

Not blown away or swept (any further) out to sea, fortunately. I have seen many whales, but none has tried to eat me so far: I'm probably not very tasty.

I am bearing up pretty well, all things considered, and coping adequately with the absence of roads. I trust you are keeping the local birdlife well fed. I look forward to seeing you before I leave Partageuse for—who knows where?—in three months' time.

How should he sign it?

"Nearly ready?" called Ralph.

"Nearly," he replied, and wrote, "*Tom.*" He sealed and addressed the envelope, and handed it to the skipper. "Any chance you could post that for me?"

Ralph looked at the address and winked. "I'll deliver it in person. Got to go past that place anyway."

CHAPTER 5

At the end of his six months, Tom savored the delights of Mrs. Mewett's hospitality once again, for an unexpected reason: the Janus vacancy had become permanent. Far from finding his marbles, Trimble Docherty had lost the few he still had, and had thrown himself over the vast granite cliff-face at Albany known as the Gap, apparently convinced he was jumping onto a boat skippered by his beloved wife. So Tom had been summoned to shore to discuss the post, do the paperwork, and take some leave before he officially took up the job. By now he had proved himself so capable that Fremantle did not bother to look elsewhere to fill the position.

"Never underestimate the importance of the right wife," Captain Hasluck had said when Tom was about to leave his office. "Old Moira Docherty could have worked the light herself, she'd been with Trimble for so long. Takes a special kind of woman to live on the Lights. When you find the right one, you want to snap her up, quick smart. Mind you, you'll have to wait a bit now . . ."

As Tom wandered back to Mrs. Mewett's, he thought about the little relics at the lighthouse—Docherty's knitting, his wife's jar of humbugs that sat untouched in the pantry. Lives gone, traces left. And he wondered about the despair of the man, destroyed by grief. It didn't take a war to push you over that edge.

Two days after his return to Partageuse, Tom sat stiff as a whalebone in the Graysmarks' lounge room, where both parents watched over their only daughter like eagles with a chick. Struggling to come up with suitable topics of conversation, Tom stuck to the weather, the wind, of which there was an abundance, and Graysmark cousins in other parts of Western Australia. It was relatively easy to steer the conversation away from himself.

As Isabel walked him to the gate afterward she asked, "How long till you go back?"

"Two weeks."

"Then we'd better make the most of it," she said, as though concluding a long discussion.

"Is that so?" asked Tom, as amused as he was surprised. He had a sense of being waltzed backward.

Isabel smiled. "Yes, that's so." And the way the light caught her eyes, he imagined he could see into her: see a clarity, an openness, which drew him in. "Come and visit tomorrow. I'll make a picnic. We can go down by the bay."

"I should ask your father first, shouldn't I? Or your mother?" He leaned his head to one side. "I mean, if it's not a rude question, how old are you?"

"Old enough to go on a picnic."

"And in ordinary numbers that would make you . . . ?"

"Nineteen. Just about. So you can leave my parents to me," she said, and gave him a wave as she headed back inside.

Tom set off back to Mrs. Mewett's with a lightness in his step. Why, he could not say. He didn't know the first thing about this girl, except that she smiled a lot, and that something inside just felt—*good.*

The following day, Tom approached the Graysmarks' house, not so much nervous as puzzled, not quite sure how it was that he was heading back there so soon.

Mrs. Graysmark smiled as she opened the door. "Nice and punctual," she noted on some invisible checklist.

"Army habits . . ." said Tom.

Isabel appeared with a picnic basket, which she handed to him. "You're in charge of getting it there in one piece," she said, and turned to kiss her mother on the cheek. "Bye, Ma. See you later."

"Mind you keep out of the sun, now. Don't want you spoiling your skin with freckles," she said to her daughter. She gave Tom a look which conveyed something sterner than the words, "Enjoy your picnic. Don't be too late back."

"Thanks, Mrs. Graysmark. We won't be."

Isabel led the way as they walked beyond the few streets that marked out the town proper and approached the ocean.

"Where are we going?" asked Tom.

"It's a surprise."

They wandered along the dirt road which led up to the headland, bordered with dense, scrubby trees on each side. These were not the giants from the forest a mile or so further in, but wiry, stocky things, which could cope with the salt and the blasting of the wind. "It's a bit of a walk. You won't get too tired, will you?" she asked.

Tom laughed. "I'll just about manage without a walking stick."

"Well I just thought, you don't have very far to walk on Janus, do you?"

"Believe me, getting up and down the stairs of the light all day keeps you in trim." He was still taking stock of this girl and her uncanny ability to tip him a fraction off balance.

The trees began to thin out the further they walked, and the sounds of the ocean grew louder. "I suppose Partageuse seems dead boring, coming from Sydney," ventured Isabel.

"Haven't spent long enough here to know, really."

"I suppose not. But Sydney—I imagine it as huge and busy and wonderful. The big smoke."

"It's pretty small fry compared to London."

Isabel blushed. "Oh, I didn't know you'd been there. That must be a *real* city. Maybe I'll visit it one day."

"You're better off here, I'd say. London's—well, it was pretty grim whenever I was there on furlough. Gray and gloomy and cold as a corpse. I'd take Partageuse any day."

"We're getting near the prettiest bit. Or I think it's the prettiest." Beyond the trees emerged an isthmus which jutted far out into the ocean. It was a long, bare strip of land a few hundred yards wide and licked by waves on all sides. "This is the *Point* of Point Partageuse," said Isabel. "My favorite place is down there, on the left, where all the big rocks are."

They walked on until they were in the center of the isthmus. "Dump the basket and follow me," she said, and without warning she whisked off her shoes and took off, running to the black granite boulders which tumbled down into the water.

Tom caught her up as she approached the edge. There was a circle of boulders, inside which the waves sloshed and swirled. Isabel lay flat on the ground and leaned her head over the edge. "Listen," she said. "Just listen to the sound the water makes, like it's in a cave or a cathedral."

Tom leaned forward to hear.

"You've got to lie down," she said.

"To hear better?"

"No. So you don't get washed away. Terrible blowhole, this. If a big wave comes without warning, you'll be down inside the rocks before you know it."

Tom lay down beside her and hung his head into the space, where the waves echoed and bellowed and washed about. "Reminds me of Janus."

"What's it like out there? You hear stories, but no one much ever actually goes there except the keeper and the boat. Or a doctor, once, years ago, when a whole ship was quarantined there with typhoid."

"It's like . . . Well, it's like nowhere else on earth. It's its own world."

"They say it's brutal, the weather."

"It has its moments."

Isabel sat up. "Do you get lonely?"

"Too busy to be lonely. There's always something needs fixi
checking or recording."

She put her head on one side, half signaling her doubt, but
it pass. "Do you like it?"

"Yep."

Now it was Isabel who laughed. "You don't exactly yack a
you?"

Tom stood up. "Hungry? Must be time for lunch."

He took Isabel's hand and helped her up. Such a petite h
with the palm covered in a fine layer of gritty sand. So delicat

Isabel served him roast beef sandwiches and ginger beer
by fruitcake and crisp apples.

"So, do you write to all the lightkeepers who go out to Ja
Tom.

"All! There aren't that many," said Isabel. You're the first
years."

Tom hesitated before venturing the next question. "
you write?"

She smiled at him and took a sip of ginger beer be
ing. "Because you're fun to feed seagulls with? Because
Because I'd never sent a letter to a lighthouse before?"
strand of hair from her eyes and looked down at the wat
rather I hadn't?"

"Oh, no, I wasn't trying to . . . I mean . . ." Tom w
on his napkin. Always slightly off balance. It was a ne
him.

Tom and Isabel were sitting at the end of the jetty
was almost the last day of 1920, and the breeze playe

wavelets against the boat hulls and plucking the ropes on the masts. The harbor lights trailed across the water's surface, and the sky was swept with stars.

"But I want to know everything," said Isabel, bare feet dangling above the water. "You can't just say, 'Nothing else to tell.'" She'd extracted the basic details of his private-school education, and his Engineering degree from Sydney University, but was growing more frustrated. "I can tell you lots—my Gran and how she taught me piano, what I remember about my granddad, even though he died when I was little. I can tell you what it's like to be the headmaster's daughter in a place like Partageuse. I can tell you about my brothers, Hugh and Alfie, and how we used to muck around with the dinghy and go off fishing down the river." She looked at the water. "I still miss those times." Curling a lock of hair around her finger, she considered something, then took a breath. "It's like a whole . . . a whole galaxy waiting for you to find out about. And I want to find out about yours."

"What else do you want to know?"

"Well, about your family, say."

"I've got a brother."

"Am I allowed to know his name, or have you forgotten it?"

"I'm not likely to forget that in a hurry. Cecil."

"What about your parents?"

Tom squinted at the light on top of a mast. "What about them?"

Isabel sat up, and looked deep into his eyes. "What goes on in there, wonder?"

"My mother's dead now. I don't keep in touch with my father." Her ιawl had slipped off her shoulder, and he pulled it back up. "Are you ·tting a bit chilly? Want to walk back?"

"Why won't you talk about it?"

"I'll tell you if you really want. It's just I'd rather not. Sometimes it's od to leave the past in the past."

"Your family's never in your past. You carry it around with you rywhere."

"More's the pity."

Isabel straightened. "It doesn't matter. Let's go. Mum and Dad'll be wondering where we've got to," she said, and they walked soberly up the jetty.

That night as he lay in bed, Tom cast his mind back to the childhood Isabel had been so keen to investigate. He had never really spoken to anyone about it. But exploring the memories now, the jagged pain was like running his tongue over a broken tooth. He could see his eight-year-old self, tugging his father's sleeve and crying, "Please! Please let her come back. Please, Daddy. I love her!" and his father wiping his hand away like a grubby mark. "You don't mention her again in this house. You hear, son?"

As his father stalked out of the room, Tom's brother, Cecil, five years older and at that stage a good measure taller, gave him a clip on the back of the head. "I told you, you idiot. I told you not to say it," and followed his father, with the same officious stride, leaving the small boy standing in the middle of the lounge room. From his pocket he took a lace handkerchief, redolent with his mother's scent, and touched it to his cheek, avoiding his tears and streaming nose. It was the feel of the cloth he wanted, the perfume, not its use.

Tom thought back to the imposing, empty house: to the silence that deadened every room with a subtly different pitch; to the kitchen smelling of carbolic, kept spotless by a long line of housekeepers. He remembered that dreaded smell of Lux flakes, and his distress as he saw the handkerchief, washed and starched by Mrs. Someone-or-other, who had discovered it in the pocket of his shorts and laundered it as a matter of course, obliterating his mother's smell. He had searched the house for some corner, some cupboard which could bring back that blurry sweetness of her. But even in what had been her bedroom, there was only polish and mothballs, as though her ghost had finally been exorcised.

In Partageuse, as they sat in the tearoom, Isabel tried again.

"I'm not trying to hide anything," Tom said. "It's just that raking over the past is a waste of time."

"And I'm not trying to pry. Only—you've had a whole life, a whole story, and I've come in late. I'm only trying to make sense of things. Make sense of you." She hesitated, then asked delicately, "If I can't talk about the past, am I allowed to talk about the future?"

"We can't rightly ever talk about the future, if you think about it. We can only talk about what we imagine, or wish for. It's not the same thing."

"OK, what do you *wish for,* then?"

Tom paused. "Life. That'll do me, I reckon." He drew a deep breath and turned to her. "What about you?"

"Oh, I wish for all sorts of things, all the time!" she exclaimed. "I wish for nice weather for the Sunday-school picnic. I wish for—don't laugh—I wish for a good husband and a houseful of kids. The sound of a cricket ball breaking a window and the smell of stew in the kitchen. The girls'll sing Christmas carols together and the boys'll kick the footy . . . I can't imagine not having children one day, can you?" She seemed to drift away for a moment before saying, "Of course, I wouldn't want one yet." She hesitated. "Not like Sarah."

"Who?"

"My friend, Sarah Porter. Used to live down the road. We used to play cubbies together. She was a bit older, and always had to be mother." Her expression clouded. "She got . . . in the family way—when she was sixteen. Her parents sent her up to Perth, out of sight. Made her give the baby to an orphanage. They said he'd be adopted, but he had a clubfoot.

"Later she got married, and the baby was all forgotten about. Then one day, she asked me if I'd come up to Perth with her, to visit the orphanage, in secret. The 'Infant Asylum,' just a few doors down from the proper madhouse. Oh, Tom, you've never seen such a sight as a ward full of motherless tots. No one to love them. Sarah couldn't breathe a word to her husband—he'd have sent her packing. He has no idea, even now. Her baby was still there: all she could do was look. The funny thing was, I was the one who couldn't stop crying. The look on their little faces. It really got to me. You might as well send a child straight to hell as send it to an orphanage."

"A kid needs its mum," said Tom, lost in a thought of his own.

Isabel said, "Sarah lives in Sydney now. I don't hear from her any more."

In those two weeks, Tom and Isabel saw each other every day. When Bill Graysmark challenged his wife about the propriety of this sudden "stepping out," she said, "Oh, Bill. Life's a short thing. She's a sensible girl and she knows her own mind. Besides, there's little enough chance these days of her finding a man with all his limbs attached. Don't look a gift horse . . ." She knew, also, that Partageuse was small. There was nowhere they could get up to anything much. Dozens of eyes and ears would report the least sign of anything untoward.

It surprised Tom how much he looked forward to seeing Isabel. Somehow she had crept under his defenses. He enjoyed her stories of life in Partageuse, and its history; about how the French had chosen that name for this spot between oceans because it meant "good at sharing" as well as "dividing." She talked about the time she fell from a tree and broke her arm, the day she and her brothers painted red spots on Mrs. Mewett's goat and knocked on her door to tell her it had measles. She told him quietly, and with many pauses, about their deaths in the Somme, and how she wished she could get her parents to smile again.

He was wary, though. This was a small town. She was a lot younger than he was. He'd probably never see her again once he went back out to the light. Other blokes might take advantage, but to Tom, the idea of honor was a kind of antidote to some of the things he'd lived through.

Isabel herself could hardly have put into words the new feeling—excitement, perhaps—she felt every time she saw this man. There was something mysterious about him—as though, behind his smile, he was still far away. She wanted to get to the heart of him.

If the war had taught her anything, it was to take nothing for granted: that it wasn't safe to put off what mattered. Life could snatch away the things you treasured, and there was no getting them back. She began to feel an urgency, a need to seize an opportunity. Before anyone else did.

The evening before he was due to go back to Janus, they were walking along the beach. Though January was only two days old, it felt like years since Tom had first landed in Partageuse, six months before.

Isabel looked out to sea, where the sun was sliding down the sky and into the gray water at the edge of the world. She said, "I was wondering if you'd do me a favor, Tom."

"Yep. What?"

"I was wondering," she said, not slowing her pace, "if you'd kiss me."

Tom half thought the wind had made the words up, and because she didn't stop walking, he tried to work out what it could have been that she really said.

He took a guess. "Of course I'll miss you. But—maybe I'll see you next time I'm back on leave?"

She gave him an odd look, and he began to worry. Even in the dying light, her face seemed red.

"I'm—I'm sorry, Isabel. I'm not too good with words . . . in situations like this."

"Situations like what?" she asked, crushed by the thought that this must be something he did all the time. A girl in every port.

"Like—saying goodbye. I'm all right on my own. And I'm all right with a bit of company. It's the switching from one to the other that gets me."

"Well, I'll make it easy for you then, shall I? I'll just go. Right now." She whipped around and started off down the beach.

"Isabel! Isabel, wait!" He ran after her and caught her hand. "I didn't want you to just go off without—well, just go off like that. And I *will* do your favor, I *will* miss you. You're—well, you're good to be with."

"Then take me out to Janus."

"What—you want to come for the trip out?"

"No. To live there."

Tom laughed. "God, you come out with some humdingers sometimes."

"I'm serious."

"You can't be," said Tom, though something in her look told him she just might.

"Why not?"

"Well, for about a hundred reasons, just off the top of my head. Most obviously because the only woman allowed on Janus is the keeper's wife." She said nothing, so he inclined his head a fraction more as if that might help him understand.

"So marry me!"

He blinked. "Izz—I hardly know you! And besides, I've never even—well, I've never even kissed you, for crying out loud."

"At long last!" She spoke as if the solution were blindingly obvious, and she stood on tiptoes to pull his head down toward her. Before he knew what was happening he was being kissed, inexpertly but with great force. He pulled away from her.

"That's a dangerous game to play, Isabel. You shouldn't go running around kissing blokes out of the blue. Not unless you mean it."

"But I do mean it!"

Tom looked at her, her eyes challenging him, her petite chin set firm. Once he crossed that line, who knew where he would end up? Oh, bugger it. To hell with good behavior. To hell with doing the right thing. Here was a beautiful girl, begging to be kissed, and the sun was gone and the weeks were up and he'd be out in the middle of bloody nowhere this time tomorrow. He took her face in his hands and bent low as he said, "Then this is how you do it," and kissed her slowly, letting time fade away. And he couldn't remember any other kiss that felt quite the same.

Finally he drew back, and brushed a strand of hair out of her eyes. "Better get you home or they'll have the troopers after me." He slipped his arm around her shoulder and guided her along the sand.

"I meant it, you know, about getting married."

"You'd have to have rocks in your head to want to marry me, Izz. There's not much money in lightkeeping. And it's a hell of a job for a wife."

"I know what I want, Tom."

He stood still. "Look. I don't want to sound patronizing, Isabel, but you're—well, you're quite a bit younger than me: I'm twenty-eight this year. And I'm guessing you haven't walked out with many fellows." He would have wagered, from the attempt at a kiss, that she hadn't walked out with any.

"What's that got to do with it?"

"Just—well, don't get confused between a thing itself and the first time you come across it. Think it over. I'll bet all the tea in China that in twelve months you'll have forgotten all about me."

"Humor me," she said, and reached up to kiss him again.

CHAPTER 6

On clear summer days, Janus seems to stretch up right to its tiptoes: you'd swear it's higher out of the water at some times than at others, not just because of the rising and ebbing of the tide. It can disappear altogether in rainstorms, disguised like a goddess in a Greek myth. Or sea mists brew up: warm air heavy with salt crystals which obstruct the passage of the light. If there are bushfires, the smoke can reach even this far out, carrying thick, sticky ash which tints the sunsets lavish red and gold, and coats the lantern-room glazing with grime. For these reasons the island needs the strongest, brightest of lights.

From the gallery, the horizon stretches forty miles. It seems improbable to Tom that such endless space could exist in the same lifetime as the ground that was fought over a foot at a time only a handful of years ago, where men lost their lives for the sake of labeling a few muddy yards as "ours" instead of "theirs," only to have them snatched back a day later. Perhaps the same labeling obsession caused cartographers to split this body of water into two oceans, even though it is impossible to touch an exact point at which their currents begin to differ. Splitting. Labeling. Seeking out otherness. Some things don't change.

On Janus, there is no reason to speak. Tom can go for months and not hear his own voice. He knows some keepers who make a point of singing, just like turning over an engine to make sure it still works. But Tom finds a freedom in the silence. He listens to the wind. He observes the tiny details of life on the island.

Now and then, as if brought in on the breeze, the memory of Isabel's kiss floats into his awareness: the touch of her skin, the soft wholeness of her. And he thinks of the years when he simply couldn't have imagined that such a thing existed. Just to be beside her had made him feel cleaner somehow, refreshed. Yet the sensation leads him back into the darkness, back into the galleries of wounded flesh and twisted limbs. To make sense of it—that's the challenge. To bear witness to the death, without being broken by the weight of it. There's no reason he should still be alive, un-maimed. Suddenly Tom realizes he is crying. He weeps for the men snatched away to his left and right, when death had no appetite for him. He weeps for the men he killed.

On the Lights, you account for every single day. You write up the log, you report what's happened, you produce evidence that life goes on. In time, as the ghosts start to dissolve in the pure Janus air, Tom dares to think of the life ahead of him—a thing that for years has been too improbable to depend on. Isabel is there in his thoughts, laughing in spite of it all, insatiably curious about the world around her, and game for anything. Captain Hasluck's advice echoes in his memory as he goes to the woodshed. Having chosen a piece of mallee root, he carries it to the workshop.

Janus Rock,

15th March 1921

Dear Isabel,

I hope this letter finds you well. I am very well. I like it out here. That probably sounds strange, but I do. The quiet suits me. There's something magical about Janus. It's like nowhere I've ever been.

I wish you could see the sunrise and sunset here. And the stars: the sky gets crowded at night, and it is a bit like watching a clock, seeing the constellations slide across the sky. It's comforting to know that they'll show up, however bad the day has been, however crook things get. That used to help in France. It put things into perspective—the stars had been around since before there were people. They just kept shining, no matter what was going on. I think of the light here like that, like a splinter of a star that's fallen to earth: it just shines, no matter what is happening. Summer, winter, storm, fine weather. People can rely on it.

Better stop rabbiting on. The point is, I am sending with this letter a little box I have carved for you. I hope it's useful. You might put jewelry in it, or hairclips and whatnot.

By now you have probably changed your mind about things, and I just wanted to say that that is all right. You are a wonderful girl, and I enjoyed the time we spent together.

The boat comes tomorrow, so I will give this to Ralph then.

Tom.

Janus Rock,

15th June 1921

Dear Isabel,

I am writing this quickly, as the boys are getting ready to leave. Ralph delivered your letter. It was good to hear from you. I am glad you liked the box.

Thank you for the photograph. You look beautiful, but not as cheeky as you are in real life. I know just where I will put it in the lantern room, so that you can see out through the window.

No, it doesn't really feel all that strange, your question. If I think about it, in the war I knew plenty of fellows who got spliced on three-day furlough back in England, then came straight back to carry on the show. Most of them thought they might not be around much longer, and probably so did their girls. With a bit of luck I will be a longer-term proposition, so think carefully. I am prepared to risk it if you are. I can apply for exceptional shore leave at the end of December, so you have got time to think it over. If you change your mind, I will understand. And if you don't, I promise I will take care of you always, and do my very best to be a good husband.

Yours,

Tom.

The next six months passed slowly. There had been nothing to wait for before—Tom had grown so used to greeting the days as ends in themselves. Now, there was a wedding date. There were arrangements to be made, permissions to be sought. In any spare minute, he would go around the cottage and find something else to put right: the window in the kitchen that didn't quite shut; the tap that needed a man's force to turn it. What would Isabel need, out here? With the last boat back, he sent an order for paint to freshen up the rooms; a mirror for the dressing table; new towels and tablecloths; sheet music for the decrepit piano—he had never touched it, but he knew Isabel loved to play. He hesitated before adding to the list new sheets, two new pillows and an eiderdown.

When, finally, the boat arrived to take Tom back for the big day, Neville Whittnish strode onto the jetty, ready to fill in during his absence.

"Everything in order?"

"Hope so," said Tom.

After a brief inspection, Whittnish said, "You know how to treat a light. I'll give you that much."

"Thanks," said Tom, genuinely touched by the compliment.

"Ready, boy?" asked Ralph as they were about to cast off.

"God only knows," said Tom.

"Never a truer word spoken." Ralph turned his eyes to the horizon. "Off we go, my beauty, got to get Captain Sherbourne, Military Cross and Bar, to his damsel."

Ralph spoke to the boat in the same way Whittnish referred to the light—living creatures, close to their hearts. The things a man could love, Tom thought. He fixed his eyes on the tower. Life would have changed utterly when he saw it again. He had a sudden pang: would Isabel love Janus as much as he did? Would she understand his world?

CHAPTER 7

"You see? Because it's this high above sea level, the light reaches over the curve of the earth—beyond the horizon. Not the beam itself, but the *loom*—the glow of it." Tom was standing behind Isabel on the lighthouse gallery, arms around her, chin reaching down to rest on her shoulder. The January sun scattered flecks of gold in her dark hair. It was 1922, and their second day alone on Janus. Back from a few days' honeymoon in Perth and straight out to the island.

"It's like seeing into the future," said Isabel. "You can reach ahead in time to save the ship before it knows it needs help."

"The higher the light, and the bigger the order of lens, the further its beam shines. This one goes just about as far as any light can."

"I've never been this high up in all my life! It's like flying!" she said, and broke away to circle the tower once more. "And what do you call the flash again—there's that word . . ."

"The *character*. Every coastal light has a different character. This one flashes four times on each twenty-second rotation. So every ship knows from the five-second flash that this is Janus, not Leeuwin or Breaksea or anywhere else."

"How do they know?"

"Ships keep a list of the lights they'll pass on their course. Time's money if you're a skipper. They're always tempted to cut the corner of the Cape—want to be first to offload their cargo and pick up a new one. Fewer days at sea saves on crew's wages, too. The light's here to ward them off, get them to pull their head in."

Through the glass Isabel could see the heavy black blinds of the lantern room. "What are they for?" she asked.

"Protection! The lens doesn't care which light it magnifies. If it can turn the little flame into a million candlepower, imagine what it can do to sunlight when the lens stands still all day. It's all very well if you're ten miles away. Not so good to be ten inches away. So you have to protect it. And protect yourself—I'd fry if I went inside it during the day without the curtains. Come inside and I'll show you how it works."

The iron door clanged behind them as they went into the lantern room, and through the opening into the light itself.

"This is a first order lens—about as bright as they come."

Isabel watched the rainbows thrown about by the prisms. "It's so *pretty*."

"The thick central bit of glass is the bull's eye. This one has four, but you can have different numbers depending on the character. The light source has to line up exactly with the height of that so it gets concentrated by the lens."

"And all the circles of glass around the bull's eyes?" Separate arcs of triangular glass were arranged around the center of the lens like the rings of a dartboard.

"The first eight *refract* the light: they bend it so that instead of heading up to the moon or down to the ocean floor where it's no good to anybody, it goes straight out to sea: they make it sort of turn a corner. The rings above and below the metal bar— See? Fourteen of them—they get thicker the further away from the center they are: they *reflect* the light back down, so all the light is being concentrated into one beam, not just going off in all directions."

"So none of the light gets away without earning its keep," said Isabel.

"You could say that. And here's the light itself," he said, gesturing to the small apparatus on the metal stand in the very center of the space, covered in a mesh casing.

"It doesn't look much."

"It isn't, now. But that mesh cover is an incandescent mantle, and it makes the vaporized oil burn bright as a star, once it's magnified. I'll show you tonight."

"Our own star! Like the world's been made just for us! With the sunshine and the ocean. We have each other all to ourselves."

"I reckon the Lights think *they've* got me all to themselves," said Tom.

"No nosy neighbors or boring relatives." She nibbled at his ear. "Just you and me . . ."

"And the animals. There's no snakes on Janus, luckily. Some islands down this way are nothing but. There's one or two spiders'll give you a nip though, so keep your eyes peeled. There are . . ." Tom was having difficulty finishing his point about the local fauna, as Isabel kept kissing him, nipping his ears, reaching her hands back into his pockets in a way that made it an effort to think, let alone speak coherently. "It's a serious . . ." he struggled on, "point I'm trying to make here, Izz. You need to watch out for—" and he let out a moan as her fingers found their target.

"Me . . ." She giggled. "I'm the deadliest thing on this island!"

"Not here, Izz. Not in the middle of the lantern. Let's"—he took a deep breath—"let's go downstairs."

Isabel laughed. "Yes, here!"

"It's government property."

"What—are you going to have to record it in the logbook?"

Tom gave an awkward cough. "Technically . . . These things are pretty delicate, and they cost more money than you or I'll ever see in a lifetime. I don't want to be the one who has to make up an excuse about how anything got broken. Come on, let's go downstairs."

"And what if I won't?" she teased.

"Well, I suppose I'll just have to"—he hoisted her onto one hip—"make you, sweetheart," he said, and carried her down the hundreds of narrow stairs.

"Oh, it's heaven here!" Isabel declared the next day as she looked out at the flat, turquoise ocean. Despite Tom's grim warnings about the weather, the wind had declared a greeting truce and the sun was again gloriously warm.

He had brought her to the lagoon, a broad pool of placid ultramarine no more than six feet deep, in which they were now swimming.

"Just as well you like it. It's three years till we get shore leave."

She put her arms around him. "I'm where I want to be and with the man I want to be with. Nothing else matters."

Tom swirled her gently in a circle as he spoke. "Sometimes fish find their way in here through the gaps in the rocks. You can scoop them up with a net, or even just with your hands."

"What's this pool called?"

"Hasn't got a name."

"Everything deserves a name, don't you think?"

"Well, you can give it one then."

Isabel thought for a moment. "I hereby christen this Paradise Pool," she said, and splashed a handful of water onto a rock. "This will be my swimming spot."

"You're usually pretty safe here. But keep your eyes open, just in case."

"What do you mean?" asked Isabel as she paddled, only half listening.

"The sharks can't usually make it through the rocks, unless there's a really high tide or a storm or something, so you're probably safe on that count . . ."

"Probably?"

"But you need to be careful about other things. Sea urchins, say. Watch out when you're walking on submerged rocks, or the spines can snap off in your foot and get infected. And stingrays bury themselves in the sand near the edge of the water—if you tread on the barb in their tail you're in trouble. If it flicks up and gets you near the heart, well . . ." He noticed that Isabel had gone silent.

"You all right, Izz?"

"It feels different somehow, when you just reel it all off like that—when we're this far from help."

Tom took her in his arms and pulled her up to the shore. "I'll look after you, sweetheart. Don't you worry," he said with a smile. He kissed her shoulders, and laid her head back on the sand, to kiss her mouth.

In Isabel's wardrobe, beside the piles of thick winter woolens, hang a few floral dresses—easy to wash, hard to hurt as she goes about her new work of feeding the chickens or milking the goats; picking the vegetables or cleaning the kitchen. When she hikes around the island with Tom she wears an old pair of his trousers, rolled up more than a foot and cinched with a cracked leather belt, over one of his collarless shirts. She likes to feel the ground under her feet, and goes without shoes whenever she can, but on the cliffs she endures plimsolls to protect her soles from the granite. She explores the boundaries of her new world.

One morning soon after she arrived, a little drunk with the freedom of it, she decided to experiment. "What do you think of the new look?" she said to Tom as she brought him a sandwich in the watch room at noon, wearing nothing at all. "I don't think I need clothes on a day as lovely as this."

He raised an eyebrow and gave her a half smile. "Very nice. But you'll get sick of it soon enough, Izz." As he took the sandwich he stroked her chin. "There's some things you have to do to survive on the Offshore Lights, love—to stay normal: eat at proper times; turn the pages of the calendar"—he laughed—"and keep your clobber on. Trust me, sweet."

Blushing, she retreated to the cottage and dressed in several layers—camisole and petticoat, shift, cardigan, then heaved on Wellington boots and went to dig up potatoes with unnecessary vigor in the sharp sunshine.

Isabel asked Tom, "Have you got a map of the island?"

He smiled. "Afraid of getting lost? You've been here a few weeks now. As long as you go in the opposite direction to the water, you'll get home sooner or later. And the light might give you a clue too."

"I just want a map. There must be one."

"Of course there is. There are charts of the whole area if you want them, but I'm not sure what good they are to you. There's nowhere much you can go."

"Just humor me, husband of mine," she said, and kissed his cheek.

Later that morning, Tom appeared in the kitchen with a large scroll, and presented it with mock ceremony to Isabel. "Your wish is my command, Mrs. Sherbourne."

"Thank you," she replied in the same tone. "That will be all, for now. You may go, sir."

A smile played on Tom's lips as he rubbed his chin. "What are you up to, missie?"

"Never you mind!"

For the next few days, Isabel went off on expeditions each morning, and in the afternoon closed the door to the bedroom, even though Tom was safely occupied with his work.

One evening, after she had dried the dinner dishes, she fetched the scroll and handed it to Tom. "This is for you."

"Thanks, love," said Tom, who was reading a dog-eared volume on the tying of rope knots. He looked up briefly. "I'll put it back tomorrow."

"But it's for *you.*"

Tom looked at her. "It's the map, isn't it?"

She gave a mischievous grin. "You won't know until you look, will you?"

Tom unrolled the paper, to find it transformed. Little annotations had appeared all over it, together with colored sketches and arrows. His first thought was that the map was Commonwealth property and that there would be hell to pay next inspection. New names had sprung up everywhere.

"Well?" Isabel smiled. "It just seemed wrong that places weren't called anything. So I've given them names, see?"

The coves and the cliffs and the rocks and the grassy fields all bore fine lettering, in which they were christened, as Paradise Pool had been: Stormy Corner; Treacherous Rock; Shipwreck Beach; Tranquil Cove; Tom's Lookout; Izzy's Cliff, and many more.

"I suppose I'd never thought of it as being separate places. It's all just Janus to me," Tom said, smiling.

"It's a world of differences. Each place deserves a name, like rooms in a house."

Tom rarely thought of the house in terms of rooms either. It was just "home." And something in him was saddened at the dissection of the island, the splitting off into the good and the bad, the safe and the dangerous. He preferred to think of it whole. Even more, he was uneasy about parts bearing his name. Janus did not belong to him: he belonged to it, like he'd heard the natives thought of land. His job was just to take care of it.

He looked at his wife, who was smiling proudly at her handiwork. If she wanted to give things names, maybe there was no harm in it. And maybe she would come to understand his way of looking at it, eventually.

When Tom gets invitations to his Battalion reunions, he always writes back. Always sends good wishes, and a bit of money toward the mess. But he never attends. Well, being on the Lights, he couldn't even if he wanted to. There are some, he knows, who will take comfort in seeing a familiar face, re-telling a story. But he doesn't want to join in. There were friends he lost—men he'd trusted, fought with, drunk with, and shivered with. Men he understood without a word, knew as if they were an extension of his body. He thinks about the language that bound them together: words that cropped up to cover circumstances no one had ever encountered before. A "pineapple," a "pipsqueak," a "plum pudding": all types of shell which might find their way into your trench. The lice were "chats," the food was "scran," and a "Blighty" was a wound that'd see you shipped back to hospital in England. He wonders how many men can still speak this secret language.

Sometimes when he wakes up next to Isabel he's still amazed, and relieved, that she isn't dead. He watches closely for her breath, just to make sure. Then he puts his head against her back and absorbs the softness of her skin, the gentle rise and fall of her body as she sleeps on. It is as great a miracle as he has ever seen.

CHAPTER 8

"Maybe all the times in my life I could have done without, maybe they were all a test to see if I deserved you, Izz."

They were stretched on a blanket on the grass, three months after Isabel's arrival on Janus. The April night was still almost warm, and tinseled with stars. Isabel lay with her eyes closed, resting in the crook of Tom's arm as he stroked her neck.

"You're my other half of the sky," he said.

"I never knew you were a poet!"

"Oh, I didn't invent it. I read it somewhere—a Latin poem? A Greek myth? Something like that, anyway."

"You and your fancy private-school education!" she teased.

It was Isabel's birthday, and Tom had cooked her breakfast and dinner, and watched her untie the bow on the wind-up gramophone which he had conspired with Ralph and Bluey to ship out to make up for the fact that the piano he had proudly shown her when she arrived was unplayable from years of neglect. All day she had listened to Chopin and Brahms, and now the strains of Handel's *Messiah* were ringing from the lighthouse, where they had set it up to let it echo in the natural sound chamber.

"I love the way you do that," said Tom, watching Isabel's index finger coil a lock of her hair into a spring, then release it and start with another.

Suddenly self-conscious, she said, "Oh, Ma says it's a bad habit. I've always done it, apparently. I don't even notice it." Tom took a strand of her hair and wound it around his finger, then let it unfurl like a streamer.

"Tell me another myth," Isabel said.

Tom thought for a moment. "You know Janus is where the word January comes from? It's named after the same god as this island. He's got two faces, back to back. Pretty ugly fellow."

"What's he god of?"

"Doorways. Always looking both ways, torn between two ways of seeing things. January looks forward to the new year and back to the old year. He sees past and future. And the island looks in the direction of two different oceans, down to the South Pole and up to the Equator."

"Yeah, I'd got that," said Isabel. She pinched his nose and laughed. "Just teasing. I love it when you tell me things. Tell me more about the stars. Where's Centaurus again?"

Tom kissed her fingertip and stretched her arm out until he had lined it up with the constellation. "There."

"Is that your favorite?"

"*You're* my favorite. Better than all the stars put together."

He moved down to kiss her belly. "I should say, 'You *two* are my favorites,' shouldn't I? Or what if it's twins? Or triplets?"

Tom's head rose and fell gently with Isabel's breath as he lay there.

"Can you hear anything? Is it talking to you yet?" she asked.

"Yep, it's saying I need to carry its mum to bed before the night gets too cold." And he gathered his wife in his arms and carried her easily into the cottage, as the choir in the lighthouse declared, "For unto us a Child is born."

Isabel had been so proud to write to her mother with the news of the expected arrival. "Oh, I wish I could—I don't know, swim ashore or something, just to let them know. Waiting for the boat is killing me!" She kissed Tom, and asked, "Shall we write to your dad? Your brother?"

Tom stood up, and busied himself with the dishes on the draining board. "No need," was all he said.

His expression, uneasy but not angry, told Isabel not to press the point, and she gently took the tea towel from his hand. "I'll do this lot," she said. "You've got enough to get through."

Tom touched her shoulder. "I'll get some more done on your chair," he said, and attempted a smile as he left the kitchen.

In the shed, he looked at the pieces of the rocking chair he was planning to make for Isabel. He had tried to remember the one on which his own mother had rocked him and told him stories. His body remembered the sensation of being held by her—something lost to him for decades. He wondered if their child would have a memory of Isabel's touch, decades into the future. Such a mysterious business, motherhood. How brave a woman must be to embark on it, he thought, as he considered the path of his own mother's life. Yet Isabel seemed utterly single-minded about it. "It's nature, Tom. What's there to be afraid of?"

When he had finally tracked down his mother, he was twenty-one and just finishing his Engineering degree. At last, he was in charge of his own life. The address the private detective gave him was a boarding-house in Darlinghurst. He had stood outside the door, his gut a whirl of hope and terror, suddenly eight again. He caught the sounds of other desperations seeping out under the doors along the narrow wooden passage—a man's sobs from the next room and a shout of "We can't go on like this!" from a woman, accompanied by a baby's screaming; somewhere further off, the fervent rhythm of a headboard as the woman who lay before it probably earned her keep.

Tom checked the penciled scrawl on the paper. Yes, the right room number. He scanned his memory again for the lullaby-gentle sound of his mother: "Ups-a-daisy, my young Thomas. Shall we put a bandage on that scrape?"

His knock went unanswered, and he tried again. Eventually, he turned the handle tentatively, and the door gave no resistance. The unmistakable scent rushed to meet him, but it was a split second before he recognized it as tainted—with cheap booze and cigarettes. In the closed-in gloom he saw an unmade bed and a tatty armchair, in shades of brown. There was a crack in the window, and a single rose in a vase had long ago shriveled.

"Looking for Ellie Sherbourne?" The voice belonged to a wiry, balding man who had appeared at the door behind him.

It was so strange to hear her name spoken. And "Ellie"—he had never imagined "Ellie." "Mrs. Sherbourne, that's right. When will she be back?"

The man gave a snort. "She won't. More's the pity, 'cause she owes me a month's rent."

It was all wrong, the reality. He couldn't make it fit with the picture of the reunion he'd planned, dreamed of, for years. Tom's pulse quickened. "Do you have a forwarding address?"

"Not where she's gone. Died three weeks ago. I was just coming in to clear the last of the stuff out."

Of all the possible scenes Tom had imagined, none had ended like this. He stood completely still.

"You planning on moving? Or moving in?" the man asked sourly.

Tom hesitated, then opened his wallet and took out five pounds. "For her rent," he said softly, and strode down the hallway, fighting tears.

The thread of hope Tom had protected so long was snapped: on a back street in Sydney, as the world was on the brink of war. Within a month he'd enlisted, giving his next of kin as his mother, at her boardinghouse address. The recruiters weren't fussy about details.

Now Tom ran his hands over the one piece of wood he had lathed, and tried to imagine what he might say in a letter to his mother today, if she were alive—how he might tell her the news of the baby.

He took up the tape measure, and turned to the next piece of wood.

"Zebedee." Isabel looked at Tom with a poker face, her mouth twitching just a touch at the corners.

"What?" he asked, pausing from his task of rubbing her feet.

"Zebedee," she repeated, putting her nose back down in the book so that he could not catch her eye.

"You're not serious? What kind of a name—"

A wounded expression crossed her face. "That's my great-uncle's name. Zebedee Zanzibar Graysmark."

Tom gave her a look, as she plowed on, "I promised Grandma on her deathbed that if I ever had a son I'd call him after her brother. I can't go back on a promise."

"I was thinking of something a bit more normal."

"Are you calling my great-uncle abnormal?"

Isabel couldn't contain herself any longer, and burst out laughing. "Got you! Got you good and proper!"

"Little minx! You'll be sorry you did that!"

"No, stop! Stop!"

"No mercy," he said, as he tickled her tummy and her neck.

"I surrender!"

"Too late for that now!"

They were lying on the grass where it gave way to Shipwreck Beach. It was late afternoon and the soft light rinsed the sand in yellow.

Suddenly Tom stopped.

"What's wrong?" asked Isabel, peeping out from under the long hair that hung over her face.

He stroked the strands away from her eyes, and looked at her in silence. She put a hand to his cheek. "Tom?"

"It bowls me over, sometimes. Three months ago there was just you and me, and now, there's this other life, just turned up out of nowhere, like . . ."

"Like a baby."

"Yes, like a baby, but it's more than that, Izz. When I used to sit up in the lantern room, before you arrived, I'd think about what life was. I mean, compared to death . . ." He stopped himself. "I'm talking rubbish now. I'll shut up."

Isabel put her hand under his chin. "You hardly ever talk about things, Tom. Tell me."

"I can't really put it into words. Where does life come from?"

"Does it matter?"

"Does it *matter*?" he queried.

"That it's a mystery. That we don't understand."

"There are times I wanted an answer. I can tell you that much. Times I saw a man's last breath, and I wanted to ask him, 'Where have you gone? You were here right beside me just a few seconds ago, and now some bits of metal have made holes in your skin, because they hit you fast enough, and suddenly you're somewhere else. How can that be?'"

Isabel hugged her knees with one arm, and with the other hand pulled at the grass beside her. "Do you think people remember this life, when they go? Do you think in heaven, my grandma and granddad, say, are knocking around together?"

"Search me," Tom said.

With sudden urgency, she asked, "When we're both dead, Tom, God won't keep us apart, will He? He'll let us be together?"

Tom held her. "Now look what I've done. Should have kept my silly mouth shut. Come on, we were in the middle of choosing names. And I was just trying to rescue a poor baby from the fate of life as Zebedee blimmin' Zanzibar. Where are we with girls' names?"

"Alice; Amelia; Annabel; April; Ariadne—"

Tom raised his eyebrows. "And she's off again . . . 'Ariadne!' Hard enough that she's going to live in a lighthouse. Let's not lump her with a name people will laugh at."

"Only two hundred more pages to go," said Isabel with a grin.

"We'd better hop to it, then."

That evening, as he looked out from the gallery, Tom returned to his question. Where had this baby's soul been? Where would it go? Where were the souls of the men who'd joked and saluted and trudged through the mud with him?

Here he was, safe and healthy, with a beautiful wife, and some soul had decided to join them. Out of thin air, in the farthest corner of the earth, a baby was coming. He'd been on death's books for so long, it seemed impossible that life was making an entry in his favor.

He went back into the lantern room, and looked again at the photograph of Isabel that hung on the wall. The mystery of it all. The mystery.

Tom's other gift from the last boat was *The Australian Mother's Manual of Efficient Child-Rearing*, by Doctor Samuel B. Griffiths. Isabel took to reading it at any available moment.

She fired information at Tom: "Did you know that a baby's kneecaps aren't made of bone?" Or, "How old do you think babies are when they can take food from a teaspoon?"

"No idea, Izz."

"Go on, guess!"

"Honestly, how would I know?"

"Oh, you're no fun!" she complained, and dived into the book for another fact.

Within weeks the pages were frilly-edged and blotted with grass stains from days spent on the headland.

"You're having a baby, not sitting for an exam."

"I just want to do things right. It's not like I can pop next door and ask Mum, is it?"

"Oh, Izzy Bella." Tom laughed.

"What? What's funny?"

"Nothing. Nothing at all. I wouldn't change a thing about you."

She smiled, and kissed him. "You're going to be a wonderful dad, I know." A question came to her eyes.

"What?" prompted Tom.

"Nothing."

"No, really, what?"

"*Your* dad. Why do you never talk about him?"

"No love lost there."

"But what was he like?"

Tom thought about it. How could he possibly sum him up? How could he ever explain the look in his eyes, the invisible gap that always surrounded him, so that he never quite made contact? "He was *right*. Always *right*. Didn't matter what it was about. He knew the rules and he stuck to them, come hell or high water." Tom thought back to the straight, tall figure that overshadowed his childhood. Hard and cold as a tomb.

"Was he strict?"

Tom gave a bitter laugh. "Strict doesn't begin to describe it." He put his hand to his chin as he speculated. "Maybe he just wanted to make sure his sons didn't kick over the traces. We'd get the strap for anything. Well, *I'd* get the strap for anything. Cecil would always be the one to tell on me—got him off lightly." He laughed again. "Tell you what, though: made army discipline easy. You never know what you're going to be grateful for." His face grew serious. "And I suppose it made it easier being over there, knowing there'd be no one who'd be heartbroken if they got the telegram."

"Oh, Tom! Don't even say such a thing!"

He drew her head into his chest and stroked her hair in silence.

There are times when the ocean is not the ocean—not blue, not even water, but some violent explosion of energy and danger: ferocity on a scale only gods can summon. It hurls itself at the island, sending spray right over the top of the lighthouse, biting pieces off the cliff. And the sound is a roaring of a beast whose anger knows no limits. Those are the nights the light is needed most.

In the worst of these storms Tom stays with the light all night if need be, keeping warm by the kerosene heater, pouring sweet tea from a thermos flask. He thinks about the poor bastards out on the ships and he thanks Christ he's safe. He watches for distress flares, keeps the dinghy ready for launch, though what good it would do in seas like that, who knows.

That May night, Tom sat with a pencil and notebook in hand, adding up figures. His annual salary was £327. How much did a pair of children's shoes cost? From what Ralph said, kids got through them at a rate of knots. Then there were clothes. And schoolbooks. Of course, if he stayed on the Offshore Lights, Isabel would teach the kids at home. But on nights like this, he wondered if it was fair to inflict this life on anyone, let alone children. The thought was nudged out by the words of Jack Throssel, one of the keepers back East. "Best life in the world for kids, I swear," he had told Tom. "All six of mine are right as rain. Always up to games and mischief: exploring caves, making cubbies. A proper gang of pioneers. And the Missus makes sure they do their lessons. Take it from me—raising kids on a light station's as easy as wink!"

Tom went back to his calculations: how he could save a bit more, make sure there was enough put by for clothes and doctors and—Lord knew what else. The idea that he was going to be a father made him nervous and excited and worried.

As his mind drifted back to memories of his own father, the storm thundered about the light, deafening Tom to any other sound that night. Deafening him to the cries of Isabel, calling for his help.

CHAPTER 9

Shall I get you a cup of tea?" Tom asked, at a loss. He was a practical man: give him a sensitive technical instrument, and he could maintain it; something broken, and he could mend it, meditatively, efficiently. But confronted by his grieving wife, he felt useless.

Isabel did not look up. He tried again. "Some Vincent's Powders?" The first aid taught to lightkeepers included "restoring the apparently drowned," treating hypothermia and exposure, disinfecting wounds; even the rudiments of amputation. They did not, however, touch on gynecology, and the mechanics of miscarriage were a mystery to Tom.

It had been two days since the dreadful storm. Two days since the miscarriage had begun. Still the blood came, and still Isabel refused to let Tom signal for help. Having stayed on watch throughout that wild night, he had finally returned to the cottage after putting out the light just before dawn, and his body begged for sleep. But entering the bedroom he had found Isabel doubled up, the bed soaked in blood. The look in her eyes was as desolate as Tom had ever seen. "I'm so, so sorry," she had said. "So, so sorry, Tom." Then another wave of pain gripped her and she groaned, and pressed her hands to her belly, desperate for it to stop.

Now she said, "What's the point in a doctor? The baby's gone." Her gaze wandered. "How hopeless am I?" she muttered. "Other women have babies as easy as falling off a log."

"Izzy Bella, stop."

"It's my fault, Tom. It must be."

"That's just not true, Izz." He drew her into his chest and kissed her hair over and over. "There'll be another. One day when we've got five kids running around and getting under your feet, this'll all feel like a dream." He pulled her shawl around her shoulders. "It's beautiful outside. Come and sit on the veranda. It'll do you good."

They sat side by side in wicker armchairs, Isabel covered with a blue checked blanket, and watched the progress of the sun across the late-autumn sky.

Isabel recalled how she had been struck by the emptiness of this place, like a blank canvas, when she first arrived; how, gradually, she had come to see into it as Tom did, attuning to the subtle changes. The clouds, as they formed and grouped and wandered the sky; the shape of the waves, which would take their cue from the wind and the season and could, if you knew how to read them, tell you the next day's weather. She had become familiar, too, with the birds which appeared from time to time, against all odds—carried along as randomly as the seeds borne on the wind, or the seaweed thrown up on the shore.

She looked at the two pine trees and suddenly wept at their aloneness. "There should be forests," she said suddenly. "I miss the trees, Tom. I miss their leaves and their smell and the fact there are so many of them—oh, Tom, I miss the animals: I bloody miss kangaroos! I miss it all."

"I know you do, Izzy, darl."

"But don't you?"

"You're the only thing in this world that I want, Izz, and you're right here. Everything else will sort itself out. Just give it time."

A sheer, velvet veil covered everything, no matter how dutifully Isabel dusted—her wedding photograph; the picture of Hugh and Alfie in their uniforms the week they joined up in 1916, grinning as if they'd just been invited to a party. Not the tallest lads in the AIF, but keen as mustard, and so dashing in their brand-new slouch hats.

Her sewing box was as neat as it needed to be, rather than pristine like her mother's. Needles and pins pierced the cushioned pale-green lining, and the panels of a christening gown lay un-united, stopped in mid-stitch like a broken clock.

The small string of pearls Tom had given her as a wedding gift sat in the box he had made for her. Her hairbrush and tortoiseshell combs were the only other things on her dressing table.

Isabel wandered into the lounge room, observing the dust, the crack in the plaster near the window frame, the frayed edge of the dark blue rug. The hearth needed sweeping, and the lining of the curtains had begun to shred from constant exposure to extremes of weather. Simply to think of fixing any of it took more energy than she could muster. Only weeks ago she had been so full of expectation and vigor. Now the room felt like a coffin, and her life stopped at its edges.

She opened the photograph album her mother had prepared for her as a going-away present, with the pictures of her as a child, the name of the photographer's studio, Gutcher's, stamped on the back of each portrait. There was one of her parents on their wedding day; a photograph of home. She trailed her finger over the table, lingering on the lace doily her grandmother had made for her own trousseau. She moved to the piano, and opened it.

The walnut was split in places. The gold leaf above the keyboard said Eavestaff, London. She had often imagined its journey to Australia, and the other lives it could have lived—in an English house, or a school, sagging under the burden of imperfect scales played by small, stumbling fingers perhaps, or even on a stage. Yet through the most unlikely of circumstances, its lot was to live on this island, its voice stolen by loneliness and the weather.

She pressed middle C, so slowly that it made no sound. The warm ivory key was as smooth as her grandmother's fingertips, and the touch brought back afternoons of music lessons, of wringing out A flat major in contrary motion, one octave, then two, then three. The sound of the cricket ball on the wood as Hugh and Alfie larked about outside while she, a "little lady," acquired "accomplishments," and listened as her grandmother explained again the importance of keeping her wrists raised.

"But it's stupid, contrary motion!" Isabel would wail.

"Well, you'd know all about contrary motion, my dear," her grandmother remarked.

"Can't I play cricket, Gran? Just a bit and then I'll come back."

"Cricket's no game for a girl. Now, come on. The Chopin étude," she would breeze on, opening a book tattooed with pencil marks and small smudged-chocolate fingerprints.

Isabel stroked the key again. She felt a sudden longing, not just for the music, but for that time when she could have rushed outside, hitched up her skirt, and stood as wicketkeeper for her brothers. She pressed the other keys, as if they might bring the day back. But the only sound was the muffled clack of the wood against the base of the keyboard, where the felt had worn away.

"What's the point?" she shrugged to Tom as he came in. "It's had it, I reckon. Just like me," and she started to cry.

Days later, the two of them stood beside the cliff.

Tom hammered the small cross he had made from some driftwood, until it was secure in the ground. At his wife's request he had carved, "31 May 1922. Remembered always."

He took the shovel and dug a hole for the rosemary bush she had moved from the herb garden. He could feel nausea rising in him as a spark of memory arced between the hammering of the cross and digging of the hole. His palms sweated, though the task required little physical effort.

Isabel watched from high on the cliff as the *Windward Spirit* docked on its next run. Ralph and Bluey would make their way up soon enough. No need to go to greet them. They slung the gangplank down, and to her surprise, a third man disembarked with them. No maintenance crews were due.

Tom came up the path while the other three lingered at the jetty. The stranger, who carried a black bag, seemed to be having some difficulty righting himself after the journey.

Isabel's face was tight with anger as Tom approached. "How dare you!"

Tom reeled. "How dare I?"

"I told you not to and you went ahead anyway! Well you can just send him back. Don't bother letting him up here. He's not wanted."

Isabel always looked like a child when she was angry. Tom wanted to laugh, and his grin infuriated her even more. She put her hands on her hips. "I told you I didn't need a doctor, but you went behind my back. I'm not having him prodding and poking about to tell me nothing I don't already know. You should be ashamed of yourself! Well, you can look after them, the whole lot of them."

"Izzy," Tom called. "Izzy, wait! Don't do your 'nana, love. He's not . . ." But she was already too far off to hear the rest of his words.

"Well?" asked Ralph as he reached Tom. "How did she take it? Pleased as Punch, I bet!"

"Not exactly." Tom stuffed his fists in his pockets.

"But . . ." Ralph looked at him in amazement. "I thought she'd be real chuffed. It took all Freda's charms to persuade him to come, and my wife doesn't use her charms freely!"

"She . . ." Tom considered whether to explain. "She got the wrong end of the stick about it. Sorry. She's chucked a wobbly. Once she does that, all you can do is batten down the hatches and wait for it to pass. Means I'll be making sandwiches for lunch, I'm afraid."

Bluey and the man approached, and after the introductions, the four of them went inside.

Isabel sat in the grass near the cove she had christened Treacherous, and seethed. She hated this—the fact that your dirty washing had to be everybody else's business. She hated the fact that Ralph and Bluey had to know. They'd probably spent the whole trip out discussing her most private shame and Lord knew what else. That Tom could ship the doctor out against her explicit wishes felt like a betrayal.

She sat watching the water, how the breeze fluffed up the waves which had been so smooth and curled earlier in the day. Hours passed. She grew hungry. She grew sleepy. But she refused to go near the cottage while the doctor was there. She concentrated instead on her surroundings. Noticing the texture of each leaf, the precise green of it. Listening to all the different pitches of wind and water and birds. She heard a foreign sound: an insistent note, short, repeated. Coming from the light? From the cottage? It was not the usual clang of metal from the workshop. She heard it again, this time at a different pitch. The wind on Janus had a way of raking sounds into separate frequencies, distorting them as they crossed the island. Two gulls came to land nearby and squabble over a fish, and the noise, faint at best, was lost.

She went back to her mulling, until she was arrested by an unmistakable sound carried on the shifting air. It was a scale: imperfect, but the pitch getting better each time.

She had never heard Ralph or Bluey mention the piano, and Tom couldn't play for toffee. It must be the wretched doctor, determined to put his fingers where they were not wanted. She had never been able to get a tune out of the piano, and now it seemed to be singing. Isabel's fury drove her up the path, ready to banish the intruder from the instrument, from her body, from her home.

She passed the outbuildings, where Tom, Ralph and Bluey were stacking sacks of flour.

"Afternoon, Isab—" Ralph attempted, but she marched past him and into the house.

She barged into the lounge room. "If you don't mind, that's a very delicate instru—" she began, but got no further, flummoxed by the sight of the piano completely stripped down, a box of tools open, and the stranger turning the nut above one of the bass copper wires with a tiny spanner as he hit its corresponding key.

"Mummified seagull. That's your problem," he said, without looking around. "Well, one of them. That and a good twenty years' worth of sand and salt and God knows what. Once I've replaced some of the felts it'll start to sound better." He continued to tap the key and turn the spanner as he spoke. "I've seen all sorts in my time. Dead rats. Sandwiches. A stuffed cat. I could write a book about the things that end up inside a piano, though I couldn't tell you how they get there. I'm betting the seagull didn't fly in by itself."

Isabel was so taken aback that she couldn't speak. Her mouth was still open when she felt a hand on her shoulder, and turned to find Tom. She flushed deep red.

"So much for surprises, eh?" he said, and kissed her cheek.

"Well . . . Well, it was . . ." Isabel's voice trailed off.

He slipped a hand around her waist and the two of them stood for a moment, forehead touching forehead, before breaking into laughter.

She sat for the next two hours, watching the tuner as he coaxed a brighter sound, getting the notes to ring out once again, louder than ever before, and he finished with a burst of the Hallelujah Chorus.

"I've done my best, Mrs. Sherbourne," he said as he packed away his tools. "Really needs to come into the workshop, but the trip out and back would do as much harm as good. She's not perfect, by a long chalk, but she'll do." He pulled the piano stool out. "Care to give it a burl?"

Isabel sat at the keyboard, and played the A flat major scale in contrary motion.

"Well, that's a sight better than before!" she said. She broke into the beginnings of a Handel aria and was wandering off into memory when someone cleared his throat. It was Ralph, standing behind Bluey in the doorway.

"Don't stop!" Bluey said, as she turned to greet them.

"I was so rude. I'm sorry!" she said, about to get up.

"Not a bit of it," said Ralph. "And here. From Hilda," he said, producing from behind his back something tied with a red ribbon.

"Oh! Shall I open it now?"

"You'd better! If I don't give her a blow-by-blow report, I'll never hear the end of it!"

Isabel opened the wrapping and found Bach's *Goldberg Variations.*

"Tom reckons you can play this sort of caper with your eyes shut."

"I haven't played them for years. But—oh, I just love them! Thank you!" She hugged Ralph and kissed his cheek. "And you too, Bluey," she said with a kiss that accidentally caught his lips as he turned.

He blushed violently and looked at the ground. "I never had much to do with it, I don't reckon," he said, but Tom protested.

"Don't believe a word of it. He drove all the way to Albany to fetch him. Took him the whole day yesterday."

"In that case, you get an extra kiss," she said, and planted another on his other cheek.

"And you too!" she said, kissing the piano tuner for good measure.

That night as he checked the mantle, Tom was serenaded by Bach, the orderly notes climbing the stairs of the lighthouse and ringing around the lantern room, flittering between the prisms. Just like the mercury that made the light go around, Isabel was—mysterious. Able to cure and to poison; able to bear the whole weight of the light, but capable of fracturing into a thousand uncatchable particles, running off in all directions, escaping from itself. He went out onto the gallery. As the lights of the *Windward Spirit* disappeared over the horizon, he said a silent prayer for Isabel, and for their life together. Then he turned to the logbook and wrote, in the "remarks" column for Wednesday, 13 September, 1922, "Visit per store boat: Archie Pollock, piano tuner. Prior approval granted."

PART TWO

CHAPTER 10

27th April 1926

Isabel's lips were pale and her eyes downcast. She still placed her hand fondly on her stomach sometimes, before its flatness reminded her it was empty. And still, her blouses bore occasional patches from the last of the breast milk that had come in so abundantly in the first days, a feast for an absent guest. Then she would cry again, as though the news were fresh.

She stood with sheets in her hands: chores didn't stop, just as the light didn't stop. Having made the bed and folded her nightgown under the pillow, she headed up to the cliff, to sit by the graves a while. She tended the new one with great care, wondering whether the fledgling rosemary would take. She pulled a few weeds from around the two older crosses, now finely crystalled with years of salt, the rosemary growing doggedly despite the gales.

When a baby's cry came to her on the wind, she looked instinctively to the new grave. Before logic could interfere, there was a moment when her mind told her it had all been a mistake—this last child had not been stillborn early, but was living and breathing.

The illusion dissolved, but the cry did not. Then Tom's call from the gallery—"On the beach! A boat!"—told her this was not a dream, and she moved as quickly as she could to join him on the way to the dinghy.

The man in it was dead, but Tom fished a screaming bundle out of the bow.

"Bloody hell!" he exclaimed. "Bloody hell, Izzy. It's—"

"A baby! Oh my Lord above! Oh Tom! Tom! Here—give it to me!"

Back in the cottage, Isabel's belly quickened at the very sight of the baby—her arms knew instinctively how to hold the child and calm her, soothe her. As she scooped warm water over the infant, she registered the freshness of her skin, taut and soft and without a wrinkle. She kissed each of the tiny fingertips in turn, gently nibbling down the nails a fraction so the child would not scratch herself. She cupped the baby's head in the palm of her hand, and with the silk handkerchief she kept for best, dabbed away a fine crust of mucus from under her nostrils, and wiped the dried salt of tears from around her eyes. The moment seemed to merge into one with another bathing, another face—a single act that had merely been interrupted.

Looking into those eyes was like looking at the face of God. No mask or pretense: the baby's defenselessness was overwhelming. That this intricate creature, this exquisite crafting of blood and bones and skin, could have found its way *to her,* was humbling. That she could have arrived now, barely two weeks after . . . It was impossible to see it as mere chance. Frail as a falling snowflake, the baby could so easily have melted into oblivion had the currents not borne her, arrow-true and safe, to Shipwreck Beach.

In a place before words, in some other language of creature to creature, with the softening of her muscles, the relaxing of her neck, the baby signaled her trust. Having come so close to the hands of death, life now fused with life like water meets water.

Isabel was awash with emotions: awe, at the grip of the miniature hands when they latched onto a single finger of her own; amusement, at the sweet little bottom which was yet to become fully distinct from the legs; reverence, for the breath which drew in the air around and transformed it into blood, into soul. And below all of these hummed the dark, empty ache.

"Look, you've made me cry, my poppet," said Isabel. "However did you manage that? You tiny little, perfect little thing." She lifted the baby from the bath like a sacred offering, laid her on a soft, white towel, and began to dab her dry, like blotting ink so as not to smudge it—as though if she were not careful she could erase it altogether. The baby lay patiently while she was dusted with talcum, a new nappy pinned. Isabel did not hesitate as she went to the chest of drawers in the nursery and chose from the various unworn garments. She took out a yellow dress with ducklings on the bodice, and fitted the child carefully into it.

Humming a lullaby, skipping bars here and there, she opened the palm of the tiny hand and considered its lines: there from the moment of birth—a path already mapped, which had brought her here, to this shore. "Oh, my beautiful, beautiful little thing," she said. But the exhausted baby was now fast asleep, taking small, shallow breaths; occasionally giving a shiver. Isabel held her in one arm as she went about putting a sheet into the cot, shaking out the blanket she had crocheted from soft lambs' wool. She could not quite bring herself to put the baby down—not just yet. In a place far beyond awareness, the flood of chemicals which until so recently had been preparing her body for motherhood, conspired to engineer her feelings, guide her muscles. Instincts which had been thwarted rushed back to life. She took the baby into the kitchen and rested her on her lap as she searched through the book of babies' names.

A lightkeeper accounts for things. Every article in the light station is listed, stored, maintained, inspected. No item escapes official scrutiny. The Deputy Director of Lights lays claim to everything from the tubes for the burners to the ink for the logs, from the brooms in the cupboard to the boot scraper by the door. Each is documented in the leather-bound Register of Equipment—even the sheep and the goats. Nothing is thrown away, nothing is disposed of without formal approval from Fremantle or, if it is very costly, Melbourne. Lord help the keeper who is down a box of mantles or a gallon of oil and cannot explain it. No matter how remote their lives, like moths in a glass case, the lightkeepers are pinned down, scrutinized, powerless to escape. You can't trust the Lights to just anyone.

The logbook tells the tale of the keeper's life in the same steady pen. The exact minute the light was lit, the exact minute it was put out the following morning. The weather, the ships that passed. Those that signaled, those that inched by on a squally sea, too intent on dealing with the waves to break into Morse or—still sometimes—international code, about where they came from or where they were bound. Once in a while, a keeper might have a little joke to himself, decorating the start of a new month with a scroll or a curlicue. He might craftily record that the Inspector of Lights has confirmed his long-service leave, on the basis that there's no nay-saying what's written there. But that's as far as liberties are taken. The log is the gospel truth. Janus isn't a Lloyds station: it's not one the ships depend on for forecasts, so once Tom closes the pages on the book, it is unlikely that any eyes will glance at it again, perhaps ever. But he feels a particular peace when he writes. The wind is still measured using the system from the age of sail: *"calm (0–2, sufficient wind for working ships)"* to *"hurricane (12—no sail can stand, even running)."* He relishes the language. When he thinks back to the chaos, the years of manipulating facts, or the impossibility of knowing, let alone describing, what the bloody hell was going on while explosions shattered the ground all around him, he enjoys the luxury of stating a simple truth.

It was therefore the logbook that first played on Tom's mind that day the boat arrived. It was second nature to him to report any little thing that might have significance, bound not only by the rules of his employment, but by Commonwealth law. His information might be only one tiny piece of a puzzle, a piece he alone could contribute, and it was vital that he do so. A distress flare, a wisp of smoke on the horizon, a bit of metal washed up that might turn out to be wreckage—all were recorded in his steady, efficient hand, the letters sloping gently and evenly forward.

He sat at the desk below the lantern room, his fountain pen waiting faithfully to report the day. A man was dead. People should be notified; inquiries made. He drew more ink into the pen, even though it was almost full. He checked back over a few details on previous pages, then went to the very first entry he had ever recorded, that gray Wednesday he had arrived on Janus six years before. The days had followed like the rise and fall of the tides since then, and through all of them—when he was dog-tired from urgent repairs, or on watch all night during a storm, or wondering what the hell he was doing there, even the desperate days of Isabel's miscarriages—there was never one when putting ink to the page made him so uneasy. But she had begged him to wait a day.

His thoughts revisited the afternoon just two weeks earlier when he had returned from fishing, to be greeted by Isabel's cries. "Tom! Tom, quick!" Running into the cottage, he had found her lying on the kitchen floor.

"Tom! Something's wrong." She was groaning between words. "It's coming! The baby's coming."

"Are you sure?"

"Of course I'm not sure!" she spat. "I don't know what's going on! I just— Oh, sweet Jesus, Tom, it hurts!"

"Let me help you up," he urged, kneeling down beside her.

"No! Don't move me." She was panting, battling the pain for each breath, moaning the phrases. "It hurts too much. Oh God make this stop!" she cried, as blood seeped through her dress and onto the floor.

This was different from before—Isabel was nearly seven months along, and Tom's previous experience was of little help. "Tell me what to do, Izz. What do you want me to do?"

She was fumbling about her clothes, trying to get her bloomers off.

Tom lifted her hips and pulled them down and over her ankles as she started to moan more loudly, twisting this way and that, her cries ringing out over the island.

The labor was as quick as it was early, and Tom watched helpless as a baby—it was unmistakably a baby, *his* baby—emerged from Isabel's body. It was bloody and small: a mocking, scale model of the infant they had so long been waiting for, drowned in a wash of blood and tissue and mess from the woman so unprepared for its arrival.

About a foot long from head to toe: no heavier than a bag of sugar. It made no movement, uttered no sound. He held it in his hands, torn between wonder and horror, not knowing what he was supposed to do, or feel.

"Give her to me!" Isabel screamed. "Give me my baby! Let me hold her!"

"A little boy," was all Tom could think of to say, as he handed the warm body to his wife. "It was a little boy."

The wind had kept up its sullen howl. The late-afternoon sun continued to shine in through the window, laying a blanket of bright gold over the woman and her almost-baby. The old clock on the kitchen wall still clicked its minutes with fussy punctuality. A life had come and gone and nature had not paused a second for it. The machine of time and space grinds on, and people are fed through it like grist through the mill.

Isabel had managed to sit up a little against the wall, and she sobbed at the sight of the diminutive form, which she had dared to imagine as bigger, as stronger—a child of this world. "My baby my baby my baby my baby," she whispered like a magic incantation that might resuscitate him. The face of the creature was solemn, a monk in deep prayer, eyes closed, mouth sealed shut: already back in that world from which he had apparently been reluctant to stray.

Still the officious hands of the clock tutted their way around. Half an hour had passed and Isabel had said nothing.

"I'll get you a blanket."

"No!" She grabbed his hand. "Don't leave us."

Tom sat beside her, his arm around her shoulders as she sobbed against his chest. The blood had started to dry at the edges of the pools on the floor. Death, blood, comforting the wounded—all were familiar. But not like this: a woman, a baby; no explosions or mud. Everything else was exactly as it should be: the willow-pattern plates stood neatly in the dish drainer; the tea towel hung over the oven door. The cake Isabel had made that morning lay upside down on the cooling rack, the tin still covered with a damp cloth.

After a while, Tom said, "What shall we do? With the—with him?"

Isabel looked at the cold creature in her arms. "Light the chip heater."

Tom glanced at her.

"Light it, please."

Still confused, but wary of upsetting her, Tom rose to his feet and went to light the water heater. When he returned, she said, "Fill the laundry tub. When the water's warm."

"If you want a bath I'll carry you, Izz."

"Not for me. I have to wash him. Then in the linen cupboard, there are the good sheets—the ones I embroidered. Will you bring one?"

"Izz, love, there'll be time for all that. You're what matters most right now. I'll go and signal. Get a boat sent out."

"No!" Her voice was fierce. "No! I don't want—I don't want anyone else here. I don't want anyone else to know. Not yet."

"But sweet, you've lost so much blood. You're white as a ghost. We should get a doctor out here to take you back."

"The tub, Tom. Please?"

When the water was warm, Tom filled the metal tub and lowered it to the floor beside Isabel. He handed her a flannel. She dipped it in the water, and gently, gently, with the cloth covering her fingertip, began to stroke the face, smoothing away the watery blood that covered the translucent skin. The baby stayed at his prayers, locked in some secret conversation with God, as she lowered the cloth into the water to rinse it. She squeezed it and began again, watching closely, perhaps hoping that the eyes might flicker, or the minuscule fingers twitch.

"Izz," Tom said softly, touching her hair, "you've got to listen to me now. I'm going to make you some tea, with a lot of sugar in it, and I need you to drink it for me, all right? And I'm going to get a blanket to put over you. And I'm going to clean things up here a bit. You don't have to go anywhere, but you have to let me take care of you now. No arguments. I'm going to give you some morphine tablets for the pain, and some iron pills, and you're going to take them for me." His voice was gentle and calm, simply reciting some facts.

Transfixed by ritual, Isabel continued to dab away at the body, the umbilical cord still attached to the afterbirth on the floor. She hardly raised her head as Tom draped a blanket over her shoulders. He came back with a bucket and a cloth, and on his hands and knees, started to sponge up the blood and mess.

Isabel lowered the body into the bath to wash it, taking care not to submerge the face. She dried it with the towel, and wrapped it in a fresh one, still with the placenta, so that it was bound up like a papoose.

"Tom, will you spread the sheet on the table?"

He moved the cake tin aside and laid out the embroidered sheet, folded in half. Isabel handed him the bundle. "Lay him down on it," she said, and he rested the little body there.

"Now we need to look after you," said Tom. "There's still hot water. Come and let's get you clean. Come on, lean on me. Slowly does it now. Slowly, slowly." Thick drops of scarlet splashed a trail as he led her from the kitchen into the bathroom, where this time it was he who dabbed her face with a flannel, rinsing it in the basin, and starting again.

An hour later, in a clean nightgown, her hair tied back in a plait, Isabel lay in bed. As Tom stroked her face, she eventually surrendered to exhaustion and the morphine tablets. Back in the kitchen, he finished cleaning up, and put the soiled linen into the laundry trough to soak. As darkness fell, he sat at the table and lit the lamp. He said a prayer over the little body. The vastness, the tiny body, eternity and the clock that accused the time of passing: it all made even less sense here than it had in Egypt or France. He had seen so many deaths. But there was something about the quietness of this one: as though, in the absence of the gunfire and the shouting, he were observing it unobscured for the first time. The men he had accompanied to the border of life would be mourned by a mother, but on the battlefield, the loved ones were far away and beyond imagining. To see a child torn away from his mother at the very moment of birth—torn away from the only woman in the world Tom cared about—was a more dreadful kind of pain. He glanced again at the shadows cast by the baby, and beside it, the cake covered with the cloth, like a shrouded twin.

"Not yet, Tom. I'll tell them when I'm ready," Isabel had insisted the following day, as she lay in bed.

"But your mum and dad—they'll want to know. They're expecting you home on the next boat. They're expecting their first grandchild."

Isabel had looked at him, helpless. "Exactly! They're expecting their first grandchild, and I've lost him."

"They'll be worried for you, Izz."

"Then why upset them? Please, Tom. It's our business. *My* business. We don't have to tell the whole world about it. Let them have their dream a bit longer. I'll send a letter when the boat comes again in June."

"But that's weeks away!"

"Tom, I just can't." A tear dropped on her nightgown. "At least they'll have a few more happy weeks . . ."

So, he had given in to her wish, and let the logbook stay silent.

But that was different—it was a personal matter. The arrival of the dinghy left no such leeway. Now he began by recording the steamer he had seen that morning, the *Manchester Queen* bound for Cape Town. Then he noted the calm conditions, the temperature, and put down his pen. Tomorrow. He would tell the whole story of the boat's arrival tomorrow, once he had sent the signal. He paused for a moment to consider whether to leave a space so that he could come back and fill it in, or whether it was best simply to imply that the boat had arrived later than it had. He left a space. He would signal in the morning and say that they had been too preoccupied with the baby to make contact sooner. The log would tell the truth, but a bit late. Just one day. He caught sight of his reflection in the glass over the "Notice under the Lighthouses Act 1911" which hung on the wall, and for a moment did not recognize the face he saw there.

"I'm not exactly an expert in this department," Tom said to Isabel on the afternoon of the baby's arrival.

"And you never will be if you stand around like that. I just need you to hold her while I check the bottle's warm enough. Come on. She won't bite," she said, smiling. "Not for now, at any rate."

The child was barely the length of Tom's forearm, but he took her as though he were handling an octopus.

"Just stay still a minute," said Isabel, arranging his arms. "All right. Keep them like that. And now"—she made a final adjustment—"she's all yours for the next two minutes." She went through to the kitchen.

It was the first time Tom had ever been alone with a baby. He stayed as if standing to attention, terrified of failing inspection. The child started to wriggle, kicking her feet and arms in a maneuver which flummoxed him.

"Steady on! Be fair on a bloke, now," he implored as he tried to get a better grip.

"Remember to keep her head supported," Isabel called. Immediately he slipped a hand up to the baby's scalp, registering its smallness in the palm of his hand. She squirmed again, so he rocked her gently. "Come on, be a sport. Play fair with your Uncle Tom."

As she blinked at him, and looked right into his eyes, Tom was suddenly aware of an almost physical ache. She was giving him a glimpse of a world he would now surely never know.

Isabel returned with the bottle. "Here." She put it into Tom's hand and guided it to the baby's mouth, demonstrating how to tap gently at her lips until she latched on. Tom was absorbed by how the process performed itself. The very fact that the baby required nothing of him stirred a sense of reverence for something far beyond his comprehension.

When Tom went back to the light, Isabel busied herself around the kitchen, preparing dinner while the child slept on. As soon as she heard a cry, she hurried to the nursery, and lifted her from the cot. The baby was fractious, and again nuzzled into Isabel's breast, starting to suck at the thin cotton of her blouse.

"Oh, my darling, are you still hungry? Old Doc Griffith's manual says to be careful not to give you too much. But maybe just a drop . . ." She warmed a little more milk and offered the bottle to the baby. But this time the child turned her head away from the teat and cried as she pawed instead at the inviting, warm nipple that touched her cheek through the cloth.

"Come on, here you are, here's the bottle, sweet thing," Isabel cooed, but the baby became more distressed, kicking her arms and legs and turning in to Isabel's chest.

Isabel remembered the fresh agony of the arrival of the milk, making her breasts heavy and sore with no baby to suckle—it had seemed a particularly cruel mechanism of nature. Now, this infant was seeking desperately for her milk, or perhaps just for comfort, now that immediate starvation had been staved off. She paused for a long moment, her thoughts swirling with the crying and the longing and the loss. "Oh, little sweetheart," she murmured, and slowly unbuttoned her blouse. Seconds later, the child had latched on fast, sucking contentedly, though only a few drops of milk came.

They had been like that for a good while when Tom entered the kitchen. "How's the—" He stopped in mid-sentence, arrested at the sight.

Isabel looked up at him, her face a mixture of innocence and guilt. "It was the only way I could get her to settle."

"But . . . Well . . ." Alarmed, Tom couldn't even frame his questions.

"She was desperate. Wouldn't take the bottle . . ."

"But—but she took it earlier, I saw her . . ."

"Yes, because she was starving. Probably literally."

Tom continued to stare, completely out of his depth.

"It's the most natural thing in the world, Tom. The best possible thing I could do for her. Don't look so shocked." She reached out a hand to him. "Come here, darl. Give me a smile."

He took her hand, but remained bewildered. And deep within, his uneasiness grew.

That afternoon, Isabel's eyes were alive with a light Tom had not seen for years. "Come and look!" she exclaimed. "Isn't she a picture? She fits just beautifully!" She gestured to the wickerwork cot, in which the child slept peacefully, her tiny chest rising and falling in a miniature echo of the waves around the island.

"Snug as a walnut in a shell, isn't she?" said Tom.

"I'd say she's not three months old yet."

"How can you tell?"

"I looked it up." Tom raised an eyebrow. "In *Dr. Griffiths*. I've picked some carrots and some turnips, and I've made a stew with the last of the mutton. I want to have a special tea tonight."

Tom frowned, puzzled.

"We need to welcome Lucy, and say a prayer for her poor father."

"If that's who he was," said Tom. "And *Lucy*?"

"Well she needs a name. Lucy means 'light,' so it's perfect, isn't it?"

"Izzy Bella." He smiled, then stroked her hair, gently serious. "Be careful, sweet. I don't want to see you upset . . ."

As Tom lit up for the evening, he still couldn't drive away the uneasiness, nor could he tell whether it came from the past—reawakened grief—or from foreboding. As he made his way down the narrow, winding stairs, across each of the metal landings, he felt a heaviness in his chest, and a sense of sliding back into a darkness he thought he had escaped.

That night, they sat down to dinner accompanied by the snuffling of the child, the occasional gurgle bringing a smile to Isabel's lips. "I wonder what will become of her?" she pondered aloud. "It's sad to think she could end up in an orphanage. Like Sarah Porter's little boy."

Later they made love for the first time since the stillbirth. Isabel seemed different to Tom: assured, relaxed. She kissed him afterward and said, "Let's plant a rose garden when spring comes. One that'll be here years after we're gone."

"I'll send the signal this morning," Tom said just after dawn, as he returned from extinguishing the light. The pearl-shell glow of day stole into the bedroom and caressed the baby's face. She had woken in the night and Isabel had brought her in to sleep between them. She put her finger to her lips as she nodded toward the sleeping infant, and rose from the bed to lead Tom into the kitchen.

"Sit down, love, and I'll make tea," she whispered, and marshaled cups, pot and kettle as quietly as she could. As she put the kettle on the stove, she said, "Tom, I've been thinking."

"What about, Izzy?"

"Lucy. It can't just be a coincidence that she turned up so soon after . . ." The sentence did not need completing. "We can't just ship her off to an orphanage." She turned to Tom and took his hands in hers. "Sweetheart, I think she should stay with us."

"Fair go now, darl! She's a lovely baby, but she doesn't belong to us. We can't *keep* her."

"Why not? Think about it. I mean, practically speaking, who's to know she's here?"

"When Ralph and Bluey come in a few weeks, *they'll* know, for a start."

"Yes, but it occurred to me last night that they won't know she's not ours. Everyone still thinks I'm expecting. They'll just be surprised she arrived early."

Tom watched, his mouth open. "But . . . Izzy, are you in your right mind? Do you realize what you're suggesting?"

"I'm suggesting kindness. That's all. Love for a baby. I'm suggesting, sweetheart," she clasped his hands tighter, "that we accept this gift that's been sent to us. How long have we wanted a baby, *prayed* for a baby?"

Turning to the window, Tom put his hands on his head and started to laugh, then stretched his arms up in appeal. "For heaven's sakes, Isabel! When I tell them about the fellow in the boat, eventually someone will know who he is. And they'll work out that there was a baby. Maybe not straightaway, but in the long run . . ."

"Then I think you shouldn't tell them."

"Not tell them?" His tone was suddenly sober.

She stroked his hair. "Don't tell them, sweetheart. We've done nothing wrong except give shelter to a helpless baby. We can give the poor man a decent burial. And the boat, well—just set it adrift again."

"Izzy, Izzy! You know I'd do anything for you, darl, but—whoever that man is and whatever he's done, he deserves to be dealt with properly. And lawfully, for that matter. What if the mother's not dead, and he's got a wife fretting, waiting for them both?"

"What woman would let her baby out of her sight? Face it, Tom: she *must* have drowned." She clasped his hands again. "I know how much your rules mean to you, and I know that this is technically breaking them. But what are those rules for? They're to save lives! That's all I'm saying we should do, sweetheart: save *this* life. She's here and she needs us and we can help her. Please."

"Izzy, I *can't*. This isn't up to me. Don't you understand?"

Her face darkened. "How can you be so hard-hearted? All you care about is your rules and your ships and your bloody light." These were accusations Tom had heard before, when, wild with grief after her miscarriages, Isabel had let loose her rage against the only person there—the man who continued to do his duty, who comforted her as best he could, but kept his own grieving to himself. Once again, he sensed her close to a dangerous brink, perhaps closer this time than she had ever been.

CHAPTER 11

An inquisitive gull watched Tom from its seaweed-cushioned rock. It followed him with an implacable eye as he wrapped the body, now pungent with that smell of the dead, in the canvas. It was hard to tell what the man might have been in life. His face was neither very old nor very young. He was slight; blond. He had a small scar on his left cheek. Tom wondered who missed him; who might have cause to love or hate him.

The old graves from the shipwreck lay on low ground, near the beach. As he set about digging the fresh hole, his muscles took over, executing their familiar task from blind memory in a ritual he had never expected to repeat.

The first time he had reported for the daily burial parade he had vomited at the sight of the corpses stretched out side by side, waiting for his shovel. After a while, it became just a job. He would hope to get the skinny bloke, or the one with his legs blown off, because he was a bloody sight easier to move. Bury them. Mark the grave. Salute, and walk away. That's how it was. Hoping for the one with the most bits blown off: Tom went cold at the thought that there had seemed nothing strange about that back then.

The shovel gave a gasp at each contact with the sandy soil. Once the ground had been patted back into a neat mound, he stopped to pray for a moment for whoever the poor wretch was, but he found himself whispering, "Forgive me, Lord, for this, and all my sins. And forgive Isabel. You know how much goodness there is in her. And you know how much she's suffered. Forgive us both. Have mercy." He crossed himself and returned to the boat, ready to drag it back into the water. He gave it a heave, and a ray of light pricked his eyes as the sun glinted off something. He peered into the hull of the dinghy. Something shiny was wedged under the rib of the bow, and resisted his first attempt to grasp it. After pulling for a moment he prised away a cold, hard shape, which came to life, jangling: a silver rattle, embossed with cherubs and hallmarked.

He turned it over and over, as if waiting for it to speak to him, to give him some kind of clue. He thrust it in his pocket: any number of stories might account for the arrival of this strange pair on the island, but only telling himself Izzy's story that the child was an orphan would allow him to sleep at night. It did not bear thinking beyond that, and he needed to avoid any proof to the contrary. He fixed his eyes on the line where the ocean met the sky like a pair of pursed lips. Better not to know.

He made sure that the boat had been picked up by the southerly current before wading back in to the beach. He was grateful for the salty stink of the green-black seaweed rotting on the rocks, which washed the smell of death from his nostrils. A tiny purple sand crab ventured out from under a ledge, sidled busily over to a dead blowfish, swollen and spiky even in death, and began to pincer little pieces from the belly into its own mouth. Tom shivered, and started the steep trek up the path.

"Most days, there's nowhere to escape the wind around here. It's all right if you're a seagull, or an albatross: see how they just sit on the currents of air, like they're having a rest?" As he sat on the veranda, Tom pointed to a great silver bird which had made its way from some other island, and seemed to hang in a still sky on a thread, despite the turbulent air.

The baby ignored Tom's finger and instead gazed into his eyes, mesmerized by the movement of his lips and the deep resonance of his chest. She cooed—a high-pitched half-hiccup. Tom tried to ignore the way his heart kicked in response, and continued his discourse. "But in that bay, just that little cove, it's one spot where you're most likely to find a bit of peace and quiet, because it faces north, and the wind hardly ever comes in due north. That side's the Indian Ocean—nice and calm and warm. Southern Ocean's on the other side—wild and dangerous as anything. You want to keep away from that fella."

The child flung an arm above her blanket in response, and Tom let her hand wrap around his index finger. In the week since her arrival, he had become accustomed to her gurgles, to her silent, sleeping presence in her cot, which seemed to waft through the cottage like the smell of baking or flowers. It worried him that he could find himself listening out for her to wake in the morning, or going by reflex to pick her up when she started to cry.

"You're falling in love with her, aren't you?" said Isabel, who had been watching from the doorway. Tom frowned, and she said with a smile, "It's impossible not to."

"All those little expressions she does . . ."

"You're going to be a beaut dad."

He shifted in his chair. "Izz, it's still wrong, not reporting it."

"Just look at her. Does she look like we've done anything wrong?"

"But—that's just it. We don't *need* to do anything wrong. We could report her now and apply to adopt her. It's not too late, Izz. We can still make it right."

"Adopt her?" Isabel stiffened. "They'd never send a baby to a lighthouse in the middle of nowhere: no doctor; no school. No *church* probably worries them the most. And even if they did put her up for adoption, they'd want to give her to some couple in a town somewhere. And besides, it takes forever to go through the rigmarole. They'd want to meet us. You'd never get leave to go and see them, and we're not due back onshore for another year and a half." She put a hand on his shoulder. "*I* know we'll cope. *I* know you're going to be a wonderful dad. But *they* don't."

She gazed at the baby, and put a finger to her soft cheek. "Love's bigger than rule books, Tom. If you'd reported the boat, she'd be stuck in some dreadful orphanage by now." She rested her hand on his arm. "Our prayers have been answered. The baby's prayers have been answered. Who'd be ungrateful enough to send her away?"

The simple fact was that, sure as a graft will take and fuse on a rosebush, the root stock of Isabel's motherhood—her every drive and instinct, left raw and exposed by the recent stillbirth—had grafted seamlessly to the scion, the baby which needed mothering. Grief and distance bound the wound, perfecting the bond with a speed only nature could engineer.

When Tom came down from the lantern room that evening, Isabel was sitting beside the first fire of the autumn, nursing the baby in the rocking chair he had made four years ago now. She hadn't noticed him, and he watched her in silence for a moment. She seemed to handle the child by sheer instinct, incorporating her into every move. He fought back his gnawing doubt. Perhaps Isabel was right. Who was he to part this woman from a baby?

In her hands was the Book of Common Prayer, to which Isabel had turned more frequently after the first miscarriage. Now, she read silently "The Churching of Women," prayers for women after childbirth. "Lo, children and the fruit of the womb: are an heritage and gift that cometh of the Lord . . ."

The next morning, Isabel stood beside Tom below the lantern room, holding the baby as he tapped out the signal. He had thought carefully about the wording. His fingers were unsteady as he began: he had been dreading sending news of the stillbirth, but this felt much worse. "*Baby arrived early stop took us both by surprise stop Isabel recovering well stop no need for medical help stop little girl stop Lucy—*" He turned to Isabel. "Anything else?"

"The weight. People always ask the weight." She thought back to Sarah Porter's baby. "Say seven pounds one ounce."

Tom looked at her in surprise at the ease with which the lie came to her. He turned back to the key and tapped out the figures.

When the reply arrived, he transcribed it and noted it in the signals book. "*Congratulations stop marvelous news stop have officially recorded increase in Janus population as per regulations stop Ralph and Bluey send cheers stop grandparents will be informed pronto stop.*" He sighed, aware of a pressure in his chest, and waited a while before going to report the response to Isabel.

In the weeks that followed, Isabel bloomed. She sang as she went about the cottage. She could not keep from showering Tom with hugs and kisses all through the day. Her smile dazzled him with its sheer uninhibited joy. And the baby? The baby was peaceful, and trusting. She did not question the embrace which held her, the hands which caressed her, the lips which kissed her and crooned, "Mamma's here, Lucy, Mamma's here," as she was rocked to sleep.

There was no denying that the child was thriving. Her skin seemed to glow with a soft halo. Isabel's breasts responded to the baby's suckling by producing milk again within weeks, the "relactation" Dr. Griffiths described in clinical detail, and the child fed without a moment's hesitation, as though the two of them had agreed some sort of contract. But Tom took to staying a fraction longer in the lantern room in the mornings after extinguishing the light. Time and again he would catch himself turning back the page of the log to 27 April, and staring at the blank space.

You could kill a bloke with rules, Tom knew that. And yet sometimes they were what stood between man and savagery, between man and monsters. The rules that said you took a prisoner rather than killed a man. The rules that said you let the stretchers cart the enemy off from no-man's-land as well as your own men. But always, it would come down to the simple question: could he deprive Isabel of this baby? If the child was alone in the world? Could it really be right to drag her away from a woman who adored her, to some lottery of Fate?

At night, Tom began to dream he was drowning, flinging his arms and legs desperately to find ground somewhere, but there was nothing to stand on, nothing to hold him afloat except a mermaid, whose tail he would grasp and who would then pull him deeper and deeper into the dark water until he awoke gasping and sweating, while Isabel slept beatifically beside him.

CHAPTER 12

Geddday, Ralph. Good to see you. Where's Blue?"

"Back here!" shouted the deckhand from the stern, hidden from view by some fruit crates. "How ya doing, Tom? Glad to see us?"

"Always, mate—you're the blokes with the grog, aren't you?" he laughed as he secured the line. The old engine chugged and spluttered as the boat drew alongside, filling the air with thick diesel fumes. It was mid-June, the first time the store boat had visited since the baby's arrival seven weeks earlier.

"Flying fox is set up. Got the winch all ready too."

"Struth, you're a bit keen, Tom!" Ralph exclaimed. "We don't want to rush things now, do we? It's a grand day. We can take our time. We've got to see the new arrival, after all! My Hilda's piled me up like a packhorse with things for the little 'un, not to mention the proud grandparents."

As Ralph strode off the gangway he grabbed Tom in a bear hug. "Congratulations, son. Bloody marvelous. Especially after—after all that's happened before."

Bluey followed suit. "Yeah, good on you. Ma sends all her best too."

Tom's eyes wandered to the water. "Thanks. Thanks a lot. Appreciate it."

As they hiked up the path, Isabel was silhouetted against a washing line of nappies strung out like signal flags flapping in the brisk wind. Strands of her hair escaped from the roll she had just pinned it in.

Ralph held his arms out as he approached her. "Well, can't you just tell, hey? Nothing makes a girl bloom like having a littlie. Roses in your cheeks and a shine in your hair, just like my Hilda used to get with each of ours."

Isabel blushed at the compliment, and gave the old man a quick kiss. She kissed Bluey too, who bowed his head and muttered, "Congratulations, Mrs. S."

"Come inside, all of you. Kettle's boiled, and there's cake," she said.

As they sat at the old deal table, Isabel's glance strayed now and then to the child asleep in her basket.

"You were the talk of every woman in Partageuse, having your baby on your own like that. Of course, the farmers' wives didn't turn a hair—Mary Linford said how she'd had three without any help. But them in town, they were mighty impressed. I hope Tom wasn't too useless?"

The couple exchanged a look. Tom was about to speak, but Isabel took his hand and squeezed it tight. "He's been wonderful. I couldn't ask for a better husband." There were tears in her eyes.

"She's a real pretty little thing, from what I can see," said Bluey. But all that peeped out from the fluffy blanket was a delicate face in a bonnet.

"She's got Tom's nose, hasn't she?" chipped in Ralph.

"Well . . ." Tom hesitated. "Not sure my nose is what you want a baby girl to have!"

"I take your point!" Ralph chuckled. "Right, Mr. Sherbourne, my friend, I need your autograph on the forms. Might as well sort them out now."

Tom was relieved to get up from the table. "Righto. Come through to the office, Captain Addicott, sir," he said, leaving Bluey cooing over the basket.

The young man reached into the cot and jangled the rattle at the baby, who was now wide awake. She watched it intently, and he jiggled it again. "You're a lucky one, aren't you, getting a fancy silver rattle! Fit for a princess: I've never seen anything so grand! Angels on the handle and everything. Angels for an angel . . . And your nice fluffy blanket . . ."

"Oh, they were left over from . . ." Isabel's voice dropped, "from before."

Bluey blushed. "Sorry. Putting my foot in it. I . . . Better get on with unloading. Thanks for the cake," and he beat a retreat through the kitchen door.

Janus Rock,

June 1926

Dear Mum and Dad,

Well, God has sent us an angel to keep us company. Baby Lucy has captured our hearts! She's a beautiful little girl—absolutely perfect. She sleeps well and feeds well. She's never any trouble.

I wish you could see her and hold her. Every day she looks a bit different, and I know by the time you see her she'll have lost her baby looks. She'll be a toddler when we come back on shore. But in the meantime, here's the nearest thing to a picture. I dipped the sole of her foot in cochineal! (You have to be inventive on the Lights . . .) See masterpiece attached.

Tom is a wonderful dad. Janus seems so different now that Lucy's here. At the moment it's pretty easy to look after her—I pop her in her basket and she comes with me when I have to get the eggs or do the milking. It might be a bit harder when she starts to crawl. But I don't want to get ahead of myself.

I want to tell you so much about her—how her hair is dark, how beautiful she smells after her bath. Her eyes are quite dark too. But I can't do her justice. She's much too wonderful to describe. I've only known her a few weeks and already I can't imagine my life without her.

Well, "Grandma and Grandpa" (!), I'd better finish this so that the boat can take it, otherwise it'll be another three months before you get it!

With fondest love,
Isabel

P.S. I've just read your letter from the boat this morning. Thanks for the beautiful bunny rug. And the doll is just lovely. The books are wonderful too. I tell her nursery rhymes all the time, so she'll like these new ones.
P.P.S. Tom says thanks for the jumper. Winter's starting to bite out here!

The new moon was barely a crescent stitched into the darkening sky. Tom and Isabel were sitting on the veranda as the light swept around far above them. Lucy had fallen asleep in Tom's arms.

"It's hard to breathe differently from her, isn't it?" he said, gazing at the baby.

"What do you mean?"

"It's like a kind of spell, isn't it? Whenever she's asleep like this, I end up breathing in the same rhythm. A bit like I end up doing things in time to the turning of the light." Almost to himself, he said, "It scares me."

Isabel smiled. "It's just love, Tom. No need to be scared of love."

Tom felt a shiver creep through him. Just as he couldn't now imagine having lived in this world without meeting Isabel, he realized that Lucy, too, was making her way inside his heart. And he wished she belonged there.

Anyone who's worked on the Offshore Lights can tell you about it—the isolation, and the spell it casts. Like sparks flung off the furnace that is Australia, these beacons dot around it, flickering on and off, some of them only ever seen by a handful of living souls. But their isolation saves the whole continent from isolation—keeps the shipping lanes safe, as vessels steam the thousands of miles to bring machines and books and cloth, in return for wool and wheat, coal and gold: the fruits of ingenuity traded for the fruits of earth.

The isolation spins its mysterious cocoon, focusing the mind on one place, one time, one rhythm—the turning of the light. The island knows no other human voices, no other footprints. On the Offshore Lights you can live any story you want to tell yourself, and no one will say you're wrong: not the seagulls, not the prisms, not the wind.

So Isabel floats further and further into her world of divine benevolence, where prayers are answered, where babies arrive by the will of God and the working of currents. "Tom, I wonder how we can be so lucky?" she muses. She watches in awe as her blessed daughter grows and thrives. She revels in the discoveries each day brings for this little being: rolling over; starting to crawl; the first, faltering sounds. The storms gradually follow winter to another corner of the earth, and summer comes, bearing a paler blue sky, a sharper gold sun.

"Up you come." Isabel laughs, and hoists Lucy onto her hip as the three of them stroll down the path to the glinting beach for a picnic. Tom picks different leaves—sea grass, pig-face—and Lucy smells them, chews on their ends, pulling faces at the strange sensations. He gathers tiny posies of rose banjine, or shows her the shimmering scales of a trevally or a blue mackerel he has caught off the rocks on the side of the island where the ocean floor drops away into sudden darkness. On still nights, Isabel's voice carries across the air in a soothing lilt as she reads Lucy tales of Snugglepot and Cuddlepie in the nursery, while Tom works on repairs in the shed.

Whatever the rights and the wrongs of it, Lucy was here now, and Isabel couldn't have been a better mother. Every night in prayer she gave thanks to God for her family, her health, her much-blessed life, and prayed to be worthy of the gifts He showered on her.

Days broke and receded like waves on the beach, leaving barely a trace of the time that passed in this tiny world of working and sleeping and feeding and watching. Isabel shed a tear when she put away some of Lucy's earliest baby things. "Seems only yesterday she was tiny, and now look at her," she mused to Tom, as she folded them carefully away in tissue paper—a dummy, her rattle, her first baby dresses, a tiny pair of kid booties. Just like any mother might do, anywhere in the world.

When the blood didn't come, Isabel was excited. When she had given up all hope of another child, her expectations were about to be confounded. She would wait a little longer, keep praying before saying anything to Tom. But she found her thoughts drifting off to daydreams about a brother or sister for Lucy. Her heart was full. Then the bleeding returned with a vengeance, heavier and more painful, in a pattern she couldn't fathom. Her head would ache, sometimes; she would sweat at night. Then months would pass with no blood at all. "I'll go and see Dr. Sumpton when we get our shore leave. No need to fuss," she told Tom. She carried on without complaint. "I'm strong as an ox, darl. There's nothing to worry about." She was in love—with her husband, and with her baby—and that was enough.

The months trailed by, marked with the peculiar rituals of the lighthouse—lighting up, hoisting the ensign, draining the mercury bath to filter out stray oil. All the usual form-filling, and compliance with the bullying correspondence from the Foreman Artificer about how any damage to the vapor tubes could only be caused by lightkeeper negligence, not faulty workmanship. The logbook changed from 1926 to 1927 in mid-page: there was no wasting paper in the CLS—the books were expensive. Tom pondered the institutional indifference to the arrival of a new year—as though the Lights were not impressed by something as prosaic as the mere effluction of time. And it was true—

the view from the gallery on New Year's Day was indistinguishable from that of New Year's Eve.

Occasionally, he would still find himself revisiting the page for 27 April 1926, until the book opened there of its own accord.

Isabel worked hard. The vegetable patch thrived; the cottage was kept clean. She washed and patched Tom's clothes, and cooked the things he liked. Lucy grew. The light turned. Time passed.

CHAPTER 13

It's coming up for a year soon," said Isabel. "The twenty-seventh of April's her birthday, near enough."

Tom was in the workshop, filing away rust from a bent door hinge. He put down the rasp. "I wonder—you know, what her real birthday is."

"The day she arrived is good enough for me." Isabel kissed the child, who was sitting astride her hip, gnawing on a crust.

Lucy reached out her arms to Tom.

"Sorry, littlie. My hands are filthy. You're better off with Mamma just now."

"I can't believe how much she's grown. She weighs a ton these days." Isabel laughed, and gave Lucy a heave to settle her higher on her hip. "I'm going to make a birthday cake." The child responded by dipping her head into Isabel's chest and dribbling bits of bread onto her. "That tooth's giving you trouble, isn't it, sweetie? Your cheeks are so red. Shall we put some teething powder on it?" Turning to Tom, she said, "See you in a while, darl. I'd better get back. Soup's still on the stove," and left for the cottage.

The steely light pierced the window and scoured Tom's workbench. He had to hammer the metal straight, and each blow rang sharply off the walls. Though he found himself striking with more force than was necessary, he couldn't stop. There was no getting away from the feeling stirred up by talk of birthdays and anniversaries. He set to work with the hammer again, the blows no less heavy, until the metal snapped from the force. He picked up the shattered halves and stared at them.

Tom looked up from the armchair. A few weeks had passed since the baby's birthday celebration.

"It doesn't matter what you read to her," said Isabel. "It's just good for her to get used to hearing different words." She deposited Lucy on his lap and went to finish making the bread.

"Dadadadad," said the child.

"Bubububub," said Tom. "So. You want a story?" The little hand reached out, but instead of pointing to the heavy book of fairy tales on the table beside them, grabbed a beige booklet, and pushed it at him. He laughed. "I don't think you'll like that one much, bunny rabbit. No pictures in it, for a start." He reached for the fairy tales, but Lucy thrust the booklet in his face. "Dadadadad."

"If that's the one you want, littlie!" He laughed again. The child opened it at a page, and pointed at the words, like she had seen Tom and Isabel do. "All right," began Tom. *"Instructions to Lightkeepers. Number twenty-nine: 'The Lightkeepers are never to allow any interests, private or otherwise, to interfere with discharge of their duties, which are of the greatest importance to the safety of navigation; and they are reminded that their retention or promotion in the Service depends upon their strict obedience to orders, adherence to the rules laid down for their guidance, industry, sobriety, and the maintenance of cleanliness and good order in their own persons and families as well as in every part of the Lighthouse establishment and premises.' Number thirty: 'Misconduct, disposition to quarrel, insobriety or immorality on the part of any keeper'"*—he paused to retrieve Lucy's fingers from his nostrils— "*'will render the offender liable to punishment or dismissal. The committing of any such offense by any member of the Lightkeeper's family will render the offender liable to exclusion from the Light-*

house station.'" He stopped. A chill had crept though him, and his heart beat faster. He was summoned back to the present by a tiny hand coming to rest on his chin. He pressed it to his lips, absently. Lucy grinned at him and gave him a generous kiss.

"Come on, let's read *Sleeping Beauty* instead," he said, and took up the fairy tales, though he found it hard to concentrate.

"Here you are—tea and toast in bed, ladies!" said Tom, resting the tray beside Isabel.

"Careful, Luce," said Isabel. She had brought the toddler into bed that Sunday after Tom had gone to extinguish the light, and the child was clambering toward the tray to reach the small cup of tea Tom had made her too—hardly more than warm milk with a drop of color.

Tom sat beside Isabel and pulled Lucy onto his knee. "Here we go, Lulu," he said, and helped her steady the cup in both hands as she drank. He was concentrating on his task, until he became aware of Isabel's silence, and turned to see tears in her eyes.

"Izzy, Izzy, what's wrong, darl?"

"Nothing at all, Tom. Nothing at all."

He brushed a tear away from her cheek.

"Sometimes I'm so happy it frightens me, Tom."

He stroked her hair, and Lucy started to blow bubbles into the tea. "Listen, Miss Muffet, you going to drink that, or have you had enough for the minute?"

The child continued to slobber into the cup, clearly pleased with the sounds.

"OK, I think we'll give it a rest for now." He eased the cup away from her, and she responded by climbing off him and onto Isabel, still blowing bubbles of spittle.

"Charming!" said Isabel, laughing through her tears. "Come here, you little monkey!" and she blew a raspberry on her tummy. Lucy giggled and squirmed and said, "'Gain! 'Gain!" and Isabel obliged.

"You two are as bad as each other!" said Tom.

"Sometimes I feel a bit drunk with how much I love her. And you. Like if they asked me to walk one of those straight lines I couldn't."

"No straight lines on Janus, so you're all right on that score," said Tom.

"Don't mock, Tom. It's like I was color-blind before Lucy, and now the world's completely different. It's brighter and I can see further. I'm in exactly the same place, the birds are the same, the water's the same, the sun rises and sets just like it always did, but I never knew what *for*, Tom." She drew the child into her. "Lucy's the what for . . . And *you're* different too."

"How?"

"I think there are bits of you you didn't know existed until she came along. Corners of your heart that life had shut down." She traced a finger along his mouth. "I know you don't like to talk about the war and everything, but—well, it must have made you numb."

"My feet. Made my feet numb more often than not—frozen mud'll do that to a bloke." Tom could manage only half a smile at the attempted joke.

"Stop it, Tom. I'm trying to say something. I'm being serious, for goodness' sake, and you just send me packing with some silly joke, like I'm a child who doesn't understand or can't be trusted with the truth."

This time Tom was deadly serious. "You *don't* understand, Isabel. No civilized person should ever *have* to understand. And trying to describe it would be like passing on a disease." He turned toward the window. "I did what I did so that people like you and Lucy could forget it ever happened. So that it would never happen again. 'The war to end all wars,' remember? It doesn't belong here, on this island. In this bed."

Tom's features had hardened, and she glimpsed a resolve she'd never seen in him before—the resolve, she imagined, that had got him through everything he'd had to endure.

"It's just . . ." Isabel began again, "well, we none of us know whether we're around for another year or another hundred years. And I wanted to make sure you knew how thankful I am to you, Tom. For everything. Especially for giving me Lucy."

Tom's smile froze at the last words, and Isabel hurried on. "You *did,* darl. You understood how much I needed her, and I know that cost you, Tom. Not many men would do that for their wife."

Jolted back from some dream world, Tom could feel his palms sweating. His heart started to race with the urge to run—anywhere, it didn't matter where, just as long as it was away from the reality of the choice he had made, which suddenly seemed to weigh like an iron collar.

"Time I was getting on with some work. I'll leave you two to have your toast," he said, and left the room as slowly as he could manage.

CHAPTER 14

When Tom's second three-year term came to an end just before Christmas 1927, the family from Janus Rock made its first journey to Point Partageuse while a relief keeper manned the light station. The couple's second shore leave, it would be Lucy's first voyage to the mainland. As Isabel had prepared for the arrival of the boat, she had toyed with finding an excuse to stay behind with the little girl in the safety of Janus.

"You OK, Izz?" Tom had asked when he saw her, suitcase open on the bed, staring blankly through the window.

"Oh. Yes," she said quickly. "Just making sure I've packed everything."

He was about to leave the room, when he doubled back and put his hand on her shoulder. "Nervous?"

She snatched up a pair of socks and rolled them together in a ball. "No, not at all," she said as she stuffed them in the case. "Not at all."

The unease Isabel had tried to hide from Tom vanished at the sight of Lucy in Violet's arms, when her parents came to greet them at the jetty.

Her mother wept and smiled and laughed all at the same time. "At last!" She shook her head in awe, inspecting every inch of the child, touching her face, her hair, her little hand. "My blessed granddaughter. Fancy waiting nearly two years to lay eyes on you! And isn't she just the image of my old Auntie Clem?"

Isabel had spent months preparing Lucy for exposure to people. "In Partageuse, Luce, there are lots and lots of people. And they'll all like you. It might be a bit strange at first, but there's no need to be scared." At bedtimes, she had told the girl stories of the town, and the people who lived in it.

Lucy responded with great curiosity to the endless supply of humans that now surrounded her. Isabel felt a twinge as she accepted the warm congratulations of townspeople on her pretty daughter. Even old Mrs. Mewett tickled the little girl under the chin when she saw her in the haberdasher's as she was buying a hairnet. "Ah, little ones," she said wistfully. "Such blessings," leaving Isabel to wonder whether she was hearing things.

Almost as soon as they arrived, Violet packed the whole family off to Gutcher's photographic studio. In front of a canvas backdrop painted with ferns and Greek columns, Lucy had been photographed with Tom and Isabel; with Bill and Violet; and on her own, perched on a grand wicker chair. Copies were ordered to take back to Janus, to send to cousins far afield, to have framed for the mantelpiece and the piano. "Three generations of Graysmark women," beamed Violet when she saw herself, with Lucy on her knee, sitting beside Isabel.

Lucy had grandparents who doted on her. God doesn't make mistakes, thought Isabel. He had sent the little girl to the right place.

"Oh, Bill," Violet had said to her husband the evening the family arrived. "Thank goodness. Thank goodness . . ."

Violet had last seen her daughter three years before, still grieving at her second miscarriage, on the couple's first shore leave. Then, Isabel had sat with her head on her mother's lap, weeping.

"It's just nature's way," Violet had said. "You have to take a breath, and get up again. Children will come along, if that's what God wants for you: just be patient. And pray. The praying's the most important thing."

She did not tell Isabel the whole truth of it, though. She did not say how often she had seen a child carried to term over the draining, withering summer or the whip-sharp winter, only to be lost to scarlet fever or diphtheria, their clothes folded away neatly until they might fit the next one down. Nor did she touch on the awkwardness of replying to a casual inquiry as to the number of children one had. A successful delivery was merely the first step of a long, treacherous journey. In this house, which had fallen silent years ago, Violet knew that only too well.

Reliable, dutiful Violet Graysmark, respectable wife of a respectable husband. She kept the moths out of the cupboards, the weeds out of the flowerbeds. She deadheaded the roses to persuade them into blooming even in August. Her lemon curd always sold out first at the church fête, and it was her fruitcake recipe which had been chosen for the local CWA booklet. True, she thanked God every night for her many blessings. But some afternoons, as the sunset turned the garden from green to a dull dun while she peeled potatoes over the sink, there just wasn't enough room in her heart to hold all the sadness. As Isabel had cried during that previous visit, Violet had wanted to wail with her, to tear her hair and tell her she knew the grief of losing the firstborn: how nothing—no person, no money, no thing that this earth could offer—could ever make up for that, and that the pain would never, never go away. She wanted to tell her how it made you mad, made you bargain with God about what offering you could sacrifice to get your child back.

When Isabel had been safely asleep and Bill was dozing beside the last of the fire, Violet went to her wardrobe and fetched down the old biscuit tin. She fished around inside it, moving aside the few pennies, a small mirror, a watch, a wallet, until she came to the envelope frayed at the edges now from years of opening. She sat on the bed, and by the yellow light of the lamp, set to reading the clumsy script, though she knew the words by heart.

Dear Mrs. Graysmark,

I hope you will forgive me writing to you: you don't know me. My name is Betsy Parmenter and I live in Kent.

Two weeks ago I was visiting my son Fred, who was sent back from the front on account of bad shrapnel wounds. He was in the 1st Southern General hospital in Stourbridge, and I have a sister who lives nearby, so I was able to visit him every day.

Well I am writing because one afternoon they brought in a wounded Australian soldier who I understand was your son Hugh. He was in a bad way, on account as you will know of being blinded and lost an arm. He could still manage some words though, and spoke very fondly of his family and his home in Australia. He was a very brave lad. I saw him each day, and at one stage there was high hopes that he would recover, but then it seems he developed blood poisoning, and he went downhill.

I just wanted you to know that I brought him flowers (the early tulips were just blooming and they're such lovely things) and some cigarettes. I think my Fred and him got along well. He even ate some fruitcake I brought in one day which was very pleasing to see and it seemed to give him pleasure. I was there the morning when he went downhill, and we all three said the Lord's Prayer and we sang "Abide With Me." The doctors eased his pain as best they could, and I think he did not suffer too much at the end. There was a vicar came and blessed him.

I would like to say how much we all appreciate the great sacrifice that your brave son made. He mentioned his brother, Alfie, and I pray that he comes back to you safe and sound.

I am sorry for the delay in writing this to you, only my Fred passed away a week after your boy and it has taken a lot of doing things as you can imagine.

With very best wishes and prayers,
(Mrs.) Betsy Parmenter

Hugh would only have known tulips from picture books, Violet thought, and it comforted her that he had perhaps touched one and felt its shape. She wondered whether tulips had a scent.

She recalled how the postman had looked grave and almost guilty a couple of weeks later as he handed her the parcel: brown paper tied with string, addressed to Bill. She was so upset that she did not even read the printing on the form: she did not need to. Many a woman had received the meager collection of things which constituted her son's life.

The receipt form from Melbourne read:

Dear Sir,

Forwarded herewith, per separate registered post, is one package containing the effects of the late No. 4497 Pte Graysmark, 28th Bn. received ex "Themistocles" as per inventory attached.

I shall be much obliged if you would kindly let me know whether it comes safely to hand, by signing and returning the enclosed printed receipt slip.

Yours faithfully
J. M. Johnson, Major,
Officer in Charge, Base Records.

On a separate slip of paper from "The Kit Store, 110 Greyhound Road, Fulham, London SW" was the inventory of the effects. Violet was struck by something as she read the list: *shaving mirror; belt; three pennies; wrist-watch with leather strap, harmonica.* How odd that Alfie's mouth organ was among Hugh's belongings. Then she looked again at the list, the forms, the letter, the parcel, and read the name more carefully. A. H. Graysmark. Not H. A. Alfred Henry, not Hugh Albert. She ran to find her husband. "Bill! Oh Bill!" she cried. "There's been the most dreadful mistake!"

It took a good deal of correspondence, on black-edged paper on the part of the Graysmarks, to find that Alfie had died within a day of Hugh, three days after arriving in France. Joining the same regiment on the same day, the brothers had been proud of their consecutive service numbers. The signalman, who had with his own eyes seen Hugh shipped out alive on a stretcher, disregarded the instruction to send the KIA telegram for A. H. Graysmark, assuming it meant H. A. The first Violet knew of her second son's death was the bland package in her hands. It was an easy enough mistake to have made on a battlefield, she had said.

Coming back last time to the house she grew up in, Isabel had been reminded of the darkness that had descended with her brothers' deaths, how loss had leaked all over her mother's life like a stain. As a fourteen-year-old, Isabel had searched the dictionary. She knew that if a wife lost a husband, there was a whole new word to describe who she was: she was now a *widow*. A husband became a *widower*. But if a parent lost a child, there was no special label for their grief. They were still just a mother or a father, even if they no longer had a son or a daughter. That seemed odd. As to her own status, she wondered whether she was still technically a sister, now that her adored brothers had died.

It was as if one of the shells from the French front line had exploded in the middle of her family, leaving a crater that she could never fill or repair. Violet would spend days tidying her sons' rooms, polishing the silver frames of their photographs. Bill became silent. Whatever topic of conversation Isabel tried to engage him in, he didn't answer, or even wandered out of the room. Her job, she decided, was not to cause her parents any more bother or concern. She was the consolation prize—what they had instead of their sons.

Now, her parents' rapture confirmed to Isabel that she had done the right thing in keeping Lucy. Any lingering shadows were swept away.

The baby had healed so many lives: not only hers and Tom's, but now the lives of these two people who had been so resigned to loss.

At Christmas lunch, Bill Graysmark said grace and in a choked voice thanked the Lord for the gift of Lucy. In the kitchen later, Violet confided to Tom that her husband had had a new lease of life from the day he had heard about Lucy's birth. "It's done wonders. Like a magic tonic."

She gazed through the window at the pink hibiscus. "Bill took the news about Hugh hard enough, but when he found out about Alfie, it fair knocked him for six. For a long time he wouldn't believe it. Said it was impossible that such a thing could have happened. He spent months writing here, there and everywhere, determined to show it was a mistake. In a way, I was glad of it: proud of him for fighting the news. But there were plenty of people hereabouts who'd lost more than one boy. I knew it was true.

"Eventually the fire went out of him. He just lost heart." She took a breath. "But these days"—she raised her eyes and smiled in wonder—"he's his old self again, thanks to Lucy. I'd wager your little girl means as much to Bill as she does to you. She's given him the world back." She reached up and kissed Tom's cheek. "Thank you."

As the women did the dishes after lunch, Tom sat out the back on the shady grass with Lucy, where she toddled about, circling back now and again to give him ravenous kisses. "Jeez, thanks, littlie!" he chuckled. "Don't eat me." She looked at him, with those eyes that sought his like a mirror, until he pulled her in to him and tickled her again.

"Ah! The perfect dad!" said a voice from behind. Tom turned to see his father-in-law approaching.

"Thought I'd come and make sure you were managing. Vi always said I had the knack with our three." As the last word came out, a shadow flitted across his face. He recovered and stretched out his arms. "Come to Grandpa. Come and pull his whiskers. Ah, my little princess!"

Lucy tottered over and stretched out her arms. "Up you come," he said, sweeping her up. She reached for the fob watch in his waistcoat pocket, and tugged it out.

"You want to know what time it is? Again?" Bill laughed, and he went through the ritual of opening the gold case and showing her the hands. She immediately snapped it shut, and thrust it back at him to reopen. "It's hard on Violet, you know," he said to Tom.

Tom brushed the grass off his trousers as he stood up. "What is, Bill?"

"Being without Isabel, and now, missing out on this little one . . ." He paused. "There must be jobs you could get around Partageuse way . . . ? You've got a university degree, for goodness' sake . . ."

Tom shifted his weight uneasily to his other foot.

"Oh, I know what they say—once a lightkeeper, always a lightkeeper."

"That's what they say," said Tom.

"And is it true?"

"More or less."

"But you could leave? If you really wanted to?"

Tom gave it thought before replying, "Bill, a man could leave his wife, if he really wanted to. Doesn't make it the right thing to do."

Bill gave him a look.

"Hardly fair to let them train you up, get the experience, and then leave them in the lurch. And you get used to it." He glanced up at the sky as he considered. "It's where I belong. And Isabel loves it."

The child reached out her arms to Tom, who transferred her to his hip in a reflex movement.

"Well, you mind you look after my girls. That's all I'm saying."

"I'll do my best. I promise you that."

The most important Boxing Day tradition in Point Partageuse was the Church Fête. A gathering of residents from the town and far beyond, it had been established long ago, by someone with an eye for business who had seen the advantage of holding the fund-raising event on a day when no one had an excuse to say they were too busy with work to attend. And, it being still Christmastime, they had no excuse not to be generous either.

As well as the sale of cakes and toffees, and jars of jam that occasionally exploded in the fierce sun, the event was famous for its sports and novelty events: the egg and spoon race, three-legged race, sack race—all were staples of the day. The coconut shy still ran, though they'd given up on the shooting gallery after the war, because the newly honed skills of the local men meant it started to lose money.

The events were open to all, and participation was something of a three-line whip. Families made a day of it, and patties and sausages were barbecued over half a forty-four-gallon drum, and sold off at sixpence a go. Tom sat with Lucy and Isabel on a blanket in the shade, eating sausages in buns, while Lucy dismantled her lunch and redistributed it on the plate beside her.

"The boys were great runners," Isabel said. "Even used to win the three-legged race. And I think Mum's still got the cup I won for the sack race one year."

Tom smiled. "Didn't know I'd married a champion athlete."

She gave him a playful slap on the arm. "I'm just telling you the Graysmark family legends."

Tom was attending to the mess that threatened to spill over from Lucy's plate when a boy with a marshal's rosette appeared beside them. Clasping a pad and pencil, he said, "'Scuse me. That your baby?"

The question startled Tom. "Pardon?"

"Just asking if that's your baby."

Though words came from Tom's mouth, they were incoherent.

The boy turned to Isabel. "That your baby, Missus?"

Isabel frowned for a second, and then gave a slow nod as she understood. "You on the round-up for the dads' race?"

"That's right." He lifted the pencil to the page and asked Tom, "How do you spell your name?"

Tom looked again at Isabel, but there was no trace of discomfort in her face. "I can spell it if you've forgotten how," she teased.

Tom waited for her to understand his alarm, but her smile didn't waver. Finally, he said, "Not really my strong point, running."

"But all the dads do it," said the boy, at what was clearly the first refusal he'd come across.

Tom chose his words carefully. "I wouldn't make the qualifying round."

As the boy wandered off to find his next conscript, Isabel said lightly, "Never mind, Lucy. I'll go in the mums' race instead. At least one of your parents is prepared to make a fool of themselves for you." But Tom didn't return her smile.

Dr. Sumpton washed his hands as, behind the curtain, Isabel dressed again. She had kept her promise to Tom to see the doctor while they were back in Partageuse.

"Nothing wrong, mechanically speaking," he said.

"So? What is it? Am I sick?"

"Not at all. It's just the change of life," the doctor said as he wrote up his notes. "You're lucky enough to have a baby already, so it's not as hard on you as it is on some women, when it comes unusually early like this. As for the other symptoms, well, I'm afraid you just have to grin and bear it. They'll pass in a year or so. It's just the way of things." He gave her a jolly smile. "And then, it'll be a blessed relief: you'll be past all the problems of menses. Some women would envy you."

As she walked back to her parents' house, Isabel tried not to cry. She had Lucy; she had Tom—at a time when many women had lost forever those they loved most. It would be greedy to want anything more.

A few days later, Tom signed the paperwork for another three-year term. The District Officer, who came down from Fremantle to see to the formalities, again paid close attention to his handwriting and signature, comparing them to his original documentation. Any sign of a tremor creeping into his hand and he wouldn't be allowed back. Mercury poisoning was common enough: if they could catch it at the stage where it just caused shaky handwriting, they could avoid sending out a keeper who like as not would be mad as a meat ax by the end of his next stint.

CHAPTER 15

Lucy's christening, originally arranged for the first week of their leave, had been postponed because of the lengthy "indisposition" of Reverend Norkells. It finally took place the day before their return to Janus in early January. That scorching morning, Ralph and Hilda walked to the church with Tom and Isabel. The only shade to be had while they waited for the doors to open was under a cluster of mallee trees beside the gravestones.

"Let's hope Norkells isn't on another bender," said Ralph.

"Ralph! Really!" said Hilda. To change the subject, she tutted at a fresh granite stone a few feet away. "Such a shame."

"What is, Hilda?" asked Isabel.

"Oh, the poor baby and her father, the ones that drowned. At least they've finally got a memorial."

Isabel froze. For a moment, she feared she might faint, and the sounds around her became distant and then suddenly booming. She struggled to make sense of the bright gold letters on the stone: *"In loving memory of Franz Johannes Roennfeldt, dearly beloved husband of Hannah, and of their precious daughter Grace Ellen. Watched over by God."* Then under that, *"Selig Sind die da Leid tragen."* Fresh flowers lay at the foot of the memorial. With this heat, they couldn't have been left more than an hour before.

"What happened?" she asked, as a tingling spread to her hands and feet.

"Ah, shocking," said Ralph with a shake of his head. "Hannah Potts as was." Isabel recognized the name immediately. "Septimus Potts, old Potts of Money, they call him. Richest fella for miles. He came here from London fifty-odd years back as an orphan with nothing. Made a fortune in timber. Wife died when his two girls were only small. What's the other one's name, Hilda?"

"Gwen. Hannah's the oldest. Both went to that fancy boarding school up in Perth."

"Then a few years back Hannah went and married a Hun . . . Well, old Potts wouldn't speak to her after that. Cut off the money. They lived in that run-down cottage by the pumping station. Old man finally came around when the baby was born. Anyway, there was a bit of a barney on Anzac Day, year before last now—"

"Not now, Ralph." Hilda cautioned with a look.

"Just telling them . . ."

"This is hardly the time or the place." She turned to Isabel. "Let's just say there was a misunderstanding between Frank Roennfeldt and some of the locals, and he ended up jumping into a rowing boat with the baby. They . . . well, they took against him because he was German. Or as good as. No need to go into all of that here, at a christening and all. Better forgotten."

Isabel had stopped taking breaths as she listened to the tale, and now gave an involuntary gasp as her body clamored for air.

"Yes, I know!" Hilda said, to show her agreement. "And it gets worse . . ."

Tom glanced urgently at Isabel, his eyes wide, sweat beading on his lip. He wondered if it was possible for others to hear his heart beating, it was thundering so wildly.

"Well, the bloke was no sailor," Ralph went on. "Had a dicky heart since he was a kid, by all accounts: he was no match for these currents. Storm blew up and no one saw hide nor hair of them again. Must have drowned. Old man Potts put up a reward for information: a thousand guineas!" He gave a shake of the head. "That would've brought 'em out of the woodwork if anyone knew anything. Even had a mind to look for them myself! Mind you—I'm no Boche-lover. But the baby . . . Barely two months old. You can't hold it against a baby now, can you? Little mite."

"Poor Hannah never recovered," sighed Hilda. "Her father only persuaded her to put up the memorial a few months ago." She paused as she pulled her gloves up. "Funny how lives turn out, isn't it? Born to more money than you can shake a stick at; went all the way to Sydney University to get a degree in something or other; married the love of her life—and you see her now sometimes, wandering about, like she's got no home to go to."

Now, Isabel felt plunged into ice, as the flowers on the memorial taunted her, threatened her with the closeness of the mother's presence. She leaned against a tree, dizzy.

"Are you all right, dear?" asked Hilda, concerned at the sudden change in her color.

"Yes. It's just the heat. I'll be all right in a minute."

The heavy jarrah doors swung open and the vicar stepped out of the church. "All ready for the big day, then?" he asked, wincing at the light.

"We've got to say something! Now! Call off the christening . . ." Tom's voice was low and urgent as he faced Isabel in the vestry while Bill and Violet showed off their granddaughter to the guests in the church.

"Tom, we can't." Her breath was shallow and her face was pale. "It's too late!" she said.

"We have to put this right! We have to tell people, *now*."

"We can't!" Still reeling, she cast about for any words that made sense. "We can't do that to Lucy! We're the only parents she's ever known. Besides, what would we say? That we suddenly remembered I didn't actually have a baby?" Her face turned gray. "What about the man's body? It's all gone too far." Every instinct told her to buy time.

She was too confused, too terrified to do anything else. She tried to sound calm. "We'll talk about it later. Right now we have to go through with the christening." A shaft of light caught the sea-green irises of her eyes, and Tom could see the fear in them. She took a step toward him and he sprang back, as if they were opposing magnets.

The vicar's footsteps rose above the murmur of the guests in the church as he approached. Tom's head spun. "*In sickness and in health. For better, for worse.*" The words, uttered by him in this church years earlier, thudded in his skull.

"All ready for you," beamed the vicar.

"Hath this child already been baptized or no?" began Reverend Norkells. Those gathered at the font replied, "No." Alongside Tom and Isabel, Ralph stood as godfather, Isabel's cousin Freda as godmother.

The godparents held candles and intoned the answers to the vicar's questions: "Dost thou, in the name of this child, renounce the devil and all his works . . . ?"

"I renounce them all," the godparents replied in unison.

As the words echoed off the sandstone walls, Tom looked sternly at his shiny new boots and concentrated on a burning blister on his heel.

"Wilt thou then obediently keep God's holy will and commandments . . . ?"

"I will."

With each promise, Tom flexed his foot against the stiff leather, immersing himself in the pain.

Lucy seemed mesmerized by the fireworks of the stained-glass windows, and it occurred to Isabel, even in her turmoil, that the child had never seen such brilliant colors.

"Oh merciful God, grant that the old Adam in this child may be so buried, that the new man may be raised up in her . . ."

Tom thought of the unmarked grave on Janus. He saw the face of Frank Roennfeldt as he had covered it with canvas—detached, expressionless—leaving Tom to be his own accuser.

Outside, the noise of children playing French cricket in the church playground peppered the air with thwacks and cries of "Owzat?" In the second row of pews, Hilda Addicott whispered to her neighbor, "Look, Tom's got a tear in his eye. Now, that's a soft heart for you. He may look a great rock of a man, but it's a real soft heart he's got."

Norkells took the child into his arms and said to Ralph and Freda, "Name this child."

"Lucy Violet," they said.

"Lucy Violet, I baptize thee in the name of the Father, and of the Son, and of the Holy Ghost," said the priest, pouring water on the head of the little girl, who let out a shriek of protest, soon accompanied by Mrs. Rafferty coaxing "Crimond" out of the decrepit wooden organ.

Before the service had finished, Isabel excused herself and hurried to the outhouse at the end of the path. The small brick space was as hot as an oven, and she shooed away flies before leaning over to retch violently. A gecko clung to the wall, watching her in silence. When she pulled the chain it scampered up to the tin roof, to safety. As she rejoined her parents, she said weakly, "Upset tummy," to head off her mother's inquiries. Holding out her arms for Lucy, she hugged her so tight that the child put her hands to Isabel's chest and levered herself away a little.

At the christening lunch at the Palace Hotel, Isabel's father sat at the table with Violet, who was wearing her blue cotton shift with the white lace collar. Her corset was pinching, and the bun into which she had tidied her hair was giving her a headache. She was determined, however, that nothing would spoil this day—the christening of her first and, she now understood from Isabel, her only grandchild.

"Tom doesn't seem his usual self, does he, Vi? Not usually much of a drinker, but he's on the whisky today." Bill shrugged, as if to convince himself. "Just wetting the baby's head, I suppose."

"I think it's just nerves—such a big day. Isabel's come over all touchy too. Probably that tummy trouble."

Over at the bar with Tom, Ralph said, "That little girl's made all the difference to your missus, hasn't she? She's like a new woman."

Tom turned his empty glass round and round in his hands. "It's brought out a different side of her, all right."

"When I think back to how she lost the baby . . ."

Tom gave an imperceptible start, but Ralph went on, ". . . that first time. It was like seeing a ghost when I came out to Janus. And the second was worse."

"Yeah. They were hard times for her."

"Oh well, God comes good in the end, doesn't he?" Ralph smiled.

"Does he, Ralph? He can't come good for everyone, can he? Couldn't come good for Fritz as well as us, say . . ."

"That's no way to be talking, boy. He's come good for you!"

Tom loosened his tie and collar—suddenly the bar felt stifling.

"You all right, mate?" asked Ralph.

"Stuffy in here. Think I'll go for a bit of a wander." But outside was no better. The air seemed solid, like molten glass that suffocated him rather than letting him breathe.

If he could talk to Isabel alone, calmly . . . Things would be all right. It could be all right, somehow. He drew himself up, taking a deep breath, and walked slowly back into the hotel.

"She's fast asleep," said Isabel as she closed the door to the bedroom, where the child lay surrounded by pillows to keep her from rolling off the edge of the bed. "She was so good today. Got through the whole christening, with all those people. Only cried when she got wet." As the day went on, her voice had lost the tremor it had acquired with Hilda's revelation.

"Oh, she's an angel," said Violet, smiling. "I don't know what we'll do with ourselves when she goes back tomorrow."

"I know. But I promise I'll write, and tell you all her news," Isabel said, and gave a sigh. "We'd better turn in, I suppose. Got to be up at the crack of dawn for the boat. Coming, Tom?"

Tom gave a nod. "Night, Violet. Night, Bill," he said, and left them to their jigsaw puzzle as he followed Isabel into the bedroom.

It was the first time they had been alone together all day, and as soon as the door was closed, he demanded, "When are we going to tell them?" His face was tight, his shoulders stiff.

"We're not," replied Isabel, in an urgent whisper.

"What do you mean?"

"We need to think, Tom. We need time. We have to leave tomorrow. All hell will break loose if we say anything, and you're supposed to be back on duty tomorrow night. We'll work out what to do once we get back to Janus. We mustn't rush into something we'll regret."

"Izz, there's a woman here in town who thinks her daughter's dead when she's alive; who doesn't know what happened to her husband. God knows what she's been through. The sooner we put her out of her misery—"

"It's all such a shock. We have to do the right thing, not just by Hannah Potts, but by Lucy as well. Please, Tom. Neither of us can think straight at the moment. Let's take this slowly. Right now, let's just try to get a bit of sleep before the morning."

"I'll turn in later," he said, "I need some fresh air," and he slipped quietly out on to the back veranda, ignoring Isabel's plea to stay.

Outside it was cooler, and Tom sat in the darkness in a cane chair, his head in his hands. Through the kitchen window, he could hear the clack-clack as Bill put the last pieces of the jigsaw back into its wooden box. "Isabel seems so keen to get back to Janus. Says she's not good with crowds any more," Bill said as he put the lid on. "You'd be hard-pressed to muster a real crowd this side of Perth."

Violet was trimming the wick of the kerosene lamp. "Well, she always was highly strung," she mused. "Between you and me, I think she just wants to have Lucy all to herself." She sighed. "It'll be quiet without the little one around."

Bill put his arm around Violet's shoulders. "Brings back memories, doesn't it? Remember Hugh and Alfie when they were tots? Grand little fellas, they were." He chuckled. "Remember that time they shut the cat in the cupboard for days?" He paused. "It's not the same, I know, but being a grandfather's the next best thing, isn't it? The next best thing to having the boys back."

Violet lit the lamp. "There were times I didn't think we'd get through it all, Bill. Didn't think we could ever have another day's happiness." She blew out the match. "Such a blessing, at last." Replacing the glass shade, she guided the way to bed.

The words reverberated in Tom's mind as he breathed in the night jasmine, its sweetness oblivious to his desperation.

CHAPTER 16

The first night back on Janus, the wind howled around the lantern room, pushing at the thick panes of glass in the tower, testing for some weak spot. As Tom lit up, his mind went over and over the argument he had had with Isabel as soon as the store boat had left.

She had been unmovable: "We can't undo what's happened, Tom. Don't you think I've been trying to find an answer?" She was clasping the doll she had just picked up from the floor, hugging it to her chest. "Lucy's a happy, healthy little girl. Ripping her away now would be—oh Tom, it'd be horrible!" She had been folding sheets into the linen press, pacing to and fro between the basket and the cupboard. "For better or worse, Tom, we did what we did. Lucy adores you and you adore her and you don't have the right to deprive her of a loving father."

"What about her loving mother? Her *living* bloody mother! How can this be fair, Izz?"

Her face flushed. "Do you think it's *fair* that we lost three babies? Do you think it's fair that Alfie and Hugh are buried thousands of miles away and you're walking around without a scratch? Of course it's not *fair*, Tom, not fair at all! We just have to take what life dishes up!"

She had landed a shot where Tom was most vulnerable. All these years later, he could not shed that sickening sensation of having cheated—not cheated death, but cheated his comrades, having come through unscathed at their expense, even though logic told him it was nothing but luck one way or another. Isabel could see that she had winded him, and softened. "Tom, we have to do what's right—for Lucy."

"Izzy, please."

She cut across him. "Not another word, Tom! The only thing we can do is love that little girl as much as she deserves. And never, never hurt her!" Clutching the doll, she hurried from the room.

Now, as he looked out over the ocean, blustery and whipped white with foam, the darkness was closing in on all sides. The line between the ocean and the sky became harder to judge, as the light faltered second by second. The barometer was falling. There would be a storm before morning. Tom checked the brass handle on the door to the gallery, and watched the light turn, steady, impervious.

As Tom attended to the light that evening, Isabel sat beside Lucy's cot, watching her drift into sleep. It had taken all her strength to get through the day, and her thoughts still swirled like the gathering storm outside. Now, she sang, almost in a whisper, the lullaby Lucy always insisted on. *"Blow the wind southerly, southerly, southerly . . ."* Her voice struggled to keep the tune. "*I stood by the lighthouse the last time we parted, Till darkness came down o'er the deep rolling sea, And no longer I saw the bright bark of my lover . . .*"

When Lucy finally nodded off, Isabel opened her little fingers to remove the pink shell the child had been clasping. The nausea that had been with her since the moment by the memorial stone intensified, and she fought it by tracing the spiral of the shell with her finger, seeking comfort in its perfect smoothness, its exact proportions. The creature that had made it was long dead, and had left only this sculpture. Then the thought taunted her that Hannah Potts's husband, too, had left his living sculpture, this little girl.

Lucy flung an arm above her head and a frown crossed her features for a moment, as her fingers closed tight around the missing shell.

"I won't let anyone hurt you, darling. I promise to keep you safe, always," Isabel murmured. Then she did a thing she had not done for some years. She got down on her knees, and bowed her head. "God, I can never hope to understand your mystery. I can only try to be worthy of what you've called me to do. Give me the strength I need to carry on." For a moment, doubt came roaring in, shaking her frame, until she managed to anchor again the rhythm of her breath. "Hannah Potts—Hannah *Roennfeldt,*" she said, adjusting to the idea, "is safely in your hands too, I know. Grant us peace. All of us." She listened to the wind outside, and to the ocean, and felt the distance restoring the sense of safety that the past two days had stripped away. She put the shell beside Lucy's bed, where she could find it easily when she woke, and left the room quietly, newly resolved.

For Hannah Roennfeldt, the January Monday that followed the christening had been a momentous one.

When she went to the letterbox, she expected to find it empty: she had checked it the previous day as part of the ritual she had crafted to pass the hours since that terrible Anzac Day evening nearly two years earlier. First, she would call at the police station, sometimes giving no more than a questioning look, to which the constable, Harry Garstone, would reply with a silent shake of the head. As she walked out, his colleague Constable Lynch might comment, "Poor woman. Fancy ending up like that . . ." and he too would shake his head, and carry on with his paperwork. Each day she would walk to a different part of the beach in search of a sign, a clue—bits of driftwood, a fragment of metal from a rowlock.

She would draw from her pocket a letter to her husband and child. Occasionally she enclosed things—a cutting from a newspaper about a circus coming to town; a nursery rhyme she had written by hand and decorated with colors. She would cast the letter into the waves in the hope that, as the ink seeped from the envelope, somewhere, in one or another of the oceans, it would be absorbed by her loved ones.

On the way back she would call at the church and sit silently in the last pew, near the statue of St. Jude. Sometimes she would stay until the marri trees laid their lanky shadows across the stained glass, and her votive candles were cold puddles of hard wax. Here, somehow Frank and Grace still existed, for as long as she sat in the shadows. When she could avoid it no longer, she would return home, opening the letterbox only once she felt strong enough to face the disappointment of its emptiness.

For two years, she had written to anyone she could think of—hospitals, port authorities, seafaring missions: anyone who might have heard tell of a sighting—but had received only courteous assurances that they would let her know if any news of her missing husband and daughter came their way.

That January morning was hot, and magpies caroled their waterfall song—notes that fell in splashes over gum trees beneath the bleached azure sky. Hannah ambled the few yards from the front veranda down the flagstone path as though in a trance. She had long ceased to notice the gardenia and the stephanotis and the proffered consolation of their sweet, creamy scent. The rusty iron letterbox creaked as she coaxed it open—it was as weary and reluctant to move as she. Inside was a scrap of white. She blinked. A letter.

Already a snail had etched a filigree track across it, the paper glistening like a rainbow around the parts it had eaten: just one trail across the corner. There was no stamp, and the hand was measured and firm.

She brought it inside and placed it on the dining table, lining up its border with the wood's gleaming edge. She sat in front of it a long while, before taking up the pearl-handled letter opener to slit the envelope, careful not to tear whatever was inside.

She drew out the paper, a small, single sheet, which read:

Don't fret for her. The baby is safe. Loved and well cared for, and always will be. Your husband is at peace in God's hands. I hope this brings you comfort.

Pray for me.

The house was dark, the brocade curtains drawn as a shield against the fierce brightness. Cicadas rasped in the grapevine on the back veranda at such a ferocious pitch that Hannah's ears buzzed.

She studied the handwriting. The words formed before her eyes, but she could not quite un-jumble them. Her heart hammered at her lungs and she struggled to breathe. She had half expected the letter to disappear when she opened it—that sort of thing had happened before: catching sight of Grace in the street, perhaps, the pink flash of one of her baby dresses, then finding it was merely a parcel of the same color, or a woman's skirt; glimpsing the silhouette of a man she would have sworn was her husband, tugging his sleeve even, to be met with the bewildered expression of someone who was no more similar to him than chalk to cheese.

"Gwen?" she called, when she could finally muster words. "Gwen, could you come in here a minute?" She summoned her sister from her bedroom, afraid that if she moved a muscle the letter might evaporate—that it might all just be a trick of the gloom.

Gwen was still carrying her embroidery. "Were you calling me, Hanny?"

Hannah did not speak, just nodded warily toward the letter. Her sister picked it up. "At least," Hannah thought, "I'm not imagining it."

Within an hour they had left the simple wooden cottage for Bermondsey, Septimus Potts's stone mansion on the hill at the edge of the town.

"And it was just there, in the letterbox, today?" he asked.

"Yes," said Hannah, still bewildered.

"Who'd do a thing like this, Dad?" asked Gwen.

"Someone who knew Grace was alive, of course!" said Hannah. She did not see the look that flashed between her father and sister.

"Hannah, dear, it's been a very long time," said Septimus.

"I know that!"

"He's just saying," Gwen said, "well, that it's odd not to have heard something sooner, and then to get this out of the blue."

"But it's *something*!" said Hannah.

"Oh, Hanny," said Gwen, shaking her head.

Later that day, Sergeant Knuckey, the senior policeman in Point Partageuse, sat awkwardly on a squat grandmother-chair, balancing a dainty teacup on his broad knee as he tried to take notes.

"And you didn't see anyone unusual around the house, Miss Potts?" he asked Gwen.

"No one." She put the milk jug back on the occasional table. "No one comes to call, usually," she said.

He jotted something down.

"Well?"

Knuckey realized Septimus was addressing a question to him. He examined the letter again. Neat handwriting. Plain paper. Not posted. From a local? Lord knew there were still people about the place who'd take comfort in watching a Hun-lover suffer. "Not much to go on, I'm afraid." He listened patiently to Hannah's protests that surely it must contain clues. He noticed that the father and sister looked a bit awkward, like when a mad aunt starts up about Jesus at the dinner table.

As Septimus showed him to the door, the sergeant replaced his hat and said quietly, "A cruel piece of mischief-making, looks like. I reckon it's about time to bury the hatchet against Fritz. All a filthy business, but there's no need for pranks like this. I'd keep it under your hat, the note. Don't want to encourage copycats." He shook hands with Septimus and made his way up the long, gum-lined drive.

Back in his study, Septimus put a hand on Hannah's shoulder. "Come on, girlie, chin up. Mustn't let this get the better of you."

"But I don't understand, Dad. She must be alive! Why would someone bother to write a note lying about something like that, completely out of the blue?"

"I tell you what, sweetheart, what's say I double the reward? I'll make it *two* thousand guineas. If anyone really knows anything, we'll soon find out." As Septimus poured his daughter another cup of tea, he was, for once, not pleased that he was unlikely to be parted with his money.

Although the figure of Septimus Potts loomed large in business round Partageuse way, there weren't many who could say they knew him well. He was fiercely protective of his family, but his chief opponent was, and always had been, Fate. Septimus was five years old when, in 1869, he disembarked at Fremantle from the *Queen of Cairo*. Around his neck he wore the little wooden sign his mother had placed there as she kissed him a distraught farewell on the dock in London. It read: "I am a good Christian boy. Please take care of me."

Septimus was the seventh and last child of a Bermondsey ironmonger who waited only three days after the baby's birth before departing this world under the hooves of a runaway carthorse. His mother had done her best to keep the family together, but after a few years, as consumption burrowed away at her, she knew she had to secure her children's future. She dispatched as many of them as she could to relatives around and about London, where they could be free help to the people who took them in. But her lastborn was too young to be anything but a drain on scarce resources, and one of his mother's last acts was to secure passage to Western Australia for him, alone.

As he put it decades later, that sort of experience either gives you a taste for death, or a thirst for life, and he reckoned death would come calling soon enough anyway. So when he was gathered up by a round, sunburned woman from the Seafarer's Mission, and sent to a "good home" in the South West, he went without complaint or question: who would have listened to either? He started a new life in Kojonup, a town well east of Partageuse, with Walt and Sarah Flindell, a couple who eked out a living as sandalwood pullers. They were a good sort of people, but shrewd enough to know that being so light, sandalwood could be loaded and maneuvered even by a child, so they agreed to take the little boy in. As for Septimus, after his time on the ship, having a floor that stayed still and people who didn't begrudge you your daily bread was paradise.

So Septimus got to know this new country to which he had been shipped like a parcel without an address, and grew to love Walt and Sarah and their practical ways. The little hut on their patch of cleared land had neither glass in the windows nor running water, but, in the early days, somehow there always seemed to be enough of what was needed.

When eventually the precious sandalwood, sometimes worth more than gold, was virtually wiped out by over-harvesting, Walt and Septimus turned instead to work on the new timber mills that were opening up around Partageuse. The building of new lighthouses along the coast meant that shipping cargo along that route changed from a sheer gamble to an acceptable commercial risk, and new railways and jetties allowed the forests to be chopped up and shipped out to anywhere in the world, right from their doorstep.

Septimus worked like a devil and said his prayers, and cadged reading and writing lessons from the Pastor's wife on Saturdays. He never spent a halfpenny he didn't have to, and never missed an opportunity to make one. The thing about Septimus was, he seemed to see opportunities where other people couldn't. Though he grew to no more than five foot seven in his boots, he carried himself like a much bigger man, and always dressed as respectably as funds allowed. At times this meant he looked almost dapper, and at the very least it meant clean clothes for church on Sunday, even if he'd had to wash them at midnight to get the sawdust out of them after an all-day shift.

All of this stood him in good stead when, in 1892, a newly made baronet from Birmingham was passing through the colony in search of somewhere exotic to invest a little capital. Septimus seized the chance to make a start in business, and convinced the baronet to put up the money for a small land deal. Septimus smartly trebled the investment, and by careful risk and shrewd re-investment of his cut, soon set himself up in business in his own right. By the time the colony joined the newly formed nation of Australia in 1901, he was one of the richest timber men for miles around.

Times had been prosperous. Septimus had married Ellen, a debutante from Perth. Hannah and Gwen were born, and their home, Bermondsey, became a watchword for style and success in the South West. Then, at one of her famous picnics in the bush, served on a dazzle of linen and silver, his cherished wife was bitten just above the ankle of her pale kid boot by a dugite, and died within the hour.

Life, thought Septimus, when his daughters had returned to the cottage the day the mysterious letter arrived: you could never trust the bastard. What it gives with one hand, it takes away with the other. Finally reconciled with Hannah when her baby was born, then the husband and child disa-bloody-ppear into nowhere, leaving his daughter a wreck. Now some troublemaker was stirring things up again. Well, you just had to count your blessings and be thankful things weren't worse.

Sergeant Knuckey sat at his desk, tapping his pencil on his blotter, watching the tiny lead trails. Poor bloody woman. Who could blame her for wanting the baby to be alive? His Irene still cried sometimes about young Billy, and it had been twenty years since he'd drowned as a tot. They'd had five more kids since then, but it was never far away, the sadness.

Really, though, there wasn't a snowflake's chance in hell that the baby was still alive. All the same, he took a fresh sheet of paper and started on a report of the incident. The Roennfeldt woman deserved the formalities, at least.

CHAPTER 17

"*Your husband is at peace in God's hands.*" Hannah Roennfeldt runs over the phrase again and again on the day of the mysterious letter. Grace is alive, but Frank is dead. She wants to be able to believe the one and not the other. Frank. Franz. She recalls the gentle man whose life was turned upside down so many times along the curious path which somehow led him to her.

The first reverse saw him ripped from his life of privilege in Vienna as a boy of sixteen, as his father's gambling debts drove them all the way to relatives in Kalgoorlie, a place so remote from Austria that even the most ardent creditor would give up the chase. From luxury to austerity, the son taking on the trade of baker in the shop run by his uncle and aunt, who since their arrival years before had changed from Fritz and Mitzie into Clive and Millie. It was important to blend in, they said. His mother understood this, but his father, with the pride and stubbornness that had triggered his financial ruin, resisted adaptation, and within the year had thrown himself under a train bound for Perth, leaving Frank as head of the household.

Months later, war brought internment as an enemy alien—first on Rottnest Island, then over East—for this boy who was now not simply uprooted and bereaved, but despised, for things done far away and beyond his control.

And never once had he complained, thought Hannah. Frank's ready, open smile was undiminished by the time she met him in Partageuse in 1922, when he came to work in the bakery.

She remembered the first time she had seen him, on the main street. The spring morning was sunny but October still brought a nip with it. He had smiled at her, and proffered a shawl she recognized as her own.

"You left it in the bookshop, just now," he said.

"Thank you. That's very kind."

"It is a beautiful shawl, with such embroidery. My mother used to have one like it. Chinese silk is very costly: it would be a pity to lose it." He gave a respectful nod, and turned to go.

"I haven't seen you here before," said Hannah. Nor had she heard his charming accent.

"I have just started at the baker's. I am Frank Roennfeldt. Pleased to meet you, ma'am."

"Well, welcome to Partageuse, Mr. Roennfeldt. I hope you'll like it here. I'm Hannah Potts." She rearranged her parcels, trying to pull the shawl over her shoulders.

"Please, allow me," he had said, draping it around her in one fluid movement. "I wish you an excellent day." Again, he flashed an open smile. The sun caught the blue of his eyes and made his fair hair shine.

As she crossed the street to her waiting sulky, she noticed a woman nearby give her a piercing look and spit on the pavement. Hannah was shocked, but said nothing.

A few weeks later, she visited Maisie McPhee's little bookshop once again. As she entered, she saw Frank standing at the counter, under attack from a matron who was waving her stick to make her point. "The very idea, Maisie McPhee!" the woman was declaring. "The very notion that you could sell books that support the Boche. I lost a son and a grandson to those animals, and I don't expect to see you, sending them money like a Red Cross parcel."

As Maisie stood speechless, Frank said, "I am sorry if I caused any offense, ma'am. It is not Miss McPhee's fault." He smiled and held the open book toward her. "You see? It is only poetry."

"Only poetry, my foot!" the woman snapped, thumping her stick on the ground. "Not a decent word ever came out of their mouths! I'd heard we had a Hun in town, but I didn't think you'd be bold enough to rub it in our faces like this! And as for you, Maisie!" She faced the counter. "Your father must be turning in his blessed grave."

"Please, I am very sorry," said Frank. "Miss McPhee, please keep the book. I did not mean to offend anyone." He put a ten-shilling note on the counter and walked out, brushing past Hannah without noticing her. The woman stormed out after him, clacking her way down the street in the opposite direction.

Maisie and Hannah looked at one another for a moment, before the shopkeeper assembled a bright smile and said, "Got your list there, Miss Potts?"

As Maisie ran her eye down the page, Hannah's attention wandered to the abandoned book. She was curious how the dainty volume bound in forest-green leather could have caused such offense. Opening it, the Gothic print on the flyleaf caught her eye: *"Das Stunden Buch*—Rainer Maria Rilke." She had learned German at school along with her French, and had heard of Rilke.

"And," she said, taking out two pound notes, "do you mind if I take this book too?" When Maisie looked at her in surprise, Hannah said, "It's about time we all put the past behind us, don't you think?"

The shopkeeper wrapped it in brown paper and tied it with string. "Well, to be honest, it saves me trying to send it back to Germany. No one else'll buy it."

At the baker's a few moments later, Hannah put the little parcel on the counter. "I wonder if you could give this to Mr. Roennfeldt please. He left it behind at the bookshop."

"He's out the back. I'll give him a cooee."

"Oh, there's no need. Thanks very much," she said, and left the shop before he had a chance to say anything else.

A few days later, Frank called on her to thank her in person for her kindness, and her life began a new path, which at first seemed like the most fortunate she could have dreamed of.

Septimus Potts's delight at the inkling that his daughter had found a local man to step out with turned to dismay when he learned he was the baker. But he remembered his own humble beginnings, and was determined not to hold the man's trade against him. When, however, he found out he was German, or practically German, his dismay became disgust. The spats with Hannah that had started soon after the courtship began made each of them, stubborn in heart and head, more entrenched in their position.

Within two months, things had come to a head. Septimus Potts paced the drawing room, trying to take in the news. "Are you out of your mind, girl?"

"It's what I want, Dad."

"*Marrying* a Hun!" He glanced at Ellen's photo in its ornate silver frame on the mantelpiece. "Your mother would never forgive me, for a start! I promised her I'd bring you up properly . . ."

"And you have, Dad, you have."

"Well something went up the spout if you're talking about hitching up with a German bloody baker."

"He's Austrian."

"What difference does that make? Do I have to take you down to the Repat Home, and show you the boys still gibbering like idiots because of the gas? Me of all people—I paid for the bloody hospital!"

"You know full well Frank wasn't even in the war—he was interned. He's never hurt a soul."

"Hannah, show some sense. You're a decent-looking girl. There's plenty of fellows hereabouts—hell, in Perth or Sydney or even Melbourne—would be honored to have you as a wife."

"Honored to have your money, you mean."

"So we're back on that now, are we? You're too good for my money, are you, my lass?"

"It's not that, Dad . . ."

"I worked like a dog to get where I am. I'm not ashamed of what I am or where I came from. But you—you've got a chance of something better."

"I just want a chance to live my own life."

"Look, if you want to do charity work you can go and live out with the natives on the mission. Or work in the orphanage. You don't have to bloody marry it, your charity career."

His daughter's face was red, her heart racing at this last slight—not only at the outrage of it, but somewhere beneath that, at the unformed fear that it might be true. What if she had only said yes to Frank to spite the suitors who chased her money? Or if she was just wanting to make up to him for all he had suffered? Then she thought of how his smile made her feel, and that way he lifted his chin to consider things she asked him, and felt reassured.

"He's a decent man, Dad. Give him a chance."

"Hannah." Septimus put a hand on her shoulder. "You know you mean the world to me." He stroked her head. "You wouldn't let your mother brush your hair, as a little 'un, did you know that? You'd say, 'Pa! I want Pa to do it!' And I would. You'd sit on my knee by the fire in the evening, and I'd brush your hair while the crumpets toasted on the flames. We'd make sure Mum didn't see where the butter had dripped on your dress. And your hair would shine like a Persian princess.

"Just wait. Just a while," her father pleaded.

If all he needed was time to get used to the idea, time to feel differently about it . . . Hannah was about to concede, when he continued, "You'll see things my way, see you're making a bad mistake"—he took one of the deep, puffed-out breaths she associated with his business decisions—"and you'll thank your lucky stars I talked you out of it."

She pulled away. "I won't be partronized. You can't stop me from marrying Frank."

"Can't save you from it, you mean."

"I'm old enough to marry without your consent and I will if I want."

"You may not give a damn what this will mean for me, but have a care for your sister. You know how folks round here will take this."

"Folks round here are xenophobic hypocrites!"

"Oh, that university education was worth every penny. So now you can put your father down with your fancy words." He looked her straight in the eye. "I never thought I'd hear myself say this, my girl, but if you marry that man it will be without my blessing. And without my money."

With the composure that had first drawn Septimus to her mother, Hannah stood straight and very still. "If that's how you want it to be, Dad, that's how it will be."

Following a small wedding, which Septimus refused to attend, the couple lived in Frank's rickety clapboard house at the edge of the town. Life was frugal, there was no doubt. Hannah gave piano lessons and taught some of the timber workers to read and write. One or two took a nasty pleasure in the thought that they employed, if just for an hour a week, the daughter of the man who employed them. But by and large, people respected Hannah's kindness and straightforward courtesy.

She was happy. She had found a husband who seemed to understand her completely, who could discuss philosophy and classical mythology, whose smile dispersed worry and made hardship easy to bear.

As the years passed, a measure of tolerance was afforded to the baker whose accent never entirely disappeared. Some, like Billy Wishart's wife, or Joe Rafferty and his mother, still made a performance of crossing the street when they saw him, but mostly, things settled down. By 1925, Hannah and Frank decided that life was certain enough, money secure enough, to bring a baby into the world, and in February 1926 their daughter was born.

Hannah recalled Frank's lilting tenor voice, as he rocked the cradle. *"Schlaf, Kindlein, schlaf. Dein Vater hüt' die Schaf. Die Mutter schüttelt's Bäumelein, da fällt herab ein Träumelein. Schlaf, Kindlein, schlaf."*

In that little room lit by a paraffin lamp, with a back that was aching, on a chair that needed mending, he had told her, "I cannot imagine a more fortunate existence." The glow in his face was not from the lamp but from the tiny creature in the cot, whose breathing made that telltale change in rhythm as she finally surrendered to sleep.

That March, the altar had been decorated with vases of daisies and stephanotis from Frank and Hannah's garden, and the sweet scent floated all the way across the empty pews to the back of the church. Hannah wore pale blue with a matching low-brimmed felt hat, and Frank his wedding suit, which still fitted, four years on. His cousin Bettina and her husband, Wilf, had come from Kalgoorlie to be godparents, and smiled indulgently at the tiny infant in Hannah's arms.

Reverend Norkells stood beside the font, fumbling slightly as he pulled one of the brightly colored tassels to turn to the correct page of the baptism rite. The clumsiness may have been connected to the whiff of alcohol on his breath. "Hath this child already been baptized or no?" he began.

It was a hot, brooding Saturday afternoon. A fat blowfly buzzed about, coming in periodically to drink at the font, only to be chased away by the godparents. It came in once too often and, swatted by Wilf with his wife's fan, plummeted into the holy water like a drunk into a ditch. The vicar fished it out without a pause as he asked, "Dost thou, in the name of this child, renounce the devil and all his works . . . ?"

"I renounce them all," the godparents replied in unison.

As they spoke, the door to the church creaked in response to a tentative push. Hannah's heart lifted at the sight of her father, led by Gwen, making his way slowly to kneel in the last pew. Hannah and her father had not spoken since the day she left home to be married, and she had expected him to respond to the christening invitation in the usual way—with silence. "I'll try, Hanny," Gwen had promised. "But you know what a stubborn old mule he is. I promise you this, though. I'll be there, whatever he says. This has gone on long enough."

Now Frank turned to Hannah. "You see?" he whispered. "God makes everything work out in his own time."

"Oh merciful God, grant that the old Adam in this child may be so buried, that the new man may be raised up in her . . ." The words echoed off the walls, and the baby snuffled and wriggled as her mother held her. When she started to grizzle, Hannah put the knuckle of her little finger to the tiny lips, which sucked contentedly. The rite continued, and Norkells took the child and said to the godparents, "Name this child."

"Grace Ellen."

"Grace Ellen, I baptize thee in the name of the Father, and of the Son, and of the Holy Ghost."

Throughout the rest of the service, the infant stared at the brightly colored glass in the windows, as fascinated as she would be when, two years later, she gazed at it again from beside the font, in another woman's arms.

When it was over, Septimus remained in his pew. As Hannah walked slowly down the aisle, the baby stirred in her blanket, winding her head a little this way and that. Hannah stopped beside her father, who stood up as she offered him his grandchild. He hesitated, before putting out his arms to cradle the baby.

"Grace Ellen. Your mother would be touched," was all he could manage before a tear escaped, and he gazed with awe at the child.

Hannah took his arm. "Come and see Frank," she said, as she led him up the aisle.

"Please, I'd like you to come in," Hannah said later, as her father stood at her gate with Gwen. Septimus was hesitant. The little clapboard cottage, barely more than a shack, reminded him of the Flindells' lean-to affair in which he grew up. Going through the door took him back fifty years in a couple of steps.

In the front room, he talked stiffly but politely to Frank's cousins. He complimented Frank on the excellent christening cake, and the small but fine assortment of food. Out of the corner of his eye he kept sizing up the cracks in the plaster, the holes in the rug.

As he was leaving, he drew Hannah aside and took out his wallet. "Let me give you a little something for—"

Hannah gently pushed his hand back down. "It's all right, Dad. We do all right," she said.

"Of course you do. But now that you've got a little one . . ."

She put a hand on his arm. "Really. It's kind of you, but we can manage on our own. Come and visit soon."

He smiled and kissed the baby on the forehead, then his daughter. "Thank you, Hanny." Then in hardly more than a mumble, he said, "Ellen would have wanted her granddaughter watched over. And I've—I've missed you."

Within a week, gifts for the baby were being delivered from Perth, from Sydney and beyond. A cot, a mahogany chest of drawers. Dresses and bonnets and things for the bath. The granddaughter of Septimus Potts would have the best that money could buy.

"Your husband is at peace in God's hands." Because of the letter, Hannah goes through both a mourning and a renewal. God has taken her husband, but has saved her daughter. She weeps not just with sorrow, but with shame, at her memories of that day.

The town draws a veil over certain events. This is a small community, where everyone knows that sometimes the contract to forget is as important as any promise to remember. Children can grow up having no knowledge of the indiscretion of their father in his youth, or of the illegitimate sibling who lives fifty miles away and bears another man's name. History is that which is agreed upon by mutual consent.

That's how life goes on—protected by the silence that anesthetizes shame. Men who came back from the war with stories they could have told about the desperate failings of comrades at the point of death say only that they died bravely. To the outside world, no soldier ever visited a brothel or acted like a savage or ran and hid from the enemy. Being over there was punishment enough. When wives have to hide the mortgage money or the kitchen knives from a husband who's lost the thread, they do it without a word, sometimes acknowledging it not even to themselves.

So for Hannah Roennfeldt, her memory of losing Frank is one she has learned she can share with no one. "Raking over coals—what's the good of that?" people would say, anxious to return to their civilized picture of life in Partageuse. But Hannah remembers.

Anzac Day. The pubs are full—full of men who were there, or who lost brothers there; fellows back from Gallipoli and the Somme and still not over the shell shock and the mustard gas, even ten years on. The twenty-fifth of April, 1926. The sly two-up games go on in the back bar, where the police turn a blind eye for this one day of the year. Hell, the police join in—it was their war too. And the Emu Bitter flows and the talk gets louder, the songs saucier. There's a lot to forget. They came back to their work on farms, to their work behind desks and in front of classes, and they got on with it—just bloody got on with it because there was no choice. And the more they drink, the harder the forgetting becomes, the more they want to take a swing at something, or at someone—fair and square, man to man. Bloody Turks. Bloody Huns. Bloody bastards.

And Frank Roennfeldt will do as well as anything. The only German in town, except he's Austrian. He's the nearest thing to the enemy they can find, so as they see him walking down the street with Hannah at dusk, they start to whistle "Tipperary." Hannah looks nervous, and stumbles. Frank instantly takes baby Grace into his arms, snatches the cardigan draped on his wife's arm to cover her, and they walk more quickly, heads down.

The boys in the pub decide this is a fine sport, and spill out onto the street. The fellows from the other pubs along the main drag come out too, then one wag decides it will be a great joke to swipe Frank's hat, and does.

"Oh, leave us alone, Joe Rafferty!" scolds Hannah. "Go back to the pub and leave us alone," and they keep up a brisk pace.

"Leave us alone!" mimics Joe in a high-pitched whimper. "Bloody Fritz! All the same, all cowards!" He turns to the mob. "And look at these two, with their pretty little baby." He's slurring his words. "You know Fritz used to *eat* babies. Roasted them alive, evil bastards."

"Go away or we'll get the police!" shouts Hannah, before freezing at the sight of Harry Garstone and Bob Lynch, the police constables, standing on the hotel veranda, schooners in hand, smirking behind their waxed mustaches.

Suddenly, like a struck match, the scene's alight: "Come on, lads, let's have some fun with the Hun-lovers!" goes up the cry. "Let's save the baby from being eaten," and a dozen drunks are chasing the couple and Hannah is falling behind because her girdle stops her from breathing properly and she's calling, "Grace, Frank! Save Grace!" and he runs with the little bundle away from the mob who are corraling him down the road to the jetty, and his heart is thumping and out of rhythm and pain shoots down his arm as he runs along the rickety planks above the water and jumps into the first rowing boat he can find, and rows out to sea, out to safety. Just until the mob sobers up and things calm down.

He's known worse, in his day.

CHAPTER 18

As Isabel goes about her day—always moving, always busy—she has a keen physical sense of where Lucy is, attached by an invisible thread of love. She is never angry—her patience with the child is infinite. When food falls to the floor, when grubby hand marks decorate the walls, they are never greeted with a cross word or a disapproving look. If Lucy wakes crying in the night, Isabel comforts her gently, lovingly. She accepts the gift that life has sent her. And she accepts the burdens.

While the child is asleep in the afternoon, she goes up to the stick crosses on the headland. This is her church, her holy place, where she prays for guidance, and to be a worthy mother. She prays too, in a more abstract way, for Hannah Roennfeldt. Hers is not to question the way things have turned out. Out here, Hannah is just a distant notion. She has no body, no existence, whereas Lucy—Isabel knows every expression of hers, every cry. She has been watching the miracle that is this little girl take shape day by day, like a gift revealed only with the passing of time. A whole personality is emerging, as the girl catches and masters words, and begins to articulate how she feels, who she is.

So Isabel sits in the chapel without walls or windows or pastor, and thanks God. And if thoughts of Hannah Roennfeldt intrude, her response is always the same. She simply cannot send this child away: it is not for her to risk Lucy's happiness. And Tom? Tom is a good man. Tom will do the right thing, always: she can rely on that. He will come to terms with things, in the end.

But a sliver of uncrossable distance has slipped between them: an invisible, wisp-thin no-man's-land.

Gradually, the rhythm of life on Janus re-establishes itself, absorbing Tom in the minutiae of its rituals. When he wakes sometimes from dark dreams of broken cradles, and compasses without bearings, he pushes the unease down, lets the daylight contradict it. And isolation lulls him with the music of the lie.

"And you know what day it is today, don't you, Luce?" asked Isabel as she pulled the jumper down over the little girl's head and extracted a hand from the end of each sleeve. Six months had passed since their return to Janus in January 1928.

Lucy tilted her head upward a fraction. "Ummm," she said, playing for time.

"Want a clue?"

She nodded.

Isabel pulled on the first little sock. "Come on. Other tootsie. Thaaat's the way. OK, the clue is that if you're a very good girl, there might be oranges tonight . . ."

"Boat!" cried the girl, sliding off her mother's knee and jumping up and down, one shoe on her foot and the other in her hand. "Boat coming! Boat coming!"

"That's right. So shall we make the house all lovely for when Ralph and Bluey come?"

"Yes!" Lucy called behind her, as she dashed to the kitchen to say, "Alf and Booey coming, Dadda!"

Tom picked her up and gave her a kiss. "No flies on you! Did you remember that all by yourself, or has someone been helping you?"

"Mamma said," she confessed with a grin, and wriggled to the ground, off to find Isabel again.

Soon, garbed in galoshes and coats, the two of them set out toward the chook house, Lucy clutching a miniature version of Isabel's basket.

"A real fashion parade," remarked Tom as he passed them on his way to the shed.

"I'd rather be warm than glamorous," said Isabel, and gave him a quick kiss. "We're on an egg expedition."

Inside the chicken coop, Lucy used two hands to pick up each egg, the task that would have taken Isabel seconds treated instead as a precious ritual. She put each egg to her cheek and reported either "Still warm!" or "Tone cold" as appropriate, then passed it to Isabel for safe storage, keeping the last one to carry in her own basket. Then, "Thank you, Daphne. Thank you, Speckle . . ." she began, and went on to thank each hen for her contribution.

In the vegetable patch, she held the spade handle with Isabel during the potato dig.

"I think I can see one . . ." said Isabel, waiting for Lucy to spot the lighter patch in the sandy soil.

"There!" said Lucy, and put her hand into the hole, retrieving a stone.

"Almost." Isabel smiled. "How about next to it? Look a little bit nearer the side."

"'Tato!" Lucy beamed as she raised the prize above her head, scattering soil in her hair, then in her eyes, which started her crying.

"Let's have a look," soothed Isabel, wiping her hands on her dungarees before attending to the eye. "There we are, now, blink for Mamma. There, all gone, Luce." And the little girl continued to open and squint shut her eyes.

"All gone," she said eventually. Then, "More 'tato!" and the hunt began again.

Inside, Isabel swept the floor in every room, gathering the sandy dust into piles in the corner, ready to gather up. Returning from a quick inspection of the bread in the oven, she found a trail leading all through the cottage, thanks to Lucy's attempts with the dustpan.

"Look, Mamma! I helping!"

Isabel took in at the miniature cyclone trail and sighed. "You could call it that . . ." Picking Lucy up, she said, "Thank you. Good girl. Now, just to make extra sure the floor's clean, let's give it an extra sweep, shall we?" With a shake of the head, she muttered, "Ah, Lucy Sherbourne, who'd be a housewife, eh?"

Later, Tom appeared at the doorway. "She all ready?"

"Yep," said Isabel. "Face washed, hands washed. No grubby fingers."

"Then up you come, littlie."

"Up the stairs, Dadda?"

"Yes, up the stairs." And she walked beside him to the tower. At the foot of the steps, she put her arms up so that he could hold her hands from behind. "Now, Bunny, let's count. One, two, three," and they proceeded, at an agonizingly slow pace, up the stairs, Tom counting every one aloud, long after Lucy gave up.

At the top, in the watch room, Lucy held out her hands. "Noclars," and Tom said, "Binoculars in a minute. Let's get you up on the table first." He sat her on top of the charts, then handed her the binoculars, keeping the weight of them in his own hands.

"Can you see anything?"

"Clouds."

"Yep, plenty of those around. Any sign of the boat?"

"No."

"You sure?" Tom laughed. "Wouldn't want you in charge of the guardhouse. What's that over there? See? Where my finger is."

She kicked her legs back and forward. "Alf and Booey! Oranges."

"Mamma says there'll be oranges, does she? Well, let's keep our fingers crossed."

It was more than an hour before the boat docked. Tom and Isabel stood on the jetty, Lucy on Tom's shoulders.

"A whole welcoming committee!" called Ralph.

"Hello!" called Lucy. "People! Hello, Alf, hello, Boo."

Bluey jumped off onto the jetty, heaving the rope Ralph threw him. "Mind out, Luce," he called to the child, now on the ground. "Don't want to get in the way of the rope." He looked at Tom. "Golly, she's a real little girl now, isn't she? No more Baby Lucy!"

Ralph laughed. "They grow up, you know, babies."

Bluey finished securing the rope. "We only see her every few months: just makes it more obvious. Kids in town, you see them every day, so you kind of don't notice them getting older."

"And suddenly they're great hulks of lads like you!" teased Ralph. As he stepped onto the jetty, he had something in one hand behind his back. "Now, who's going to help me take the things off the boat?"

"Me!" said Lucy.

Ralph gave Isabel a wink as he produced a tin of peaches from behind his back. "Well then, here's something very, very heavy for you to carry."

Lucy took the tin with both hands.

"Gosh, Luce, better be careful with that! Let's take it up to the house." Isabel turned to the men. "Give me something to take up if you like, Ralph." He clambered back to fish out the mail and a few light parcels. "See you up at the house in a bit. I'll have the kettle on."

After lunch, as the adults finished cups of tea at the kitchen table, Tom said, "Lucy's a bit quiet . . ."

"Hmmm," said Isabel. "She's supposed to be finishing her drawing for Mum and Dad. I'll go and check." But before she could leave the room, Lucy entered the kitchen, dressed in a petticoat of Isabel's that trailed to the floor, a pair of her shoes with heels, and the string of blue glass beads that Isabel's mother had sent out with that morning's boat.

"Lucy!" said Isabel. "Have you been in my things?"

"No," said the girl, eyes wide.

Isabel blushed. "I don't usually parade my underwear around," she said to the visitors. "Come on, Lucy, you'll catch your death of cold like that. Let's get your clothes back on. And let's have a talk about going through Mamma's things. And about telling the truth." Smiling as she left the room, she didn't catch the brief expression that crossed Tom's features at her last remark.

Lucy trots happily behind Isabel as they go to gather the eggs. She is mesmerized by the newly hatched chicks which appear from time to time, and holds them under her chin to feel their golden fluffiness. When she helps pick carrots and parsnips, sometimes she tugs so hard that she tumbles over backward, showered with soil. "Lucy-Goosy!" laughs Isabel. "Up you get now."

At the piano, she sits on Isabel's knee and bashes away at notes. Isabel holds her index finger and helps her press out "Three Blind Mice," then the child says, "By myself, Mamma," and starts her cacophony again.

She sits for hours on the kitchen floor, wielding colored pencils on the back of obsolete CLS forms, producing random squiggles to which she proudly points and says, "This is Mamma, Dadda, and Lulu Lighthouse." She takes for granted the 130-foot castle-tower in her backyard, with a star in it. Along with words such as "dog" and "cat"—fanciful concepts from books—she masters the more concrete "lens" and "prism" and "refraction." "It's *my* star," she tells Isabel one evening as she points to it. "Dadda gave it to me."

She tells Tom snatches of stories, about fish, about seagulls, about ships. As they walk down to the beach, she delights in taking a hand each from Tom and Isabel and getting them to swing her in the air between them. "Lulu Lighthouse!" is her favorite phrase, and she uses it when she draws herself in splodgy pictures, or describes herself in stories.

The oceans never stop. They know no beginning or end. The wind never finishes. Sometimes it disappears, but only to gather momentum from somewhere else, returning to fling itself at the island, to make a point which is lost on Tom. Existence here is on a scale of giants. Time is in the millions of years; rocks which from a distance look like dice cast against the shore are boulders hundreds of feet wide, licked round by millennia, tumbled onto their sides so that layers become vertical stripes.

Tom watches Lucy and Isabel as they paddle in Paradise Pool, the girl enraptured by the splashing and the saltiness and the starfish she has found, brilliant blue. He watches her fingers clutch the creature, her face alight with excitement and pride, as though she has made it herself. "Dadda, look. My starfish!" Tom has trouble keeping both time scales in focus: the existence of an island and the existence of a child.

It astounds him that the tiny life of the girl means more to him than all the millennia before it. He struggles to make sense of his emotions—how he can feel both tenderness and unease when she kisses him goodnight, or presents a grazed knee for him to kiss better with the magic power that only a parent has.

For Isabel, too, he is torn between the desire he feels for her, the love, and the sense that he cannot breathe. The two sensations grate at one another, unresolved.

Sometimes, alone in the light, he finds his mind seeking out Hannah Roennfeldt. Is she tall? Is she plump? Is there some trace of her in Lucy's face? When he tries to imagine her, he sees only hands, covering a weeping face. He shudders, and returns to his immediate task.

This child is healthy and happy and adored, in this little world beyond the reach of newspapers and gossip. Beyond the reach of reality. There are weeks at a time when Tom can almost rest in the story of a normal, happy family, as if it is some kind of opiate.

"We mustn't let Dadda know. Not until I tell you."

Lucy looked at Isabel gravely. "I mustn't tell," she said, nodding. "Can I have a biscuit?"

"In a minute. Let's just finish wrapping these." The September boat in 1928 had brought several extra parcels, which Bluey had managed to smuggle to Isabel in moments when Ralph distracted Tom with unloading. Engineering a birthday surprise for Tom was no easy feat: it involved writing to her mother months in advance with the list of requests. As Tom was the only one with a bank account, it also required a promise to pay next time they were ashore.

Tom was both easy and difficult to buy for: he would be happy with whatever he got, but he didn't really want anything. She had settled on a Conway Stewart fountain pen and the latest edition of Wisden: something practical and something entertaining. When she had asked Lucy one night as they sat outside, what she wanted to give Dadda, the little girl had twirled her hair around her finger as she thought for a moment and said, "The stars."

Isabel had laughed. "I'm not sure we can manage that, Luce."

The child had said crossly, "But I want to!"

An idea came to Isabel. "What if we gave him a *map* of the stars—an atlas?"

"Yes!"

Now, as they sat in front of the hefty book, Isabel asked, "What do you want to write in the front?" She held the pen, her fingers around Lucy's, to inscribe in jerky letters, as instructed, "For my Dadda, love for ever and ever . . ."

"More," Lucy insisted.

"More what?"

"More 'ever.' 'Ever and ever and ever and ever . . .' "

Isabel laughed, and "ever and ever and ever and ever" trailed like a caterpillar across the page. "What comes next? Shall we say, 'From your loving daughter Lucy'?"

"From Lulu Lighthouse."

The little girl started shaping the letters with her mother, but got bored and climbed off her knee in mid-stroke.

"Mamma finish it," she commanded casually.

So Isabel completed the signature, and added in brackets, "(Per Isabel Sherbourne, scribe and general factotum of the above-mentioned signatory)."

When Tom unwrapped the parcel, a difficult maneuver with Lucy's hands over his eyes, he said, "It's a book . . ."

"It's a antless!" shouted Lucy.

Tom took in the present. *"Brown's star atlas, showing all the bright stars, with full instructions how to find and use them for navigational purposes and Board of Trade examinations."* He smiled slowly, and turned to Isabel. "Lucy's a clever girl, isn't she, organizing this?"

"Read, Dadda. Inside. I did writing."

Opening the cover, Tom saw the long dedication. He still smiled, but there was something about the words "For ever and ever and ever and ever and ever . . ." that stabbed him. Forever was an impossible concept, particularly for this child, in this place. He put his lips to the top of Lucy's head. "It's just beaut, Lulu Lighthouse. The loveliest present I've ever had."

CHAPTER 19

"At least if we can win this one, it won't be a complete washout," said Bluey. The Australian cricket team had lost the first four test matches of the 1928/29 Ashes series on home ground, and the March boat arrived while the final test was still going on in Melbourne. Bluey had been regaling Tom with highlights as they did the unloading. "Bradman got his century. Still not out. Gave Larwood all sorts of trouble, the paper said. I tell you what, though—the match's been going four days already. Looks like we're in for a long one this time."

While Ralph went to the kitchen to deliver another of Hilda's regular presents to Lucy, Tom and the deckhand finished stacking away the last of the flour sacks in the shed.

"I got a cousin works there, you know," Bluey said, nodding at the stencil of the Dingo brand on the calico.

"Up at the flour mill?" asked Tom.

"Yeah. Reckons it pays good. And all the free flour he wants."

"Every job's got its perks."

"Sure. Like I get as much fresh air as I can breathe, and as much water as I need to swim in." Bluey laughed. He looked round, to be sure there was no sign of the skipper. "Reckons he can get me a job there any time I want." He paused. "Or sometimes, I think of working—in a grocer's, maybe," he said, making the jump in subject with a studied, casual tone.

This wasn't like Bluey. Occasionally he'd discuss the Sheffield Shield results, or report winning a bit of money on the horses. He'd talk about his brother Merv, who'd died on the first day at Gallipoli, or the formidable Ada, his widowed mother. Tom sensed something different today. "What's brought this on?"

Bluey gave one of the sacks a kick to straighten it. "What's it like, being married?"

"What?" Tom was startled at the change of tack.

"I mean—is it good?"

Tom kept his eyes on the inventory. "Something you want to tell me, Blue?"

"No."

"Righto." Tom nodded. If he waited long enough, the story would make sense. It usually did. Eventually.

Bluey straightened another sack. "Her name's Kitty. Kitty Kelly. Her dad owns the grocer's. We've been walking out together."

Tom raised his eyebrows and gave a smile. "Good for you."

"And I—well, I don't know—I thought maybe we should get married." The look on Tom's face prompted him to add, "We don't *have* to get married. It's nothing like that. Struth, we've never even—I mean, her dad keeps a pretty close eye on things. And her mother. So do her brothers. And Mrs. Mewett's her mum's cousin, so you know what the family's like."

Tom laughed. "So what's your question?"

"It's a big step. I know everyone does it eventually, but I just wondered—well, how you *know* . . ."

"I'm hardly a full bottle on it. Only been married the once and I'm still getting the hang of it. Why don't you ask Ralph? He's been hitched to Hilda since Methuselah was a boy; raised a couple of kids. Seems to have made a fair job of it."

"I can't tell Ralph."

"Why not?"

"Kitty reckons that if we get married I'll have to give up working on the boat, and come and work in the grocery business. Reckons she's too scared I'll get drowned one day and not come home from work."

"Cheery sort of soul, eh?"

Bluey looked worried. "But, you know, seriously. What's it like being married? Having a kid and all that?"

Tom ran his hand through his hair as he considered the question for some time, deeply uneasy. "We're hardly your typical setup. Not many families like us around the place—out on a lighthouse in the middle of nowhere. The honest answer is, it depends which day you ask me. It brings its share of good things, and its share of hard ones. It's a lot more complicated than being on your own, I can tell you that much."

"Ma says I'm too young and I don't know my own mind."

Tom smiled in spite of himself. "I think your Ma'll probably still be saying that when you're fifty. Anyway, it's not about your mind. It's about your gut. Trust your gut, Blue." He hesitated. "But it's not always plain sailing, even when you've found the right girl. You've got to be in it for the long haul. You never know what's going to happen: you sign up for whatever comes along. There's no backing out."

"Dadda, look!" Lucy appeared at the doorway of the shed, brandishing Hilda's stuffed tiger. "It growls!" she said. "Listen," and she turned it upside down to produce the noise.

Tom picked her up. Through the small window he could see Ralph making his way down the path toward them. "Aren't you the lucky one?" He tickled her neck.

"Lucky Lucy!" she laughed.

"And being a dad? What's that like?" asked Bluey.

"It's like this."

"No, go on. I'm really asking, mate."

Tom's face grew serious. "Nothing can prepare you for it. You wouldn't believe how a baby gets through your defenses, Bluey. Gets right inside you. A real surprise attack."

"Make it growl, Dadda," urged Lucy. Tom gave her a kiss and turned the creature upside down again.

"Keep it under your hat, all this, could you, mate?" asked Bluey. Reconsidering, he said, "Well, everyone knows you're quiet as the grave anyway," and he made his own version of a tiger's growl for the little girl.

Sometimes, you're the one who strikes it lucky. Sometimes, it's the other poor bastard who's left with the short straw, and you just have to shut up and get on with it.

Tom was hammering a plank onto the wall of the chookhouse, to cover a hole the wind had blown in it the night before. Spent half his life trying to protect things from the wind. You just had to get on with things, do what you could do.

Bluey's questions had stirred up old feelings. But every time Tom thought about the stranger in Partageuse who had lost her child, Isabel's image took her place: she'd lost children, and would never have any more. She had known nothing about Hannah when Lucy arrived. Just wanted what was best for the baby. And yet. He knew it wasn't just for Lucy's sake. There was a need in Isabel that he could now never fill. She had given up everything: comforts, family, friends—everything to be with him out here. Over and over he told himself—he couldn't deprive her of this one thing.

Isabel was tired. The supplies had just come in and she'd set about replenishing food—making bread, baking a fruitcake, turning a sack of plums into jam that would last out the year. She'd left the kitchen for barely a moment—the moment Lucy had chosen to step closer to the stove to smell the delicious mixture, and had burned her hand on the jam pan. It wasn't severe, but enough to keep the child from sleeping soundly. Tom had bandaged the burn and given her a small dose of aspirin, but by nightfall she was still unsettled.

"I'll take her up to the light. I can keep an eye on her. I've got to finish the paperwork for the inventory anyway. You look done in."

Exhausted, Isabel conceded.

Holding the child in one arm, and a pillow and blanket in the other, Tom carried her gently up the stairs, and laid her on the chart table in the watch room. "There you are, littlie," he said, but she was already dozing.

He set about adding up columns of figures, totting gallons of oil and boxes of mantles. Above him, in the lantern room the light turned steadily, with its slow, low hum. Far below, he could see the single oil light from the cottage.

He had been working for an hour when some instinct made him turn, and he found Lucy watching him, her eyes glittering in the soft light. When his gaze met hers she smiled, and yet again Tom was caught off guard by the miracle of her—so beautiful, so undefended. She raised her bandaged hand, and examined it. "I been in the wars, Dadda," she said, and a frown crept over her features. She held her arms out.

"You go back to sleep, littlie," Tom said, and tried to turn back to his work. But the child said, "'Ullaby, Dadda." And she kept her arms extended.

Tom lifted her onto his lap and rocked her gently. "You'd get nightmares if I sang to you, Lulu. Mamma's the singer, not me."

"I hurt my hand, Dadda," she said, raising her injury as proof.

"You did, didn't you, bunny rabbit?" He kissed the bandage delicately. "It'll soon be better. You'll see." He kissed her forehead, and stroked her fine blonde hair. "Ah, Lulu, Lulu. However did you find your way here?" He looked away, out into the solid blackness. "However did you turn up in my life?"

He could feel her muscles surrender as she edged toward sleep. Gradually her head weighed loosely against the crook of his arm. In a whisper even he could hardly hear, he asked the question that gnawed at him constantly: "However did you make me feel like this?"

CHAPTER 20

"I never knew he'd tried to get in touch." Tom was sitting beside Isabel on the veranda. He was turning over and over an ancient, battered envelope, addressed to him "c/o 13th Battalion, AIF." On every available inch of space were scrawled forwarding addresses and instructions, culminating in an authoritative command in blue pencil to *"return to sender"*—to Edward Sherbourne, Esquire, Tom's father. The letter had arrived in a small packet three days earlier, when the June boat brought news of his death.

The letter from Church, Hattersley & Parfitt, Solicitors, observed the formalities and provided only the facts. Throat cancer; 18 January 1929. It had taken them some months to track Tom down. His brother Cecil was the exclusive beneficiary, save for the bequest to Tom of a locket of his mother's, enclosed in the letter which had pursued Tom across the world.

He had opened the packet after he had lit up that evening, sitting in the lantern room, numb at first as he read the stern, spiky handwriting.

"Merrivale"
Sydney

16th October 1915

Dear Thomas,

I am writing because I know that you have enlisted. I am not much of a one for words. But with you so far away now, and with the possibility that harm may come to you before we have an opportunity to meet again, it seems writing is the only way.

There are many things I cannot explain to you without denigrating your mother, and I have no wish to do any more harm than has already been done. Some things, therefore, will be left unsaid. I am at fault in one respect, and it is this I wish to remedy now. I enclose a locket which your mother asked me to let you have, when she left. It has her likeness in it. At the time, I felt it was better for you not to be reminded of her, and I therefore did not pass it on. It was not an easy decision to make, to determine that your life would be better without her influence.

Now that she is dead, I feel it right to fulfil her request, if rather late.

I have tried to raise you as a good Christian. I have tried to ensure you had the best available education. I hope I have instilled in you a sense of right and wrong: no amount of worldly success or pleasure can redeem the loss of your immortal soul.

I am proud of the sacrifice you have made by enlisting. You have grown into a responsible young man, and after the war, I would be pleased to find you a position in the business. Cecil has the makings of a fine manager, and I expect will run the factory successfully after my retirement. But I am sure a suitable place can be found for you.

It pained me that I had to hear of your embarkation through others. I would have welcomed the opportunity to see you in uniform, to see you off, but I gather that since tracing your mother and learning she had passed away, you wish to have nothing further to do with me. Therefore, I leave it up to you. If you choose to reply to this letter, I shall be most pleased. You are, after all, my son, and until you too are a father, you will not fully understand all it means to say that.

If, however, you do not wish to respond, I shall respect your choice, and shall not trouble you again. I shall nonetheless pray for your safety in battle, and your return to these shores, victorious.

Your affectionate father,
Edward Sherbourne

It seemed a lifetime since Tom had spoken to this man. How it must have cost him, to write such a letter. That his father had made an attempt to contact him after their bitter separation was not just a surprise but a shock. Nothing seemed certain any more. Tom wondered whether his father's coldness protected a wound all along. For the first time he glimpsed something beyond the stony exterior and, just for an instant, he could imagine a man of high principle, hurt by a woman he loved, but unable to show it.

Tom had sought out his mother for a particular reason. As he had stood at the boardinghouse door, shoes polished, fingernails cut, he had rehearsed the words one last time. "I'm sorry I got you into trouble." At the time he felt as shaky as the child who had waited thirteen years to say the words. He thought he might be sick. "All I said was that I'd seen a motorcar. That there had been a motorcar at the house. I didn't know—"

It was only years later that he had understood the full magnitude of his tale-telling. She had been declared an unfit mother, and banished from his life. But his pilgrimage to seek forgiveness was too late, and he would never now hear his mother absolve him from the guilt of betrayal, innocent though it had been. Words had a way of getting into all sorts of places they weren't meant to. Best keep things to yourself in life, he'd learned.

He looked at the picture of his mother in the locket. Perhaps each of his parents had loved him, however brokenly. He felt a sudden surge of anger at his father's almost casual assumption of the right to separate him from his mother: so sincere, yet so destructive.

It was only when a droplet sent the ink running in miniature rivers that Tom noticed he was crying. *"Until you too are a father, you will not fully understand . . ."*

Beside him now on the veranda, Isabel was saying, "Even though you hadn't seen him for years, he was still your dad. You only ever get one of them. It's bound to affect you, sweetheart."

Tom wondered if Isabel caught the irony of her own words.

"Come on, Luce, come and have some cocoa," she called without pausing.

The little girl ran up and grasped the beaker with both hands. She wiped her mouth with her forearm instead of her grubby hand, then handed back the cup. "Ta-ta!" she called out cheerily. "I riding to Pataterz now to see Grandma and Grandpa," and ran back to her hobbyhorse.

Tom looked at the locket in the palm of his hand. "For years, I thought she hated me because I gave away her secret. I never knew about the locket . . ." His lower lip pressed upward and he pursed his mouth. "It would have made a difference."

"I know there's nothing I can say. I just wish I could—I don't know—make it better for you."

"Mamma, I hungry," called Lucy as she came back.

"No wonder, with all that running about!" said Isabel, and swept her up in her arms. "Come on. Come and give Dadda a hug. He's sad today." And she sat the child on his lap, so that they could both hug him tightly.

"Smile, Dadda," said the little girl. "Like this," she said, and grinned.

The light came in crooked through the clouds, seeking refuge from the rain that hovered in the distance. Lucy sat on Tom's shoulders, beaming at her towering view.

"This way!" she exclaimed, stabbing a finger to her left. Tom altered course and carried her down the field. One of the goats had chewed its way out of a temporary pen, and Lucy had insisted on helping to find it.

There was no sign of the creature in the cove. Well, it couldn't have got far. "We'll look somewhere else," said Tom. He strode up toward the flat of the land once more, and turned in a circle. "Where to now, Lulu? You pick."

"Down there!" she pointed again, to the other side of the island, and they set off.

"How many words do you know that sound like goat?"

"Boat!"

"That's right. Any more?"

The child tried again. "Boat?"

Tom laughed. "What do you wear when it's cold?"

"My jumper."

"Yes, but what do you wear when it's cold that sounds like goat? Starts with a 'kuh' sound."

"Coat!"

He tickled her tummy. "Coat, boat, goat. Talking of which . . . Look, Luce, down there, near the beach."

"She's there! Let's run, Dadda!"

"Let's not, bunny rabbit. Don't want to scare her away. We'll take it quietly."

Tom was so preoccupied that he hardly noticed at first where the animal had chosen its new pasture.

"Down you get, little one." He lifted Lucy high over his shoulders and lowered her to the grass. "You be good and stay here while I go and get Flossie. I'm going to tie this rope to her collar, then she'll come back nice and easy.

"Right, Flossie. Come on, now, no buggering about." The goat looked up and trotted a few paces away. "Enough of that. Stay still," Tom caught it by the collar and fastened the rope. "There. That's that. All right, Lulu—" Turning, he felt a tingling in his arms, a split second before his conscious mind realized why. Lucy was sitting on a slight mound, where the grass grew more thickly than on the flatter land around it. Usually, he avoided this part of the island, which to him seemed permanently shadowed and gloomy, no matter how bright the day.

"Look, I found a seat, Dadda," she said, beaming.

"Lucy! Off that right now!" he shouted before he could stop himself.

Lucy's face puckered and tears came at the shock—she had never been shouted at before, and started to bawl.

He raced to pick her up. "Sorry, Lulu. I didn't mean to scare you," he said, ashamed of his response. Trying to hide his horror, he hurried a few steps away. "That's not a good place to sit, love."

"Why not?" she wailed. "It's my special seat. It's magic."

"It's just . . ." He snuggled her head into the crook of his neck. "It's just not a good place to sit, sweetie." He kissed the top of her head.

"Are I naughty?" asked Lucy, confused.

"No. Not naughty. Not you, Lulu." He kissed her cheek and brushed her fair hair out of her eyes.

But as he held her, he was for the first time in years acutely aware that the hands that now touched her were the hands that had heaved her father into the grave. Eyes closed, he recalled the sensation in his muscles, the weight of the man, and contrasted it with the weight of the daughter. Lucy seemed the heavier of the two.

He felt a patting on his cheeks. "Dadda! Look at me!" the child said.

He opened his eyes, and looked at her in silence. Finally, with a deep breath, he said, "Time to take Flossie home. Why don't you hold the rope?"

She nodded, and he wrapped it around her hand, carrying the weight of her back up the hill on his hip.

That afternoon, in the kitchen, Lucy was about to climb onto a chair, but first turned to Tom. "Is this a good place to sit, Dadda?"

He didn't look up from the door handle he was repairing. "Yes, that's a good place, Lulu," he replied without thinking.

When Isabel went to sit beside her, Lucy exclaimed, "No! Mamma, off that chair! That's *not* a good place to sit."

Isabel laughed. "It's where I always sit, sweetie. I think it's a lovely seat."

"It's *not* a good place. Dadda says!"

"What's she talking about, Dadda?"

"I'll tell you later," he said, and took up his screwdriver, hoping Isabel would forget.

But she did not.

Once she had tucked Lucy into bed, Isabel asked again, "What was all that palaver about where to sit? She was still worried about it when I sat on her bed for the story. Told me you'd be very cross."

"Oh, just a game she came up with. She'll probably have forgotten it by tomorrow."

But Lucy had summoned up the ghost of Frank Roennfeldt that afternoon, and the memory of his face now haunted Tom every time he looked in the direction of the graves.

"Until you too are a father . . ." He had thought a great deal about Lucy's mother, but it was only now that the full sacrilege of his treatment of her father came home to him. Thanks to him, the man could never have a priest or a pastor mark his passing with due ritual; never be allowed to live, even in memory, in Lucy's heart, as was a father's right. For a moment, just a few feet of sand had separated Lucy from her true heritage—from Roennfeldt and generations of his family. Tom went cold at the realization that he may have killed relatives—it seemed almost likely—of this man who had created her. Suddenly, vivid and accusing, the faces of the enemy wakened from the tomb beneath memory to which he had confined them.

The next morning, as Isabel and Lucy went to collect the eggs, Tom set about straightening things in the lounge room, putting Lucy's pencils in a biscuit tin, stacking up her books. Among them, he found the prayer book Ralph had given her at her christening, and from which Isabel often read to her. He flicked through the feathery pages, edged with gold. Morning prayers, communion rites . . . Going through the psalms, his eyes came to rest on number 37, *"Noli aemulari." "Fret not thyself because of the ungodly: neither be thou envious among the evil-doers. For they shall be cut down like the grass: and be withered even as the green herb."*

Isabel and Lucy, the little girl carried piggyback, came in, laughing at something. "Gosh, this is clean! Have magic pixies been in?" asked Isabel.

Tom shut the book, and put it on top of the pile. "Just trying to put things in order," he said.

A few weeks later, Ralph and Tom were sitting, backs resting against the stone wall of the storage shed, having unloaded the last of the September supplies. Bluey was down on the boat, sorting out a problem with the anchor chain, and Isabel was in the kitchen with Lucy, making gingerbread men. It had been a hard morning, and the two men sat sharing a bottle of beer in the first tentative spring sunshine.

For weeks, Tom had been anticipating this moment, considering how he could approach the subject when the boat arrived. He cleared his throat before asking, "Have you ever . . . done anything wrong, Ralph?"

The old man cocked Tom a look. "What the bloody hell's that supposed to mean?"

The words had come out awkwardly, despite all Tom's planning. "I'm talking about—well—how you put something right when you've buggered it up. How you fix it." His eyes were focused on the black swan on the beer label, and he struggled to keep his nerve. "I mean something serious."

Ralph took a swig of beer and looked at the grass as he nodded slowly. "Want to say what? None of my business, of course—not trying to stick me beak in."

Tom was very still, sensing bodily the relief that would follow the unburdening of the truth about Lucy. "My father dying got me thinking about everything I've done wrong in life, and about how to put it right before I die." He opened his mouth to go on, but an image of Isabel bathing their stillborn son silenced him, and he balked.

"I'll never even know their names . . ." He was surprised at how readily the space had been filled with other thoughts, other guilt.

"Whose names?"

Tom hesitated, poised on the edge of a chasm, deciding whether to dive. He drank some beer. "The men I killed." The words fell, blunt and heavy.

Ralph weighed up his response. "Well, that's what you do in a bloody war. Kill or be killed."

"The more time passes, the madder everything I've done seems." Tom had a sense of being physically trapped in each separate past moment, held in some vise that pressed into him every bodily sensation, every guilt-filled thought that had mounted up over years. He struggled for breath. Ralph was completely still, waiting.

Tom turned to him, suddenly shaking. "Jesus Christ, I just want to do the right thing, Ralph! Tell me what the right fucking thing to do is! I—I just can't stand this! I can't do it any more." He threw the bottle to the ground and it shattered on a rock, as his words dissolved into a sob.

Ralph put an arm around him. "There now, boy. Easy does it, easy does it. I've been around a shade longer than you. Seen all sorts. Right and wrong can be like bloody snakes: so tangled up that you can't tell which is which until you've shot 'em both, and then it's too late."

He looked at Tom: a long, wordless look. "The question I'd ask is, how would raking over the coals make things better? You can't put any of that right now." The words, devoid of judgment or animosity, twisted like a knife in Tom's guts just the same. "Christ—the quickest way to send a bloke mad is to let him go on re-fighting his war till he gets it right."

Ralph scraped at a callus on his finger. "If I'd had a son, I'd be proud if he turned out half as well as you. You're a good bloke, Tom. A lucky bloke, with that wife and daughter of yours. Concentrate on what's best for your family now. Fella upstairs's given you a second chance, so I reckon he's not too fussed about whatever you did or didn't do back then. Stick to now. Put right the things you can put right today, and let the ones from back then go. Leave the rest to the angels, or the devil or whoever's in charge of it."

"The salt. You can never get rid of the salt. It eats away like a cancer if you don't watch out." It was the day after his talk with Ralph, and Tom was muttering to himself. Lucy sat beside him inside the giant glass cocoon of the lens, feeding her rag doll imaginary sweets as he buffed and polished the bronze fittings. Her blue eyes beamed up at him.

"Are you Dolly's dadda too?" she asked.

Tom stopped. "I don't know. Why don't you ask Dolly?"

She leaned to whisper something to the doll, then announced, "She says no. You're just *my* Dadda."

Her face had lost its round shape, and was now giving hints of her future self—blonde hair rather than the earlier dark shade, and enquiring eyes, fair skin. He wondered whether she would begin to resemble her mother, or her father. He thought back to the face of the blond man he had buried. Dread crawled up his spine as he imagined her asking him harder questions as the years went on. He thought, too, how his reflection in the mirror now offered glimpses of his own father's face at his age. Likeness lies in wait. Partageuse was small: a mother might fail to recognize her infant in the face of a toddler, but eventually, wouldn't she see herself in the grown woman? The thought gnawed away at him. He dabbed the rag into the tin of polish and rubbed again, until the sweat trickled into the corners of his eyes.

That evening, Tom was leaning against the veranda post, watching the wind blow the sun into night. He had lit up, and the tower was now settled down until dawn. He had gone over Ralph's advice again and again. *Put right the things you can put right today.*

"Here you are, darl," said Isabel. "She's gone off to sleep. I had to read *Cinderella* three times!" She put an arm around Tom and leaned into him. "I love the way she pretends to read as she turns the pages. Knows the stories by heart."

Tom did not reply, so Isabel kissed him below the ear and said, "We could always have an early night. I'm tired, but not too tired . . ."

He was still looking out at the water. "What does Mrs. Roennfeldt look like?"

It took a moment for Isabel to register that the reference was to Hannah Potts. "What on earth do you want to know that for?"

"Why do you think?"

"She doesn't look a bit like her! Lucy's blonde with blue eyes—she must have got that from her father."

"Well she sure as hell didn't get it from us." He turned to face her. "Izzy, we've got to say something. We have to tell her."

"*Lucy?* She's too young to—"

"No, Hannah Roennfeldt."

Isabel looked horrified. "What for?"

"She deserves to know."

She shivered. In dark moments, she had wondered whether it was worse to believe your daughter was dead, or that she was alive and you would never see her; she had imagined Hannah's torment. But even a moment's agreement with Tom would be fatal, she knew. "Tom. We've done this one to death. It just isn't right to put your niggling conscience above Lucy's welfare."

"*Niggling conscience?* For the love of God, Isabel, we're not talking about swiping sixpence from the collection plate! We're talking about a child's life! And a woman's life, for that matter. Every moment of our happiness is on *her* tab. That can't be right, no matter how much we try to think our way out of it."

"Tom, you're tired and you're sad and you're confused. In the morning you'll think differently. I'm not going to talk about it any more tonight." She touched his hand, and fought to mask the tremble in her voice. "We're—we're not in a perfect world. We have to live with that."

He stared at her, seized by the sensation that perhaps she didn't exist. Perhaps none of this existed, for the inches between them seemed to divide two entirely different realities, and they no longer joined.

Lucy is particularly fond of looking at the photographs taken of her as a baby on her visit to Partageuse. "That's me!" she tells Tom, as she sits on his knee and points to the picture on the table. "But I was only little then. Now I'm a big girl."

"You certainly are, sweetie. Four next birthday."

"That," she says, pointing authoritatively, "is Mamma's mamma!"

"Quite right. Mamma's mamma is Grandma."

"And that's Dadda's dadda."

"No, that's *Mamma's* dadda. That's Grandpa."

Lucy looks skeptical.

"Yeah, it's confusing, I know. But Grandma and Grandpa aren't my mum and dad."

"Who are your mum and dad?"

Tom shifted Lucy from one knee to the other. "My mum and dad were called Eleanora and Edward."

"Are they my grandma and grandpa too?"

Tom sidestepped the question. "They both died, sweetie."

"Ah," said Lucy, and nodded seriously, in a way that made him suspect she had no idea what he was talking about. "Like Flossie."

Tom had forgotten about the goat that had become ill and died a few weeks earlier. "Well, yes, like Flossie died."

"Why did your mamma and dadda die?"

"Because they were old and sick." He added, "It was a long time ago."

"Will I die?"

"Not if I can help it, Lulu."

But lately, every day with this child seemed a precarious thing.

The more she had access to words, the greater her ability to excavate the world around her, carving out the story of who she was. It gnawed away at Tom that her understanding of life and of herself would be founded on a single, enormous lie: a lie he himself had helped craft and refine.

Every surface in the light room gleamed: Tom had always kept it diligently, but now he waged war on every screw, every fitting, until it surrendered a brilliant sheen. These days he smelled permanently of Duraglit. The prisms sparkled and the beam shone, unhindered by a speck of dust. Every cog in the works moved smoothly. The apparatus had never functioned with more precision.

The cottage, on the other hand, had suffered. "Couldn't you just put a bit of putty in that crack?" Isabel asked, as they sat in the kitchen after lunch.

"I'll do it once I'm ready for the inspection."

"But you've been ready for the inspection for weeks—for months, for that matter. It's not as if the King's coming, is it?"

"I just want it shipshape, that's all. I've told you, we're in with a chance for the Point Moore posting. We'd be on land, close to Geraldton. Near people. And we'd be hundreds of miles from Partageuse."

"Time was you couldn't bear the thought of leaving Janus."

"Yeah, well, times change."

"It's not time that's changed, Tom," she said. "You're the one who always says that if a lighthouse looks like it's in a different place, it's not the lighthouse that's moved."

"Well you work out what has," he said as he picked up his spanner and headed off down to the storage sheds, without looking back.

That night, Tom took a bottle of whisky, and went to watch the stars from near the cliff. The breeze played on his face as he traced the constellations, and tasted the burn of the liquid. He turned his attention to the rotation of the beam, and gave a bitter laugh at the thought that the dip of the light meant that the island itself was always left in darkness. A lighthouse is for others; powerless to illuminate the space closest to it.

CHAPTER 21

The celebration at Point Partageuse three months later was big by South West standards. The Superintendent of the Mercantile Marine Office had come all the way from Perth, together with the State Governor. The town worthies were there—the Mayor, the Harbormaster, the vicar, as well as three of the last five lightkeepers. They had gathered to commemorate the day on which Janus was first lit, forty years earlier in January 1890. The occasion brought with it a grant of brief special shore leave for the Sherbourne family.

Tom ran his finger between his neck and the starched collar which imprisoned it. "I feel like a Christmas goose!" he complained to Ralph as the two stood backstage, looking out from behind the curtains. Already sitting in neat rows on the stage were municipal engineers and Harbor and Lights employees who had been associated with Janus over the years. Outside the open windows, the summer's night was alive with the chirrup of crickets. Isabel and her parents sat on one side of the hall, Bill Graysmark holding Lucy on his knee while she rabbited nursery rhymes.

"Just keep your mind on the free beer, son," Ralph whispered to Tom. "Even Jock Johnson can't blather on too long tonight—that getup must be killing him." He nodded in the direction of the bald, perspiring man bedecked with ermine-collared robe and mayoral chain who was pacing about, preparing to address the gathering in the rickety town hall.

"I'll join you in a minute," Tom said. "Call of nature." And he headed out to the toilet behind the hall.

On the way back, he noticed a woman who seemed to be staring at him.

He checked that his flies were buttoned; glanced behind him, in case she was observing someone else. Still she looked at him, and as she got closer, she said, "You don't remember me, do you?"

Tom looked at her again. "Sorry, think you've got the wrong person."

"It was a long time ago now," she said, blushing. In that instant something in her expression changed, and he recognized the face of the girl on the boat on his first trip to Point Partageuse. She had aged, and was thin now, with shadows under her eyes. He wondered if she had some sort of illness. He remembered her, in her nightgown, wide-eyed with fear and pinned to the wall by some drunken fool. The memory belonged to a different man, a different lifetime. Once or twice over the years, he'd wondered what had become of her, and of the cove who'd bailed her up. He had never bothered to mention the incident to anyone, Isabel included, and instinct told him it was too late to tell her about it now.

"I just wanted to say thank you," the woman began, but was interrupted by a voice calling from the back door of the hall. "We're about to start. Best be getting in."

"Excuse me," said Tom. "Got to go, I'm afraid. See you afterward, perhaps."

As soon as he took up his seat onstage, proceedings got under way. There were speeches, a few anecdotes from some of the older lightkeepers; the unveiling of a model of the original structure.

"This model," the Mayor announced proudly, "was paid for by our local benefactor, Mr. Septimus Potts. I'm delighted that Mr. Potts and his charming daughters, Hannah and Gwen, are attending our little gathering tonight, and I'd ask you to show your thanks in the usual way." He gestured to an older man sitting beside two women, the first of whom, Tom realized with a sick lurch, was the girl from the boat. He glanced at Isabel, who smiled stiffly as she applauded with the rest of the audience.

The Mayor continued, "And of course, ladies and gentlemen, we also have with us tonight the current lightkeeper on Janus, Mr. Thomas Sherbourne. I'm sure Tom would be delighted to say a few words about life on Janus Rock today." He turned to Tom, and gestured him to the podium.

Tom froze. No one had mentioned a speech. He was still reeling from the realization that he had met Hannah Roennfeldt. The audience clapped. The Mayor beckoned him again, more forcefully this time. "Up you get, sport."

For just a second, he wondered whether everything, from the day the boat had washed up, might be just one terrible, merciful nightmare. But there in the audience he could see Isabel, the Pottses and Bluey, oppressively real and inescapable. He got to his feet, heart thudding, and walked to the lectern as if to the gallows.

"Struth," he began, sending a ripple of laughter through the audience. "I wasn't expecting this." He wiped his palms on the sides of his trousers, and gripped the lectern for support. "Life on Janus today . . ." He stopped, lost in a thought, and repeated, "Life on Janus today . . ." How could he explain the isolation? How could he make anyone know the world there, as far removed from their experience as another galaxy? The Janus bubble had shattered like glass: here he was, in a crowd, in an ordinary, real room, full of people, of other lives. In the presence of Hannah Roennfeldt. There was a long silence. A few cleared their throats, others shifted in their seats.

"Janus Light was designed by some pretty smart characters," he said. "And built by some pretty brave ones. I just try and do them justice. Keep the light burning." He sought refuge in the technical, in the practical, which he could talk about without having to think. "People imagine the light must be huge, but it's not—the actual luminescence comes from a flame of vaporized oil that burns in an incandescent mantle. It gets magnified and directed through a giant set of glass prisms twelve feet high, called a first order Fresnel lens, which bends the light into a beam so intense you can see it more than thirty miles away. Amazing to think a little thing can become so strong that you can see it miles off . . . My job—my job's to keep it clean. Keep it turning.

"It's like being in a different world, out there, and a different time: nothing changes except the seasons. There are dozens of lighthouses all around the coast of Australia: plenty more fellows like me, trying to make the ships safe, keeping the light for whoever might need it, even though we'll mostly never see them or know who they are.

"Can't think what else to say, really. Except you can never tell what the tide's going to bring in from one day to the next—everything that two whole oceans fling at us." He could see the Mayor checking his pocket watch. "Well, I reckon that's kept you away from the spread for long enough: this is thirsty weather. Thanks," he concluded, turning abruptly to sit down, to moderate applause from the bemused audience.

"You all right, mate?" Ralph asked in a whisper. "You look a bit green about the gills."

"Not too keen on surprises," was all Tom said.

Mrs. Captain Hasluck loved a party. Her penchant was rarely indulged in Partageuse, so tonight she was beside herself with delight. She relished her duty, as Harbormaster's wife, to encourage the guests to mix, especially seeing as there were visitors from Perth. She glided here and there, introducing people, reminding them of names and suggesting things they had in common. She kept an eye on Reverend Norkells's sherry intake; engaged the Superintendent's wife in small talk about the difficulty of laundering the gold braid on uniforms. She even managed to persuade old Neville Whittnish to tell the story of the day he saved the crew of a schooner whose cargo of rum had caught fire out near Janus in 1899. "Of course, that was before Federation," he said. "And long before the Commonwealth got its hands on the Lights in 1915. A lot more red tape since then." The State Governor's wife nodded dutifully and wondered if he knew he had dandruff.

Mrs. Captain looked about for her next task, and saw her opportunity. "Isabel, dear," she said, laying a hand on her elbow. "What an interesting speech Tom gave!" She cooed to Lucy, who was perched on Isabel's hip, "You're up very late this evening, young lady. I hope you're being a good girl for Mummy."

Isabel smiled. "Good as gold."

In a crochet-hook maneuver, Mrs. Hasluck reached out to gather in the arm of a woman who was just passing. "Gwen," she said. "You know Isabel Sherbourne, don't you?"

Gwen Potts hesitated a moment. She and her sister were several years older than Isabel, and having been to boarding school in Perth, neither of them knew her well. Mrs. Captain registered the hesitation. "*Graysmark.* You'd know her as Isabel Graysmark," she said.

"I—well, I know who you are, of course," she said with a polite smile. "Your father's the headmaster."

"Yes," replied Isabel, nausea creeping into her belly. She looked around, as though trying to escape with her eyes.

Mrs. Captain was beginning to regret the introduction. The Potts girls had never really mixed much with the locals. And then, after all that business with the German, well, the sister . . . Oh dear . . . She was considering how to rescue the situation when Gwen gestured to Hannah, standing a few feet away.

"Hannah, did you realize Mr. Sherbourne who gave that speech just now is married to Isabel Graysmark? You know, the headmaster's daughter."

"No, I didn't know," said Hannah, whose thoughts seemed elsewhere as she approached.

Isabel froze, unable to speak, as a gaunt face slowly turned toward her. She clutched Lucy tighter and tried to utter a greeting, but no words came.

"What's your little one's name?" asked Gwen with a smile.

"Lucy." It was only by supreme effort that Isabel managed not to run from the room.

"Lovely name," said Gwen.

"Lucy," said Hannah, as if pronouncing a word from a foreign language.

She was staring at the child, and reached out to touch her arm.

Isabel flinched with terror at the look in Hannah's eyes as she surveyed the little girl.

Lucy seemed hypnotized by the woman's touch. She studied the dark eyes, and neither smiled nor frowned, as though concentrating on a puzzle. "Mamma," she said, and both women blinked. She turned to Isabel. "Mamma," she said again, "I'm sleepy," and rubbed her eyes.

For the briefest of moments, Isabel pictured herself handing Hannah the child. She was the mother. She had the right. But she was hallucinating. No, she had thought about it so many times. There was no going back on her decision. Whatever God meant by this, Isabel had to stay with the plan, go along with His will. She cast about in her mind for something to say.

"Oh look," said Mrs. Hasluck, seeing Tom approach, "here's the man of the moment," and pulled him in as she moved off to another little group. Tom had been anxious to catch Isabel and slip away, as people converged on the trestle tables of sausage rolls and sandwiches. As he realized who Isabel was talking to, his neck tingled, and his pulse raced harder.

"Tom, this is Hannah and Gwen Potts," said Isabel, attempting a smile.

Tom stared as his wife, with Lucy on her hip, put her hand on his arm.

"Hello," said Gwen.

"Pleased to meet you again, properly," said Hannah, finally tearing her eyes from the child.

Tom could find no words.

"'Properly'?" queried Gwen.

"We actually met years ago, but I never knew his name."

Now Isabel was looking anxiously from one to the other.

"Your husband was very gallant. Rescued me from a fellow who—well, who was bothering me. On a boat from Sydney." She answered Gwen's silent question. "Oh, I'll tell you about it later. It's all a long time ago now." To Tom, she said, "I had no idea you were on Janus."

There was a heavy silence as they stood, inches from each other.

"Dadda," said Lucy finally, and held out her arms to him. Isabel resisted, but the child put her arms around his neck and Tom let her climb on to him and rest her head against his chest, listening to the drumbeat of his heart.

Tom was about to take the chance to move away, when Hannah touched his elbow. "I liked what you said, by the way, about the light being there for whoever needed it." She took a moment to work up to her next words. "Could I ask you something, Mr. Sherbourne?"

The request filled him with dread, but he said, "What's that?"

"It may seem a strange question, but do ships ever rescue people far out to sea? Have you ever heard of boats being picked up? Survivors taken to the other side of the world, perhaps? I was just wondering whether you'd ever come across stories . . ."

Tom cleared his throat. "When it comes to the ocean, anything's possible, I suppose. Anything at all."

"I see . . . Thank you." Hannah took a deep breath, and looked again at Lucy. "I took your advice," she added. "About that fellow on the boat back then. Like you said, he had enough problems." She turned to her sister. "Gwen, I'm ready for home. I'm not much of a one for this kind of do. Will you say goodbye to Dad for me? I don't want to interrupt him." Then to Tom and Isabel, "Excuse me." She was about to leave when Lucy gave a sleepy "Ta-ta" and a wave. Hannah tried to smile. "Ta-ta," she replied. Through tears she said, "You have a very lovely daughter. Excuse me," and hurried to the door.

"So sorry about that," Gwen said. "Hannah had a terrible tragedy a few years ago. Family lost at sea—her husband, and a daughter who would have been about your girl's age by now. She's always asking that sort of thing. Seeing little ones sets her off."

"Dreadful," Isabel managed to mutter.

"I'd better go and see she's all right."

As Gwen left, Isabel's mother joined them. "Aren't you proud of your daddy, Lucy? Isn't he a clever fellow, giving speeches and what have you?" She turned to Isabel. "Shall I take her home? You and Tom can enjoy the party. Must be years since you've been to a dance."

Isabel looked to Tom for a response.

"I promised Ralph and Bluey I'd have a beer with them. Not my cup of tea, all this." Without another glance at his wife, he strode out into the darkness.

Later that night, when Isabel looked into the mirror as she washed her face, for an instant it was Hannah's features she glimpsed in the glass, etched with distress. She splashed more water on her skin, to wash away the unbearable image along with the sweat of the encounter. But she couldn't make the picture go away, nor could she tame the other, almost imperceptible wire of fear that came from learning that Tom had met her. She couldn't say why it made things worse, but somehow, it felt as if solid ground had moved imperceptibly beneath her feet.

The encounter had been shocking. To see close up the darkness in Hannah Roennfeldt's eyes. To smell the faded sweetness of powder on her. To feel, almost physically, the hopelessness that hung about her. But at the very same time, she had tasted the possibility of losing Lucy. The muscles in her arms stiffened now, as if to hold on to the child. "Oh God," she prayed, "God, bring peace to Hannah Roennfeldt. And let me keep Lucy safe."

Tom had still not come home. She went into Lucy's room to check on her. She took a picture book gently from her hand as she slept, and laid it on the dressing table. "Night night, my angel," she whispered, and kissed her. As she stroked her hair, she found herself comparing the shape of Lucy's face with the vision of Hannah in the mirror, looking for something in the curve of the chin or the arch of an eyebrow.

CHAPTER 22

Mamma, can we have a cat?" Lucy asked the next morning as she followed Isabel into the Graysmarks' kitchen. The child had been fascinated by the exotic marmalade creature called Tabatha Tabby that patrolled the house. She had seen cats in storybooks, but this was the only one she had ever touched.

"Oh, I don't think a cat would be very happy on Janus, sweetie pie. He wouldn't have any friends to play with." Isabel's voice had a distracted air.

"Dadda, can we please have a cat?" asked the child without missing a beat, oblivious to the tension in the air.

Tom had got home after Isabel was asleep, and risen before anyone else. He was sitting at the table, flipping through a week-old copy of the *West Australian*.

"Lulu, why don't you take Tabatha out into the garden for an adventure—go hunting for mice," he said.

She hauled the compliant animal up by its middle and stumbled to the door.

Tom turned to Isabel. "How much longer, Izz? How much bloody longer?"

"What?"

"How can we do it? How can we carry on with this every day? You knew the poor woman had gone out of her mind because of us. Now you've seen her with your own eyes!"

"Tom, there's nothing we can do. I know it and so do you." But Hannah's face came back to her, her voice. As Tom set his jaw, she searched for some way of placating him. "Perhaps . . ." she ventured, "perhaps—when Lucy's older, perhaps we can tell Hannah then, when it won't be so devastating . . . But that's years away, Tom, years."

Astounded both by the concession and by its inadequacy, he pressed on. "Isabel, what's it going to take? It can't wait years. Imagine her life! You even *knew* her!"

Fear awoke in Isabel in earnest. "And it turns out you did too, Tom Sherbourne. But you kept that pretty quiet, didn't you?"

Tom was taken aback by the counter-attack. "I don't *know* her. I met her. Once."

"When?"

"On the boat from Sydney."

"That's what's brought this on though, isn't it? Why didn't you ever tell me about her? What did she mean, 'You're very gallant'? What are you hiding?"

"What am *I* hiding? That's rich."

"I know nothing about your life! What else have you kept secret, Tom? How many other shipboard romances?"

Tom stood up. "Stop it! Stop it right there, Isabel! You're carrying on like a two-bob watch over Hannah Roennfeldt to change the subject because you know I'm right. Makes no odds whether I'd seen her before or not."

He tried an appeal to reason. "Izz. You saw what she's become. That's *our* doing." He turned away from her. "I saw things . . . I saw things in the war, Izz. Things I've never told you and never will. Christ, I *did* things . . ." His fists were closed tight and his jaw stiff. "I swore I'd never make anyone suffer after that, not if I could help it. Why do you think I went on the Lights anyway? I reckoned I could maybe do a bit of good, maybe save some poor bastard from being wrecked. And now look what I've gotten into. I wouldn't want a *dog* to have to go through what Hannah Roennfeldt's been through!" He searched for words. "Christ, I learned in France that you're bloody lucky if you've got tucker for tea and teeth to chew it with." He balked at the images that flooded his mind. "So when I met you, and you even looked twice at me, I thought I was bloody well in heaven!"

He stopped for a moment. "What are we, Izzy? What do we think we're playing at, for crying out loud? I swore I'd stay with you through thick and thin, Isabel, *thick and thin*! Well all I can say is, things have got pretty bloody thin," he said, and strode away down the hall.

The child stood in the back doorway, watching the end of the argument, spellbound. She had never heard so many words come from Tom's mouth, never so loud. Never seen him cry.

"She's gone!" Isabel's words greeted Tom as he returned to the Graysmarks' that afternoon, in the company of Bluey.

"Lucy! I left her outside playing with the cat while I went to pack. I thought Mum was watching her, and she thought *I* was watching her."

"Calm down. Calm down, Izz," he said, and put a hand on each arm. "Take it quietly. When did you last see her?"

"An hour ago? Two at the most."

"When did you realize she'd gone?"

"Just now. Dad's gone to look for her, up in the bush at the back." Partageuse frilled in and out of native bush land at its fringes, and beyond the Graysmarks' neat, lawned garden lay acres of scrub that led into forest.

"Tom, thank goodness you're back." Violet came rushing on to the veranda. "I'm so sorry—it's all my fault. I should have checked on her! Bill's gone to search up along the old logging track . . ."

"Are there any other places she's likely to have gone?" Tom's methodical, practical reflex came to the fore. "Anywhere you and Bill told her stories about?"

"She could be anywhere," said Violet, shaking her head.

"Tom, there are snakes. Redbacks. God help us!" Isabel implored.

Bluey spoke up. "I used to spend all day in that bush when I was a kid, Mrs. S. She'll be all right. We'll find her, no trouble. Come on, Tom."

"Izz—Bluey and I'll head into the bush, see if we can find any tracks. You have another look around the garden and out the front. Violet, double-check the house—all the cupboards and under the beds. Anywhere she could have followed the cat. If we don't find her in the next hour, we'll have to send for the police, get the black-trackers out."

Isabel flashed him a look at the mention of police.

"It won't come to that," said Bluey. "She'll be right as rain, Mrs. S., you wait and see."

It was only when they were out of earshot of the women that Bluey said to Tom, "Let's hope she's been making a racket as she goes. Snakes sleep during the day. They'll get out of your way if they hear you coming. But if they're surprised . . . Has she ever wandered off before?"

"She's never had any-bloody-where to wander to," Tom said sharply, then, "Sorry, Blue. Didn't mean to— It's just she hasn't really got much of a feel for distance. On Janus, everywhere's close to home."

They walked on, calling the child's name as they went, and waiting in vain for a reply. They were following the remnants of a path, now mostly overgrown at adult height, where branches reached over the empty space below. But at her height, Lucy would have met no resistance.

About fifteen minutes in, the path opened out into a clearing, then forked in opposite directions. "Loads of these trails," said Bluey. "They'd clear a route, back in the old days, when they went scouting for good timber country. There are still soaks here and there, so you've got to watch out. They're usually covered over," he said, referring to the wells dug to get at groundwater.

The child from the lighthouse has little fear. She knows not to go too near cliff edges. She understands that spiders can bite, and should be avoided. She is clear that she mustn't try to swim unless Mamma or

Dadda is beside her. In the water, she can tell the difference between the fin of a friendly dolphin, which goes up and down, and of a shark, which stays steady as it cuts the surface. In Partageuse, if she pulls the cat's tail it might scratch her. These are the boundaries of danger.

So as she follows Tabatha Tabby beyond the borders of the garden, she has no concept of getting lost. After a while she can no longer see the cat, but by then it is too late—she is too far away simply to retrace her steps, and the more she tries, the further she wanders.

Eventually, she comes to a clearing, where she sits down by a log. She takes in her surroundings. There are soldier ants, which she knows to avoid, and she makes sure she's a good distance from the trail they're making. She's not concerned. Mamma and Dadda will find her.

As she sits there, drawing patterns in the sandy soil with a twig, she notices a strange creature, longer than her finger, approach from under the log. It's like nothing she's ever seen before: a long body, and legs like an insect or a spider, but two fat arms like one of the crabs Dadda catches sometimes on Janus. Fascinated, she touches it with the twig, and its tail rapidly curls up in a beautiful arch, pointing to its head. In that moment, a second creature appears, a few inches away.

She is mesmerized by the way the insects follow her twig, trying to grab it with their crab claws. A third one emerges from under the log. The seconds pass slowly.

As they reach the clearing, Tom gives a start. He sees a small, shod foot protruding from behind a log.

"Lucy!" He races to the log, where the little girl sits playing with a stick. He freezes as he recognizes the shape clinging to the end of the twig as a scorpion. "Jesus, Lucy!" He grabs the little girl under her arms and lifts her high in the air as he dashes the scorpion to the ground and crushes it under his foot. "Lucy, what the hell are you doing?" he cries.

"Dadda! But you killed it!"

"Lucy, that's dangerous! Did it bite you?"

"No. It likes me. And look," she says, opening the wide pocket at the front of her smock, proudly displaying another scorpion. "I got one for *you.*"

"Don't move!" he says, feigning calm and returning her to the ground. He lowers the twig into the pocket until the scorpion locks onto it, then slowly raises it and flings it onto the dirt, stamping on it.

He inspected her arms and legs for signs of bites or stings. "Are you sure it didn't sting you? Does it hurt anywhere?"

She shook her head. "I did an aventure!"

"You certainly did an adventure all right."

"Have a close look," said Bluey. "You can't always see the puncture marks. But she doesn't look drowsy. That's a good sign. Tell you the truth, I was more worried she was at the bottom of one of those soaks."

"Ever the optimist," muttered Tom. "Lucy, darl, we don't have scorpions on Janus. They're dangerous. You mustn't ever touch them." He hugged her. "Where on earth have you been?"

"I did play with Tabatha. You said to." Tom felt a stab as he recalled his instruction earlier that morning to go outside with the cat. "Come on, sweetie. We've got to get you back to Mamma." His mouth seemed newly aware of the significance of the word, as the previous night's events came back to him.

Isabel rushed from the veranda to meet them at the edge of the garden. She grabbed Lucy and sobbed with relief.

"Thank God," said Bill, standing beside Violet. Her put his arms around her. "Thank the blessed Lord. And thanks to you too, Bluey," he said. "You've saved our lives."

All thoughts of Hannah Roennfeldt were swept from Isabel's mind that afternoon, and Tom knew he couldn't raise the subject again. But he was haunted by her face. The figure who had existed in the abstract was now a living woman, suffering every minute because of what he had done. Every aspect of her—the gaunt cheeks, the harrowed eyes, the chewed fingernails—were vivid in his conscience. Hardest to bear was the respect she had shown him, the trust.

Time and again, Tom wondered at the hidden recesses of Isabel's mind—the spaces where she managed to bury the turmoil his own mind couldn't escape.

When Ralph and Bluey cast off from Janus the following day, having delivered the family back to the light, the younger man said, "Cripes, things seemed a bit frosty between them, don't you reckon?"

"Piece of free advice, Blue—never try and work out what's going on in someone else's marriage."

"Yeah, I know, but, well, you'd think they'd be relieved that nothing happened to Lucy yesterday. Isabel was acting like it was Tom's fault she'd wandered off."

"Keep out of it, boy. Time you brewed us up some tea."

CHAPTER 23

It was one of the mysteries of the Great Southern District, the riddle of what happened to baby Grace Roennfeldt and her father. Some people said it just proved you still couldn't trust a Hun: he was a spy and had finally been called back to Germany after the war. Made no difference that he was Austrian. Others, familiar with the oceans, didn't bat an eyelid at his disappearance: "Well, what was he thinking, setting off into these waters? Must have had kangaroos in his top paddock. Wouldn't have lasted five minutes." There was a general sense that somehow it was God expressing disapproval for Hannah's choice of spouse. Forgiveness is all very well, but look at the sorts of things his lot had done . . .

Old Man Potts's reward took on mythic status. Over the years, it lured people from the Goldfields, from up north, from Adelaide even, who saw a chance to make their fortune by coming up with a piece of splintered driftwood and a theory. In the early months, Hannah listened keenly to every tale that was spun of a sighting, every memory of a baby's cry heard from the shore on the fateful night.

With time, even her eager heart could not fail to see the holes in the stories. When she would suggest that a baby's dress which had been "discovered" on the shore did not match the one Grace had been wearing, the reward prospector would urge her, "Think! You're overcome with grief. How could you be expected to remember what the poor child was dressed in?" Or, "You know you'd sleep more easily if you just accepted the evidence, Mrs. Roennfeldt." Then they would make some sour remark as they were ushered from the parlor by Gwen, who thanked them for their trouble and gave them a few shillings for the journey home.

That January, the stephanotis was in bloom again, the same voluptuous scent heavy in the air, but it was an ever more gaunt Hannah Roennfeldt who continued her ritual journey—though less often now—to the police station, the beach, the church. "Completely off her rocker," Constable Garstone muttered as she wandered out. Even Reverend Norkells urged her to spend less time in the stony darkness of the church and to "look for Christ in the life around her."

Two nights after the lighthouse celebrations, as Hannah lay awake, she heard the groan of the hinges on the letterbox. She looked at the clock, whose eerie numerals signaled three a.m. A possum, perhaps? She crept out of bed and peered from the corner of the curtain, but saw nothing. The moon had hardly risen: no light anywhere save for the faint glow of the stars which dusted the sky. Again, she heard the iron clang of the box, this time caught by the breeze.

She lit a storm-lantern and ventured through the front door, careful not to wake her sister, only vaguely wary of disturbing any snakes which might be taking advantage of the inky blackness to hunt for mice or frogs. Her pale feet made no sound on the path.

The door to the letterbox swung gently back and forward, giving glimpses of a shape inside. As she held the lantern closer, the outline of a small oblong emerged—a parcel. She pulled it out. Not much bigger than her hand, it was wrapped in brown paper. She looked about for any hint of how it had got there, but the darkness curled around her lamp like a closing fist. She hurried back to her bedroom, fetching her sewing scissors to cut the string. The package was addressed to her, in the same neat hand as before. She opened it.

As she pulled out layer upon layer of newspaper, something made a noise with each movement. As the last of the packing was removed, there, returning the soft glimmer of the lantern, was the silver rattle her father had commissioned in Perth for his granddaughter. There was no mistaking the embossed cherubs on the handle. Beneath the rattle was a note.

She is safe. She is loved and cared for. Please pray for me.

Nothing more. No date, no initial, no sign.

"Gwen! Gwen, quick!" She hammered on her sister's door. "Look at this! She's alive! Grace is alive. I knew it!"

Gwen stumbled from her bed, ready to hear yet another outlandish idea. But confronted by the rattle, she became instantly alert, for she had sat with her father at the counter in Caris Brothers up in Perth as he discussed the design with the silversmith. She touched it warily, as though it were an egg that might hatch a monster.

Hannah was weeping and smiling, laughing at the ceiling, at the floor. "I told you, didn't I? Oh, my darling Grace! She's alive!"

Gwen laid a hand on her shoulder. "Let's not get carried away, Hannah. We'll go and see Dad in the morning and get him to come with us to the police. They'll know what to do. Now, go back to sleep. You'll need a clear head tomorrow."

Sleep was out of the question. Hannah was terrified that if she closed her eyes she might wake up. She went out to the backyard and sat in the swinging seat where once she had sat with Frank and Grace, and looked at the thousands of stars that dotted the hemisphere; they soothed her with their steadiness, like pinpricks of hope in the night. Little lives could barely be heard or felt on a canvas this vast. Yet she had the rattle, and the rattle brought her hope. This was no hoax. This was a talisman of love—a symbol of her father's forgiveness; a thing touched by her child and those who treasured her. She thought back to her Classics studies, and the tale of Demeter and Persephone. Suddenly this ancient story was alive for her, as she contemplated her daughter's return from wherever she had been held captive.

She felt—no, she *knew*—she was coming to the end of a dreadful journey. Once Grace was back with her, life would begin again—together they would harvest the happiness so long denied them both. She found herself laughing at funny memories: Frank struggling to change a nappy; her father's attempt at composure when his granddaughter brought up her recent feed onto the shoulder of his best suit. For the first time in years, her belly was tight with excitement. If she could just make it to the morning.

When a glimmer of doubt crept into her thoughts, she turned her mind to the specific: the way Grace's hair was slightly thinner at the back from rubbing against her sheet; the way her fingernails had little half-moons at their base. She would anchor her child in memory and draw her home by sheer will—by ensuring that in one place on this earth there was the knowing of every aspect of her. She would love her home to safety.

The town was full of talk. It was a dummy had been found. No, a teething ring. It was something that proved the baby was dead; it was something that proved she was alive. The father had killed her; the father had been murdered. From the butcher's to the greengrocer's, from the farrier's to the church hall, the story acquired and shed facts and frills as it passed from mouth to ear, always with a "tut" or a pursing of lips to disguise the thrill of each teller.

"Mr. Potts, we're not for a minute doubting you can recognize your own purchases. But I'm sure you'll appreciate that it doesn't prove the child's alive." Sergeant Knuckey was trying to calm the now ruddy-faced Septimus, who stood before him, chin up, chest out, like a prizefighter.

"You've got to investigate it! Why would someone have waited until now to hand it in? In the middle of the night? Not tried to claim the reward?" His whiskers seemed even whiter as his face grew more puce.

"All due respect, but how the bloody hell would I know?"

"That's enough of that language, thank you very much! There are ladies present!"

"I apologize." Knuckey pursed his lips. "We will be investigating, I can assure you."

"How, exactly?" demanded Septimus.

"We . . . I . . . You have my word that I will."

Hannah's heart sank. It would be the same as before. Still, she took to staying up late into the night, watching the letterbox, waiting for a sign.

"Right, I'll need a picture of this, Bernie," announced Constable Lynch. Standing at the counter of Gutcher's studio, he produced the silver rattle from a felt bag.

Bernie Gutcher looked askance. "Since when have you been interested in babies?"

"Since it was about evidence!" the policeman replied.

It took time for the photographer to set up his equipment, and as he did, Lynch looked around the walls at the portraits illustrating choices of style and frame. His gaze passed evenly over an array of examples that included the local football team, Harry Garstone and his mother, and Bill and Violet Graysmark with their daughter and granddaughter.

A few days later, a photograph was duly pinned to the noticeboard outside the police station, showing the rattle next to a ruler for scale, and asking for anyone who recognized it to come forward. Beside it was a notice from Septimus Potts, Esquire, announcing that the reward for information leading to the safe return of his granddaughter Grace Ellen Roennfeldt now stood at *three* thousand guineas, and that all approaches would be treated in the strictest confidence.

Down Partageuse way, a thousand guineas could buy you a farm. Three thousand—well, with three thousand guineas there was no telling what you could do.

"Are you sure?" Bluey's mother asked again as she paced the kitchen, her hair still in the rag curlers in which she had slept. "Think, boy, for God's sake!"

"No. I can't be sure—not completely sure—it was so long ago. But I'd never seen anything that flash before, and in a baby's cot!" His hands shook as he rolled a cigarette, and he fumbled the match as he lit it. "Ma, what am I going to do?" Beads of sweat were forming on his forehead beneath his red curls. "I mean, maybe there's some reason for it. Or maybe I was just dreaming." He drew fiercely on his cigarette, and exhaled a thought. "P'raps I should wait until the next trip out to Janus and ask him then, man to man."

"Man to monkey, more like! You're more lame-brained than I thought if that's your idea of what to do. Three thousand guineas!" She waved three fingers in his face. "Three thousand guineas is more than you'd make on that godforsaken boat in a hundred years!"

"But it's *Tom* we're talking about. And Isabel. As if they'd do anything wrong. And even if it *is* the same rattle—it could have just washed up and they found it. You should see some of the stuff that ends up on Janus. He found a musket once! And a rocking horse."

"No wonder Kitty Kelly sent you packing. Not an ounce of ambition. Not an ounce of common sense."

"Ma!" Bluey was stung by his mother's jibe.

"Put a fresh shirt on. We're going to the station."

"But it's Tom! It's a mate, Mum!"

"It's *three blessed thousand guineas*! And if you don't get in first, old Ralph Addicott might be down there spinning them the same story." She added, "Kitty Kelly's not going to look down her nose at a man with that much money, is she? Now brush your hair. And put that wretched cigarette out."

CHAPTER 24

At first Tom thought he was imagining the shape of the *Windward Spirit* as it approached, lashed by the tail end of the cyclone which had been whirling down the West Australian coast. He called to Isabel, to check if she saw it too. They had been back on Janus only a week. No boat was due again until the middle of March, when it was scheduled to take them to the mainland before their transfer to Point Moore. Perhaps it had engine trouble on the way from another job? Perhaps Ralph or Bluey had been injured in all the wild weather?

The swell was treacherous, and it had taken all the skill of the crew to dock the vessel without smashing it into the jetty. "Any port in a storm, eh, Ralph?" Tom shouted above the wind as the boat came alongside, but the old man did not respond.

When, instead of Bluey emerging from the back of the boat, Tom recognized the craggy, timeless features of Neville Whittnish, his confusion deepened. Four policemen followed.

"Crikey, Ralph! What's all this?"

Again Ralph failed to reply. A chill crept through Tom. He looked up the slope and saw Isabel edging back, out of sight of the jetty. One of the policemen staggered down the gangway like a drunk, and took a moment to adjust to the stationary dock. The others followed.

"Thomas Edward Sherbourne?"

"That's right."

"Sergeant Spragg, Albany police. This is my assistant, Constable Strugnell. Sergeant Knuckey and Constable Garstone you may recognize from Point Partageuse station."

"Can't say I do."

"Mr. Sherbourne, we're here about Frank Roennfeldt and his daughter, Grace."

It was a king-hit, knocking the breath out of him for a moment. His neck was stiff, his face suddenly waxy-pale. The waiting was over. It was like finally getting the signal for a hop-over after days of waiting in the trenches.

The sergeant fished something from his pocket—a piece of cardboard that flipped about in the blustery wind. He held it steady between both hands.

"Do you recognize this, sir?"

Tom took in the photograph of the rattle. He glanced up at the cliff as he considered his reply: Isabel was gone. Time balanced on a fulcrum—there would be no going back after this.

He gave a great sigh, as though relieved of a physical weight, and hung his head, eyes closed. He felt a hand on his shoulder. It was Ralph's: "Tom. Tom, son . . . What the bloody hell's been going on out here?"

While the police question Tom alone, Isabel retreats to the little crosses near the cliff. The rosemary bushes move in and out of focus, like her thoughts. She is shaking as she goes over the scene: the shortest of the policemen, the youngest, had been very solemn as he showed her the photograph, and could not have failed to see her eyes widen and her breath stop at the sight.

"Someone sent the rattle to Mrs. Roennfeldt, last week."

"Last week?"

"Looks like the same person as sent her a letter getting on for two years ago."

This last news was too much to make sense of.

"We'll want to ask you some questions once we've spoken to your husband, but in the meantime, perhaps you should—" He shrugged awkwardly. "Don't go too far."

Isabel looks out over the cliff: there is so much air, yet she struggles for breath as she pictures Lucy, having an afternoon sleep while in the room next door, police question her father. They will take her away. Her mind races: she can hide her somewhere on the island. She can—she can set off in the boat with her. She calculates quickly—the rescue boat is always ready to launch at an instant. If she can pretend she's taking Lucy . . . where? Anywhere, it doesn't matter. She can get the girl to the boat and they can be off the island before anyone realizes they've gone. And if they get into the right current, they'll head north . . . She pictures the two of them, making land far up toward Perth, together, safe. Logic intervenes to remind her of the risks of the southerly current and the certain death of the Southern Ocean. Urgently she explores another route. She can swear that the child is her own, that the dinghy washed up with *two* dead bodies, and they kept only the rattle. She clutches at any possibility, no matter how absurd.

The same impulse keeps returning: "I must ask Tom what to do." Then she feels sick, as she remembers this is all Tom's doing. It hits her just as when she woke in the night after learning of her brother Hugh's death and thought, "I must tell Hugh the awful news."

Gradually, some part of her concedes there is no escape, and fear gives way to anger. Why? Why could he not just leave things be? Tom is supposed to protect his family, not rip it apart. Deep beneath awareness, a tar-thick feeling has been disturbed, and now looks for a safe harbor. Her thoughts spiral into darkness—he has been planning this for two years. Who is this man who could lie to her, tear her baby away? She remembers the sight of Hannah Roennfeldt touching his arm, and wonders what really happened between them. She retches violently onto the grass.

The ocean thundered against the cliff, showering spittle right up to where Isabel stood, hundreds of feet above the water, on the edge. The spray had soaked into the crosses and her dress was damp with it.

"Izzy! Isabel!" Tom's voice was all but blown off the island by the gale.

A petrel was wheeling in the air, circling, circling, before plummeting hard as lightning into the jagged swell to retrieve a herring. But luck and the storm were on the side of the fish, and it wriggled from the bird's beak, falling back to the waves.

Tom covered the few hundred yards to his wife. The petrel continued to hover on the storm currents, knowing that the tumult of the water would make easy pickings of any fish not sheltered in the deepest reefs.

"We haven't got much time," Tom said, pulling Isabel close. "Lucy'll be awake any minute." The police had been questioning him for the past hour, and two of them were now heading down toward the old graves on the other side of the island, armed with shovels.

Isabel searched his face as though he were a stranger. "The policeman said someone sent Hannah Roennfeldt a rattle . . ."

He held her gaze, but said nothing.

". . . that someone wrote to her *two years ago,* to say her baby was alive." She wrestled with the implications a little longer. "Tom!" was all she could say, her eyes wide with terror. "Oh, Tom!" she said again, stepping backward.

"I had to do *something,* Izzy. God knows I've tried to explain. I just wanted her to know her child was safe."

She looked at him, as if trying to make sense of words shouted from far away, though he was standing so close that strands of her hair blew into his face. "I trusted you, Tom." She bunched her hair in her fists as she stared at him, openmouthed as she struggled for words. "What in God's name have you done to us? What have you done to Lucy?"

She saw resignation in his shoulders, relief in his eyes. As she dropped her hands, her hair swept across her face again like a mourning veil and she began to sob. "Two years! Has everything been a lie for *two years*?"

"You saw the poor bloody woman! You saw what we'd done."

"And she means more to you than our family?"

"It's not *our* family, Izz."

"It's the only family we'll ever have! What on earth's going to happen to Lucy?"

He clasped her arms. "Look, just do what I say and you'll be all right. I've told them it was me, all right? I've told them keeping Lucy was all my idea—said you didn't want to, but I forced you. As long as you go along with that no one will touch you . . . They're taking us back to Partageuse. Izzy, I promise I'll protect you." He pulled her close to him again and touched his lips to the top of her head. "It doesn't matter what happens to me. I know they'll send me to jail, but when I get out, we'll still—"

Suddenly she launched at him, her fists pounding at his chest. "Don't talk about 'we,' Tom! Not after what you've done!" He made no effort to stop her. "You made your choice! You don't give a tinker's damn about Lucy, or me. So don't"—she searched for words—"don't expect me to care what the bloody hell happens to you from now on."

"Izz—come on now, you don't know what you're saying!"

"Don't I?" Her voice was shrill. "I know they'll take our daughter away. You can't begin to understand, can you? What you've done—it's unforgivable!"

"Christ, Izz—"

"You might as well have *killed* me, Tom! Killing *me* is better than killing our child. You're a monster! A cold, selfish monster!"

Tom stood, absorbing the words that hurt more than the blows. He searched her face for some hint of the love she had sworn for him over and over, but she was full of icy fury, like the ocean all around.

The petrel plummeted again, arising triumphant with a fish it had imprisoned in its beak so that only the mouth, feebly opening and closing, showed that it ever existed.

"It's too rough to start back now," Ralph told Sergeant Knuckey. Sergeant Spragg, the senior policeman from Albany, had been making a great to-do about the need to set out at once. "He can bloody swim if he's that keen to get back," was all the skipper said.

"Well Sherbourne can stay on the boat, under guard. I'm not having him cooking up stories with his wife, thank you very much," Spragg had insisted.

Sergeant Knuckey looked at Ralph and raised his eyebrows, the angle of his mouth betraying his opinion of his colleague.

As sunset approached, Neville Whittnish strode briskly down to the boat. "What do you want?" asked Constable Strugnell, who was taking his guard duty seriously.

"I'll need Sherbourne to do a handover. Has to come with me to light up." Although Whittnish spoke rarely and briefly, his tone never countenanced contradiction.

Strugnell was wrong-footed, but regained sufficient composure to say, "Right, well I'll have to accompany him."

"No unauthorized personnel in the light. Commonwealth rules. I'll bring him back when I've finished with him."

Tom and the keeper walked in silence to the tower. When they reached the door, Tom said quietly, "What was all that about? You don't need me to light up."

The old man said simply, "Never seen a light as well kept. None of my business what else you've done. But you'll want to say goodbye to her. I'll wait down here," and he turned his back, looking out through the rounded window to size up the storm.

So, one last time, Tom climbed the hundreds of stairs. One last time, he performed the alchemy of brilliance from sulphur and oil. One last time, he sent his signal to mariners for miles about: beware.

By the next morning, the storm has abated, and the sky is once again serene blue. The beaches are decked with banks of yellow foam and seaweed thrown up by the waves. As the boat pulls away from Janus Rock, a school of dolphins plays about the bow for a time, their slithering gray forms rising and subsiding like water spouts, now closer, now further away. Isabel, eyes swollen and red, sits on one side of the cabin, Tom on the other. The policemen talk among themselves of rosters and the best way to get a shine on their boots. At the stern, the rotting tarpaulin exhales the odor of its dreadful contents.

On Isabel's lap, Lucy asks again, "Where are we going, Mamma?"

"Back to Partageuse, sweetheart."

"Why?"

Isabel throws Tom a look. "I really don't know why, Luce, my darling. But we have to go." She hugs her tight.

Later, the child climbs down from her mother's knee and clambers up onto Tom. He holds her wordlessly, trying to imprint everything about her: the smell of her hair, the softness of her skin, the shape of her tiny fingers, the sound of her breath as she puts her face so close to his.

The island swims away from them, fading into an ever more miniature version of itself, until it is just a flash of memory, held differently, imperfectly by each passenger. Tom watches Isabel, waits for her to return his glance, longs for her to give him one of the old smiles that used to remind him of Janus Light—a fixed, reliable point in the world, which meant he was never lost. But the flame has gone out—her face seems uninhabited now.

He measures the journey to shore in turns of the light.

PART THREE

CHAPTER 25

As soon as they disembarked, Sergeant Spragg drew a pair of handcuffs from his pocket and strode toward Tom. Vernon Knuckey stopped him with just a shake of the head.

"It's correct procedure," said the Albany sergeant, who outranked Vernon in importance of station.

"Never mind that. There's a little girl here," Knuckey said, nodding toward Lucy, who ran to Tom, grabbing his leg.

"Dadda! Dadda, pick me up!"

Naked distress flashed across his face as the girl's eyes met his, with this most routine of requests. At the top of a peppermint tree, a pair of willy wagtails chittered away. Tom swallowed hard, digging his nails into his palms. "Look, Lulu! Look at the funny birds up there. You don't see those at home, do you?" Keeping his eyes on the birds, he urged, "Go and have a proper look."

Two motorcars were parked near the jetty, and Sergeant Spragg addressed Tom. "This way. Into the first one."

Tom turned back toward Lucy, now distracted by the play of the birds wiggling their long black tails. He was about to reach out a hand to her, but imagined her anguish: best if he slipped away.

She caught sight of his movement and stretched out her arms. "Dadda, wait! Pick me up!" she urged again, her tone betraying her sense that something was wrong.

"Now, if you please," urged Spragg, taking Tom's elbow.

As Tom walked away, every step more awful, Lucy pursued him, arms still outstretched. "Dadda, wait for Lulu," she begged, wounded and confused. When she tripped and fell face down on the gravel, letting out a scream, Tom could not go on, and spun around, breaking free of the policeman's grip.

"Lulu!" He scooped her up and kissed her scratched chin. "Lucy, Lucy, Lucy, Lucy," he murmured, his lips brushing her cheek. "You're all right, little one. You'll be all right."

Vernon Knuckey looked at the ground and cleared his throat.

Tom said, "Sweetheart, I have to go away now. I hope—" He stopped. He looked into her eyes and he stroked her hair, finally kissing her. "Goodbye, littlie."

The child showed no sign of letting go, so Knuckey turned to Isabel. "Mrs. Sherbourne?"

Isabel prised her from Tom. "Come on now, sweet thing. You're all right. Mamma's got you," she said, though the girl continued to call, "Dadda, I want to go with *you,* Dadda!"

"Happy now, Tom? This is what you wanted, isn't it?" Tears ran down Isabel's face and on to Lucy's cheek.

For a moment, Tom stood paralyzed by the sight of the two of them—the pain etched on their faces—the two he had promised Bill Graysmark he would protect and care for. Eventually, he managed to say, "Christ, Izz—I'm sorry."

Kenneth Spragg had lost patience, and grabbed him by the arm again, shoving him along to the car. As Tom ducked into the back of the vehicle, Lucy began to howl. "Dadda, don't go! Please, Dadda! *Please!*" Her face was crumpled and red and tears ran into her open mouth, as Isabel tried in vain to console her. "Mamma, stop the men! They naughty, Mamma! They being nasty to Dadda!"

"I know, darling, I know." She put her lips to Lucy's
murmured, "Sometimes men do very bad things, swee
bad things." As she said the words, she knew there was
come.

Ralph watched the scene from the deck of the boat. When he
to Hilda, he looked at her: really looked at her for perhaps the
in twenty years.

"What's that for?" asked his wife, disconcerted by the att

"Just—oh, just for nothing," he said, and drew her in
hug.

In his office, Vernon Knuckey addressed Kenneth Spragg. "I
you again, Sergeant. You're not taking him to Albany this a
He'll be transferred in good time, when I've had a chance to
more questions."

"He'll end up as our prisoner. Lighthouses are Comm
remember, so we do this the right way."

"I know the rules as well as you." Every policeman this sid
knew how Kenneth Spragg loved to throw his weight around
a chip on his shoulder about not enlisting, and tried to mak
by carrying on like a sergeant bloody major. "He'll be sent to
due course."

"I want a crack at Sherbourne—I'll soon get to the b
things. I'm here now. I'll take him with me."

"If you want him that badly you can bloody well come b
this station."

"Telephone Perth."

"What?"

"Let me telephone Perth. If I hear it from District C

I'll leave him here. Otherwise he's in the motorcar and off to Albany."

It had taken Isabel so long to persuade the distraught child to get into the second motorcar that Tom was already in a cell by the time they arrived at the police station.

In the waiting area, Lucy sat on Isabel's knee, fractious and exhausted by the long journey and the strange goings-on. She kept touching Isabel's face—patting and prodding it to get a response. "Where's Dadda? I want to see him." Isabel was pale, her forehead set in an absent frown. Time and again, her thoughts would drift off, her attention focused on a notch in the wood of the counter, or the call of a distant magpie. Then, Lucy's fingers, prodding with another question, would bring her back to the sickening knowledge of where she was.

An old man who had come to pay a fine for letting his cattle stray onto the highway stood at the counter, waiting for his receipt. He whiled away the time by trying to tempt Lucy into a game of peek-a-boo.

"What's your name?" he asked.

"Lucy," she said shyly.

"That's what you think," muttered Harry Garstone with a sardonic smile, as his pen scratched across the receipt form.

At that moment, Dr. Sumpton arrived from his surgery, puffing, bag in hand. He nodded perfunctorily at Isabel, but avoided eye contact. She blushed scarlet, recalling his last examination of her, and its devastating conclusion.

"Through here, sir," said Garstone, ushering him into a room at the back. The constable returned to Isabel. "The child has to be examined by the medico. If you'd just give her to me."

"Examined? What for? There's nothing wrong with her!"

"You don't get a say in this, Mrs. Sherbourne."

"I'm her—" Isabel stopped herself before the word came out. "She doesn't need a doctor. Please. Show some common decency!"

The policeman grabbed the child and took her away, screaming

and struggling. The shrill cries rang throughout the station, reaching as far as Tom's cell, where they seemed even louder as he imagined what might be happening to her.

In Knuckey's office, Spragg replaced the receiver and scowled at his Partageuse counterpart. "All right. You've got your way for now . . ." Hoisting up his belt, he changed tactics. "The woman should be in the cells too, as far as I'm concerned. She's probably in it up to her neck."

"I've known that girl all her life, Sergeant," said Knuckey. "She never so much as missed church. You heard Tom Sherbourne's story: sounds like she's his victim too."

"His *story*! I'm telling you, she's not all butter wouldn't melt. Let me at him on my own and we'll soon find out how that Roennfeldt chap really died . . ."

Knuckey was well aware of Spragg's reputation in that department too, but overlooked the comment. "Look. I don't know Sherbourne from a bar of soap. Could be Jack the Ripper, for all I can tell. If he's guilty, he's for the high jump. But locking up his wife for the hell of it's not going to help anyone, so just hold your horses. You know as well as I do that a married woman isn't criminally responsible for anything her husband makes her do." He lined up a stack of papers with the corner of his blotter. "This is a small town. Mud sticks. You don't throw a girl in the cells unless you're pretty bloody sure of your facts. So we'll take it a step at a time."

Once the thin-lipped Sergeant Spragg had stalked out of the station, Knuckey entered the examination room and re-emerged with Lucy.

"The doctor's given her the all-clear," he said, then he lowered his voice. "We're going to take the child to her mother now, Isabel. I'd be grateful if you didn't make it any harder on anyone than it has to be. So if you—if you'd like to say goodbye to her?"

"Please! Don't do this!"

"Don't make things worse." Vernon Knuckey, who for years had observed the plight of Hannah Roennfeldt, sure she was basking in a sad delusion, now looked at this woman and wondered the same thing.

Believing she was back safe in her mother's arms, the child gripped her tight as Isabel kissed her cheek, unable to take her lips away from the soft skin. Harry Garstone put his hands around the girl's waist and yanked at her.

Even though everything in the past twenty-four hours had been leading to this, even though it was a fear Isabel had harbored from the day she had first laid eyes on Lucy as a baby, still, the moment ripped through her.

"Please!" she pleaded through tears. "Have some pity!" Her voice reverberated around the bare walls. "Don't take my baby away!"

As the girl was wrenched from her screaming, Isabel fainted onto the stone floor with a resounding crack.

Hannah Roennfeldt could not sit still. She consulted her watch, the mantel clock, her sister—anyone who could tell her how much time had passed. The boat had set out for Janus yesterday morning, and each minute since then had inched uphill like Sisyphus.

It was almost unbelievable that she might soon hold her daughter again. Since the news of the rattle, she had daydreamed about her return. The hugs. The tears. The smiles. She had picked frangipani blossoms from the garden and put them in the nursery, so that the scent filled the little cottage. Smiling and humming, she dusted and cleaned, and sat the dolls up on the chest of drawers. Then doubts would dart in: what would she eat? This had prompted her to send Gwen shopping for apples and milk and sweets. Before her sister returned, Hannah suddenly wondered whether she should be giving the child something else. She, who hardly ate, went next door to Mrs. Darnley, who had five little ones, to check what she should feed a child Grace's age. Fanny Darnley, always keen to have a tale to tell, immediately let slip to Mr. Kelly at the grocer's that Hannah had gone completely mad and was catering for ghosts, for word had not yet got around. "You don't like to speak ill of your neighbors, but—well, there's a reason why we have lunatic asylums, isn't there? I'm not keen on someone who's a shingle short living so close to my kids. You'd feel the same in my place."

The telephone call had been perfunctory. "You'd best come down in person, Mr. Graysmark. We've got your daughter here."

Bill Graysmark arrived at the police station that afternoon in a state of confusion. With the phone call, his mind had jumped straight to a vision of Isabel's body lying on a slab, awaiting collection. He had hardly heard the rest of the words that came through the newly connected telephone: death was the most obvious conclusion to jump to. Not a third child. He could not have lost *all* his children—surely God would not allow that? His mind could make no sense of words about the Roennfeldt baby, and something scrambled about Tom and a body.

At the station he was ushered into a back room, where his daughter sat on a wooden chair, her hands on her lap. He had been so convinced of her death that at the sight of her, tears came to his eyes.

"Isabel. Isabubba!" he whispered, pulling her up with a hug. "I thought I'd never see you again."

It took him a few seconds to notice her peculiar state: she did not hug him back; she did not look at him. She slumped down again in the chair, lifeless and pale.

"Where's Lucy?" he asked, first of his daughter, then of Constable Garstone. "Where's little Lucy? And Tom?" His mind was fast at work again: they must have drowned. They must have—

"Mr. Sherbourne's in the cells, sir." The policeman stamped a piece of paper on the desk. "He'll be transferred to Albany after a committal hearing."

"Committal hearing? What the devil? Where's Lucy?"

"The child's with her mother, sir."

"The child is demonstrably *not* with her mother! What have you done with her? What's this all about?"

"Looks like the child's *real* mother is Mrs. Roennfeldt."

Bill assumed he must have misheard whatever it was Garstone had said, and blundered on, "I demand you release my son-in-law right this minute."

"I'm afraid I can't do that, sir. Mr. Sherbourne is under arrest."

"*Arrest?* What the hell for?"

"So far, falsification of Commonwealth records. Breach of duty as a public servant. That's just for starters. Then there's child stealing. And the fact that we dug up Frank Roennfeldt's remains out on Janus Rock."

"Are you out of your mind?" He turned to his daughter, suddenly understanding her pallor and dreamy state. "Don't you worry about this, dear. I'll sort it out. Whatever it's about, it's obviously all a terrible mistake. I'll get to the bottom of it."

"I don't think you understand, Mr. Graysmark," began the policeman.

"You're damn right I don't understand. There'll be the devil to pay over this! Dragging my daughter into a police station because of some ridiculous story. Slandering my son-in-law." He turned to his daughter. "Isabel—tell him it's all nonsense!"

She sat, still and expressionless. The policeman cleared his throat. "Mrs. Sherbourne refuses to say anything, sir."

Tom feels the stillness of the cell weigh upon him, as dense and as liquid as mercury. For so long, his life has been shaped by the sound of the waves and the wind, the rhythm of the light. Suddenly, everything has stopped. He listens to the whipbird declaring its territory with song from high in the karri trees, oblivious.

The solitude is familiar, carrying him back to his time alone on Janus, and he wonders if the years with Isabel and with Lucy were just imagined. Then he puts his hand in his pocket and retrieves the child's lilac satin ribbon, recalling her smile as she handed it to him when it slipped off. "Hold this please, Dadda." When Harry Garstone had tried to confiscate it at the station, Knuckey had snapped, "Oh, for God's sake, boy. He's hardly going to choke us with that bloody thing, is he!" and Tom had folded it safely away.

He cannot reconcile the grief he feels at what he has done and the profound relief that runs through him. Two opposing physical forces, they create an inexplicable reaction overpowered by a third, stronger force—the knowledge of having deprived his wife of a child. As fresh and raw as being spiked on a meat hook, he feels loss: what Hannah Roennfeldt must have felt; what Isabel has felt so many times, and grips her again now. He begins to wonder how he could have inflicted such suffering. He begins to wonder what the bloody hell he's done.

He struggles to make sense of it—all this love, so bent out of shape, refracted, like light through the lens.

Vernon Knuckey had known Isabel since she was a tot. Her father had taught five of his children. "Best thing you can do is take her home," he had told Bill gravely. "I'll talk to her tomorrow."

"But what about—"

"Just take her home, Bill. Take the poor girl home."

"Isabel. Darling!" Her mother hugged her as soon as she stepped through the front door. Violet Graysmark was as confused as anyone, but when she saw the state of her daughter, did not dare ask questions. "Your bed's made up. Bill—fetch her bag through."

Isabel drifted in, blank-faced. Violet guided her to an armchair, then hurried to the kitchen and returned with a glass. "Warm water and brandy. For your nerves," she said. Isabel sipped the drink mechanically, and put the empty glass on the occasional table.

Violet brought a rug and tucked it over her knees, though the room was perfectly warm. Isabel began to stroke the wool, tracing her index finger in straight lines over the tartan. She was so absorbed that she did not seem to hear when her mother asked, "Is there anything I can get you, pet? Are you hungry?"

Bill put his head around the door and beckoned Violet out to the kitchen. "Has she said anything?"

"Not a word. I think she's in shock."

"Well that makes two of us. I can't make head or tail of it. I'm going to the station first thing in the morning to get a straight story. That Hannah Roennfeldt's been daft as a brush for years now. And as for old man Potts: thinks he can throw his weight around because of his dough." He pulled the ends of his waistcoat down over his belly. "I'm not going to be pushed around by some lunatic and her father, no matter how much money he's got."

That night, Isabel lay in her narrow childhood bed, now foreign, constricting. A light wind pushed at the lace curtains, and outside, the chirrup of the crickets reflected the sparkling stars. On a night like this, only moments ago, it seemed, she had lain sleepless and excited at the prospect of her wedding the following morning. She had thanked God for sending her Tom Sherbourne: for letting him be born, for keeping him safe through the war, for wafting him on some breeze of Fate to her shore, where she was the first person he saw as he landed.

She tried to recall that state of ecstatic anticipation, the sense that life, after all the grief and loss the war had brought, was about to bloom. But the feeling was lost: now it all seemed a mistake, a delusion. Her happiness on Janus was distant, unimaginable. For two years, Tom had been lying with every word and every silence. If she hadn't noticed that deception, what else had she missed? Why had he never said a word about meeting Hannah Roennfeldt? What was he hiding? In a sickening flash she saw a picture of Tom and Hannah and Lucy, a happy family. The thoughts of betrayal which had assailed her on Janus now came back darker, more insinuating. Perhaps he had other women and other lives. Perhaps he had deserted a wife—*wives*—back East . . . and children . . . Fantasy seemed plausible, compelling, as it poured into the gap between her memory of the eve of her wedding and this dreadful, oppressive present. A lighthouse warns of danger—tells people to keep their distance. She had mistaken it for a place of safety.

To have lost her child. To have seen Lucy terrified and distraught at being torn from the only people in the world she really knew: this was already unbearable. But to know it had happened because of her own husband—the man she adored, the man she'd given her life to—was simply impossible to grasp. He'd claimed to care for her, yet he'd done the thing guaranteed to destroy her.

This focusing outward, on Tom, painful as it was, saved her from a more intolerable examination. Slowly, taking shape among the shadows in her mind, was an almost solid sensation: an urge to punish; the fury of a wild thing deprived of her young. Tomorrow, the police would question her. By the time the stars had faded in the wakening sky, she had convinced herself: Tom deserved to suffer for what he had done. And he himself had handed her the weapons.

CHAPTER 26

The police station at Point Partageuse, like many of the town's buildings, was made from local stone, and timber cut from the surrounding forest. It was an oven in summer and an icebox in winter, which led to irregularities in uniform on days of extreme temperatures. When it rained too heavily, the cells flooded and bits of the ceiling sagged—even fell in once, killing a prisoner. Perth was too stingy to stump up the money to fix the structure properly, so it had a permanently wounded air, more bandaged than repaired.

Septimus Potts was sitting at a table near the front counter, filling in a form with the few details he could recall about his son-in-law. He was able to give Frank's full name and date of birth—they had featured on the invoice for the memorial stone. But as for place of birth, parents' names . . . "Look, I think we can safely assume he had parents, young man. Let's stick to the point here," he blustered, putting Constable Garstone onto the back foot with a technique honed over years of business deals. The constable conceded it would do for the writing-up of the initial charge sheet against Tom. The day of the disappearance was easy enough—Anzac Day, 1926; but the date of Frank's death?

"You'll have to ask Mr. Sherbourne that," Potts was saying sourly, as Bill Graysmark entered the station.

Septimus turned around, and the men glared at one another like two old bulls. "I'll just go and get Sergeant Knuckey," spluttered the constable, sending his chair clattering to the ground as he sprang up. He rapped out a machine-gun knock on the sergeant's door, and returned after a moment to summon Bill, who barged past Potts and into Knuckey's office.

"Vernon!" he launched at the sergeant as soon as the door was closed. "I don't know what's been going on, but I demand that my granddaughter be returned to her mother, right now. Dragging her off like that! She's not even four years old, for goodness' sake." He gestured toward the front of the station. "What happened to the Roennfeldts was all very sad, but Septimus Potts can't just snatch away my granddaughter to make up for what he's lost."

"Bill," said the sergeant, "I realize how hard this must be for you . . ."

"Realize, my foot! Whatever this is, it's got completely out of hand, presumably on the word of a woman who's been off with the fairies for years."

"Have a drop of brandy . . ."

"I don't need a drop of brandy! I need a drop of common sense, if that's not too much to ask around here. Since when do you put men in jail on the unsubstantiated claims of—of a madwoman?"

Knuckey sat down at his desk and rolled his pen between his fingertips. "If you mean Hannah Roennfeldt, she hasn't said anything against Tom. Bluey Smart started it all—he's the one identified the rattle." He paused. "Isabel hasn't spoken to us at all so far. Refuses to say a word." He examined the pen as it turned, and said, "That's pretty odd, don't you think, if it's all just a mistake?"

"Well, she's clearly overcome, having her child snatched like that."

Knuckey looked up. "Can you answer me this, then, Bill: why hasn't Sherbourne denied it?"

"Because he . . ." The words came out before he had registered the policeman's answer, and he doubled back: "What do you mean, he hasn't denied it?"

"Out on Janus, he told us the baby had washed up in a dinghy with a dead man, and that he'd insisted they should keep her. Assumed the mother had already drowned because of a cardigan they found. Said Isabel wanted to report the whole thing and he stopped her. He blamed her for not producing children for him. Looks like it's all been a pack of lies since then—a complete charade. We've got to investigate, Bill." He hesitated, then lowered his voice. "Then there's the question of *how* Frank Roennfeldt died. Who knows what Sherbourne's got to hide? Who knows what he's forced Isabel to keep quiet about? It's a very nasty business."

The town had not seen such excitement in years. As the editor of the *South Western Times* put it to his colleague in the pub, "It's the next best thing to Jesus Christ himself turning up and shouting us all a beer. We've got a mother and baby reunited, a mysterious death, and old Potts of Money giving away his dough like it's—well, Christmas! Folks can't get enough of it."

The day after the child's return, Hannah's house is still decorated with crêpe-paper streamers. A new doll, its dainty porcelain face glowing in the afternoon light, sits abandoned on a chair in the corner, eyes wide in silent appeal. The clock on the mantelpiece ticks stolidly, and a music box stretches out "Rock-a-bye Baby" with a macabre, threatening air. It is drowned out by the cries coming from the backyard.

On the grass, the child is screaming, her face puce with fear and fury, the skin on her cheeks stretched tight and her tiny teeth exposed like keys on a miniature piano. She is trying to escape Hannah, who is picking her up each time she wrestles free and screams again.

"Grace, darling. Shh, shh, Grace. Come on, please."

The child yells hopelessly again, "I want my mamma. I want Dadda. Go 'way! I don't like you!"

There had been a great to-do when the police had reunited the mother with her child. Photographs had been taken, and thanks and praise lavished on the officers and on God in equal measure. Again, the tongues of the town were busy spreading news, tickling the air with tales of the dreamy look on the face of the child, the joyful smile of the mother. "The poor tot—she was so sleepy by the time she was delivered to her mum. Looked like an angel. You can only thank the good Lord that she was got out of the clutches of that dreadful man!" said Fanny Darnley, who had made it her business to extract the details from Constable Garstone's mother. Grace had been not drowsy, however, but on the fringes of consciousness, dosed with a strong sleeping draft by Dr. Sumpton when it was clear that she was hysterical at being parted from Isabel.

Now Hannah was locked in a stand-off with her terrified daughter. She had kept her so close to her heart all these years that it had never occurred to her that the child might not have done the same. When Septimus Potts came into the garden, he would have been hard-pressed to say which of the two figures he saw was more distressed.

"Grace, I'm not going to hurt you, my darling. Come to Mummy," Hannah was pleading.

"I'm not Grace! I'm Lucy!" cried the child. "I want to go home! Where's Mamma? You're not my mummy!"

Wounded more by each outburst, Hannah could only murmur, "I've loved you so long. So long . . ."

Septimus remembered his own helplessness as Gwen, at about the same age, had continued to demand her mother, as though he were hiding his late wife somewhere about the house. It still got him in the guts.

Hannah caught sight of her father. His expression betrayed his assessment of the situation, and humiliation washed through her.

"She just needs some time to get used to you. Be patient, Hanny," he said. The girl had found a safe nook behind the old lemon tree and the Cape gooseberry, where she stayed poised, ready to dart off.

"She's got no idea who I am, Dad. No idea. Of course. She won't come near me," Hannah wept.

"She'll come round," said Septimus. "She'll either get tired and fall asleep there, or get hungry and come out. Either way, it's just a question of waiting."

"I know, I know she has to get used to me again."

Septimus put an arm around her shoulder. "There's no 'again' about it. You're a whole new person for her."

"*You* try. Please, see if you can get her to come out . . . She ran away from Gwen too."

"She's seen enough new faces for one day, I'd say. She doesn't need my ugly mug on top of everything else. Just give her a bit of peace and quiet."

"What did I do wrong, to deserve all this, Dad?"

"None of this is your fault. She's your daughter, and she's right where she belongs. Just give it time, girlie. Give it time." He stroked her hair. "And I'll see to it that that Sherbourne fellow gets what's coming to him. That's a promise."

As he made his way back through the house, he found Gwen, standing in the shadows of the passageway, watching her sister. She shook her head and whispered, "Oh, Dad, it's just awful watching the poor little creature. It's enough to break your heart, all her crying." She gave a deep sigh. "Perhaps she'll get used to things," she said with a shrug, though her eyes said otherwise.

In the country around Partageuse, every life-form has its defenses. The ones you need to worry about least are the fast-movers, who survive by disappearing: the racehorse goanna, the parrots they call "twenty-eights," the brush-tailed possum. They're off at the slightest glint of trouble: retreat, evasion, camouflage—those are their survival tricks. Others are deadly only if you're the one in their sights. The tiger snake, the shark, the trapdoor spider: they'll use their means of attack to defend themselves against humans if threatened.

The ones to fear most stay still, unnoticed, their defenses undetected until you trigger them by accident. They make no distinctions. Eat the pretty heart-leaf poison bush, say, and your heart will stop. Such things are only trying to protect themselves. But Lord help you if you get too close. Only when Isabel Sherbourne was threatened were her defenses awakened.

Vernon Knuckey sat rapping his fingers on his desk as Isabel waited in the next room to be questioned. Partageuse was a fairly quiet place for a policeman. The odd assault or a bit of drunk and disorderly was the most the average week would dish up. The sergeant could have moved to Perth for promotion, and the chance to witness darker crimes—uglier scars on lives that meant less to him. But he had seen enough strife in the war to last him a lifetime. Petty thieving and fines for sly grog would do him. Kenneth Spragg, on the other hand, was itching to move to the Big Smoke. He'd go to town on this one if he got half a chance. Literally—he'd be treating it as his ticket up the ladder to Perth. He neither knew nor cared about anyone in Partageuse, thought Knuckey: Bill and Violet, for example, and the boys they had lost. He thought of all the years he'd seen little Isabel, with a beautiful voice and a face to match, singing in the church choir at Christmas. Then his thoughts swung to old Potts, devoted to those girls of his since his wife died, and crushed by Hannah's choice of husband. As for poor Hannah herself . . . Nothing to write home about on the looks front, but a real brain box, and a very decent sort. Always thought she had a screw loose believing her child would show up after all these years, but just look how things had turned out.

He took a deep breath as he turned the handle of the door and entered. Addressing Isabel, he was efficient, respectful. "Isabel—Mrs. Sherbourne—I have to ask you some more questions. I know he's your husband, but this is a very serious matter." He took the cap off his pen, and rested it on the paper. A puddle of black leaked from the nib, and he stroked it this way and that, stretching the ink out in lines from its central point.

"He says you wanted to report the boat's arrival and he stopped you. Is that right?"

Isabel looked at her hands.

"Says he resented you for not giving him children, and took things into his own hands."

The words struck deep within her. In telling the lie, had Tom revealed a truth?

"Didn't you try to talk sense into him?" Knuckey asked.

Truthfully, she said, "When Tom Sherbourne thinks he's doing the right thing, there's no persuading him otherwise."

He asked gently, "Did he threaten you? Assault you, physically?"

Isabel paused, and the fury of her sleepless night flooded back. She clung to silence like a rock.

Often enough Knuckey had seen the wives and daughters of timber workers bullied into submission with just a look by great hulks of men. "You were afraid of him?"

Her lips tightened. No words came out.

Knuckey put his elbows on the desk, and leaned forward. "Isabel, the law recognizes that a wife can be powerless at the hands of her husband. Under the Criminal Code, you're not responsible for anything he made you do or stopped you from doing, so you needn't worry on that score. You won't be punished for his crimes. Now, I need to ask you a question, and I want you to think very carefully. Remember, you can't get into trouble for anything he forced you into." He cleared his throat. "According to Tom, Frank Roennfeldt was dead when the boat washed up." He looked her in the eye. "Is that true?"

Isabel was taken aback. She could hear herself saying, "Of course it's true!" But before her mouth could open, her mind rushed again to Tom's betrayal. Suddenly overwhelmed—by the loss of Lucy, by anger, by sheer exhaustion, she closed her eyes.

The policeman prompted softly, "Is it true, Isabel?"

She fixed her gaze on her wedding ring as she said, "I've got nothing to say," and burst into tears.

Tom drank the tea slowly, watching the swirling steam vanish in the warm air. The afternoon light angled in through the high windows of the sparsely furnished room. As he rubbed the stubble on his chin, it brought back sensations from the days when shaving was impossible, and washing likewise.

"Want another one?" asked Knuckey evenly.

"No. Thanks."

"You smoke?"

"No."

"So. A boat washes up at the lighthouse. Out of nowhere."

"I told you all this out on Janus."

"And you'll tell me again as many times as I like! So. You find the boat."

"Yes."

"And it's got a baby in it."

"Yes."

"What state's the baby in?"

"Healthy. Crying, but healthy."

Knuckey was writing notes. "And there's a bloke in the boat."

"A body."

"A man," said Knuckey.

Tom looked at him, sizing up the rephrasing.

"You're pretty used to being the king of the castle out on Janus, are you?"

Tom considered the irony, which anyone who knew about life on the Lights would have registered, but he didn't answer. Knuckey went on, "Reckon you can get away with things. No one around."

"It had nothing to do with getting away with things."

"And you decided you might as well keep the baby out there. Isabel had lost yours. No one would ever know. That it?"

"I told you: I made the decision. Made Isabel go along with it."

"Knock your wife around, do you?"

Tom looked at him. "Is that what you think?"

"That why she lost the baby?"

Shock registered on Tom's face. "Did *she* say that?"

Knuckey stayed silent, and Tom took a deep breath. "Look, I've told you what happened. She tried to talk me out of it. I'm guilty of whatever you say I'm guilty of, so let's just get this over, and leave my wife out of it."

"*Don't* try to tell me what to do," Knuckey snapped. "I'm not your batman. I'll do what *I* decide to do when *I'm* good and ready." He pushed his chair out from the desk, and folded his arms. "The man in the boat . . ."

"What about him?"

"What state was he in, when you found him?"

"He was dead."

"You sure about that?"

"I've seen enough bodies in my time."

"Why should I believe you about this one?"

"Why should I lie?"

Knuckey paused, and let the question hang in the air, for his prisoner to feel the answer weigh down upon him. Tom shifted in his chair. "Exactly," said Knuckey. "Why should you lie?"

"My wife'll tell you he was dead when the boat washed up."

"The same wife you admit you forced to lie?"

"Look, it's completely different, sheltering a child and—"

"Killing someone?" Knuckey cut in.

"*Ask* her."

"I have," said Knuckey quietly.

"Then you know he was dead."

"I don't know anything. She refuses to talk about it."

Tom felt a hammer blow to his chest. He avoided Knuckey's eyes. "What *has* she said?"

"That she's got nothing to say."

Tom hung his head. "Christ all bloody mighty," he muttered under his breath, before responding, "Well all I can do is repeat what I said. I never saw that man alive." He knitted his fingers together. "If I can just see her, talk to her . . ."

"No chance of that. Besides the fact that it's not allowed, I get the impression she wouldn't talk to you if you were the last person on earth."

Quicksilver. Fascinating, but impossible to predict. It could bear the ton of glass in the light, but try to put your finger on a drop of it, and it would race away in any direction. The image kept coming into Tom's mind as he sat thinking about Isabel after Knuckey's questioning. He thought back to the days after the last stillbirth, when he had tried to comfort her.

"We'll be all right. If it's just you and me for the rest of our lives, that's enough for me."

Her eyes had slid up to meet his and her expression chilled him. It was despairing. Defeated.

He moved to touch her, but she drew away. "You'll get better. Things'll get better. Just give it time."

Without warning, she stood up and rushed to the door, doubling up for a moment from pain, before limping into the night.

"Izzy! For God's sake, stop. You'll hurt yourself!"

"I'll do more than that!"

The moon balanced in the warm, windless sky. The long, white nightgown Isabel had worn on their wedding night four years before glowed like a paper lantern as she stood, a tiny white dot, in an ocean of darkness. "I can't bear it!" she screamed in a voice so loud and shrill that the goats started from their sleep and began to move with a jangle of bells in their paddock. "I can't bear it any more! God, why do you make me live when my children die? I'd be better off dead!" She stumbled toward the cliff.

He rushed to gather her into his arms. "Calm down, Izz." But she broke free and ran again, half hobbling when the pain got too bad.

"Don't tell me to calm down, you stupid, stupid man! It's *your* fault. I hate this place! I hate you! I want my baby!" The light scythed a path far above, leaving her untouched by its beam.

"You didn't want him! That's why he died. He could tell you didn't care!"

"Come on, Izz. Come back inside."

"You don't *feel* anything, Tom Sherbourne! I don't know what you did with your heart but it's not inside you, that's for sure!"

A person could only take so much. He'd seen it often enough. Lads who'd turned up full of ginger and ready to give Fritz hell, who'd survived the shelling and the snow and the lice and the mud, for years sometimes. Then something in them just packed up and went home—went somewhere deep inside where they couldn't be touched. Or sometimes they turned on you, came at you with a bayonet, laughing like a maniac and crying at the same time. Christ, when he thought back to his own state by the time it was all over . . .

Who was he to judge Isabel? She'd reached her edge, that was all. Everyone had one. Everyone. And in taking Lucy away, he had driven her to it.

Late that night, Septimus Potts pulled off his boots and wiggled his toes in his fine woolen socks. He groaned at the familiar creaking of his back. He was sitting on the side of the solid jarrah bed carved out of a tree from his own forest. The only sound in the enormous room was the ticking of the carriage clock on the nightstand. He gave a sigh as he took in the finery—the starched linen, the gleaming furniture, the portrait of his late wife, Ellen—by the light of the electric lamps, shaded by frosted rose glass. The image of his granddaughter, distraught and cowering that afternoon, was still vivid: Baby Grace, given up for dead by everyone but Hannah. Life. Who the bloody hell could tell how it was going to turn out?

That distress, that despair at the loss of a mother—he never imagined he would see it again after Ellen's death, until confronted by his granddaughter in the garden. Just when he thought he'd seen all the tricks life could play, out it came with a new one, like an evil card sharp. He knew what the little girl was going through. A doubt seeped into a corner of his mind. Perhaps—perhaps it *was* cruel to keep her from the Sherbourne girl . . .

He looked again at the portrait of Ellen. Grace had the same jawline. Maybe she would grow up to be as beautiful as her grandmother. He wandered off into imaginings of Christmases and birthdays along the way. A happy family, that's all he wanted. He thought of Hannah's tortured face; remembered with guilt that same look when he'd tried to stop her marrying Frank.

No. This was the place for the child, with her true family. She'd have the top brick off the chimney. Eventually she'd get used to her real home and her real mother. If Hannah could just bear up that long.

He felt tears in his eyes, and anger fought its way to the surface. Someone should pay. Someone should be made to suffer the way his daughter had been made to suffer. Who could possibly come across a tiny baby and keep her, like a driftwood souvenir?

He drove out the intrusive doubt. He couldn't change the past, and the years he had refused to acknowledge Frank's existence, but he could make it up to Hannah now. Sherbourne would be punished. He would see to it.

He switched off the lamp, watching the moonlight glimmer on the silver framing Ellen's photograph. And he pushed away thoughts of what the Graysmarks must be feeling that night.

CHAPTER 27

Since her return, Isabel found herself constantly on the lookout for Lucy—where had she got to? Was it time for bed? What would she give her for lunch? Then her brain would correct her, remind her how things were now, and she would go through the agony of loss all over again. What was happening to her daughter? Who was feeding her? Undressing her? Lucy would be beside herself.

The image of the little girl's face as she was forced to swallow the bitter sleeping draft made Isabel's throat tighten. She tried to blot it out with other memories: Lucy playing in the sand; Lucy holding her nose as she jumped into the water; her face as she slept at night—at ease, safe, perfect. There was no more wonderful sight in the world than your child sleeping. Isabel's whole body bore the imprint of the little girl: her fingers knew the smoothness of her hair as she brushed it; her hips remembered the weight of her, and the tight locking of her legs around her waist; the warm softness of her cheek.

While she wandered through these scenes, sucking comfort from them like nectar from a dying flower, she was aware of something dark behind her, something she could not bear to look at. It would come to her in dreams, blurred and dreadful. It would call to her, "Izzy! Izzy, love . . ." but she could not turn around, and her shoulders would shoot up to her ears as if to escape a grasp. She would awaken, breathless and sick to the stomach.

All the while, Isabel's parents took her silence for misplaced loyalty. "There's nothing I can say," were her only words that day she first came home, and she repeated them whenever Bill and Violet tried to broach the subject of Tom and what had happened.

The cells at the back of the police station usually had to do no more than keep a drunk long enough to sleep it off, or give an angry husband time to see sense and promise not to take his temper out with his fists. Half the time, whoever was on duty didn't bother to lock the cell door, and if it was someone they knew, on a shift that was dragging, more often than not they'd have them out in the office playing cards, on the strict understanding that they wouldn't try to shoot through.

Today Harry Garstone was particularly excited, at last in charge of a serious criminal. He was still spitting chips that he'd been off duty the night a year ago when they brought in Bob Hitching from Karridale. The fellow had never been right in the head since Gallipoli. Got carried away with a meat cleaver and did in his brother from the next-door farm because they didn't see eye-to-eye over their mother's will. Ended up swinging for it. So now, Garstone was delighting in the niceties of procedure. He got the rule book out to check that he was following it to the letter.

When Ralph had asked to see Tom, the constable had made a great show of consulting the book, sucking his teeth, and sliding a pout from one side of his letterbox mouth to the other. "Sorry, Captain Addicott. I wish I could let you, but it says here—"

"Don't give me any of your nonsense, Harry Garstone, or I'll be on to your mother."

"It's quite specific, and—"

The walls in the station were thin, and the constable was interrupted by the voice of Vernon Knuckey, who rarely bothered to rise from his seat for such communications. "Don't be so bloody wet, Garstone. It's the lighthouse keeper in the cell, not Ned bloody Kelly. Let the man through."

The deflated constable gave the keys a vigorous jangle in protest as he led Ralph through a locked door, down some stairs and along a dark corridor until he arrived at a few cells with bars.

In one of them, Tom sat on a canvas bunk that folded out from the wall. He took in Ralph's face—drawn and gray.

"Tom," said the skipper.

"Ralph." Tom gave a nod.

"Came as soon as I could. Hilda says hello," he said, "and Blue," emptying his pockets of greetings like small change.

Tom nodded again.

The two sat in silence. After a while, Ralph said, "If you'd rather I left you . . ."

"No, it's good to see you. Just not much to say, sorry. All right if we don't talk for a bit?"

Ralph was full of questions, both his own and his wife's, but he sat out the silence on a rickety chair. The day was warming up and the wooden walls creaked, like a creature stretching as it awoke. Honeyeaters and willy-wagtails chirruped outside. Once or twice a vehicle sputtered down the road, drowning out the clicking of the crickets and cicadas.

Thoughts clamored in Ralph's mind and made it to his tongue, but he managed to stop them just in time. He put his hands under his thighs, to overcome his urge to shake Tom by the shoulders. Unable to resist any longer, he finally barked out, "In God's name, Tom, what's going on? What's all this about Lucy being the Roennfeldt baby?"

"It's true."

"But—How . . . What in hell . . . ?"

"I've explained it to the police, Ralph. I'm not proud of what I've done."

"Is this—is this what you were talking about putting right, that time on Janus?"

"It's not as simple as that." There was a long pause.

"Tell me what happened."

"Not much point, Ralph. I made a bad decision, back then, and it's time for me to pay for it."

"For God's sake, boy, at least let me help you!"

"There's nothing you can do. I'm in this one alone."

"Whatever you've done, you're a good man and I won't see you go down like this." He stood up. "Let me get you a decent lawyer—see what he makes of it all."

"Not much a lawyer can do now either, Ralph. A priest might be more use."

"But it's all tommy rot, what's being said about you!"

"Not all of it, Ralph."

"You tell me straight to my face that this was all your doing! That you threatened Isabel! You look me in the eye and tell me, and I'll leave you in peace, boy."

Tom inspected the grain of the timber in the wall.

"You see?" exclaimed Ralph in triumph. "You can do no such thing!"

"I was the one with the duty, not her." Tom looked at Ralph, and considered if there was anything at all he could tell him, explain to him, without jeopardizing Isabel. Finally, he said, "Izzy's suffered enough. She can't take any more."

"Putting yourself in the firing line's no way of dealing with it. This has all got to be sorted out properly."

"There's no sorting out, Ralph, and there's no going back. I owe her this."

Miracles were possible: it was official. In the days following Grace's return, Reverend Norkells experienced a decided increase in his congregation, particularly among the womenfolk. Many a mother who had given up hope of seeing her darling son again, and many a war widow, took to prayer with renewed vigor, no longer feeling foolish about praying for the hopeless. St. Jude had never received so much attention. Dull aches of loss reawakened, as raw longing was soothed by that balm so long exhausted—hope.

Gerald Fitzgerald was sitting opposite Tom, the table between them strewn with papers and pink legal tape from the brief. Tom's lawyer was short and balding, like a jockey in a three-piece suit, wiry but nimble. He had come down on the train from Perth the night before, and had read the brief over dinner at The Empress.

"You've been formally charged. Partageuse gets a circuit magistrate every two months, and he's just been, so you'll be held in custody here until he's back. You're a damn sight better off on remand here than Albany jail, that's for sure. We'll use the time to prepare for the committal hearing."

Tom looked at him with a question.

"That's the preliminary hearing to decide whether you've got a case to answer. If you have, you'll get committed for trial in Albany, or Perth. Depends."

"On what?" asked Tom.

"Let's go through the charges," said Fitzgerald, "and you'll find out." Once again he cast his eye over the list before him. "Well, they've certainly spread the net wide enough. WA Criminal Code, Commonwealth Public Service Act, WA Coroners Act, Commonwealth Crimes Act. A real dog's breakfast of State and Commonwealth charges." He smiled and rubbed his hands together. "That's what I like to see."

Tom raised an eyebrow.

"Means they're scraping around, not sure what they can get you on," the lawyer went on. "Neglect of Statutory Duty—that's two years and a fine. Improperly dealing with a body—two years hard labor. Failing to report a dead body—well," he scoffed, "that's just a ten-pound fine. Making a false statement to register a birth—two years hard labor and a two-hundred-pound fine." He scratched his chin.

Tom ventured, "What about the—the child-stealing charge?" It was the first time he had used the phrase, and he flinched at the sound of the words.

"Section 343 of the Criminal Code. Seven years hard labor." The lawyer screwed up his mouth and nodded to himself. "Your advantage, Mr. Sherbourne, is that the law covers the *usual*. Statutes are drafted to catch what happens *most* of the time. So section 343 applies to . . ." he picked up the dog-eared statute and read from it, "'any person who, with intent to deprive any parent of the possession of a child . . . forcibly or fraudulently takes or entices away, or detains the child . . .'"

"Well?" Tom asked.

"Well they'll never get up on that. Luckily for you, most of the time, babies don't leave their mothers unless someone takes them away. And they don't usually find their way to barely inhabited islands. You see? They can't make out the necessary elements of the offense. You didn't 'detain' the baby: legally speaking, she could have left any time she wanted. You certainly didn't 'entice her away.' And they can never prove 'intention to deprive' because we'll say you honestly believed the parents were dead. So I reckon I can get you off that one. And you're a war hero, a Military Cross and Bar. Most courts will still go easy on a bloke who risked his life for his country and never had a whiff of trouble."

Tom's face relaxed, but the lawyer's expression changed, as he continued, "But what they don't like, Mr. Sherbourne, is a liar. In fact, they dislike it so much that the penalty for perjury is seven years hard labor. And if that liar stops the real culprit getting what's coming to them, then that's perverting the course of justice, and that's another seven years. Do you get my drift?"

Tom gave him a look.

"The law likes to make sure that the right people are getting punished. Judges are a bit particular about that sort of thing." He stood up, and wandered to the window, gazing up through the bars into the trees beyond. "Now, if I walked into a court, and told a story of a poor woman, beside herself with grief over the loss of her stillborn baby—a woman who wasn't right in the head for a bit, couldn't tell right from wrong—and if I told the story of how her husband, who was a decent bloke, who'd always done his duty, but who, just this once, trying to make things better for his wife, let his heart get the better of his common sense, and went along with her idea . . . Well, I could sell that to a judge. I could sell it to a jury. The Court's got what we call 'the prerogative of mercy'—the right to impose a lesser sentence, for the wife too.

"But at the moment, I've got a man who by his own admission is not only a liar, but a bully. A man who, presumably worried that people will think he's got no lead in his pencil, decides to keep a tiny baby, and forces his wife to lie about it."

Tom straightened his back. "I've said what I've said."

Fitzgerald continued, "Now, if you're the sort of man who really would do something like that, then, for all the police know, you're the sort of person who might go even a step further to get what you want. If you're the sort of man who takes what he wants because he can, and who's prepared to make his wife act under duress, then perhaps you're the sort of man who's prepared to *kill* to get what he wants. We all know you did enough of that during the war." He paused. "That's what they might say."

"They haven't charged me with that."

"So far. But from what I hear, that copper from Albany's dying to get his hands on you. I've come across him before, and I can tell you, he's a right bastard."

Tom took a deep breath, and shook his head.

"And he's very excited that your wife won't corroborate your story about Roennfeldt being dead when you found him." He twirled the crimson tape from the brief around his finger. "She must really hate your guts." As he unwound it, he said slowly, "Now, she could hate your guts because you made her lie about keeping a baby. Or even because you killed a man. But I reckon it's more likely she hates your guts because you gave the game away."

Tom made no response.

"It's up to the Crown to prove how he died. With a bloke who's been underground for nearly four years, that's no easy task. Not that much left of him. No broken bones. No fractures. Documented history of heart trouble. Normally, that would probably lead to an open verdict by the Coroner. If you came clean and told the whole truth."

"If I plead guilty to all the charges—say I made Isabel go along with me, and there's no other evidence—no one can touch her: is that right?"

"Yes, but—"

"Then I'll take what's coming to me."

"Trouble is, there might be a lot more coming to you than you've bargained for," Fitzgerald said as he put the papers back in his briefcase. "We've got no idea what your wife's going to say you did or didn't do, if she ever decides to talk. If I were in your shoes, I'd be doing some damned hard thinking."

If people used to stare at Hannah before she got Grace back, they stared a lot harder afterward. They had expected some sort of miraculous transformation, like a chemical reaction, as mother and daughter met. But they were disappointed on that score: the child looked distressed and the mother distraught. Far from getting a bloom back in her cheeks, Hannah grew more gaunt, as every one of Grace's screams made her wonder whether she had done the right thing in reclaiming her.

Old logbooks from Janus had been requisitioned by the police as they examined the handwriting on the letters to Hannah: there was no mistaking the sure, steady penmanship in both. Nor was there any question as to the rattle Bluey had identified. It was the baby herself who had altered beyond recognition. Hannah had handed Frank a tiny, dark-haired infant weighing twelve pounds, and Fate had handed back to her a frightened, willful blonde changeling who could stand on her own two feet, walk, and scream until her face was scarlet and her chin wet with tears and dribble. The confidence Hannah had gained in handling her baby in the first weeks of her life was swiftly eroded. The rhythms of intimacy, the unspoken understandings, which she had assumed she could just pick up again, were lost to her: the child no longer responded in a way she could predict. They were like two dancers whose steps were foreign to one another.

Hannah was terrified by the moments when she lost patience with her daughter, who at first would eat and sleep and be bathed only after pitched battles, and later simply withdrew into herself. In none of her years of daydreams, or even her nightmares, had her imagination managed anything as awful as this.

In desperation, she took the child to Dr. Sumpton.

"Well," said the rotund doctor as he put his stethoscope back on his desk, "physically she's perfectly healthy." He pushed the jar of jelly beans in Grace's direction. "Help yourself, young lady."

The girl, still terrified from her first encounter with him at the police station, stayed mute, and Hannah offered her the jar. "Go on. Any color you like, darling." But her daughter turned her head away, and took up a strand of hair to curl around her finger.

"And she's been wetting the bed, you say?"

"Often. At her age, surely you'd normally expect—"

"You hardly need me to remind you that these aren't *normal* circumstances." He rang a bell on his desk and, after a discreet knock, a white-haired woman entered.

"Mrs. Fripp, take little Grace out to sit with you while I have a word to her mother, would you?"

The woman smiled. "Come on, dear, let's see if we can find a biscuit for you somewhere," she said, and led the listless child away.

Hannah began. "I don't know what to do, what to say. She still keeps asking for"—she stumbled—"for Isabel Sherbourne."

"What have you said about her?"

"Nothing. I've told her that I'm her mother and I love her and—"

"Well, you have to say *something* about Mrs. Sherbourne."

"But what?"

"My suggestion is that you just tell her she and her husband had to go away."

"Go away where, why?"

"It doesn't really matter at that age. Just as long as she has an answer to her question. She'll forget eventually—if there's nothing around to remind her of the Sherbournes. She'll get used to her new home. I've seen it often enough with adopted orphans and so forth."

"But she gets into such a state. I just want to do the right thing for her."

"You don't make an omelette without breaking eggs, I'm afraid, Mrs. Roennfeldt. Fate's dealt this little girl a pretty tough set of cards, and there's nothing you can do about that. Eventually those two will fade from her mind, as long as she doesn't keep in contact with them. And in the meantime, give her a drop of the sleeping draft if she's too anxious or unsettled. Won't do her any harm."

CHAPTER 28

"You stay away from that man, you hear me?"

"I've got to go and see him, Ma. He's been in the lockup for ages! This is all my fault!" lamented Bluey.

"Don't talk rubbish. You've reunited a baby with her mother, and you're about to pocket three thousand guineas reward." Mrs. Smart took the iron from the stove, and pressed the tablecloth harder with each sentence. "Use your loaf, boy. You've done your bit, now just keep out of it!"

"He's in more trouble than the early settlers, Ma. I don't reckon this is gonna turn out good for him."

"That's not your lookout, sonny. Now out the back and get on with weeding the rose bed."

By reflex, Bluey took a step toward the back door, as his mother muttered, "Oh, to have been left with the halfwit son!"

He stopped, and to her astonishment, pulled himself up to his full height. "Yeah, well I may be a halfwit, but I'm not a dobber. And I'm not the sort of bloke that deserts his mates." He turned and headed for the front door.

"Just where do you think you're going, Jeremiah Smart?"

"Out, Ma!"

"Over my dead body!" she snapped, blocking his way.

She was all of five feet tall. Bluey topped six foot. "Sorry," he said as he picked his mother up by the waist as easily as a piece of sandalwood, and put her down lightly to one side. He left her, jaw agape, eyes flaming, as he walked out of the door and down the front path.

Bluey took in the scene. The tiny space, the slop bucket in the corner, the tin mug on a table that was bolted to the floor. In all the years he had known Tom, he had never seen him unshaven; never seen his hair uncombed, his shirt creased. Now he had dark gulleys under his eyes, and his cheekbones rose like ridges above his square jaw.

"Tom! Good to see you, mate," declared the visitor, in a phrase that brought them both back to days of jetty landings and long voyages, when they were, truly, glad to see one another.

Bluey tried to look at Tom's face, but could not negotiate the space between the bars, so either the face or the bars were out of focus. He searched for a few moments before coming up with, "How are things?"

"I've been better."

Bluey fidgeted with the hat in his hands until he screwed up his courage. "I'm not going to take the reward, mate." The words tumbled out. "Wouldn't be right."

Tom looked off to his side for a moment. "Thought there must have been some reason you didn't come out with the troopers." He sounded uninterested rather than angry.

"I'm sorry! Ma made me do it. I never should have listened to her. I wouldn't touch the money with a barge pole."

"Might as well be you gets it as some other bloke. Makes no difference to me now."

Whatever Bluey was expecting from Tom, it was not this indifference. "What happens next?"

"Buggered if I know, Blue."

"Is there anything you need? Anything I can get you?"

"A bit of sky and some ocean'd be nice."

"I'm serious."

"So am I." Tom took a deep breath as he considered a thought. "There *is* something you could do. You could look in on Izzy for me. She'll be at her parents'. Just . . . see she's OK. She'll be taking it hard. Lucy meant the world to her," and he stopped because a crack had found its way into his voice. "Tell her—I understand. That's all. Tell her that I understand, Bluey."

Though the young man felt utterly out of his depth, he took his commission like a sacred charge. He would convey the message as if his own life depended on it.

Once Bluey had gone, Tom lay down on the bunk, and wondered again how Lucy was; how Isabel was coping. He tried to think of any other way he could have done things, starting from that very first day. Then he remembered Ralph's words—"no point in fighting your war over and over until you get it right." Instead, he sought comfort in perspective: in his mind's eye, he mapped out on the ceiling the exact position the stars would be in that night, starting with Sirius, always the brightest; the Southern Cross; then the planets—Venus and Uranus—all easily visible in the sky over the island. He traced the constellations as they slid their way across the roof of the world from dusk till dawn. The precision of it, the quiet orderliness of the stars, gave him a sense of freedom. There was nothing he was going through that the stars had not seen before, somewhere, some time on this earth. Given enough time, their memory would close over his life like healing a wound. All would be forgotten, all suffering erased. Then he remembered the star atlas and Lucy's inscription: "for ever and ever and ever and ever," and the pain of the present flooded back.

He said a prayer for Lucy. "Keep her safe. Let her have a happy life. Let her forget me." And for Isabel, lost in the darkness, "Bring her home, back to her self, before it's too late."

Bluey shuffled his feet and silently rehearsed his speech again as he stood at the Graysmarks' front door. When it opened, Violet stood before him, her face wary.

"Can I help you?" she asked, the formality a shield against any new unpleasantness.

"Afternoon, Mrs. Graysmark." When she made no acknowledgment, he said, "I'm Bl— Jeremiah Smart."

"I know who you are."

"I wonder if—do you think I could have a word with Mrs. Sherbourne?"

"She's not up to visitors."

"I—" He was about to give up, but remembered Tom's face, and persisted, "I won't hold her up. I just have to—"

Isabel's voice drifted out from the darkened lounge room. "Let him in, Ma."

Her mother scowled. "You'd better come through. Mind you wipe your feet," and she stared at his boots while he wiped, and wiped them again, on the brush doormat, before following her.

"It's all right, Ma. No need to stay," said Isabel from her chair.

Isabel looked as bad as Tom, Bluey thought: gray-skinned and empty. "Thanks for—for seeing me . . ." He faltered. The rim of his hat was damp where he clutched it. "I've been to see Tom."

Her face clouded and she turned away.

"He's in a real bad way, Mrs. S. A real bad way."

"And he sent you to tell me that, did he?"

Bluey continued to fidget with his hat. "No. He asked me to give you a message."

"Oh?"

"He said to tell you he understands."

She could not keep the surprise from her face. "Understands what?"

"Didn't say. Just said to tell you."

Her eyes remained fixed on Bluey, but she was not looking at him.

After a long time, in which he blushed deeper at being stared at, she said, "Well then, you've told me." She rose slowly to her feet. "I'll show you out."

"But—well?" asked Bluey, shocked.

"Well what?"

"What should I tell him back? I mean—a message or something?" She didn't answer. "He's always been good to me, Mrs. S . . . You both have."

"It's through here," she said, guiding him to the front door.

As she closed it behind him, she leaned her face against the wall, shaking.

"Oh, Isabel, darling!" her mother exclaimed. "Come and have a lie-down, there's a girl," she said, and led her to her room.

"I'm going to be sick again," said Isabel, and Violet maneuvered the old china basin onto her daughter's lap just in time.

Bill Graysmark prided himself on being a good judge of people. As a headmaster, he got to observe human character in the process of formation. He was rarely wrong about which ones would do well for themselves in life, and which would come a cropper. Nothing in his gut told him Tom Sherbourne was a liar, or a violent man. Just to see him with Lucy was enough to show that the child hadn't the least fear of him. And he couldn't have asked for someone to cherish his daughter more.

But, having lost the only grandchild he would ever have, Bill's loyalty was to his one surviving child. His instinctive judgment was elbowed aside: blood was thicker than water—God knows he'd learned that the hard way.

"It's a terrible business, Vernon. A terrible business. Poor Isabel's a wreck," he said, as they sat in the corner of the pub.

"As long as she gives evidence against Tom," said Knuckey, "she's got nothing to worry about."

Bill questioned him with a look.

"She's not criminally liable for anything he made her do, so she just needs to put her side of the story. She's what we call 'competent but not compellable' as a witness for this sort of case," the policeman explained. "Her evidence is admissible—the Court says it's as good as anyone's. But you can't force a wife to testify against her husband. And of course, he's got the right to remain silent. We can't make him say anything against her either, if he doesn't want to, and he's made it quite clear he's not going to say a word." He paused. "Isabel—did she ever seem, well, uneasy about the child?"

Bill shot him a glance. "Let's not get dragged off the point here, Vernon."

Knuckey let it pass. He mused aloud, "Being a lighthouse keeper's a position of trust, you know. Our whole country—the whole world, if you want to look at it that way—depends on them being men of good character: honest, decent. We can't have them running around falsifying government records, coercing their wives. Let alone doing whatever it was he did to Frank Roennfeldt before he buried him." He registered the alarm on Bill's face, but continued, "No. Best put a stop to that sort of thing right away. Magistrate will be here in a few weeks for the committal hearing. Given what Sherbourne's said so far, well . . . He'll probably be sent to Albany, where the Court's got power to dish out harsher penalties. Or they could really take against him and drag him up to Perth. Spragg's looking for any hint that the fellow wasn't dead when he reached Janus." As he drained the last of his beer, he said, "Things don't look good for him, Bill, I can tell you that much."

"Do you like books, darling?" Hannah ventured. She had been trying everything she could think of to build a bridge with her daughter. She herself had loved stories as a child, and one of the few memories she could still muster of her own mother was being read *The Tale of Peter Rabbit,* one sunny afternoon on the lawns of Bermondsey. She remembered clearly the pale blue silk of her mother's blouse, the scent she wore—something floral and rare. And her mother's smile—the greatest treasure of all. "What's that word?" she was asking Hannah. "You know that word, don't you?"

"Carrot," Hannah had proclaimed proudly.

"Clever Hannah!" Her mother had smiled. "You're as bright as a button." The memory faded out there, like the end of a story, so she would start it again, over and over.

Now she tried to tempt Grace with the same book. "You see? It's about a rabbit. Come and read it with me."

But the child looked at her sullenly. "I want my Mamma. I hate the book!"

"Oh, come on, you haven't even looked at it." She took a breath and tried again. "Just one page. Let's read one page and if you don't like it, we'll stop."

The girl snatched the book from her hands and threw it at her, the corner striking Hannah's cheek, narrowly missing her eye. Then she darted from the room, running straight into Gwen, who was coming in at the same moment.

"Hey, hey there, missie!" said Gwen. "What have you done to Hannah? Go and say sorry!"

"Leave her be, Gwen," said Hannah. "She didn't mean any harm. It was an accident." She picked up the book and put it carefully on the shelf. "I thought I might try her with some chicken soup for dinner tonight. Everyone likes chicken soup, don't they?" she asked, without much conviction.

Hours later, she was on her hands and knees, mopping up the soup her daughter had vomited on the floor.

"When you think about it, what did we ever really know about him? All the stories about being from Sydney—that could all be a furphy. All we know for certain is that he's not from Partageuse." Violet Graysmark was speaking to Bill when their daughter was safely asleep. "What sort of man is he? Waits until she can't live without the child, then whisks her away." Her eyes were on the framed photograph of her granddaughter. She had removed it from the mantelpiece, and was stowing it under the linen in her underwear drawer.

"But, well, what do you make of it, Vi? Really?"

"For heaven's sake. Even if he didn't hold a gun to her head, he's still responsible. She was clearly beside herself with losing that third baby. And to blame her for it . . . It was up to him to stick to the rules then and there, if that's what he was going to do. Not start backtracking years later, when so many people were affected. We live with the decisions we make, Bill. That's what bravery is. Standing by the consequences of your mistakes."

Bill said nothing, and as she rearranged the dainty bags of lavender, she continued, "It was rubbing salt in the wound, to put his own guilty conscience above what it would do to Isabel or to Lucy, or"—she put her hand on his—"to us, for that matter, dear. Not a thought for us in any of this business. As if we hadn't had enough to deal with along the way." A tear glistened in her eye. "Our little granddaughter, Bill. All that love . . ." She closed the drawer slowly.

"Come on, Vi, dear. I know it's hard on you. I know," said her husband, and he hugged his wife close, noticing her hair was shot through with gray these days. The two of them stood in the embrace, Violet weeping, Bill saying, "I was such a fool to believe the bad days were over." Without warning, a great sob escaped him, and he hugged her tighter still, as if it might physically halt this new shattering of his family.

Having cleaned up the floor, and with her daughter finally asleep, Hannah sits by the little bed and gazes at her. In the day, it is impossible. Grace hides her face if she thinks she is being watched. She turns her back, or runs into another room.

Now, by the light of a single candle, Hannah can observe every aspect of her, and in the curve of her cheek, in the shape of her eyebrows, she sees Frank. It makes her heart swell, and she can almost believe that if she spoke to the sleeping figure, it would be Frank who answered. The flame, throwing shadows that twitch with the rhythm of her daughter's breath, catches the golden glint of her hair, or the glistening of a fine filament of dribble that trails from the corner of the translucent pink mouth.

Hannah is only slowly aware of the wish that has formed itself at the back of her mind: that Grace could stay asleep, for days, for years, if need be, until all memory of those people, of that life, has ebbed away. She feels that peculiar hollowness inside her, which came the first time she saw distress on the face of the returned child. If only Frank were here. He would know what to do, how to get through this. No matter how many times life knocked him down, he was always straight back on his feet, with a smile and no hard feelings.

Hannah casts her mind back to see a tinier figure—her perfect baby, a week old—and hears again Frank's lullaby, *"Schlaf, Kindlein, schlaf,"* "Sleep, little child, sleep." She recalls the way he would gaze into the cot and whisper to her in German. "I'm whispering her good things for her dreams," he would say. "As long as one has good things in the mind, one can be happy. This I know."

Now, Hannah straightens her back. Just the memory is enough to give her courage to face the next day. Grace is her daughter. Something in the child's soul will surely remember, recognize her, eventually. She just needs to take things a day at a time, as her father says. Soon enough, the little girl will be hers again, will be the joy she was on the day she was born.

Quietly, she blows out the candle, and makes her way from the room by the light which slides along the floor from the open door. When she climbs into her own bed, she is struck by how empty it feels.

Isabel paces. It is three o'clock in the morning, and she has slipped out through the back door of her parents' house. A ghost gum has trapped the moon between two of its long branches like spindly fingers. The dry grass crackles faintly under her bare feet as she walks on it—from the jacaranda to the flame tree, from the flame tree to the jacaranda: the place of the old wicket, all those years ago.

She is flicking in and out of understanding, in and out of being, in that fluttering of thoughts that came originally with the loss of her first baby, and grew with the snatching away of two more, and now Lucy. And the Tom she loved, the Tom she married, has disappeared too in the fog of deceit—slipping away when she wasn't looking: running off with notes to another woman; plotting to take her daughter away.

"I understand." Tom's message is puzzling. Her gut tightens in a knot of fury and longing. Her thoughts fly out in all directions, and just for a moment she has a bodily memory of being nine, on a runaway horse. The tiger snake on the track. A sudden rearing and off the horse shot, between the trunks, heedless of the branches and the child clinging desperately to its mane. Isabel had lain flat against its neck until its fear and its muscles were exhausted, and it finally came to a halt in a clearing nearly a mile away. "There's nothing you can do," her father had said. "Once a horse bolts, you can only say your prayers and hang on for all you're worth. Can't stop an animal that's caught in a blind terror."

There's no one she can talk to. No one who will understand. What sense can her life make by itself, without the family she lived for? She runs her fingers over the bark of the jacaranda and finds the scar—the mark Alfie carved in it to show her height, the day before he and Hugh left for France. "Now, I'll be checking how much you've grown when we come back, Sis, so mind you get on with it."

"When will you be back, really?" she had asked.

The boys had shot one another a look—both worried and excited. "By the time you reach here," Hugh had said, and nicked the bark six inches higher. "Once you get there, we'll be home to bother you again, Bella."

She never grew that tall.

The scurrying of a gecko brings her back to the present, back to her predicament. The questions harangue her as the moon languishes in the branches above: who is Tom, really? This man she thought she knew so well. How could he be capable of such betrayal? What has her life with him been? And who were the souls—that blending of her blood with his—who failed to find their way into being within her? A goblin thought jumps onto her shoulder: what's the point of tomorrow?

The weeks following Grace's return were more harrowing for Hannah than the weeks following her loss, as she was faced with truths which, long pushed away, were now inescapable. Years really had passed. Frank really was dead. Part of her daughter's life had gone and could never be brought back. While Grace had been absent from Hannah's days, she had been present in someone else's. Her child had lived a life without her: without, she caught herself thinking, a moment's thought for her. With shame, she realized she felt betrayed. By a baby.

She remembered Billy Wishart's wife, and how her joy at the return of a husband she had believed dead on the Somme had turned to despair. The gas victim who came home to her was as much a stranger to himself as to his family. After struggling for five years, one morning when the ice was thick on the water in their tank, she had stood on an upturned milking bucket in the cowshed and hanged herself, leaving her children to cut her down because Billy still couldn't grip a knife.

Hannah prayed for patience and strength and understanding. Every morning, she asked God to help her get through to the end of the day.

One afternoon as she was passing the nursery, she heard a voice. She slowed her pace and tiptoed closer to the door, which was ajar. She felt a thrill to see her daughter playing with her dolls at last: all her attempts to get her to play had been rejected. Now pieces of a toy tea set were strewn about on the bedcovers. One doll still wore its exquisite lace dress, but the other had been stripped to a camisole and long bloomers. On the lap of the one with the skirt lay a wooden clothes peg. "Dinnertime," said the skirted doll, as the child held the tiny teacup to the clothes peg and made "nyum nyum" noises. "Good little girl. Now time for bed, sweetie. Ni-nigh," and the doll lifted the peg to its lips to kiss it. "Look, Dadda," it went on, "Lucy's sleeping," as it touched the clothes peg with a dainty hand. "Goodnight, Lulu, good night, Mamma," said the doll in bloomers. "Got to light up now. Sun's nearly down." And off the doll trotted under the blanket. The doll with the skirt said, "Don't worry, Lucy. The witch can't catch you, I maked her dead."

Before she knew what she was doing, Hannah marched in and snatched the dolls away. "That's enough of those silly games, you hear me?" she snapped, and smacked her daughter's hand. The child's limbs stiffened but she did not cry—she just watched Hannah silently.

Instantly, Hannah was flooded with remorse. "Darling, I'm sorry! I'm so sorry. I didn't mean to hurt you." She remembered the doctor's instructions. "They've gone, those people. They did a bad thing, keeping you away from home. And they've gone now." Grace looked puzzled at the mention of home, and Hannah sighed. "One day. One day it'll make sense."

By lunchtime, as Hannah sobbed in the kitchen, ashamed of her outburst, her daughter was playing the game again, with three clothes pegs instead. Hannah stayed up late into the night, stitching and cutting, so that in the morning, the child awoke to a new rag doll on her pillow—a little girl, with "Grace" embroidered on her pinafore.

"I can't bear the thought of what it must be doing to her, Ma," said Isabel, as the two women sat together on wicker chairs under the eaves at the back of the house. "She'll be missing us, missing home. The poor little thing won't know what on earth's going on."

"I know, dear. I know," replied her mother.

Violet had made her a cup of tea and settled it on to her lap. Her daughter had altered dreadfully—sunken eyes shadowed beneath in gray; hair dull and tangled.

Isabel spoke aloud the thought that had occurred to her, perhaps to understand it better. "There's never been a funeral . . ."

"What do you mean?" asked Violet. Isabel was not making much sense, these days.

"Everyone I've lost—they've just been ripped away—into nothing. Maybe a funeral would have made it—I don't know—made a difference. With Hugh there's the photo of the grave in England. Alfie's just a name on that memorial. My first three babies—*three,* Mum—never had so much as a hymn sung for them. And now . . ." her voice broke into tears, "Lucy . . ."

Violet had been glad she'd never given her sons a funeral: a funeral was proof. Indisputable. A funeral meant admitting that your boys were absolutely dead. And buried. It was a betrayal. No funeral meant that one day they might waltz into the kitchen and ask what was for dinner and laugh with her about that silly mistake which had led her to believe for a moment—imagine that!—that they'd gone forever.

She considered her words carefully. "Sweetheart, Lucy's not *dead.*" Isabel seemed to shrug off the comment, and her mother frowned. "None of this is your fault, dear. I'll never forgive that man."

"I thought he loved me, Mum. He told me I was the most precious thing in the world to him. Then he did such a dreadful thing . . ."

Later, as Violet polished the silver frames of the pictures of her sons, she went over the situation in her mind for the umpteenth time. Once a child gets into your heart, there's no right or wrong about it. She'd known women give birth to children fathered by husbands they detested, or worse, men who'd forced themselves on them. And the woman had loved the child fiercely, all the while hating the brute who'd sired it. There's no defending yourself from love for a baby, Violet knew too well.

CHAPTER 29

"Why are you protecting her?"

The question arrested Tom, who eyed Ralph warily through the bars. "Plain as the nose on your bloody face, mate. As soon as I mention Isabel, you go all queer and make no sense."

"I should have protected her better. Protected her from me."

"Don't talk bilge."

"You've been a good friend to me, Ralph. But—there's a lot about me you don't know."

"And there's a lot about you I do, boy."

Tom stood up. "Did the engine get sorted out? Bluey said you'd been having problems with it."

Ralph looked at him carefully. "It's not looking good."

"She's served you well, over the years, that boat."

"Yep. I've always trusted her, and I didn't think she'd ever let me down. Fremantle wants to decommission her." He looked Tom in the eye. "We're all dead soon enough. Who are you to throw away the best years of your life?"

"The best years of my life were over a long time ago, Ralph."

"That's codswallop and you know it! It's about time you got on your feet and did something! For Christ's sake wake up to your bloody self!"

"What are you suggesting I do, Ralph?"

"I'm suggesting you tell the bloody truth, whatever it is. The only place lying leads is trouble."

"Sometimes that's the only place telling the truth gets you, too . . . People can only take so much, Ralph. Christ—I know that better than anyone. Izzy was just an ordinary, happy girl until she got tangled up with me. None of this would have happened if she hadn't come out to Janus. She thought it'd be paradise. She had no idea what she was in for. I should never have let her come out."

"She's a grown woman, Tom."

He looked at the skipper, weighing his next words. "Ralph, I've had this coming a long time. Sins catch up with you in the end." He sighed, and looked up at a spiderweb in the corner of his cell, where a few flies hung like forlorn Christmas decorations. "I should have been dead years ago. God knows I should have copped a bullet or a bayonet a hundred times over. I've been on borrowed time a long while." He swallowed hard. "It's tough enough on Izz being without Lucy. She'd never survive time in— Ralph, this is one thing I can do for her. It's as close to making it up to her as I'll ever get."

"It's not fair." The child repeats this phrase over and over, not in a whingeing tone, but in a desperate appeal to reason. Her expression is that of someone trying to explain an English phrase to a foreigner. "It's not fair. I want to go home."

Sometimes, Hannah manages to distract her for a few hours. Making cakes with her. Cutting out paper dolls. Putting crumbs out for the fairy wrens, so that the tiny creatures come right to the door and hop about on legs as fine as fuse wire, enthralling Grace while they peck daintily at the stale bread.

When she sees Grace's expression of delight at the tabby cat they pass one day, she asks around town if anyone has any kittens, and a tiny black creature with white paws and face becomes part of the household.

Grace is interested, but suspicious. "Go on, he's yours. All for you," says Hannah, putting the kitten gently into her hands. "So you have to help look after him. Now, what do you think his name should be?"

"Lucy," says the child, without hesitation.

Hannah balks. "I think Lucy's a little girl's name, not a cat's name," she says. "What about a proper cat's name?"

So Grace gives the only cat's name she knows. "Tabatha Tabby."

"Tabatha Tabby it is," Hannah says, resisting the urge to tell her it's not a tabby cat, and it's not a girl. At least she's got the child to speak.

The next day, when Hannah says, "Come on, shall we give Tabatha some mince?" Grace responds, fiddling with a strand of hair, "She doesn't like you. She only likes me." There's no malice. Just explaining a fact.

"Perhaps you should let her see Isabel Sherbourne," Gwen suggested after a particularly fierce round between mother and child over putting on a pair of shoes.

Hannah looked horrified. "Gwen!"

"I know it's the last thing you want to hear. But I'm just saying . . . maybe if Grace thought you were a friend of her mother's, that might help somehow."

"A *friend* of her mother's! How could you even say such a thing! Besides, you know what Dr. Sumpton said. The sooner she forgets about that woman, the better!"

But she could not escape the fact that her daughter had been irrevocably embossed with the stamp of those other parents, that other life. When they walked by the beach, Grace strained to get to the water. At night, whereas most children would be pleased to identify the moon, Grace could point to the brightest star of the evening and declare, "Sirius! And the Milky Way," in a voice so confident that it frightened Hannah, and made her hurry inside, saying, "Time for bed now. In we go."

Hannah prayed to be freed from resentment, from bitterness. "Lord, I'm so blessed to have my daughter back. Show me the right thing to do." But straightaway she would imagine Frank, thrown into an unmarked grave in a piece of canvas. She remembered the look on his face the first time he had held his daughter, as though she had presented him with the whole of heaven and earth in that pink blanket.

It was not up to her. It was only right that Tom Sherbourne should be dealt with according to the law. If a court decided he should go to jail—well, an eye for an eye, the Bible said. She would let justice take its course.

But then she would remember the man who had stepped in to save her from God knew what, years ago on that boat. She remembered how safe she'd suddenly felt in his presence. The irony made her catch her breath even now. Who could tell what someone was like on the inside? She'd seen that air of authority he'd adopted with the drunk. Did he think he was above the rules? Or beyond them? But the two notes, that beautiful handwriting: "Pray for me." So she would return to her prayers, and pray for Tom Sherbourne too: that he be dealt with justly, even though some part of her wanted to see him suffer for what he had done.

The following afternoon, Gwen slipped her arm into her father's, as they walked along the grass. "I miss this place, you know," she said, looking back toward the grand limestone homestead.

"It misses you, Gwenny," her father replied. After a few more steps he said, "Now that Grace is home with Hannah, perhaps it's time you came back to your old Dad . . ."

She bit her lip. "I'd love to. I really would. But . . ."

"But what?"

"I don't think Hannah can manage yet." She pulled away and faced her father. "I hate to be the one to say it, Dad, but I don't know she'll ever cope. And that poor little girl! I didn't know a child could be that miserable."

Septimus touched her cheek. "I know a little girl who used to be that miserable. Fair broke my heart, you did. Went on for months after your mother died." He stooped to smell one of the old red roses, just past its full, velvet bloom. He breathed the scent deep into his lungs, then put his hand on his back to straighten up.

"But that's the sad thing," insisted Gwen. "*Her* mother's not dead. She's here in Partageuse."

"Yes. *Hannah* is right here in Partageuse!"

She knew her father well enough not to press the point. They continued to walk in silence, Septimus inspecting the flower beds, Gwen trying not to hear the sound of her niece's distress, so sharply etched in her mind.

That night, Septimus thought hard about what to do. He knew a thing or two about little girls who had lost their mother. And he knew a thing or two about persuasion. When he had settled on his plan, he nodded off to a dreamless sleep.

In the morning, he drove to Hannah's, and announced, "Right. All ready? We're going on a mystery outing. It's about time Grace got to know Partageuse a bit better; learned where she's from."

"But I'm in the middle of mending the curtains. For the church hall. I promised Reverend Norkells . . ."

"I'll take her by myself. She'll be right as rain."

The "mystery outing" began with a trip to Potts's Timber Mill. Septimus had remembered how, as children, Hannah and Gwen had delighted in feeding apples and cube sugar to the Clydesdales there. The wood was moved by rail these days, but the mill still kept some of the old draft horses for emergencies, when rain washed away sections of rail track in the forest.

Patting one of the horses, he said, "This, young Grace, is Arabella. Can you say 'Arabella'?

"Rig her up to the cart, there's a good lad," said Septimus to the stable hand, who jumped to. A short while later, he led Arabella into the yard, drawing a sulky.

Septimus hoisted Grace on to the seat, before climbing up beside her. "Let's have an explore, shall we?" he said, and gave a giddy-up to the old horse's reins.

Grace had never seen such a big horse. She had never been in a real forest—the closest she had got was her ill-starred adventure in the scrubland behind the Graysmarks' house. For most of her life, she had only ever seen two trees—the Norfolk pines on Janus. Septimus followed the old milling tracks through the towering karri, pointing out kangaroos and goannas here and there: the child was engrossed in the fairy-tale world. From time to time she picked out a bird or a wallaby. "What's that?" And her grandfather would name the creature.

"Look, a baby kangaroo," she said, pointing to a marsupial hopping slowly near the track.

"That's not a baby 'roo. That little chap's a quokka. Like a kangaroo but tiny. That's as big as he'll ever get." He patted her head. "It's good to see you smile, girlie. I know you've been sad . . . You miss your old life." Septimus considered for a moment. "I know what that's like because—well, that's what happened to me."

The girl gave a puzzled look, and he continued, "I had to say goodbye to my mum, and go across the sea, all the way to Fremantle on a sailing ship. When I was just a little bit older than you. Hard to imagine, I know. But I came here, and I got a new mum and dad, called Walt and Sarah. They looked after me from then on. And they loved me just like my Hannah loves you. So sometimes, you don't just have one family in your life."

Grace's face gave no clue as to what she had made of this conversation, so he changed tack. As the horse walked on gently, the sun came dappling through the high branches here and there. "Do you like the trees?"

Grace nodded.

Septimus pointed to some saplings. "See—little trees, growing back. We chop down the big old ones, and new ones take their places. Everything grows back, if you give it time. By the time you're my age, that tree'll be a giant. It'll come good." A thought occurred to him. "This forest will belong to *you* one day. It'll be your forest."

"*My* forest?"

"Well, it belongs to me, and one day it'll belong to your mummy and your Auntie Gwen, and then it'll be yours. What do you think of that?"

"Can I giddy up the horse?" she asked.

Septimus laughed. "Give me your hands and we'll hold the reins together."

"Here she is, safe and sound," said Septimus as he delivered Grace to Hannah.

"Thanks, Dad." She bobbed down to her daughter's level. "Did you have a lovely day?"

Grace nodded.

"And did you pat the horses?"

"Yes," she said softly, rubbing her eyes.

"It's been a long day, sweetie. It's time for a bath, and then we'll get you to bed."

"He gived me the forest," said Grace, with the trace of a smile, and Hannah's heart skipped.

After Grace's bath that evening, Hannah sat on the little girl's bed. "I'm so glad you had a good day. Tell me all about the things you saw, sweetheart."

"A quotta."

"Pardon?"

"A quotta that's little and hops."

"Ah! A quokka! Sweet little things, aren't they? And what else?"

"A big horse. I drove it."

"Do you remember its name?"

The girl thought. "Araballa."

"Arabella, that's right. She's lovely. She's got friends there too—Samson, and Hercules, and Diana. Arabella's quite old now, you know. But she's still very strong. Did Granddad show you the timber whims she can pull?" The girl looked confused, and Hannah said, "The great big carts, with just two huge wheels. That's how they used to pull the big trees out of the forest once they cut them down." The child shook her head, and Hannah said, "Oh, my darling. There's so much I want to show you. You'll love the forest, I promise."

As Grace drifted off to sleep, Hannah stayed beside her, planning. She would show her the wildflowers when spring came. She would get a little pony for her—a Shetland, perhaps, so they could ride through the narrow forest trails together. A vista of decades suddenly opened out in her imagination, and she dared to explore them. "Welcome home," she whispered to her sleeping daughter. "Welcome home at last, my darling," and she went about her duties that evening humming under her breath.

CHAPTER 30

Partageuse has only so many people, and only so many places those people can be. Sooner or later, you're bound to bump into someone you'd rather avoid.

It had taken days for Violet to persuade her daughter to leave the house. "Come on, just come for a walk with me while I pop into Mouchemore's. I need some more wool for that bedcover I'm doing." No more sweet cardigans. No more diminutive Liberty lawn dresses. These days she was back to crocheting blankets for the last of the wretches languishing in the Repat home. Well, it kept her hands busy, even if it couldn't always occupy her mind.

"Mum, really, I don't feel up to it. I'll just stay here."

"Oh, come on, darling."

As the pair walked down the street, people tried not to look too obviously. A few offered polite smiles, but there was none of the old "How are things, Vi?" or "See you at church on Sunday?" No one was sure how to treat this mourning that wasn't for a death. Some crossed the street to avoid them. Townsfolk read the newspapers to extract what gobbets they could, but things had gone quiet of late.

As Violet and her daughter passed through the doors of the haberdasher's, Fanny Darnley, on her way out, gave a little gasp, and halted outside, wide-eyed with alarm and relish.

The shop smelled of lavender polish, and old roses from the potpourri set out in a basket near the cash register. High up the walls on all sides ranked bolts of cloth—damasks and muslins, linens and cottons. There were rainbows of thread and clouds of balled wool. Cards of lace—thick, thin, Brussels, French—lay on the table where Mr. Mouchemore was serving an elderly woman. All the way from the counter at the far end, a row of tables lined the store on each side, with chairs for the comfort of customers.

Seated at one of the tables with their backs to Isabel were two women. One was blonde; the other, who was dark-haired, was considering a bolt of pale lemon linen unrolled before her. At her side, glum and fidgeting with a rag doll, was a little blonde girl, immaculately turned out in a pink smocked dress, her white socks trimmed with lace.

As the woman examined the cloth, asking the attendant questions about price and quantity, the little girl's eyes drifted up to see who had come in. She dropped the doll and scrambled down from the chair. "Mamma!" she called, dashing to Isabel. "Mamma! Mamma!"

Before anyone could take in what had happened, Lucy had wrapped her arms around Isabel's legs and was holding as fast as a crab.

"Oh Lucy!" Isabel bundled her up and hugged her, letting the child snuggle into her neck. "Lucy, my darling!"

"That bad lady took me, Mamma! She did smack me!" the child whimpered, pointing.

"Oh, my poor, poor sweetheart!" Isabel was squeezing the girl to her, sobbing at the touch of her, the legs fitting snugly around her waist and the head slotting automatically into the space beneath her chin, like the final piece of a jigsaw. She was oblivious to anything and anyone else.

Hannah watched, stricken: humiliated, and despairing at the magnetic pull Isabel exerted on Grace. For the first time, the enormity of the theft came home to her. Right in front of her was the evidence of all that had been stolen. She saw the hundreds of days and the thousands of embraces the two had shared—the love usurped. She was aware of a trembling in her legs, and she feared she might fall to the ground. Gwen put a hand on her arm, unsure of what to do.

Hannah tried to fend off the humiliation, and the tears it brought. The woman and child were knitted together like a single being, in a world no one could enter. She felt sick as she fought to stay upright, to maintain some fragment of dignity. Struggling to breathe calmly, she picked up her bag from the counter and walked as steadily as she could toward Isabel.

"Grace darling," she tried. The child was still burrowing into Isabel, and neither moved. "Grace dear, it's time to come home." She reached out a hand to touch the little girl, who screamed: not a squeal but a full-throated, murderous cry that bounced off the windows.

"Mamma, make her go 'way! Mamma, *make her*!"

The small crowd looked on, the men perplexed and the women horrified. The little girl's features were distorted and purple. "Please, Mamma!" She was begging, a tiny hand on each side of Isabel's face, shouting the words at her as though to overcome distance or deafness. Still, Isabel remained mute.

"Perhaps we could—" Gwen's sentence was cut off by her sister.

"Let her go!" Hannah shouted, unable to address Isabel by name. "You've done enough," she went on more quietly, in a voice edged with bitterness.

"How can you be so cruel?" Isabel burst out. "You can see the state she's in! You don't know the first thing about her—about what she needs, how to look after her! Have some common sense, if you can't have any kindness to her!"

"Let go of my daughter! Now!" demanded Hannah, shaking. She was desperate to get out of the shop, to break the magnetic hold. She pulled the child away and held her around the waist, as she resisted and screamed, "Mamma! I want Mamma! Let me go!"

"It's all right, darling," she said. "I know you're upset, but we can't stay," and she went on, trying to soothe the child with words while keeping a strong enough grip on her to stop her wriggling out of her arms and running away.

Gwen glanced at Isabel, and shook her head in despair. Then she turned to her niece. "Shh, shh, love. Don't cry," and she dabbed at her face with a delicate lace handkerchief. "Come home and we'll find you a toffee. Tabatha Tabby will be missing you. Come on, darling." The words of reassurance, from Hannah and from Gwen, continued in a gentle stream as the trio made their way out. At the door, Gwen turned again to behold Isabel, and the desperation in her eyes.

For a moment, no one stirred. Isabel stared into thin air, not daring to move her limbs so as not to lose the feel of her daughter. Her mother eyed the shop assistants, defying them to comment. Finally, the boy who had been unraveling the linen picked up the bolt and started to re-roll it.

Larry Mouchemore took that as the cue to say to the old woman he had been serving, "And it was just the two yards you wanted? Of the lace?"

"Ye-yes, just the two yards," she replied, as normally as she could, though she tried to pay him with a hair comb rather than the coins she had meant to extract from her handbag.

"Come on, dear," said Violet softly. Then louder, "I don't think I want the same wool this time. I'll look at the pattern again and then decide."

Fanny Darnley, gossiping to a woman beside her on the pavement, froze as the two women came out, only her eyes daring to follow them down the street.

Knuckey walks along the isthmus of Point Partageuse, listening to the waves launch themselves at the shore on both sides. He comes here to clear his head, in the evenings after tea. He's dried the dishes his wife washed. He still misses the days when there were kids around to do it with them, and they'd make a game of it. Mostly grown up, now. He smiles at a memory of little Billy, forever three years old.

Between his finger and thumb he is turning a shell, cool and rounded like a coin. Families. God knows what he'd be without his family. Most natural thing in the world, it was, for a woman to want a baby. His Irene would have done anything to get Billy back. Anything. When it comes to their kids, parents are all just instinct and hope. And fear. Rules and laws fly straight out the window.

The law's the law, but people are people. He thinks back to the day that started the whole sorry business: the Anzac Day when he was up in Perth for his aunt's funeral. He could have gone after the lot of them, the mob, Garstone included. All the men who used Frank Roennfeldt to take the pain away, just for a moment. But that would have made things worse. You can't confront a whole town with its shame. Sometimes, forgetting is the only way back to normality.

His thoughts returned to his prisoner. That Tom Sherbourne was a puzzle. Closed as a Queensland nut. No way of knowing what was inside the smooth, hard shell, and no weak spot to put pressure on. Bloody Spragg was desperate for a go at him. He'd stalled him as long as he could, but he'd have to let him come and question Sherbourne soon. Down in Albany, or in Perth, who knew what they'd make of him. Sherbourne was his own worst enemy, the way he was carrying on.

At least he'd managed to keep Spragg away from Isabel. "You know we can't compel a wife to talk, so stay away from her. If you put pressure on her, she could clam up for good. Is that what you want?" he'd asked the sergeant. "You leave her to me."

Christ, all this was too much. A quiet life in a quiet town, that's what he'd signed up for. And now he was supposed to make sense of all this. A bastard of a case, this was. A real bastard. His job was to be fair, and thorough. And to hand it over to Albany when the time came. He threw the shell into the water. Didn't even make a splash, drowned by the roar of the waves.

Sergeant Spragg, still sweating from the long journey from Albany, flicked a piece of fluff from his sleeve. Slowly, he turned back to the papers in front of him. "Thomas Edward Sherbourne. Date of birth, 28 September 1893."

Tom offered no response to the statement. The cicadas clicked shrilly from the forest, as though they were the sound of the heat itself.

"Quite the war hero, too. Military Cross and Bar. I've read your citations: captured a German machine-gun nest single-handed. Carried four of your men to safety under sniper fire. And the rest." Spragg let a moment pass. "You must have killed a lot of people in your time."

Tom remained silent.

"I said"—Spragg leaned toward him over the table—"you must have killed a lot of people in your time."

Tom's breathing remained steady. He looked straight ahead, his face expressionless.

Spragg thumped the table. "When I ask you a question you'll bloody well answer it, understand me?"

"When you ask me a question, I will," said Tom quietly.

"Why did you kill Frank Roennfeldt? That's a question."

"I didn't kill him."

"Was it because he was German? Still had the accent, by all accounts."

"He didn't have an accent when I came across him. He was dead."

"You'd killed plenty of his sort before. One more would have made no difference, would it?"

Tom let out a long breath, and folded his arms.

"That's a question too, Sherbourne."

"What's all this about? I've told you I'm responsible for keeping Lucy. I've told you the man was dead when the boat washed up. I buried him, and that's my responsibility too. What more do you want?"

"Oh, he's so brave, so honest, copping it sweet like that, prepared to go to jail," Spragg mimicked in a singsong. "Well it doesn't wash with me, mate, you understand? It's a bit too much like you're trying to get away with murder."

Tom's stillness riled him even more, and he went on, "I've seen your type before. And I've had enough of bloody war heroes. Came back here and expected to be worshipped for the rest of your lives. Looking down on anyone who didn't have a uniform. Well the war's long over.

God knows we saw plenty of you get back and go right off the rails. The way you survived over there isn't the way to survive in a civilized country and you won't get away with it."

"This has got bugger all to do with the war."

"Someone's got to take a stand for common decency, and I'm the one who's going to do it here."

"And what about common *sense,* Sergeant? For Christ's sake, think about it! I could have denied everything. I could have said that Frank Roennfeldt wasn't even *in* the boat, and you'd have been none the wiser. I told the truth because I wanted his wife to know what had happened, and because he deserved a decent burial."

"Or maybe you told *half* the truth because you wanted to ease your conscience and get let off with a slap on the wrist."

"I'm asking you what makes sense."

The sergeant eyed him coldly. "Seven men, it says you killed in your little machine-gun escapade. That looks to me like the work of a violent man. Of a ruthless killer. Your heroics might just be the death of you," he said, gathering up his notes. "It's hard to be a hero when you're swinging from a rope." He closed the file and called to Harry Garstone to take the prisoner back to the cells.

CHAPTER 31

Since the incident at Mouchemore's, Hannah hardly sets foot outside the house, and Grace has regressed, becoming more withdrawn, despite her mother's best efforts.

"I want to go home. I want my mamma," the girl whimpers.

"I *am* your mummy, Grace, darling. I know it must be confusing for you." She puts a finger under the little girl's chin. "I've loved you since the day you were born. I waited so long for you to come home. One day you'll understand, I promise."

"I want my dadda!" the child rejoins, smacking the finger away.

"Daddy can't be with us. But he loved you very much. So very much." And she pictures Frank, his baby in his arms. The child looks at Hannah with bewilderment, sometimes anger, and eventually resignation.

Walking home from a visit to her dressmaker the following week, Gwen ran over and over the situation. She worried what would become of her niece: it was a sin for a child to suffer that much, surely. She couldn't stand idly by any longer.

As she passed the edge of the park where it fringed into bush, her eye was drawn to a woman sitting on a bench, staring into the distance. She noticed first the pretty shade of her green dress. Then she realized it was Isabel Sherbourne. She hurried past, but there was no risk of Isabel seeing her: she was in a trance. The following day, and the next, Gwen saw her in the same place, in the same dazed state.

Who could say if the idea had already come to her before the to-do over Grace tearing all the pages out of her storybook? Hannah had scolded her, then stood in tears as she tried to gather up the pages of the first book Frank had ever bought for his daughter—Grimms' fairy tales in German, elaborately illustrated with watercolor plates. "What have you done to Daddy's book? Oh, darling, how could you?" The girl responded by scrambling under her bed and curling into a ball, out of reach.

"There's so little left that's Frank . . ." Hannah sobbed again as she looked at the ruined pages in her hands.

"I know, Hanny. I know. But Grace doesn't. She didn't do it on purpose." She put a hand on her shoulder. "Tell you what, you go and have a lie-down while I take her out."

"She needs to get used to being in her own home."

"We'll just go to Dad's. He'll love it, and the fresh air will do her good."

"Really, no. I don't want—"

"Come on, Hanny. You really could do with a rest."

Hannah sighed. "All right. But just straight there and back."

As they started down the street, Gwen handed her niece a toffee. "You'd like a lolly, wouldn't you, Lucy?"

"Yes," the child replied, then cocked her head to one side as she noticed the name.

"Now you be a good girl, and we'll go and visit Granddad."

The girl's eyes flickered at the mention of the man with the big horses and big trees. She wandered along, sucking the toffee. She did not smile, but neither did she scream or howl, Gwen noted.

Strictly speaking, there was no need to pass the park. They could have got to Septimus's house more quickly by taking the route by the cemetery and the Methodist chapel.

"Are you tired, Lucy? Why don't we have a bit of a breather? It's a long way to Granddad's, and you're only a little mite . . ." The girl merely continued to open and close her thumb and fingers like pincers, experimenting with the stickiness of the toffee residue. Out of the corner of her eye, Gwen saw Isabel on the bench. "You run ahead now, that's a good girl. You run to the bench and I'll follow." The child did not run, but ambled, dragging her rag doll along the ground. Gwen kept her distance and watched.

Isabel blinked. "Lucy? Sweetheart!" she exclaimed, and gathered her into her arms before it occurred to her to see how she'd got there.

"Mamma!" cried the child, gripping her tightly.

Isabel turned and at a distance saw Gwen, who gave a nod, as if to say "Go on."

Whatever the woman was doing or why, Isabel did not care. She wept as she hugged the girl and then held her at arm's length to see her better. Somehow, despite everything, perhaps Lucy could still be hers. A warmth spread through her at the idea.

"Oh, you've got thin, little one! You're skin and bone. You must be a good girl and eat. For Mamma." Gradually she took in the other changes to her daughter: hair parted on the other side; a dress made of fine muslin sprinkled with daisies; new shoes with butterflies on the buckles.

Relief swept over Gwen to see her niece's response. She was watching a completely different child, suddenly safe with the mother she loved. She left them together for as long as she dared, before approaching. "I'd better take her now. I wasn't sure you'd be here."

"But—I don't understand . . ."

"It's all so dreadful. So hard on everyone." She shook her head and sighed. "My sister's a good woman, really she is. She's been through so much." She nodded in the child's direction. "I'll try to bring her again. I can't promise. Be patient. That's all I'm saying. Be patient and perhaps . . ." She left the sentence hanging. "But please, don't tell anyone. Hannah wouldn't understand. She'd never forgive me . . . Come on now, Lucy," she said, and held her arms out to the girl.

The child clung to Isabel. "No, Mamma! Don't go!"

"Come on, sweet thing. Be good for Mamma, won't you? You need to go with this lady now, but I'll see you again soon, I promise."

Still the child clung. "If you're good now, we can come again." Gwen smiled, pulling her carefully away.

Some remnant of the rational stopped Isabel from acting on the impulse to snatch the child away. No. If she could be patient, the woman had promised to bring her again. Who knew what else might change with time?

It took Gwen a long while to calm her niece. She cuddled her, and carried her, taking every opportunity to distract her with riddles and snatches of nursery rhymes. She wasn't sure yet how she would make her plan work, but she simply couldn't bear to see the poor child kept from her mother any longer. Hannah had always had a stubborn streak, and Gwen feared it was blinding her now. She wondered how likely it was that she could keep the meeting from Hannah. Even if she couldn't, it was worth trying. When Grace had finally quietened down, Gwen asked, "Do you know what a secret is, sweetheart?"

"Yes," she mumbled.

"Good. So we're going to play a game about secrets, OK?"

The little girl looked up at her, waiting to understand.

"You love Mamma Isabel, don't you?"

"Yes."

"And I know you want to see her again. But Hannah might be a bit cross, because she's very sad, so we mustn't tell her, or Granddad, all right?"

The child's face tightened.

"We have to keep this a special secret, and if anyone asks what we did today, you just say we went to Granddad's. You mustn't tell about seeing your mamma. Understand, love?"

The girl kept her lips pursed as she nodded gravely, the confusion showing in her eyes.

"She's an intelligent child. She knows Isabel Sherbourne isn't dead—we saw her at Mouchemore's." Hannah sat again in Dr. Sumpton's consulting room, this time without her daughter.

"I'm telling you, as a professional, that the only cure for your daughter is time, and keeping her away from Mrs. Sherbourne."

"I just wondered—well, I thought if I could get her to talk to me—about her other life. Out on the island. Would it help?"

He took a puff of his pipe. "Think of it like this—if I'd just taken your appendix out, the last thing to be doing would be to open up the wound every five minutes and prod about again to see if it had healed. I know it's hard, but it's a case of least said, soonest mended. She'll get over it."

But she showed no sign of getting over it, as far as Hannah could see. The child became obsessed with putting her toys in order and making her bed neat. She smacked the kitten for knocking over the dolls' house, and kept her mouth snapped shut like a miser's purse, not wanting to let slip any sign of affection to this imposter mother.

Still, Hannah persevered. She told her stories: about forests and the men who worked in them; about school in Perth and the things she'd done there; about Frank, and his life in Kalgoorlie. She would sing her little songs in German, even though the child paid no particular attention. She made clothes for her dolls and puddings for her dinner. The little girl responded by drawing pictures. Always the same pictures. Mamma and Dadda and Lulu at the lighthouse, its beam shining right to the edge of the page, driving away the darkness all around.

From the kitchen, Hannah could see Grace sitting on the lounge room floor, talking to her clothes pegs. These days she was more anxious than ever, except when she was around Septimus, so her mother was glad to see her playing quietly. She came a little closer to the door, to listen.

"Lucy, eat a toffee," said a peg.

"Yum," said another peg, as it gobbled the thin air the child delivered with her fingertips.

"I've got a special secret," said the first peg. "Come with Auntie Gwen. When Hannah is asleep."

Hannah watched intently, a cold sickness spreading through her.

From the pocket of her pinafore, Grace took a lemon and covered it with a handkerchief. "Goodnight, Hannah," said Auntie Gwen. "Now we visiting Mamma in the park."

"Pwoi, pwoi." Two other pegs pressed against one another with kisses. "My darling Lucy. Come on, sweetheart. Off we go to Janus." And the pegs trotted along the rug for a bit.

The whistling of the kettle startled the child, and she turned and saw Hannah in the doorway. She threw the pegs down, saying, "Bad Lucy!" and smacked her own hand.

Hannah's horror at the charade turned to despair at this last admonishment: this was how her daughter saw her. Not as the mother who loved her, but as a tyrant. She tried to stay calm as she considered what to do.

Her hands shook a little as she made some cocoa and brought it in. "That was a nice game you were playing, darling," she said, battling the tremor in her voice.

The child sat still, neither speaking nor drinking from the beaker in her hand.

"Do you know any secrets, Grace?"

The girl nodded slowly.

"I bet they're lovely secrets."

Again, the little chin moved up and down, while the eyes tried to work out what rules to follow.

"Shall we play a game?"

The child slid her toe back and forth in an arc on the floor.

"Let's play a game where I guess your secret. That way it's still a secret, because you haven't told me. And if I guess it, you can have a lolly as a prize." The child's face tensed as Hannah smiled awkwardly. "I guess . . . that you went to visit the lady from Janus. Is that right?"

The child began to nod, and then stopped. "We saw the man in the big house. His face was pink."

"I won't be cross with you, darling. It's nice to visit sometimes, isn't it? Did the lady give you a nice big hug?"

"Yes," she said slowly, trying to work out as the word came out whether this was part of the secret or not.

As Hannah took the washing off the line half an hour later, her stomach was still churning. How could her own sister have done such a thing? The expression on the faces of the customers at Mouchemore's came back to her, and she had a sense that they could see something she couldn't—everyone, Gwen included, was laughing behind her back. She left a petticoat dangling by one peg as she headed back into the house and stormed into Gwen's room.

"How could you?"

"What on earth's wrong?" asked Gwen.

"As if you don't know!"

"What, Hannah?"

"I know what you did. I know where you took Grace."

It was Hannah's turn to be taken aback as tears sprang to her sister's eyes and she said, "That poor little girl, Hannah."

"What?"

"The poor thing! Yes, I took her to see Isabel Sherbourne. In the park. And I let them speak to each other. But I did it for *her*. The child doesn't know whether she's Arthur or Martha. I did it for *her,* Hanny—for Lucy."

"Her name's Grace! Her name's Grace and she's my daughter and I just want her to be happy and—" Her voice lost its force as she sobbed, "I miss Frank. Oh God, I miss you, Frank." She looked at her sister. "And you take her to the wife of the man who buried him in a ditch!

How could you even think of it? Grace has to forget about them. Both of them. *I'm* her mother!"

Gwen hesitated, then approached her sister, and hugged her gently. "Hannah, you know how dear you are to me. I've tried to do everything I possibly can to help you—since that day. And I've tried so hard since she came home. But that's the trouble. It's not *her* home, is it? I can't bear to watch her suffer. And I can't bear how much it hurts you."

Hannah took a breath between a gulp and a gasp.

Gwen straightened her shoulders. "I think you should give her back. To Isabel Sherbourne. I just don't think there's any other way. For the child's sake. And for yours, Hanny dear. For yours."

Hannah drew back, her voice steely. "She will never see that woman again, as long as I live. Never!"

Neither sister saw the small face peeping through the crack in the door; the little ears that heard everything in that strange, strange house.

Vernon Knuckey sat across the table from Tom. "I thought I'd seen every sort there was, until you turned up." He looked at the page in front of him again. "A boat washes up and you say to yourself, 'That looks like a fine baby. I can keep it, and no one will ever know.'"

"Is that a question?"

"Are you trying to be difficult?"

"No."

"How many children had Isabel lost?"

"Three. You know that."

"But *you* were the one who decided to keep the baby. Not the woman who had lost three? All *your* idea, because you thought people wouldn't think you were a real man without fathering kids. How bloody wet do you think I am?"

Tom said nothing, and Knuckey leaned in toward him, his voice softening. "I know what it's like, to lose a little one. And I know what it did to my wife. Fair went mad with it for a bit." He waited, but got no reply. "They'll go easy on her, you know."

"They won't bloody touch her," said Tom.

Knuckey shook his head. "Committal hearing'll be next week, when the Beak comes to town. From then on, you're Albany's problem, and Spragg'll welcome you with open arms and Christ knows what else. He's taken against you, and down there, there'll be nothing I can do to stop him."

Tom made no response.

"Anyone you want me to tell about the hearing?"

"No. Thanks."

Knuckey gave him a look. He was about to leave, when Tom said, "Can I write to my wife?"

"Of course you can't bloody write to your wife. You can't interfere with potential witnesses. If this is the way you're going to play it, you play it by the rules, mate."

Tom sized him up. "Just a bit of paper and a pencil. You can read it if you want . . . She's my wife."

"And I'm the police, for God's sake."

"Don't tell me you never bent a rule—never turned a blind eye for some poor bastard . . . A piece of paper and a pencil."

Ralph delivered the letter to Isabel that afternoon. She took it from him reluctantly, hand trembling.

"I'll leave you to get on with reading, then." He reached out to touch her forearm. "That man needs your help, Isabel," he said gravely.

"And so does my little girl," she said, with tears in her eyes.

When he left, she took the letter to her bedroom and stared at it. She raised it to her face to smell it, to find a trace of her husband, but there was nothing distinctive about it—no trace of the man. She picked up some nail scissors from the dressing table and began to slit the corner, but something froze her fingers. Lucy's face swam before her, screaming, and she shuddered at the knowledge that it was Tom who had caused that. She put the scissors down, and slipped the letter into a drawer, closing it slowly and without a sound.

The pillowcase is wet with tears. A scythe of moon hangs in the window, too feeble to light even its own path through the sky. Hannah watches it. There is so much of the world she wishes she could share with her daughter, but the child and the world have somehow been snatched away.

Sunburn. At first, she is puzzled at the memory that has presented itself, unbidden, irrelevant. An English governess, unfamiliar with the very concept of sunburn, let alone its treatment, had put her in a bath of hot water "to take the heat out" of the burn she had got from bathing too long in the bay when her father was away. "There's no use complaining," the woman had told the ten-year-old Hannah. "It's doing you good, the pain." Hannah had continued to scream until finally the cook had come to see who was being murdered, and hauled her out of the steaming water.

"Have you ever heard such nonsense in all your life!" the cook had declared. "The last thing you do to a burn is *burn* it. You don't need to be Florence flipping Nightingale to know that much!"

But Hannah had not been angry, she remembers. The governess had truly believed she was doing the right thing. She only wanted what was best for her. She was inflicting pain only to help her.

Suddenly furious at the weakling moon, she hurls the pillow across the room and slams her fist into the mattress, over and over. "I want my *Grace* back," she mouths silently, through her tears. "This isn't *my* Grace!" Her baby had died, after all.

Tom heard the rattle of the keys.

"Afternoon," said Gerald Fitzgerald, guided in by Harry Garstone. "Sorry I'm late. Train hit a herd of sheep just outside Bunbury. Slowed us up a bit."

"I wasn't going anywhere." Tom shrugged.

The lawyer arranged his papers on the table. "Committal hearing's in four days."

Tom nodded.

"Changed your mind yet?"

"No."

Fitzgerald sighed. "What are you waiting for?"

Tom looked at him, and the man repeated. "What are you damn well waiting for? The bloody cavalry's not coming over the hill, mate. No one's coming to save you, except me. And I'm only here because Captain Addicott's paid my fee."

"I asked him not to waste his money."

"It doesn't have to be a waste of money! You could let me earn it, you know."

"How?"

"Let me tell the truth—give you the chance to walk away a free man."

"You think destroying my wife could make me a free man?"

"All I'm saying is—half of these charges we can put up a decent defense to, whatever you've done: at least put them to proof. If you plead not guilty, the Crown's got to prove every element of every offense. That bloody Spragg and his kitchen-sink charges: let me have a go at him, if only for the sake of my professional pride!"

"If I plead guilty to everything, they'll leave my wife alone, you've said. You know the law. And I know what I want to do."

"Thinking about it and doing it are two different things, you'll find. Hell of a place, Fremantle jail. Bastard of a way to spend twenty years."

Tom looked him in the eye. "You want to know a bastard of a place to spend time? You go to Pozieres, Bullecourt, Passchendaele. You go there, then tell me how awful a place is where they give you a bed and food and a roof over your head."

Fitzgerald looked down at his papers and made a note. "If you tell me to enter a guilty plea, that's what I'll do. And you'll go down for the whole kit and caboodle. But you need your bloody head read, as far as I'm concerned . . . And you'd better pray to the Good Lord bloody Jesus that Spragg doesn't up the charges once you get to Albany."

CHAPTER 32

"What the devil's the matter?" demanded Vernon Knuckey, as Harry Garstone closed the door behind him and stood dumbly in the sergeant's office.

Garstone shuffled his feet and cleared his throat, jerking his head back toward the front of the police station.

"Get to the point, Constable."

"There's a visitor."

"For me?"

"Not for you, sir."

Knuckey shot him a warning look.

"It's for Sherbourne, sir."

"Well? You know what to do, for Pete's sake. Write 'em down and send 'em in."

"It's—Hannah Roennfeldt, sir."

The sergeant sat up. "Oh." He closed a file on his desk and rubbed his chin. "I suppose I'd better have a word."

Knuckey stood near the counter in the front of the station. "It's not usual procedure to let the victim's family members see the accused, Mrs. Roennfeldt."

Hannah held the sergeant with a silent, steady gaze, forcing him into speech again.

"It really would be out of the ordinary, I'm afraid. All due respect . . ."

"But not against the rules? Against the law?"

"Look, ma'am. It's going to be hard enough for you when it all comes to Court. Take it from me: it's a distressing thing, a trial like this. You really don't want to be stirring things up for yourself before it even starts."

"I want to see him. I want to look him in the eye, the man who killed my child."

"*Killed* your child? Steady on now."

"The baby I lost is never coming back, Sergeant, never. Grace will never be the same."

"Look, I'm not sure what you mean, Mrs. Roennfeldt, but in any case I—"

"I'm entitled to that much, don't you think?"

Knuckey sighed. The woman was a pitiful sight. She'd been haunting the town for years now. Maybe this would let her lay her ghosts to rest. "If you wait here . . ."

Tom had risen to his feet, still puzzled by the news. "Hannah Roennfeldt wants to talk to *me*? What for?"

"You're not obliged, of course. I can send her away."

"No . . . ," Tom said. "I'll see her. Thank you."

"Up to you."

A few moments later, Hannah entered, followed by Constable Garstone bearing a small wooden chair. He placed it a few feet from the bars.

"I'll leave the door open, Mrs. Roennfeldt, and wait outside. Or I can stay here if you'd prefer?"

"There's no need. I won't be long."

Garstone gave one of his pouts and jangled his keys. "Right. I'll leave you to it, ma'am," he said, and marched back down the corridor.

Hannah stared in silence, taking in every inch of Tom: the small hook-shaped shrapnel scar just below his left ear; the unattached earlobes, the fingers that were long and fine despite their calluses.

He submitted to her inspection without flinching, like quarry offering itself up to a hunter at close range. All the while, scenes flashed through his mind—the boat, the body, the rattle, each fresh and vivid. Then other memories—writing the first letter late at night in the Graysmarks' kitchen, the churning in his gut as he chose the words; the smoothness of Lucy's skin, her giggle, the way her hair floated like seaweed as he held her in the water at Shipwreck Beach. The moment he discovered he had known the mother of the child all along. He could feel the sweat on his back.

"Thank you for letting me see you, Mr. Sherbourne . . ."

If Hannah had sworn at him or hurled her chair at the bars, Tom would have been less shocked than at this civility.

"I realize you didn't have to."

He gave just a slight nod.

"Strange, isn't it?" she went on. "Until a few weeks ago, if I'd thought of you at all, it would have been with gratitude. But it turns out you were the one I should have been afraid of that night, not the drunk. 'Being over there changes a man,' you said. 'Can't tell the difference between right and wrong.' I finally understand what you meant."

In a steady voice she asked, "I need to know: was this really all your doing?"

Tom nodded, slowly and gravely.

Pain flitted across Hannah's face, as if she had been slapped. "Are you sorry for what you did?"

The question stabbed him, and he focused on a knot in the floorboard. "I'm sorrier than I can say."

"Didn't you even think for a moment that the child might have had a mother? Didn't it occur to you that she might be loved and missed?" She looked about the cell, then back to Tom. "*Why?* If I could understand *why* you did it . . ."

His jaw was rigid. "I really can't say why I did what I did."

"Try. Please?"

She deserved the truth. But there was nothing he could say to her without betraying Isabel. He had done what mattered—Lucy had been returned, and he was taking the consequences. The rest was just words. "Really. I can't tell you."

"That policeman from Albany thinks you killed my husband. Did you?"

He looked her straight in the eye. "I swear to you, he was already dead when I found him . . . I know I should have done things differently. I'm truly sorry how much harm the decisions I've made since that day have done. But your husband was already dead."

She took a deep breath, about to leave.

"Do what you like to me. I'm not asking for forgiveness," Tom said, ". . . but my wife—had no choice. She loves that little girl. She cared for her like she was the only thing in the world. Show her some mercy."

The bitterness in Hannah's face faded to weary sadness. "Frank was a lovely man," she said, and walked slowly back down the corridor.

In the dim light, Tom listened to the cicadas that seemed to tick the seconds away, thousands at a time. He became aware of opening and closing his hands, as though they might take him somewhere his feet could not. He looked at them, and for a moment, considered all they had done. This collection of cells and muscles and thoughts was his life—and yet surely there was more to it. He came back to the present, to the hot walls and the thick air. The last rung of the ladder that might lead him out of hell had been taken away.

For hours at a time, Isabel put Tom from her mind: as she helped her mother around the house; as she looked at the paintings Violet had kept, done by Lucy during her brief visits back; as she felt ever more deeply the grief of losing her child. Then thoughts of Tom would creep back and she pictured the letter Ralph had delivered, banished to the drawer.

Gwen had promised to bring Lucy to see her again, but she hadn't appeared at the park in the days afterward, even though Isabel had waited for hours. But she must stay firm, while there was the merest sliver of a hope of seeing her daughter again. She must hate Tom, for Lucy's sake. And yet. She took the letter out, observed the tear in the corner where she had begun to open it. She put it back, and hurried out to the park, to wait, just in case.

"Tell me what you want me to do, Tom. You know I want to help you. Please, just tell me what to do." Bluey's voice was tight and his eyes glistened.

"Nothing more needs doing, Blue." Tom's cell was hot, and smelled of carbolic from the mopping an hour earlier.

"I wish to Christ I'd never seen that bloody rattle. Should have kept me trap shut." He gripped the bars. "That sergeant from Albany came to see me, asking all sorts of questions about you—whether you were handy with your fists, whether you were a drinker. He's been to see Ralph, too. People are talking about—they're talking about murder, for Pete's sake, Tom. Down the pub they're talking about *hanging*!"

Tom looked him in the eye. "Do you believe them?"

"Of course I don't believe them. But I believe that sort of talk takes on a life of its own. And I believe that an innocent bloke can be accused of something he never did. It's no use saying sorry when he's dead." Bluey's expression continued to implore Tom silently.

"There are things that are hard to explain," Tom said. "There are reasons why I did what I did."

"But *what* did you do?"

"I did some things that have ruined people's lives, and now it's time to pay."

"They're saying how Old Man Potts reckons that if a bloke's wife won't stick up for him, then he must have done something pretty crook."

"Thanks, mate. You're a real comfort."

"Don't go down without a fight, Tom. Promise me!"

"I'll be right, Blue."

But as Bluey's footsteps echoed away, Tom wondered how true that was. Isabel had not responded to his letter, and he had to face the fact that it could be for the very worst of reasons. Still, he had to hold on to what he knew of her, of who he knew her to be.

On the outskirts of the town are the old timber workers' cottages, meager clapboard constructions ranging from the derelict to the respectable. They're set on smaller blocks of land, near the pumping station that brings the town its water. One of them, Isabel knows, is where Hannah Roennfeldt lives, and where her treasured Lucy has been taken. Isabel has waited in vain for Gwen to appear. In desperation, she now seeks Lucy out. Just to see where she is. Just to know she is coping. It's midday and there isn't a soul in the broad street, braided with jacarandas.

One of the houses is particularly well kept. Its wood is newly painted, its grass cut, and, unlike the others, it's bounded by a tall hedge, more effective than a fence in keeping prying eyes away.

Isabel goes to the laneway at the back of the houses, and from behind the hedge, hears the rhythmic squeak of iron. She peers through a tiny gap in the foliage, and her breath comes faster as she sees her little girl, riding a tricycle up and down the pathway. All alone, she has no expression of happiness or sadness, just fierce concentration as she pedals. She is so close: Isabel could almost touch her, hold her, comfort her. Suddenly, it's absurd that she can't be with the child—as if the whole town has gone mad, and she is the only sane one left.

She considers things. The train comes once a day from Perth down to Albany, and once a day from Albany to Perth. If she waited until the last minute to get on, might there be a chance that no one would notice her? That the child's absence mightn't be discovered? In Perth, it would be easier to melt into anonymity. Then she could get to Sydney by the boat. England, even. A new life. The fact that she has not a shilling to her name—has never held a bank account—doesn't seem to stop her. She watches her daughter, and weighs up her next action.

Harry Garstone hammered on the Graysmarks' door. Bill answered, after peering through the glass to see who it could be at this hour.

"Mr. Graysmark," the constable said, and gave a peremptory nod.

"Evening, Harry. What brings you here?"

"Official business."

"I see," said Bill, braced for more grim news.

"I'm looking for the Roennfeldt girl."

"Hannah?"

"No, her daughter. Grace."

It took Bill a moment to realize he meant Lucy, and he gave the policeman a questioning look.

"Have you got her here?" Garstone asked.

"Of course I haven't got her. Why on earth . . . ?"

"Well, she's not with Hannah Roennfeldt. She's gone missing."

"Hannah lost her?"

"Or she was taken. Is your daughter at home?"

"Yes."

"Sure?" he asked, just faintly disappointed.

"Of course I'm sure."

"Been here all day, has she?"

"Not all day, no. What are you on about? Where's Lucy?"

By now Violet was standing behind Bill. "Whatever's the matter?"

"I need to see your daughter, Mrs. Graysmark," said Garstone. "Could you get her, please?"

Reluctantly, Violet went to Isabel's room, but it was empty. She hurried out to the back, where she found her sitting on the swinging seat, staring into space.

"Isabel! It's Harry Garstone!"

"What does he want?"

"I think you'd better come and see him," Violet said, and something in her tone made Isabel follow her mother through the house to the front door.

"Evening, Mrs. Sherbourne. I'm here about Grace Roennfeldt," Garstone began.

"What about her?" asked Isabel.

"When did you last see her?"

"She hasn't been near her since she came back," her mother protested, before correcting herself. "Well, she did . . . come across her, by accident, at Mouchemore's, but that's the only time—"

"That right, Mrs. Sherbourne?"

Isabel didn't speak, so her father said, "Of course it's right. What do you think she—"

"No, Dad. Actually, I did see her."

Both parents turned, mouths open in confusion.

"At the park, three days ago. Gwen Potts brought her to see me." Isabel considered whether to say more. "I didn't go looking for her—Gwen brought her to me, I swear. Where's Lucy?"

"Gone. Disappeared."

"When?"

"I thought you might be able to tell me that," said the policeman. "Mr. Graysmark, do you mind if I have a look around? Just to be sure."

Bill was about to protest, but the new information from Isabel worried him. "There's nothing to hide in this house. Look where you like."

The policeman, who still remembered getting the cane from Bill Graysmark for cheating on a maths test, made a show of opening wardrobes and peering under beds, though he did so with a trace of nerves, as though it wasn't impossible that the headmaster might still give him six of the best. Finally, he returned to the hallway. "Thank you. If you see her, make sure you let us know."

"Let you know!" Isabel was outraged. "Haven't you started a search? Why aren't you out looking for her?"

"That's not your concern, Mrs. Sherbourne."

As soon as Garstone had gone, Isabel turned to her father. "Dad, we've got to find her! Where on earth could she be? I've got to go and—"

"Hold your horses, Izz. Let me see if I can get some sense out of Vernon Knuckey. I'll telephone the station, and see what's going on."

CHAPTER 33

From her earliest days, the child from Janus Rock has experienced the extremes of human life as the norm. Who knows what visceral memories of her first trip to the island, and the scene that caused it, linger in her body? Even if that has been erased completely, her days at the lighthouse, in a world inhabited by only three people, have seeped into her very being. Her bond with the couple who raised her is fierce and beyond questioning. She cannot name the sensation of losing them as grief. She has no word for longing or despair.

But she aches for Mamma and Dadda, pines for them and spends her days thinking of them, even now she has been onshore for many weeks. She must have done something very naughty to make Mamma cry so much. As for the woman with the dark hair and the dark eyes who says she is her real mother . . . lying is wrong. So why does this sad lady insist on telling such a big lie, and to everyone? Why do the grown-ups let her?

She knows Mamma is here in Partageuse. She knows the bad men took Dadda away, but doesn't know where. She has heard the word "police" many times, but has only the vaguest notion of what they are. She has overheard many conversations. People in the street, muttering, "What a to-do, what a dreadful situation." Hannah saying she will never see Mamma again.

Janus is enormous, yet she knows every inch of it: Shipwreck Beach, Treacherous Cove, Windy Ridge. To get home, she need only look for the lighthouse, Dadda always says. She knows, for she has heard it said many times, that Partageuse is a very small place.

While Hannah is in the kitchen, and Gwen is out, the little girl goes to her room. She looks about her. Carefully, she buckles on her sandals. In a satchel, she puts a drawing of the lighthouse with Mamma and Dadda and Lulu. She adds the apple the lady gave her this morning; the pegs she uses as dolls.

She closes the back door quietly, and searches the hedge at the back of the garden, until she finds a narrow gap just wide enough to slip through. She has seen Mamma at the park. She will go there. She will find her. They will find Dadda. They will go home.

It is late in the afternoon when she embarks on her mission. The sun is slanting in from the side of the sky, and the shadows of the trees are already stretched like rubber to improbable lengths.

Having scrambled through the hedge, the girl drags her satchel along the ground as she makes her way through low scrub behind the house. The sounds here are so different from Janus. So many birds, calling to one another. As she wanders, the scrub becomes more dense, and the vegetation greener. She isn't frightened of the skinks she sees skittering now, black and quick and scaly, through the undergrowth. Skinks won't hurt her, she knows well. But she doesn't know that, unlike Janus, here not everything black and slithering is a skink. She has never had to make the vital distinction between the lizards that have legs, and those that don't. She has never seen a snake.

By the time the little girl reaches the park, the light is fading. She runs to the bench, but finds no trace of her mother. Hauling her satchel up after her, she sits there, taking in the empty surroundings. From the satchel she pulls out the apple, bruised from the journey, and takes a bite.

At this hour, the kitchens of Partageuse are busy places, filled with testy mothers and hungry children. There is much washing of hands and faces, grubby from a day's skirmishing in trees or walking back from the beach. Fathers allow themselves a beer from the Coolgardie safe, mothers oversee saucepans boiling potatoes and ovens incubating stews. Families gather, safe and whole, at the end of another day. And darkness seeps into the sky second by second, until the shadows no longer fall but rise from the ground and fill the air completely. Humans withdraw to their homes, and surrender the night to the creatures that own it: the crickets, the owls, the snakes. A world that hasn't changed for hundreds of thousands of years wakes up, and carries on as if the daylight and the humans and the changes to the landscape have been an illusion. No one walks the streets.

By the time Sergeant Knuckey has arrived at the park, there is only a satchel on the park bench, and an apple core with small teeth marks, though ants have overrun the remains now.

As the night falls, lights begin to twinkle in the gloom. Dots in the darkness, sometimes from a gas lamp in a window; sometimes electric lights, from the newer houses. The main street of Partageuse has electric street lights strung along its length on either side. The stars, too, illuminate the clear air, and the Milky Way rubs a bright smudge across the darkness.

Some of the bright dots among the trees sway like fiery fruit: people with lanterns are searching the bush. Not just police, but men from Potts's Timber Mill, men from Harbor and Lights. Hannah waits anxiously at home, as she's been instructed. The Graysmarks walk the bush paths, calling the child's name. Both "Lucy" and "Grace" fill the air, though only one child is lost.

Clutching her drawing, of Mamma and Dadda and the light, the child recalls the story of the Wise Men finding their way to Baby Jesus by a star. She has spotted the light of Janus, out to sea: it's not far at all—the light never is. Though there's something not quite right. The flash has a red beam between the white ones. Still she follows it.

Down toward the water she heads, where the swell has picked up for the night and the waves have taken the shore hostage. At the lighthouse, she will find Mamma and Dadda. She makes her way down toward the long, thin isthmus—the "Point" of Point Partageuse, where years before, Isabel taught Tom to lie down when looking into the blowhole, to avoid being swept away. Every step takes the little girl closer to the light, out in the ocean.

But it's not Janus's beam she's following. Each light has a different character, and the flash of red that punctuates the white in this one tells mariners that they're nearing the shoals at the mouth of Partageuse Harbor, nearly a hundred miles away from Janus Rock.

The wind picks up. The water churns. The child walks. The darkness abides.

From his cell, Tom heard voices carried on the air outside. "Lucy? Lucy, are you there?" Then "Grace? Where are you, Grace?"

Alone in the cells, Tom called out toward the front of the station, "Sergeant Knuckey? Sergeant?"

There was a rattling of keys, and Constable Lynch appeared. "Want something?"

"What's going on? There are people outside, calling Lucy."

Bob Lynch thought about his response. The bloke deserved to

know. Nothing he could do about it anyway. "She's gone missing, the little girl."

"When? How?"

"A few hours ago. Ran off, by the looks."

"Christ Almighty! How the bloody hell did that happen?"

"No idea."

"Well what are they doing about it?"

"They're looking."

"Let me help. I can't just sit here." The expression on Lynch's face was reply enough. "Oh for crying out loud!" said Tom. "Where am I likely to get to?"

"I'll let you know if I hear anything, mate. Best I can do." And with another metallic clang, he was gone.

In the darkness, Tom's thoughts turned to Lucy, always curious to explore her surroundings. Never afraid of the dark. Perhaps he should have taught her to be fearful. He had failed to prepare her for life beyond Janus. Then another thought came to him. Where was Isabel? What was she capable of in her current state? He prayed she hadn't taken things into her own hands.

Thank Christ it wasn't winter. Vernon Knuckey could feel the coolness setting in as midnight approached. The kid was wearing a cotton dress and a pair of sandals. At least in January she had a chance of making it through the night. In August she'd have been blue with cold by now.

No point in searching at this hour. Sun'd be up not long after five. Better to have people fresh and alert when the light was on their side. "Spread the word," he said as he met Garstone at the end of the road. "We're calling it off for tonight. Get everyone to the station at first light, and we'll start again."

It was one a.m., but he needed to clear his head. He set off on the familiar route of his evening walk, still carrying his lantern, which took a swing at the dark with each of his steps.

In the little cottage, Hannah prayed. "Keep her safe, Lord. Protect her and save her. You've saved her before . . ." Hannah worried—perhaps Grace had used up her share of miracles? Then she soothed herself. It didn't take a miracle for a child to survive a single night here. She just needed to avoid bad luck. That was a different thing altogether. But that thought was pushed aside by the more panicked, more urgent fear. Exhausted, a thought came to her with a twisted clarity. Perhaps God didn't want Grace to be with her. Perhaps she was to blame for everything. She waited, and prayed. And she made a solemn pact with God.

There's a kicking at the door of Hannah's house. Though the lights are off, she's still wide awake, and springs up to open it. Before her stands Sergeant Knuckey, with Grace's body in his arms, her limbs floppy.

"Oh dear Lord!" Hannah lunges for her. Her eyes are fixed on the girl, not the man, so she doesn't see that he's smiling.

"Almost tripped over her down on the Point. Fast asleep," he says. "She's got nine lives, this one, that's for sure." And though he's grinning, there's a tear in his eye, as he recalls the weight of the son he couldn't save, decades before.

Hannah barely registers his words as she hugs her daughter, who sleeps on in her arms.

That night, Hannah laid Grace beside her in her bed, listening to every breath, watching every turn of the head or kick of a foot. But the relief of feeling her daughter's warm body was overshadowed by a darker knowing.

The first sound of rain, like gravel scattered on the tin roof, carried Hannah back to her wedding day: to a time of leaking ceilings and buckets in their humble cottage, and love and hope. Above all, hope. Frank, with his smile, and his cheerfulness no matter what the day brought. She wanted Grace to have that. She wanted her daughter to be a happy little girl, and she prayed to God for the courage and strength to do the things needed to allow it.

When the thunder woke the child, she looked sleepily at Hannah, and snuggled in closer to her, before returning to her dreams, leaving her mother to weep silently, remembering her vow.

The black house spider has returned to its web in the corner of Tom's cell, and is going over and over the higgledy-piggledy threads, setting the shape in order to a design which only it can know—why the silk must be in this particular place, at this particular tension or angle. It comes out at night to repair its web, a funnel of fibers that accumulate dust and form haphazard patterns. It is weaving its arbitrary world, always trying to mend, never abandoning its web unless forced.

Lucy is safe. The relief fills Tom's body. But there is still no word from Isabel. No sign that she has forgiven him, or that she ever will. The helplessness he felt at being unable to do anything for Lucy now strengthens his resolve to do what he can for his wife. It is the one freedom left to him.

If he is going to have to live his life without her, somehow it makes it easier to let go, to let things take their course. His mind wanders into memory. The *woomph* of the oil vapor igniting into brilliance at the touch of his match. The rainbows thrown by the prisms. The oceans spreading themselves before him about Janus like a secret gift. If Tom is to take his leave of the world, he wants to remember the beauty of it, not just the suffering. The breaths of Lucy, who trusted two strangers, bonding with their hearts like a molecule. And Isabel, the old Isabel, who lit the way for him back into life, after all the years of death.

A light rain wafts the steam of forest scents into his cell: the earth, the wet wood, the pungent smell of banksias with their flowers like big, feathery acorns. It occurs to him that there are different versions of himself to farewell—the abandoned eight-year-old; the delusional soldier who hovered somewhere in hell; the lightkeeper who dared to leave his heart undefended. Like Russian dolls, these lives sit within him.

The forest sings to him: the rain tapping on the leaves, dripping into the puddles, the kookaburras laughing like madmen at some joke beyond human comprehension. He has the sensation of being part of a connected whole, of being enough. Another day or another decade will not change this. He is embraced by nature, which is waiting, ultimately, to receive him, to re-organize his atoms into another shape.

The rain is falling more heavily, and in the distance, thunder grumbles at being left behind by the lightning.

CHAPTER 34

The Addicotts lived in a house which, but for a few yards of sea grass, would have been paddling its toes in the ocean. The timber and brick were kept in good order by Ralph, and Hilda coaxed a small garden from the sandy soil at the back: zinnias and dahlias as garish as dancing girls bordered a trail to a little aviary in which finches chirped gaily, to the puzzlement of the native birds.

The smell of marmalade drifted through the windows and met Ralph as he trudged up the front path the day after Lucy had been found. As he took his cap off in the hallway, Hilda rushed to intercept him, the wooden spoon in her hand glistening like an orange lollipop. She put a finger to her lips and led him to the kitchen. "In the lounge room!" she whispered, eyes wide. "Isabel Sherbourne! She's been waiting for you."

Ralph shook his head. "World's gone bloody haywire."

"What does she want?"

"That's the trouble, I reckon. She can't make up her mind *what* she wants."

The small, tidy lounge room of the sea captain was decorated not with ships in bottles or scale models of men-o'-war, but icons. The Archangels Michael and Raphael, the Madonna and child, and numerous saints, stared at any visitors with stern calm from their place in eternity.

The glass of water beside Isabel was almost empty. Her eyes were fixed on an angel, his sword and shield in hand, poised over a serpent at his feet. Heavy clouds dimmed the room, so that the paintings seemed faint pools of gold, hovering in darkness.

She didn't notice Ralph come in, and he watched her for a while before saying, "That was the first one I got. I fished a Russian sailor out of the drink, near Sevastopol, forty-odd years ago. Gave it to me as a thank-you." He spoke slowly, pausing now and then. "I picked up the others along the way in my merchant marine days." He gave a chuckle. "I'm hardly the Holy Joe sort, and I couldn't tell you the first thing about painting. But there's something about this lot that makes them talk back to you. Hilda says they keep her company when I'm away."

He put his hands in his pockets and nodded toward the picture Isabel was looking at. "I've bent that fella's ear in my time, I can tell you. Archangel Michael. There he is with his sword in his hand, but he's got his shield half raised, too. Like he's still making up his mind about something."

The room fell silent, and the wind seemed to rattle the windows more urgently, demanding Isabel's attention. All the way to the horizon, the waves thrashed in chaos, and the sky began to smudge with another approaching shower. Her mind was thrust back to Janus—back to the vast emptiness, back to Tom. She started to cry, in great sobs like waves, washing her back onto familiar shore at last.

Ralph sat down beside her, and held her hand. She wept and he sat, and nothing at all was said for a good half hour.

Finally, Isabel ventured, "Lucy ran away last night because of *me,* Ralph—trying to find me. She could have died. Oh, Ralph, it's all such a mess. I can't talk to Mum and Dad about it . . ."

Still the old man stayed silent, holding Isabel's hand, looking at the fingernails, bitten to the quick. He nodded his head slowly, just a touch. "She's alive. And she's safe."

"I only ever wanted her to be safe, Ralph. From the moment she arrived on Janus, I wanted to do what was best. She needed us. And we needed *her*." She paused. "*I* needed her. When she just *appeared*—out of nowhere—it was a miracle, Ralph. I was sure she was meant to be with us. It was so crystal clear. A little baby had lost her parents, *we*'d lost a little baby . . .

"I love her so much." She blew her nose. "Out there . . . Ralph, you're one of the only people in the world who knows what it's like on Janus. One of the only people who can imagine. But even *you*'ve never waved the boat off: stood on that jetty and heard the sound of the engine die away, watched the boat get smaller and smaller. You don't know what it's like to say goodbye to the world for years at a time. Janus was *real*. *Lucy* was real. Everything else was just make-believe.

"By the time we found out about Hannah Roennfeldt—oh, it was too late then, Ralph. I just didn't have it in me to give Lucy up: I couldn't do that to her."

The old man sat, breathing slowly and deeply, nodding now and again. He resisted any urge to question or contradict her. Keeping silent was the best way to help her; to help everyone.

"We were such a happy family. Then, when the police came to the island—when I heard what Tom had done—nothing felt safe. Nowhere was safe. Not even inside myself was safe. I was so hurt, and so angry. And terrified. Nothing made sense, from the moment the policeman told me about the rattle."

She looked at him. "What have I done?" The question wasn't rhetorical. She was searching for a mirror, something to show her what she could not see.

"Can't say that concerns me as much as what you're going to do now."

"There's nothing I *can* do. Everything's ruined. There's no point in anything any more."

"That man loves you, you know. That's got to be worth something."

"But what about Lucy? She's my *daughter*, Ralph." She searched for a way to explain. "Can you imagine asking Hilda to give away one of her children?"

"This isn't giving away. This is giving *back,* Isabel."

"But wasn't Lucy given to us? Isn't that what God was asking of us?"

"Maybe He was asking you to look after her. And you did. And maybe now He's asking you to let someone else do that." He puffed out a breath. "Hell, I'm not a priest. What do I know about God? But I do know that there's a man about to give up everything—*everything*—to protect you. Do you think that's right?"

"But you saw what happened yesterday. You know how desperate Lucy is. She needs me, Ralph. How could I explain it to her? You can't expect her to understand, not at her age."

"Sometimes life turns out hard, Isabel. Sometimes it just bites right through you. And sometimes, just when you think it's done its worst, it comes back and takes another chunk."

"I thought it had done all it could to me, years ago."

"If you think things are bad now, they'll be a whole lot worse if you don't speak up for Tom. This is serious, Isabel. Lucy's young. She's got people who want to care for her, and give her a good life. Tom's got no one. I never saw a man who less deserved to suffer than Tom Sherbourne."

Under the watchful gaze of saints and angels, Ralph continued, "God knows what got into the pair of you out there. There's been lie upon lie, all with the best intentions. But it's gone far enough. Everything you've done to help Lucy has hurt someone else. Good God, of course I understand how hard it must be for you. But that Spragg's a nasty piece of work and I wouldn't put anything past him. Tom's your husband. For better or worse, in sickness and in health. Unless you want to see him in jail, or—" He couldn't finish the sentence. "I reckon this is your last chance."

"Where are you going?" An hour later, Violet was alarmed at the state of her daughter. "You've only just walked in the door."

"I'm going out, Ma. There's something I have to do."

"But it's bucketing down. Wait till it stops, at least." She gestured to a pile of clothes on the floor beside her. "I've decided to go through some of the boys' things. Some of their old shirts, their boots: they might be some good to someone. I thought I could give them to the church." A quiver crept into her voice. "But it would be nice to have some company while I sort them."

"I have to go to the police station, now."

"What on earth for?"

Isabel looked at her mother, and for a moment almost dared tell her. But she said, "I need to see Mr. Knuckey.

"I'll be back later," she called behind her, heading down the passageway to the front door.

As she opened it, she was startled by a silhouette in the doorway, about to ring the bell. The figure, soaked with rain, was Hannah Roennfeldt. Isabel stood speechless.

On the doorstep, Hannah spoke quickly, keeping her eyes on a bowl of roses on the table behind Isabel, fearing that to look at her directly would make her change her mind. "I've come to say something—just to say it and go. Don't ask me anything, please." She thought back to the vow she had made to God just hours ago: there was no reneging. She took a breath, like a run-up. "Anything could have happened to Grace last night. She was so desperate to see you. Thank God she was found before she came to any harm." She looked up. "Can you have any idea what it feels like? To see the daughter you conceived and carried, the daughter you bore and nursed, call someone else her mother?" Her eyes darted to one side. "But I have to accept that, however much it hurts. And I can't put my happiness above hers.

"The baby I had—Grace—isn't coming back. I can see that now. The plain fact is, she can live without me, even if I can't live without her. I can't punish her for what happened. And I can't punish you for your husband's decisions."

Isabel began to protest, but Hannah spoke over her. With her eyes fixed again on the roses, she said, "I knew Frank to his very soul. Perhaps I only ever knew Grace a very little." She looked Isabel in the eye.

"Grace loves you. Perhaps she belongs to you." With great effort, she pushed on to her next words: "But I need to know that justice is done. If you swear to me now that this was all your husband's doing—swear on your life—then I'll let Grace come to live with you."

No conscious thought went through Isabel's mind—it was by sheer reflex that she said, "I swear."

Hannah continued, "As long as you give evidence against that man, as soon as he's safely locked away, Grace can come back to you." Suddenly she was in tears. "Oh, God help me!" she said, and rushed away.

Isabel is dazed. She runs over and over what she has just heard, wondering whether she has made it up. But there are the wet footprints on the veranda; the trail of drops from Hannah Roennfeldt's furled umbrella.

She looks through the fly-wire door so close up that the lightning seems to be divided into tiny squares. Then the thunder rolls in and shakes the roof.

"I thought you were going to the police station?" The words crash into Isabel's thoughts, and for a moment she has no idea where she is. She turns and notices her mother. "I thought you'd already gone. What happened?"

"There's lightning."

"At least Lucy won't be frightened," Isabel catches herself thinking as the sky cracks open with a brilliant flash. From when she was a baby, Tom has taught the girl to respect, but not fear, the forces of nature—the lightning that might strike the light tower on Janus, the oceans that batter the island. She thinks of the reverence Lucy showed in the lantern room: not touching the instruments, keeping her fingers off the glass. She recalls an image of the child in Tom's arms, waving and laughing from up on the gallery to Isabel at the washing line on the ground. "Once upon a time there was a lighthouse . . ." How many of

Lucy's stories started that way? "And there did be a storm. And the wind blew and blew and the lightkeeper made the light shine, and Lucy did help him. And it was dark but the lightkeeper wasn't scared because he had the magic light."

Lucy's tortured face comes to her mind. She can keep her daughter, keep her safe and happy, and put all this behind them. She can love her and cherish her and watch her grow . . . In a few years, the tooth fairy will spirit away milk teeth for threepence, then gradually Lucy will get taller and together they will talk about the world and about—

She can keep her daughter. If. Curled in a ball on her bed, she sobs, "I *want* my daughter. Oh, Lucy, I can't bear it."

Hannah's declaration. Ralph's entreaty. Her own false oath, betraying Tom as surely as he ever betrayed her. Around and around like a merry-go-round of possibilities they whirl and jumble, pulling her with them, first in one direction, then another. She hears the words that have been spoken. But the one voice that is absent is Tom's. The man who now stands between her and Lucy. Between Lucy and her mother.

Unable to resist its call any longer, she edges to the drawer, and takes out the letter. She opens the envelope slowly.

Izzy, love,

I hope you're all right, and keeping your strength up. I know your mum and dad will be taking good care of you. Sergeant Knuckey's been good enough to let me write to you, but he'll be reading this before you do. I wish we could talk face-to-face.

I'm not sure if or when I'll be able to speak to you again. You always imagine you'll get the chance to say what needs to be said, to put things right. But that's not always how it goes.

I couldn't go on the way things were—I couldn't live with myself. I'm sorrier than I'll ever be able to say for hurting you.

We each get a little turn at life, and if this ends up being how my turn went, it will still have been worth it. My time should have been up years ago. To have met you, when I thought life was over, and been loved by you—if I lived another hundred years I couldn't ask for better than that.

I've loved you as best as I know how, Izz, which isn't saying much. You're a wonderful girl, and you deserved someone a lot better than me.

You're angry and hurt and nothing makes sense, and I know what that feels like. If you decide to wash your hands of me, I won't blame you.

Perhaps when it comes to it, no one is just the worst thing they ever did. All I can do is to ask God, and to ask you, to forgive me for the harm I've caused. And to thank you for every day we spent together.

Whatever you decide to do, I'll accept it, and I'll stand by your choice.

I will always be your loving husband,

Tom

As though it is a picture, not a note, Isabel traces her fingertip over the letters, following the steady lean, the graceful loops—as though that is how to make sense of the words. She imagines his long fingers on the pencil as it traveled across the page. Over and over, she traces "Tom," the word somehow both foreign and familiar. Her mind wanders to the game they would play, where she would draw letters with her finger on his naked back for him to guess, then he would do the same on hers. But the recollection is swiftly countered by the memory of Lucy's touch. Her baby's skin. She imagines Tom's hand again, this time as it wrote the notes to Hannah. Like a pendulum, her thoughts swing back and forward, between hatred and regret, between the man and the child.

She lifts her hand from the paper and reads the letter again, this time trying to make out the meaning of the words on the page, hearing Tom's voice pronounce them. She reads it over and over, feeling as though her body is being rent in two, until finally, shaking with sobs, she makes her decision.

CHAPTER 35

When it rains in Partageuse, the clouds hurl down water and soak the town to its very bones. Millennia of such deluges have brought forth the forests from the ancient loam. The sky darkens and the temperature plummets. Great gulleys are carved across dirt roads, and flash floods make them impassable by motorcars. The rivers quicken, finally scenting the ocean from which they have so long been parted. They will not be stopped in their urgency to get back to it—to get home.

The town goes quiet. The last few horses stand forlornly with their wagons as the rain drips off their blinkers, and bounces off the motorcars which far outnumber them these days. People stand under the wide verandas of shops in the main street, arms folded, mouths turned down in grimaces of defeat. At the back of the schoolyard, a couple of tearaways stamp their feet in puddles. Women look in exasperation at washing not retrieved from lines, and cats slink through the nearest convenient doorway, meowing their disdain. The water rushes down the war memorial, where the gold lettering is faded now. It springs off the church roof and, through the mouth of a gargoyle, onto the new grave of Frank Roennfeldt. The rain transforms the living and the dead without preference.

"Lucy won't be frightened." The thought occurs in Tom's mind, too. He recalls the feeling in his chest—that strange shiver of wonder for the little girl, when she would face down the lightning and laugh. "Make it go bang, Dadda!" she would cry, and wait for the thunder to roll in.

"Bugger it!" exclaimed Vernon Knuckey. "We've sprung a bloody leak again." The runoff from the hill above the station was rather more than a "leak." Water was pouring into the back of the building, set lower than the front. Within hours, Tom's cell was six inches deep in water, entering from above and below. The house spider had abandoned its web for somewhere safer.

Knuckey appeared, keys in hand. "Your lucky day, Sherbourne."

Tom did not understand.

"Usually happens when it rains this much. The ceiling in this part tends to collapse. Perth's always saying they're going to fix it, but they just send some cove to put a bit of flour and water glue on it, as far as I can see. Still, they get a bit dark with us if the prisoners cark it before trial. You'd better come up the front for a while. Till the cell drains." He left the key unturned in the lock. "You're not going to be stupid about this, are you?"

Tom looked at him squarely, and said nothing.

"All right. Out you come."

He followed Knuckey to the front office, where the sergeant put one handcuff on his wrist and another around an exposed pipe. "Not going to be *flooded* with customers as long as this holds out," he said to Harry Garstone. He chuckled to himself at his pun. "Ah, Mo McCackie, eat your heart out."

There was no sound except the rain, thundering down, turning every surface into a drum or a cymbal. The wind had fled, and nothing outside moved except the water. Garstone set to with a mop and some towels, attempting to redeem the situation inside.

Tom sat looking through the window at the road, imagining the view from the gallery at Janus now: the keeper would feel like he was in a cloud, with the sudden air inversion. He watched the hands on the clock inch their way around the dial as if there were all the time in the world.

Something caught his attention. A small figure was making its way toward the station. No raincoat or umbrella, arms folded, and bent forward as though leaning on the rain. He recognized the outline instantly. Moments later, Isabel opened the door. She looked straight ahead as she made for the counter, where Harry Garstone had stripped to the waist and was busy trying to mop up a puddle.

"I've . . ." Isabel began.

Garstone turned to see who was speaking.

"I've got to see Sergeant Knuckey . . ."

The flustered constable, half-naked and mop in hand, blushed. His eyes flicked toward Tom. Isabel followed his gaze, and gasped.

Tom jumped to his feet, but could not move from the wall. He reached a hand to her, as she searched his face, terrified.

"Izzy! Izzy, love!" He strained at the handcuffs, stretching his arm to the very fingertips. She stood, crippled by fear and regret and shame, not daring to move. Suddenly, her terror got the better of her, and she turned to dash out again.

It was as though Tom's whole body had been brought back to life at the sight of her. The thought that she might vanish again was more than he could bear. He pulled again at the metal, this time with such force that he wrenched the pipe from the wall, sending water gushing high into the air.

"Tom!" Isabel sobbed as he caught her in his arms, "Oh Tom!" her body shaking despite the strength of his hold. "I've got to tell them. I've got to—"

"Shh, Izzy, shh, it's all right, darl. It's all right."

Sergeant Knuckey appeared from his office. "Garstone, what in the name of Christ—" He stopped at the sight of Isabel in Tom's arms, the two of them soaking from the pipe's downpour.

"Mr. Knuckey, it's not true—none of it's true!" cried Isabel. "Frank

Roennfeldt was dead when the boat washed up. It was *my* idea to keep Lucy. I stopped him reporting the boat. It's my fault."

Tom was holding her tight, kissing the top of her head. "Shh, Izzy. Just leave things be." He pulled away and held her shoulders as he bent his knees and looked straight into her eyes. "It's all right, sweetheart. Don't say any more."

Knuckey shook his head slowly.

Garstone had hastily replaced his tunic and was smoothing his hair into some sort of order. "Shall I arrest her, sir?"

"For once in your bloody life, show some sense, Constable. Get busy and fix the blinking pipe before we all drown!" Knuckey turned to the others, who were staring intently at one another, their silence a language in itself. "And as for you two, you'd better come into my office."

Shame. To her surprise, it was shame Hannah felt more than anger, when Sergeant Knuckey visited her with news of Isabel Sherbourne's revelation. Her face burned as she thought back to her visit to Isabel just the previous day, and to the bargain she had struck.

"When? When did she tell you this?" she asked.

"Yesterday."

"What time yesterday?"

Knuckey was surprised by the question. What bloody difference could it make? "About five o'clock."

"So it was after . . ." Her voice died away.

"After what?"

Hannah blushed even deeper, humiliated at the thought that Isabel had refused her sacrifice, and disgusted at having been lied to. "Nothing."

"I thought you'd want to know."

"Of course. Of course . . ." She was concentrating not on the policeman, but on a windowpane. It needed cleaning. The whole house needed cleaning: she had hardly touched it for weeks. Her thoughts climbed this familiar trellis of housework, keeping her on safe territory, until she managed to haul them back. "So—where is she now?"

"She's on bail, at her parents'."

Hannah picked at a hangnail on her thumb. "What will happen to her?"

"She'll face trial alongside her husband."

"She was lying, all that time . . . She made me believe . . ." She shook her head, lost in another thought.

Knuckey took a breath. "All a pretty rum business. A decent sort, Isabel Graysmark was, before she went to Janus. Being out on that island didn't do her any good at all. Not sure it does anyone any good. After all, Sherbourne only got the posting because Trimble Docherty did away with himself."

Hannah wasn't sure how to put her question. "How long will they go to prison for?"

Knuckey looked at her. "The rest of their lives."

"The rest of their lives?"

"I'm not talking about the jail time. Those two will never be free now. They'll never get away from what's happened."

"Neither will I, Sergeant."

Knuckey sized her up, and decided to take a chance. "Look, you don't get a Military Cross for being a coward. And you don't get a Bar to go with it unless—well, unless you saved a lot of your side's lives by risking your own. Tom Sherbourne's a decent man, I reckon. I'd go so far as to say a good man, Mrs. Roennfeldt. And Isabel's a good girl. Three miscarriages she had out there, with no one to help her. You don't go through the things those two have been through without being bent out of shape."

Hannah looked at him, her hands still, waiting to see where he was going.

"It's a God-awful shame to see a fellow like that in the position he's in. Not to mention his wife."

"What are you saying?"

"I'm not saying anything that won't occur to you in a few years' time. But it'll be too late by then."

She turned her head a fraction, as if to understand him better.

"I'm just asking, is it really what you want? A trial? Prison? You've got your daughter back. There might be some other way . . ."

"Some other way?"

"Spragg'll lose interest now that he's had to drop his murder malarkey. As long as this is still a Partageuse matter, I've got some leeway. And maybe Captain Hasluck could be persuaded to put in a word for him with the Lights. If you were minded to speak up for him too. Ask for clemency . . ."

Hannah's face reddened again, and without warning she jumped to her feet. Words that had been building up for weeks, for years, words Hannah didn't know were there, burst from her. "I'm sick of this! I'm sick of being pushed around, of having my life ruined by the whims of other people. You have no idea what it's like to be in my position, Sergeant Knuckey! How dare you come into my house and make such a suggestion? How *bloody* dare you!"

"I didn't mean to—"

"Let me finish! I've had enough, do you understand me?" Hannah was shouting now. "No one is ever going to tell me how to live my life again! First it's my father telling me who I can marry, then it's the whole bloody town turning on Frank like a mob of savages. Then Gwen tries to convince me to give Grace back to Isabel Graysmark, and I *agree*—I actually agree! Don't look so shocked: you don't know everything that goes on around here!

"And it turns out the woman lied to my face! How dare you? How dare you presume to tell me, to even suggest to me, that I should, yet again, put someone else first!" She pulled herself up straight. "Get out of my house! Now! Just go! Before I"—she picked up the thing nearest to hand, a cut glass vase—"throw this at you!"

Knuckey was too slow in getting to his feet and the vase caught him on the shoulder, ricocheting against the skirting board, where it smashed in a dazzle of shards.

Hannah stopped, not sure whether she was imagining what she had done. She stared at him, waiting for a clue.

He stood perfectly still. The curtain flapped with the breeze. A fat blowfly buzzed against the fly wire. A last fragment of glass gave a dull tinkle as it finally succumbed to gravity.

After a long silence, Knuckey said, "Make you feel better?"

Still Hannah's mouth was open. She had never in her life hit anyone. She had rarely sworn. And she had definitely never done either to a police officer.

"I've had a lot worse thrown at me."

Hannah looked at the floor. "I apologize."

The policeman bent to pick up some of the bigger pieces of glass, and put them on the table. "Don't want the little one cutting her feet."

"She's at the river with her grandfather," muttered Hannah. Gesturing vaguely toward the glass, she added, "I don't usually . . ." but the sentence trailed off.

"You've had enough. I know. Just as well it was me you threw it at and not Sergeant Spragg." He allowed a trace of a smile at the thought.

"I shouldn't have spoken like that."

"People do, sometimes. People who've had less to contend with than you. We're not always in full control of our actions. I'd be out of a job if we were." He picked up his hat. "I'll leave you in peace. Let you think about things. But there isn't a lot of time left. Once the magistrate gets here and sends them off to Albany, there's nothing I can do about it."

He walked through the door into the dazzle of daylight, where the sun was burning the last of the clouds away from the east.

Hannah fetched the dustpan and brush, her body moving without any apparent instruction. She swept up the shards of glass, checking carefully for any overlooked splinters. She took the dustpan into the kitchen and emptied it onto old newspaper, wrapping the glass safely and taking it outside to the rubbish bin. She thought of the story of Abraham and Isaac, how God tested Abraham right to the limit, to see whether he would surrender the thing dearest to him in the world. Only as the knife was poised above the child's neck did God direct him to a lesser sacrifice. She still had her daughter.

She was about to go back inside when she caught sight of the Cape gooseberry bush, and remembered that terrible day after Grace's return when her daughter had wedged herself behind it. As she sank to her knees on the grass and sobbed, the memory of a conversation with Frank floated into her awareness. "But how? How can you just get over these things, darling?" she had asked him. "You've had so much strife but you're always happy. How do you do it?"

"I choose to," he said. "I can leave myself to rot in the past, spend my time hating people for what happened, like my father did, or I can forgive and forget."

"But it's not that easy."

He smiled that Frank smile. "Oh, but my treasure, it is so much less exhausting. You only have to forgive once. To resent, you have to do it all day, every day. You have to keep remembering all the bad things." He laughed, pretending to wipe sweat from his brow. "I would have to make a list, a very, very long list and make sure I hated the people on it the right amount. That I did a very proper job of hating, too: very Teutonic! No"—his voice became sober—"we always have a choice. All of us."

Now, she lay down on her belly in the grass, feeling the strength of the sun sap hers. Exhausted, half aware of the bees and the scent of dandelions beside her, half aware of the sour sops under her fingers where the grass was overgrown, finally she slept.

Tom still feels the touch of Isabel's wet skin, even though the cell is now drained, his clothes dry, and his reunion with her yesterday evening just a memory. He wants it both to be real, and to be an illusion. If it's real, his Izzy has come back to him, as he prayed she would. If it's an illusion, she's still safe from the prospect of prison. Relief and dread mix in his gut, and he wonders if he will ever feel her touch again.

In her bedroom, Violet Graysmark is weeping. "Oh, Bill. I just don't know what to think, what to do. Our little girl could go to jail. The pity of it."

"We'll get through it, dear. She'll get through it, too, somehow." He does not mention his conversation with Vernon Knuckey. Doesn't want to get her hopes up. But there might be the shadow of a chance.

Isabel sits alone under the jacaranda. Her grief for Lucy is as strong as ever: a pain that has no location and no cure. Putting down the burden of the lie has meant giving up the freedom of the dream. The pain on her mother's face, the hurt in her father's eyes, Lucy's distress, the memory of Tom, handcuffed: she tries to fend off the army of images, and imagines what prison will be like. Finally, she has no more strength. No more fight in her. Her life is just fragments, that she will never be able to reunite. Her mind collapses under the weight of it, and her thoughts descend into a deep, black well, where shame and loss and fear begin to drown her.

Septimus and his granddaughter are by the river, watching the boats. "Tell you who used to be a good sailor: my Hannah. When she was little. She was good at everything as a little one. Bright as a button. Always kept me on my toes, just like you." He tousled her hair. "My saving Grace, you are!"

"No, I'm Lucy!" she insists.

"You were called Grace the day you were born."

"But I want to be *Lucy.*"

He eyes her up, taking the measure of her. "Tell you what, let's do a business deal. We'll split the difference, and I'll call you Lucy-Grace. Shake hands on it?"

Hannah was awoken from her sleep on the grass by a shadow over her face. She opened her eyes to find Grace standing a few feet away, staring. Hannah sat up and smoothed her hair, disoriented.

"Told you that'd get her attention," laughed Septimus. Grace gave a faint smile.

Hannah began to stand but Septimus said, "No, stay there. Now, Princess, why don't you sit on the grass and tell Hannah all about the boats. How many did you see?"

The little girl hesitated.

"Go on, remember how you counted them on your fingers?"

She held up her hands. "Six," she said, showing five fingers on one hand, and three on the other, before folding two of them down again.

Septimus said, "I'll go and have a rummage in the kitchen and get us some cordial. You stay and tell her about the greedy seagull you saw with that big fish."

Grace sat on the grass, a few feet from Hannah. Her blonde hair shone in the sun. Hannah was caught: she wanted to tell her father about Sergeant Knuckey's visit, ask his advice. But she had never seen Grace this ready to talk, to play, and couldn't bear to ruin the moment. Out of habit, she compared the child with her memory of her baby, trying to recapture her lost daughter. She stopped. *"We always have a choice."* The words ran through her mind.

"Shall we make a daisy chain?" she asked.

"What's a daisy train?"

Hannah smiled. "*Chain.* Here, we'll make you a crown," she said, and started to pick the dandelions beside her.

As she showed Grace how to pierce a stem with her thumbnail and thread the next stem through it, she watched her daughter's hands, the way they moved. They were not the hands of her baby. They were the hands of a little girl she would have to get to know all over again. And who would have to get to know her, too. *"We always have a choice."* A lightness fills her chest, as if a great breath has rushed through her.

CHAPTER 36

As the sun dangled above the horizon, at the end of the jetty at Partageuse Tom stood waiting. He caught sight of Hannah, approaching slowly. Six months had passed since he had last seen her, and she seemed transformed: her face fuller, more relaxed. When she finally spoke, her voice was calm. "Well?"

"I wanted to say I'm sorry. And to thank you. For what you did."

"I don't want your thanks," she said.

"If you hadn't spoken up for us it would have been a lot more than three months I spent in Bunbury jail." Tom said the last two words with difficulty: the syllables felt thick with shame. "And Isabel's suspended sentence—that was mostly thanks to you, my lawyer said."

Hannah looked off into the distance. "Sending her to jail wouldn't have fixed anything. Nor would keeping you there for years. What's done's done."

"All the same, it can't have been an easy decision for you."

"The first time I saw you, it was because you came to save me. When I was a complete stranger, and you owed me nothing. That counts for something, I suppose. And I know that if you hadn't found my daughter, she would have died. I tried to remember that too." She paused. "I don't forgive you—either of you. Being lied to like that . . . But I'm not going to get dragged under by the past. Look what happened to Frank because of people doing that." She stopped, twisting her wedding ring for a moment. "And the irony is, Frank would have been the first one to forgive you. He'd have been the first one to speak in your defense. In defense of people who make mistakes.

"It was the only way I could honor him: doing what I know he would have done." She looked at him, her eyes glistening. "I loved that man."

They stood in silence, looking out at the water. Eventually, Tom spoke. "The years you missed with Lucy—we can never give them back. She's a wonderful little girl." Hannah's expression made him add, "We'll never come near her again, I promise you."

His next words caught in his throat, and he tried again. "I've got no right to ask anything. But if one day—maybe when she's grown up—she remembers us and asks about us, if you can bear to, tell her we loved her. Even though we didn't have the right."

Hannah stood, weighing something in her mind.

"Her birthday's the eighteenth of February. You didn't know that, did you?"

"No." Tom's voice was quiet.

"And when she was born, she had the cord wrapped around her neck twice. And Frank . . . Frank used to sing her to sleep. You see? There are things I know about her that you don't."

"Yes." He nodded gently.

"I blame you. And I blame your wife. Of course I do." She looked straight at him. "I was so scared that my daughter might never love me."

"Love's what children do."

She turned her eyes to a dinghy nudging the jetty with each wave, and frowned at a new thought. "No one ever mentions it around here—how Frank and Grace came to be in that boat in the first place. Not a soul ever apologized. Even my father doesn't like to talk about it. At least you've said you're sorry. Paid the price for what you did to him."

After a while, she said, "Where are you living?"

"In Albany. Ralph Addicott helped find me work at the harbor there when I got out, three months ago now. Means I can be near my wife. The doctors said she needed complete rest. For the moment, she's better off in the nursing home, where she can be properly cared for." He cleared his throat. "Best let you go. I hope life turns out well for you, and for Lu—for Grace."

"Goodbye," Hannah said, and made her way back down the jetty.

The setting sun dipped the gum leaves in gold as Hannah walked up the path at her father's house to collect her daughter.

"This little piggy stayed home . . ." Septimus was saying, giving his granddaughter's toe a wiggle as she sat on his knee on the veranda. "Oh, look who's here, Lucy-Grace."

"Mummy! Where did you go?"

Hannah was struck anew by her daughter's version of Frank's smile, Frank's eyes, of his fair hair. "Maybe I'll tell you one day, little one," she said, and kissed her lightly. "Shall we go home now?"

"Can we come back to Granddad tomorrow?"

Septimus laughed. "You can visit Granddad any time you like, Princess. Any time you like."

Dr. Sumpton had been right—given time, the little girl had gradually gotten used to her new—or perhaps it was her old—life. Hannah held out her arms and waited for her daughter to climb into them. Her own father smiled. "That's the way, girlie. That's the way."

"Come on, darling, off we go."

"I want to walk."

Hannah put her down and the child allowed herself to be led out through the gate and along the road. Hannah kept her pace slow, so that Lucy-Grace could keep up. "See the kookaburra?" she asked. "He looks like he's smiling, doesn't he?"

The girl paid little attention, until a machine-gun burst of laughter came from the bird as they drew closer. She stopped in astonishment, and watched the creature, which she had never seen so close up. Again, it rattled off its raucous call.

"He's laughing. He must like you," said Hannah. "Or maybe it's going to rain. The kookas always laugh when the rain's coming. Can you make his sound? He goes like this," and she broke into a fair imitation of its call, which her mother had taught her decades ago. "Go on, you have a go at it."

The girl could not manage the complicated call. "I'll be a seagull," she said, and came out with a pitch-perfect imitation of the bird she knew best, a shrill, harsh barracking. "Now you do it," she said, and Hannah laughed at her own unsuccessful attempts.

"You'll have to teach me, sweetheart," she said, and the two of them walked on together.

On the jetty, Tom thinks back to the first time he saw Partageuse. And the last. Between them, Fitzgerald and Knuckey had traded off charges and whittled down Spragg's "kitchen sink." The lawyer had been eloquent in showing that the child-stealing charge wouldn't stand and that all related charges must therefore also fall. The guilty plea to the remaining administrative counts, tried in Partageuse rather than Albany, could still have brought a severe penalty, had Hannah not spoken articulately in their defense, urging clemency. And Bunbury jail, halfway up to Perth, was less brutal than Fremantle or Albany would have been.

Now, as the sun dissolves into the water, Tom is aware of a nagging reflex. Months after leaving Janus, his legs still prepare to climb the hundreds of stairs to light up. Instead, he sits on the end of the jetty, watching the last few gulls on the lilting water.

He considers the world that has carried on without him, its stories unfolding, whether he is there to see them or not. Lucy is probably already tucked into bed. He imagines her face, left naked by sleep. He wonders what she looks like now, and whether she dreams about her time on Janus; whether she misses her light. He thinks of Isabel, too, in her little iron bed in the nursing home, weeping for her daughter, for her old life.

Time will bring her back. He promises her. He promises himself. She will mend.

The train for Albany will be leaving in an hour. He will wait until dark to walk through town, back to the station.

In the garden of the nursing home at Albany a few weeks later, Tom sat at one end of the wrought-iron bench, Isabel at the other. The pink zinnias were past their best now, ragged and tinged with brown. Snails had started on the leaves of the asters, and their petals had been carried off in clumps by the southerly wind.

"At least you're starting to fill out again, Tom. You looked so dreadful—when I first saw you again. Are you managing all right?" Isabel's tone was concerned, though distant.

"Don't worry about me. It's you we've got to concentrate on now." He watched a cricket settle on the arm of the bench, and start up a chirrup. "They say you're all right to leave whenever you want, Izz."

She bowed her head and tucked a strand of hair behind an ear. "There's no going back, you know. There's no undoing what happened—what we've both been through," she said. Tom looked at her steadily, but she didn't meet his gaze as she murmured, "And besides, what's left?"

"Left of what?"

"Of anything. What's left of—our life?"

"There's no going back on the Lights, if that's what you mean."

Isabel sighed sharply. "It's not what I mean, Tom." She pulled a piece of honeysuckle from the old wall beside her, and examined it. As she shredded a leaf, then another, the fine pieces fell in a jagged mosaic on her skirt. "Losing Lucy—it's as if something has been amputated. Oh, I wish I could find the words to explain it."

"The words don't matter." He reached a hand to her, but she shrank away.

"Tell me you feel the same," she said.

"How does saying that make anything better, Izz?"

She pushed the pieces into a neat pile. "You don't even understand what I'm talking about, do you?"

He frowned, struggling, and she looked away at a billowing white cloud which threatened the sun. "You're a hard man to know. Sometimes living with you was just lonely."

He paused. "What do you want me to say to that, Izzy?"

"I wanted us to be happy. All of us. Lucy got under your skin. Opened up your heart somehow, and it was wonderful to see." There was a long silence, before her expression changed with the return of a memory. "All that time, and I didn't know what you'd done. That every time you touched me, every time you—I had no idea you'd been keeping secrets."

"I tried to talk about it, Izz. You wouldn't let me."

She jumped to her feet, the fragments of leaf spiraling to the grass. "I wanted to make you hurt, Tom, like you hurt me. Do you realize that? I wanted revenge. Haven't you got anything to say about that?"

"I know you did, sweet. I know. But that time's over."

"What, so you forgive me, just like that? Like it's nothing?"

"What else is there to do? You're my wife, Isabel."

"You mean you're stuck with me . . ."

"I mean I promised to spend my life with you. I still want to spend my life with you. Izz, I've learned the hard way that to have any kind of a future you've got to give up hope of ever changing your past."

She turned away, and pulled some more honeysuckle from its vine. "What are we going to do? How are we going to live? I can't go on looking at you every day and resenting you for what you did. Being ashamed of myself, too."

"No, love, you can't."

"Everything's ruined. Nothing can ever be put right."

Tom rested a hand on hers. "We've put things right as well as we can. That's all we can do. We have to live with things the way they are now."

She wandered along the path beside the grass, leaving Tom on the seat. After a full circuit of the lawn, she returned. "I can't go back to Partageuse. I don't belong there any more." She shook her head and watched the progress of the cloud. "I don't know where I belong these days."

Tom stood up, and put his hand on her arm. "You belong with me, Izz. Doesn't matter where we are."

"Is that true any more, Tom?"

She was holding the strand of honeysuckle, stroking the leaves absently. Tom plucked one of the creamy blooms from it. "We used to eat these, when we were kids. Did you?"

"Eat them?"

He bit the narrow end of the flower and sucked the droplet of nectar from its base. "You only taste it for a second. But it's worth it." He picked another, and put it to her lips to bite.

CHAPTER 37

Hopetoun, 28th August 1950

There was nothing much in Hopetoun now, except for the long jetty that still whispered of the glory days when the town served as the port for the Goldfields. The port itself had closed in 1936, a few years after Tom and Isabel had moved here. Tom's brother, Cecil, had outlived his father by barely a couple of years, and when he died, the money was enough to buy a farm outside the town. Their property was small by local standards, but still edged the coast for several miles, and the house stood on a ridge just inland, looking down over the sweep of beach below. They lived a quiet life. They went into town occasionally. Farmhands helped with the work.

Hopetoun, on a wide bay nearly four hundred miles east of Partageuse, was far enough away that they weren't likely to bump into anyone from there, but close enough for Isabel's parents to make the journey at Christmas, in the years before they died. Tom and Ralph wrote to each other once in a while—just a greeting, short, plain, but deeply felt all the same. Ralph's daughter and her family had moved into his little cottage after Hilda died, and looked after him well, though his health was frail these days. When Bluey married Kitty Kelly, Tom and Isabel sent a gift, but they didn't attend the wedding. Neither of them ever returned to Partageuse.

And the best part of twenty years flowed past like a quiet country river, deepening its path with time.

The clock chimes. Almost time to leave. It's a short drive to town these days, with the sealed roads. Not like when they first arrived. As Tom ties his tie, a stranger with gray hair catches a glimpse of him, just a flick of an eye, then he remembers it's himself in the mirror. Now, the suit hangs more loosely on his frame, and there is a gap between the collar and the neck inside it.

Through the window, the waves rise, sacrificing themselves in a blizzard of white, far out to sea. The ocean gives not the slightest hint that any time has passed, ever. The only sound is the buffeting of the August gales.

Having placed the envelope in the camphor chest, Tom closes the lid reverently. Soon enough, the contents will lose all meaning, like the lost language of the trenches, so imprisoned in a time. Years bleach away the sense of things until all that's left is a bone-white past, stripped of feeling and significance.

The cancer had been finishing its work for months, nibbling the days from her, and there had been nothing to do but wait. He had held her hand for weeks, sitting by her bed. "Remember that gramophone?" he would ask, or "I wonder whatever happened to old Mrs. Mewett?" And she would smile faintly. Sometimes, she mustered the energy to say, "Don't forget the pruning, will you?" Or, "Tell me a story, Tom. Tell me a story with a happy ending," and he would stroke her cheek and whisper, "Once upon a time there was a girl called Isabel, and she was the feistiest girl for miles around . . ." And as he told the story, he would watch the sunspots on her hand, and notice how the knuckles swelled slightly, these days, and the ring moved loosely on the skin between the joints.

Toward the end, when she could no longer sip water, he had given her the corner of a damp flannel to suck, and smeared lanolin on her lips to stop them cracking with the dryness. He had caressed her hair, now shot-through with silver, tied in a heavy plait down her back. He had watched her thin chest rise and fall with that same uncertainty he remembered in Lucy's when she first arrived on Janus: each breath a struggle and a triumph.

"Are you sorry you ever met me, Tom?"

"I was born to meet you, Izz. I reckon that's what I was put here for," he said, and kissed her cheek.

His lips remembered that very first kiss decades before, on the windy beach in the setting sun: the bold, fearless girl guided only by her heart. He remembered her love for Lucy, instant and fierce and without question—the sort of love that, had things been different, would have been returned for a lifetime.

He had tried to show Isabel his love, in every act of every day for thirty years. But now, there would be no more days. There could be no more showing, and the urgency drove him on. "Izz," he said, hesitating. "Is there anything you want to ask me? Anything you want me to tell you? Anything at all. I'm not very good at this, but, if there is, I promise I'll try my best to answer."

Isabel attempted a smile. "Means you must think it's nearly over then, Tom." She nodded her head a little, and patted his hand.

He held her gaze. "Or maybe that I'm just finally ready to talk . . ."

Her voice was weak. "It's all right. There's nothing more I need, now."

Tom stroked her hair, looking a long while into her eyes. He put his forehead to hers, and they stayed, unmoving, until her breathing changed, growing more ragged.

"I don't want to leave you," she said, clutching his hand. "I'm so scared, love. So scared. What if God doesn't forgive me?"

"God forgave you years ago. It's about time you did too."

"The letter?" she asked anxiously. "You'll look after the letter?"

"Yes, Izz. I'll look after it." And the wind shook the windows as it had done decades ago on Janus.

"I'm not going to say goodbye, in case God hears and thinks I'm ready to go." She squeezed his hand again. After that, words were beyond her. Now and then she would open her eyes and there would be a sparkle in them, a light that brightened as her breathing got shallower and harder, as if she had been told a secret and suddenly understood something.

Then, on that last evening, just as the waning moon parted wintry clouds, her breathing changed in the way Tom knew all too well, and she slipped away from him.

Even though they had electricity, he sat with just the soft glow of the kerosene lamp to bathe her face: so much gentler, the light of a flame. Kinder. He stayed by the body all night, waiting until dawn before telephoning the doctor. Standing to, like in the old days.

As Tom walks down the path, he snaps off a yellow bud from one of the rosebushes Isabel planted when they first moved here. Its fragrance is already strong, and takes him back almost two decades to the picture of her, kneeling in the freshly dug bed, hands pressing down the earth around the young bush. "We've finally got our rose garden, Tom," she had said. It was the first time he had seen her smile since she had left Partageuse, and the image stayed with him, as clear as a photograph.

There is a small gathering at the church hall after the funeral. Tom stays as long as politeness demands. But he wishes the people really knew who they were mourning: the Isabel he had met on the jetty, so full of life and daring and mischief. His Izzy. His other half of the sky.

Two days after the funeral, Tom sat alone, in a house now empty and silent. A plume of dust fanned out in the sky, signaling the arrival of a car. One of the farmhands coming back, probably. As it got closer, he looked again. It was expensive, new, with Perth number plates.

The car drew up near the house, and Tom came to the front door.

A woman emerged and took a moment to smooth down her blonde hair, gathered in a twist at the nape of her neck. She looked around her, then walked slowly up to the veranda, where Tom now waited.

"Afternoon," he said. "You lost?"

"I hope not," replied the woman.

"Can I help you?"

"I'm looking for the Sherbournes' property."

"You've found it. I'm Tom Sherbourne." He waited for clarification.

"Then I'm not lost." She gave a tentative smile.

"I'm sorry," said Tom, "it's been a long week. Have I forgotten something? An appointment?"

"No, I haven't got an appointment, but it's you I've come to see. And . . ." she hesitated, "Mrs. Sherbourne. I heard she was very ill."

Tom was puzzled, and she said, "My name's Lucy-Grace Rutherford. Roennfeldt as was . . ." She smiled again. "I'm Lucy."

He looked in disbelief. "Lulu? Little Lulu," he said, almost to himself. He didn't move.

The woman blushed. "I don't know what I should call you. Or . . . Mrs. Sherbourne." Suddenly a thought crossed her face and she asked, "I hope she won't mind. I hope I haven't intruded."

"She always hoped you'd come."

"Wait. I've brought something to show you," she said, and headed back to the car. She reached into the front seat, and returned carrying a bassinet, her face a mixture of tenderness and pride.

"This is Christopher, my little boy. He's three months old."

Tom saw peeping out from a blanket a child who so exactly resembled Lucy as a baby that a tingle crept through him. "Izzy would have loved to have met him. It would have meant so much to her, that you came."

"Oh. I'm so sorry . . . When did . . . ?" She let the words trail off.

"A week ago. Her funeral was on Monday."

"I didn't know. If you'd prefer I left . . ."

He continued to look at the baby for a good while, and when he eventually raised his head, there was a wistful smile about his lips. "Come in."

Tom brought in a tray with teapot and cups, as Lucy-Grace sat looking out at the ocean, the baby beside her in the basket.

"Where do we begin?" she asked.

"What say we just sit quietly for a bit?" Tom replied. "Get used to things." He sighed. "Little Lucy. After all these years."

They sat silently, drinking their tea, listening to the wind which came roaring up from the ocean, occasionally banishing a cloud long enough to let a shaft of sunlight slice through the glass and on to the carpet. Lucy breathed in the smells of the house: old wood, and fire smoke, and polish. She didn't dare look directly at Tom, but glanced around the room. An icon of St. Michael; a vase of yellow roses. A wedding photo of Tom and Isabel looking radiantly young and hopeful. On the shelves were books about navigation and light and music, some, such as the one called *Brown's Star Atlas,* so big that they had to lie flat. There was a piano in the corner, with sheet music piled on top of it.

"How did you hear?" Tom asked eventually. "About Isabel?"

"Mum told me. When you wrote to Ralph Addicott, to let him know how ill she was, he went to see my mother."

"In Partageuse?"

"She lives back down there now. Mum took me to Perth when I was five—wanted to start again. She only moved back to Partageuse when I joined the WAAF in 1944. After that, well, she seemed settled there with Aunty Gwen at Bermondsey, Granddad's old place. I stayed in Perth after the war."

"And your husband?"

She gave a bright smile. "Henry! Air Force romance . . . He's a lovely man. We got married last year. I'm so lucky." She looked out at the distant water and said, "I've thought of you both so often, over the years. Wondered about you. But it wasn't"—she paused—"well, it wasn't until I had Christopher that I really understood: why you two did what you did. And why Mum couldn't forgive you for it. I'd kill for my baby. No question."

She smoothed her skirt. "I remember some things. At least I think I do—a bit like snatches from a dream: the light, of course; the tower; and a sort of balcony around it—what's it called?"

"The gallery."

"I remember being on your shoulders. And playing the piano with Isabel. Something about some birds in a tree and saying goodbye to you?

"Then, it all sort of jumbled together and I don't remember much. Just the new life up in Perth, and school. But most of all, I remember the wind and the waves and the ocean: can't get it out of my blood. Mum doesn't like the water. Never swims." She looked at the baby. "I couldn't come sooner. I had to wait for Mum to . . . well, to give her blessing, I suppose."

Watching her, Tom caught flashes of her younger face. But it was difficult to match the woman with the girl. Difficult too, at first, to find the younger man within himself who had loved her so deeply. And yet. And yet he was still there, somewhere, and for a moment, clear as a bell, he had a memory of her voice piping, "Dadda! Pick me up, Dadda!"

"She left something for you," he said, and went to the camphor chest. Reaching inside, he took the envelope and handed it to Lucy-Grace, who held it for a moment before opening it.

My Darling Lucy,

It has been a long time. Such a long time. I promised I'd stay away from you, and I've stuck to my word, however hard that was for me.

I'm gone now, which is why you have this letter. And it brings me joy because it means that you came to find us. I never gave up hope that you would.

In the chest with this letter are some of the earliest things of yours: your christening gown, your yellow blanket, some of the drawings you did as a tot. And there are things I made for you over the years—linen and so forth.

I kept them safe for you—things from that lost part of your life. In case you came in search of it.

You are a grown woman now. I hope life has been kind to you. I hope that you can forgive me for keeping you. And for letting you go.

Know that you have always been beloved.

With all my love.

The delicately embroidered handkerchiefs, the knitted bootees, the satin bonnet: they were folded carefully in the camphor chest, hidden way, way below the things from Isabel's own childhood. Tom did not know, until then, that Isabel had kept them. Fragments of a time. Of a life. Finally, Lucy-Grace unrolled a scroll, tied with a satin ribbon. The map of Janus, decorated by Isabel so long ago: Shipwreck Beach, Treacherous Cove—the ink still bright. Tom felt a pang as he remembered the day she had presented it to him, and his terror at the breach of the rules. And he was suddenly awash again with the loving and the losing of Isabel.

As Lucy-Grace read the map, a tear trailed down her cheek, and Tom offered her his neatly folded handkerchief. She wiped her eyes, considering a thought, and finally said, "I never had the chance to say thank you. To you and to . . . to Mamma, for saving me, and for taking such good care of me. I was too little . . . and then it was all too late."

"There's nothing to thank us for."

"I'm only alive because of you two."

The baby started to cry, and Lucy bent to pick him up. "Shh, shh, bubba. You're all right. You're all right, bunny rabbit." She rocked him up and down and the crying subsided. She turned to Tom. "Do you want to have a hold?"

He hesitated. "I'm a bit out of practice these days."

"Go on," she said, and passed the little bundle gently into his arms.

"Well, look at you," he said, smiling. "Just like your mummy when she was a baby, aren't you? Same nose, same blue eyes." As the child held him with a serious gaze, long-forgotten sensations flooded back. "Oh, Izzy would have loved to meet you." A bubble of saliva glistened on the baby's lips, and Tom watched the rainbow the sunlight made there. "Izzy would have just loved you," he said, and he fought the crack in his voice.

Lucy-Grace looked at her watch. "I'd better be heading off, I suppose. I'm staying at Ravensthorpe tonight. Don't want to be driving in the dusk—there'll be 'roos on the road."

"Of course." Tom nodded toward the camphor chest. "Shall I help you put the things in the car? That is, if you'd like to take them. I'll understand if you'd rather not."

"I don't want to take them," she said, and as Tom's face fell, she smiled, "because that way we'll have an excuse to come back. One day soon, maybe."

The sun is just a sliver shimmering above the waves as Tom lowers himself into the old steamer chair on the veranda. Beside him, on Isabel's chair, are the cushions she made, embroidered with stars and a sickle moon. The wind has dropped, and clouds scarred with deep orange brood on the horizon. A pinpoint of light pierces the dusk: the Hopetoun lighthouse. These days it's automatic—no need for keepers since the main port closed. He thinks back to Janus, and the light he cared for there for so long, every one of its flashes still traveling somewhere into the darkness far out toward the universe's edge.

His arms still feel the tiny weight of Lucy's baby, and the sensation unlocks the bodily memory of holding Lucy herself, and before that, the son he held in his arms so briefly. How different so many lives would have been if he had lived. He breathes the thought for a long while, then sighs. No point in thinking like that. Once you start down that road, there's no end to it. He's lived the life he's lived. He's loved the woman he's loved. No one ever has or ever will travel quite the same path on this earth, and that's all right by him. He still aches for Isabel: her smile, the feel of her skin. The tears he fought off in front of Lucy now trail down his face.

He looks behind him, where a full moon is edging its way into the sky like a counterweight on the twin horizon, heaved up by the dying sun. Every end is the beginning of something else. Little Christopher has been born into a world Tom could never have imagined. Perhaps he'll be spared a war, this boy? Lucy-Grace, too, belongs to a future Tom can only guess at. If she can love her son half as well as Isabel loved her, the boy will be all right.

There are still more days to travel in this life. And he knows that the man who makes the journey has been shaped by every day and every person along the way. Scars are just another kind of memory. Isabel is part of him, wherever she is, just like the war and the light and the ocean. Soon enough the days will close over their lives, the grass will grow over their graves, until their story is just an unvisited headstone.

He watches the ocean surrender to night, knowing that the light will reappear.

ACKNOWLEDGMENTS

This book has many midwives. So many people have played a part in bringing it into the world that to name them individually would take a separate volume. I have, I hope, thanked them in person along the way, but would like to acknowledge their importance again here. Each has contributed something unique and invaluable: some at a specific moment; some over a longer period; some over a lifetime.

Thank you—each and every one of you—for helping me tell this story. I am blessed by your kindness.

LOG OF Cape Otway LIGHTHOUSE STATION April 22nd

Day and Date.	Hour.	Wind. Direction.	Wind. Force.	Weather.	Bar	Ther.	Remarks.
Friday 21st	6 a.m.	S.E.	4	cm	29.92	57	Keeper & Assist Wareham
	Noon	S.E.	5	cm	30.00	58	loading firewood in the
	6 p.m.	S.S.E.	4	om	30.01	58	morning Assist Myers
	Mdgt.	S.E.	2	om	30.04	57	cleaning office & lookout
							Assist Meyer & Johansson
							loading firewood in the after
Saturday 22nd	6 a.m.	East	2	Bcm	30.09	57	W. McLoney
	Noon	East	3	Bcm	29.96	59	Assist Wareham loading
	6 p.m.	East	3	cm	29.98	59	firewood, Employed at
	Mdgt.	North	2	om	29.90	58	Lighthouse & Shipping duties
							Waggon load of Stores arrived
							W. McLoney
Sunday 23rd	6 a.m.	N.W.	3	cm	29.84	57	Employed at Lighthouse
	Noon	West	1	Bc	29.83	60	& Shipping duties
	6 p.m.	East	3	om	29.80	60	
	Mdgt.	S.E.	2	omp	29.81	57	W. McLoney
Monday 24th	6 a.m.	S.E.	3	O2mp	29.80	57	Assist Meyer Johansson
	Noon	E.S.E.	3	cmp	29.93	59	& Wareham employed
	6 p.m.	S.E.	3	om	29.91	58	loading firewood Wag.
	Mdgt.	East	4	Bcm	29.95	58	arrived with last load
							of Stores 4.30pm.
							W. McLoney
Tuesday 25th	6 a.m.	East	5	cqm	29.88	57	Employed cutting firewood
	Noon	E.N.E.	5	cm	29.88	60	Waggon left for Lavers
	6 p.m.	East	3	cm	29.80	60	Hill 12 Noon
	Mdgt.	East	4	cm	29.74	58	
							W. McLoney